Soldiers in the Shadows

UNKNOWN WARRIORS WHO CHANGED THE COURSE OF HISTORY

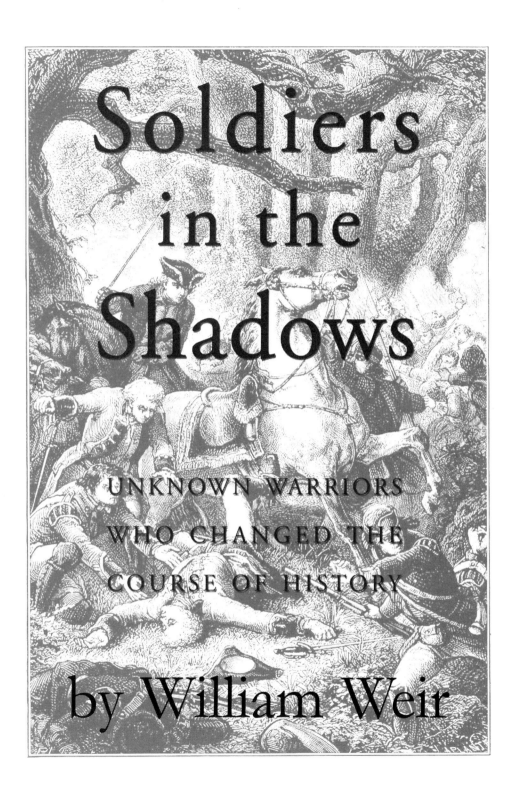

Soldiers in the Shadows

UNKNOWN WARRIORS
WHO CHANGED THE
COURSE OF HISTORY

by William Weir

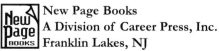
New Page Books
A Division of Career Press, Inc.
Franklin Lakes, NJ

Soldiers in the Shadows
Edited and Typeset by John J. O'Sullivan
Cover design by Foster & Foster, Inc.
Printed in the U.S.A. by Book-mart Press
Graphical elements ©2002 *www.arttoday.com*

To order this title, please call toll-free 1-800-CAREER-1 (NJ and Canada: 201-848-0310) to order using VISA or MasterCard, or for further information on books from Career Press.

The Career Press, Inc., 3 Tice Road, PO Box 687,
Franklin Lakes, NJ 07417
www.careerpress.com
www.newpagebooks.com

Library of Congress Cataloging-in-Publication Data

Weir, William, 1928-
    Soldiers in the shadows : unknown warriors who changed the course of history / by William Weir.
      p. cm.
    Includes bibliographical references (p.) and index.
    ISBN 1-56414-629-4 (cloth)
    1. Soldiers—Biography. 2. Soldiers—United States—Biography. I. Title.

U51 .W45 2002
355'.0092'2—dc21
[B]
                                                                2002071840

Dedication

For Joan and Jim, a sunny and most unshadowy couple.

Acknowledgments

Writing about people who are all but forgotten means somebody has to do a lot of digging for information. So for this book, as for all my previous ones, I turned to my favorite band of literary archaeologists: the librarians at the Guilford, Connecticut, Free Library. Research Librarian Stephanie Johnson and her "upstairs crew"—Nona Boomer, Penny Colby, Carol Dudley, Suellen Proteau, and Jackie Stevens—have demonstrated time-after-time that if it's been published, they can find it.

My thanks, too, to my agent, John White, who got me this job; to Mike Lewis of Career Press/New Page, who was not afraid to recommend something a bit off his house's beaten track; to Stacey Farkas, editorial director at Career Press/New Page; to John J. O'Sullivan, associate editorial director, who got this into a readable format; and all the people in Franklin Lakes who helped put this rogues gallery together and get it to readers.

As always, my deepest gratitude goes to my wife, Anne, who, juggling a seemingly overwhelming schedule of state, municipal, and private activities, managed to read every chapter and make valuable comments.

—William Weir
Guilford, Connecticut
June 22, 2002

Contents

Foreword

Just about anyone can tell you something about Alexander the Great, Julius Caesar, or Napoleon. But how many people can tell you anything about William Walker, Fred Ward, or Fred Funston? Alexander, Caesar, and Napoleon changed history, of course. But so did Walker, Ward and Funston. Further, they were Americans and they didn't live millennia or centuries ago. (The earliest operated just before the Civil War.)

To move up the time scale, everyone has heard of T.E. Lawrence, Erwin Rommel, and Bernard Montgomery. But what about Paul von Lettow-Vorbeck, Erskine Childers, and Orde Wingate. They were involved in the same wars, and what they did had more lasting significance. Of course, those three were foreigners, but so were Lawrence, Rommel, and Montgomery. A couple of Americans whose greatest achievements were even later—Matthew Ridgway and Edward Lansdale—are not much better known. All of these men contributed in one way or another to ending European domination of the world.

William Walker was the most famous person in pre-Civil War America, but now is almost totally forgotten. Forgotten, too is Fred Ward, who almost single-handedly dragged the world's largest country into modern times. If Fred Funston and his operation in the Philippines had been remembered in the 1960s, our involvement in Vietnam might not have turned out to be the awful mess it was. (Funston was one of America's greatest counter-guerrilla fighters. The other was Edward Lansdale, who also performed in the Philippines.)

America has also produced some great guerrilla fighters who are largely forgotten. John Singleton Mosby, the Confederate private who carved "Mosby's Confederacy" out of what is now suburban Washington D.C., was one of them. So was Captain Jack, a Modoc Indian, who, with a handful of followers, stymied more than a thousand U.S. soldiers for months in northern California.

Mosby and Captain Jack fought rear guard actions against a changing world. The others were actively engaged in changing the world. The old world was a world of masters and servants, a world of colonies and mother countries, a world where most Europeans deemed other people to be innately inferior. Most of those other people were non-European and non-white, although there were exceptions, such as the Irish and the Jews. The forgotten soldiers in this book changed that.

Walker, the earliest, trained and equipped Nicaraguans for modern war and was instrumental in eliminating what was, in practice, a British protectorate over Central America. He failed to realize his own dream, a Republic of Central America, partly because of the nationalist sentiments he himself had aroused. Ward, who took part in one of Walker's earlier expeditions, created a modern Chinese army. After his death, he was revered as one of the creators of modern China and as a Confucian demigod. Mosby, as contrary a character as any in American history, fought against the new order as a Confederate, then helped its progress as a diplomat in China and as a federal officer in the American West. Captain Jack did his best to bring the new order to his people by accommodation with the whites. He failed, fighting heroically in a war he didn't want to fight.

Funston was a colonialist. His humanitarian—and effective—tactics contrasted starkly with the brutal methods of his colleagues. His work laid the foundation for a modern, unified Philippine nation. Von Lettow-Vorbeck was also a colonial warrior, but in his campaigns against the Allies, he proved that black soldiers were in no way inferior to white soldiers. The much-discussed awakening of Africa began with this Prussian officer. Erskine Childers, born in England but raised in Ireland, was the key man in the liberation of Ireland, and he showed other colonies how they could do the same. In Ethiopia, Orde Wingate repeated the lesson von Lettow-Vorbeck had taught Europe's armies. He is also remembered as one of the founders of Israel's national army. And in Burma, he took the first step toward modern air cavalry tactics.

Matthew Ridgway stopped a new attempt at European colonization, this time by the Soviet Union in Korea. China, of course, was also heavily involved in the Communist attack, but Kim Il Sung, the North Korean leader, had been born in Russia, and both his army and that of the Chinese were at that time equipped and backed by the Soviet Union. Ed Lansdale, whatever his motives were, was an anti-colonialist in action. He secured the election of Ramon Magsaysay and established an independent democracy in the Philippines that not even Ferdinand Marcos could destroy. Then he went to Vietnam and might have accomplished the same thing if he had not been frustrated by conventional military and political thinking in Washington.

This is not a collection of character profiles, but snippets of history. They are taken from the period that runs from just before the Civil War to just before the Vietnam War. During that time, European hegemony, which began in the 16th century, began to fade away. Not surprisingly, the same characters appear in more than one episode. Characters are not the sole, or even the main, focus. Strategy, tactics, and the shape of a changing world get more emphasis than personal eccentricities. I'll spend little time on the subjects' childhoods...and even less on their sex lives. What drove William Walker to risk his life in mad expeditions to Latin America is unknown and probably unknowable. But it's irrelevant. What he did is known and very relevant. Edward Lansdale was a professional dissembler. Some of his thoughts and motives will never be known. But what he did has as much to do with the modern Philippines as the acts of the garrulous Fred Funston. As a personality, Matthew Ridgway is as interesting as mashed potatoes. He was straight-arrow all the way—a brave, incorruptible, orthodox general. What he did is fascinating. He took an army, almost demoralized under the leadership of America's greatest military hero, and turned it into an efficient and victorious machine.

None of these leaders operated in a vacuum. Their contemporaries included the famous such as President William McKinley, who raised manipulation to the level of an art. They also included the infamous, such as Cornelius Vanderbilt, who was willing to destroy a nation to protect his transportation franchise across the isthmus of Nicaragua. Their opponents were not despicable. They also included people such as Vanderbilt's henchman, Sylvanius Spencer, perhaps the most underrated mercenary in history. Spencer personally frustrated Walker's scheme for a Republic of Central America. Von Lettow-Vorbeck was opposed by no less than Jan Christian Smuts, a soldier-statesman who played a leading part in both World Wars (as well as a prominent part in the chapter on Erskine Childers and the Irish War of Independence.) In this case, it was Smuts who was frustrated. Another of von Lettow-Vorbeck's opponents was Richard Meinertzhagen who, coincidentally, greeted Adolf Hitler with "Heil Meinertzhagen!" and tried to have his old enemy appointed ambassador to Britain. Meinertzhagen failed to persuade the German dictator because he, like Orde Wingate, was a gentile Zionist. Wingate's opponents included many of his own people, especially the South Africans after his Ethiopian victories. And he got the most respect from his strongest enemy, the bold Japanese general Mutagachi Renya. When he heard of Wingate's death, Mutagachi later wrote, "I realized what a loss this was to the British Army and said a prayer for the soul of this man in whom I had met my match."

History is made by many, many people, most of them unknown. This is an attempt to remember some of them.

Soldiers
in the Shadows

Part 1

*Filibusters Shake
the Establishment*

1

The "Gray-Eyed Man of Destiny": William Walker

Death in the morning

company of soldiers guarded a short, skinny man in torn, dirty clothing. The man carried a crucifix, and two priests walked beside him. They towered over him. The prisoner was only five feet, four inches tall and weighed little more than 100 pounds.

The soldiers stood the man against a stone wall, and the priests anointed him in the sacrament of extreme unction—the sacrament of the dying. Then the priests walked away and turned their backs. An officer offered the prisoner a blindfold and asked if he had a final statement. The little man declined to make a statement and refused the blindfold.[1] He gazed at the soldiers in the firing squad with the piercing gray eyes that were known throughout Central America. The officer returned to the firing squad and gave the order to fire. A line of muskets belched fire. The prisoner fell forward. The soldiers moved aside, and a second squad stepped up and fired a second volley at the prostrate body. Then the officer walked up to the body and put a pistol bullet through its head. Some accounts say there were three volleys.[2] In any case, it was a lot of shooting to kill one small, frail man. But the prisoner was no ordinary man.

He was William Walker.

Mention William Walker today and 99 times out of 100 all you'll get is a blank look. But at the middle of the last century, William Walker was known all over Europe and the Americas. In his native land, thousands greeted him as a hero and others scorned him as no better than a pirate. He was perhaps the most famous—or infamous—American of his time. He was a filibuster.

Today, a filibuster is a senatorial gab-fest. In the 19th century, it was a North American who attempted to carve out an empire for himself, usually in Latin America. Aaron Burr was a filibuster,[3] as was Sam Houston.[4]

The making of a filibuster

Those who knew Walker when he was growing up would not have been surprised if he accomplished great things. But they never would have expected what happened.

Walker was born in Nashville, Tennessee, in 1824, 36 years before he faced that Honduran firing squad. His father, a prosperous Nashville merchant, wanted William to go into the ministry. William, a quiet, bookish child, seemed to have all the qualifications: he avoided rough play; never swore in all his life; and hated drinking, gambling, and womanizing. His brother recalled that William considered smiling a sign of weakness. There is only one recorded instance of him laughing.[5] He certainly had the intelligence to be a minister: he graduated summa cum laude from the University of Nashville at the age of 15. He got a second degree (the equivalent of an M.A.) two years later.[6]

But the boy was shy and withdrawn. The idea of preaching before a congregation terrified him. He had the ability to preach: he had been president of his college debating society, but that was in a structured, academic environment. So instead, he studied medicine at the University of Pennsylvania and again graduated summa cum laude. He took advanced courses at the University of Edinburgh. Edinburgh, in his father's native land, was considered the leading medical school in the English-speaking world. Walker felt at home in the dour Scottish capital, but he spent only two months at the university. He decided he already knew everything its professors could teach him. So he went to Paris to study at the Sorbonne. He was repelled by the worldly atmosphere of "the city of light," but even more repelled by the way medicine was practiced in France. In his 13 months in Paris, he said later, he saw the rich pampered to the extent that their comfort took precedence over medical necessity, but the poor received almost no treatment. The only thing he learned was the French language. He went on to Heidelberg where he stayed six months and learned German, if nothing else. Then he traveled around Europe, visiting England, Sweden, and Spain. He stayed in England long enough to develop a dislike of the English from what he found to be the patronizing attitude of the English toward Americans. He stayed in Spain long enough to become fluent in Spanish.

In the spring of 1845, Dr. Walker returned to Nashville and opened an office. When he arrived, he found his mother bedridden with what three physicians diagnosed as "neuralgia, melancholia and rheumatism." He examined her, too, but he was unable to prescribe a cure. That fall, his mother died. According to Walker's sister Alice, it was his frustration at being unable to cure the person he cared most for in all the world that led him to abandon medicine. He denounced medicine as a profession based not on science but on myths and superstitions.

Walker not only abandoned medicine, he abandoned Nashville. He read law for a few weeks in the office of a Nashville attorney and then moved to New Orleans. Walker went into partnership with Edmund Randolph, a well-connected young lawyer who would become his best friend. Walker's personality made it difficult for him to attract clients, and he didn't like to appear in court. Instead, he preferred the research and writing side of the job. He was also totally unable to bring himself to engage in the sort of out-of-court dickering so essential to lawyers at that time. After a year, he gave up law.

William Walker, the insignificant-looking "Gray-Eyed Man of Destiny," also called "King of the Filibusters." (Library of Congress)

In the meantime, he had fallen in love with a beautiful New Orleans socialite, Ellen Galt Martin. Ellen was deaf, so William learned sign language. The warmth of Ellen's love began to thaw out the frozen William Walker. Before he could ask her to marry, he had to have some means of support. He tried journalism. He joined a new newspaper, the *New Orleans Crescent*, and quickly became an editor. With his knowledge of Europe and foreign languages, he was able to take over foreign news coverage. Then he was allowed to write editorials.

Ellen Martin was an ardent Abolitionist. William Walker, although a Southerner, had grown up in a family that considered slavery an abomination. His father refused to own slaves.[7] He had no love for the South's "peculiar institution." His editorials repeatedly attacked the institution of slavery and its extension. He called for its gradual abolition. Walker received death threats, but he kept on writing, achieving a reputation as a wild radical. He even advocated female suffrage.

Walker developed a small personal following, which did wonders for his self-confidence and his ego. Only one other member of the staff had his own coterie of fans—a young writer named Walt Whitman. Walker was promoted to co-publisher.

His future seemed assured. Then New Orleans suffered one of its periodic cholera epidemics, and Ellen Martin was stricken. Walker took a leave of absence to help his beloved. For three weeks he stayed by her bed. Then she died, and Walker's world turned upside down. A few weeks later, he left New Orleans without saying goodbye to anyone or leaving a forwarding address.

Ten months later, he appeared in San Francisco. His clothes were patched; he was heavily tanned, and he carried a sword cane and a pistol. He looked older than his 26 years, and he looked hard. San Francisco was a rough town in 1850, but in spite of Walker's size, people tried not to quarrel with him. There were plenty of newspapers in San Francisco, but few experienced newsmen. Walker got a job on the *San Francisco Herald*. Once again he was writing editorials.

And once again, Walker launched an editorial crusade. This time it was against crime and corruption. Crime and corruption were widespread in the United States in 1850, but San Francisco was undoubtedly the nation's capital for murder, vice, and civic corruption. Walker zeroed in on the chief judge of the state district court, Levi Parsons. Parsons tried to have the publisher and editors of the *Herald* charged with libel, but a grand jury refused to indict. He jailed Walker for contempt.

Four thousand armed men gathered outside the courthouse. The crowd offered Judge Parsons a choice: release Walker or be lynched.[8] It was Walker himself who dispersed the crowd. His lawyer, Edmund Randolph, who had also gone to California, appeared before the mob and said that Walker adamantly opposed extralegal violence. He wanted the law to take its course. Randolph had applied for a writ of habeas corpus. The crowd went home, grumbling, as Walker wrote editorials from his cell. The crowds again began gathering outside the police station where Walker was held. The sheriff and police feared they would try to break Walker out by force and refused to guard him. Again Walker poured oil on the waters. He pried open a window of his cell and addressed the crowd. "I rely on American justice," he shouted, "and the right will prevail!"[9]

Public opinion was too much for the court system, and Walker was released. However, crimes continued to be committed and criminals continued to go unpunished. And Walker continued writing. The *Herald* was burned out twice along with many of its advertisers. The second case of arson was one too many. San Francisco citizens formed the first Committee of Public Safety, and the Committee's vigilantes began hanging criminals. Although Walker had opposed vigilante action on his own behalf, he warmly supported the vigilantes.

Parsons tried another way to silence the editorial gadfly. So one of his friends, Graham Hicks, challenged Walker to a duel. Dueling was common in San Francisco at the time, but it was rarely fatal. (This is surprising, because most duels were conducted at eight paces with percussion revolvers which had rifled barrels.) The procedure sounds like a recipe for a murder-suicide.[10] Although it was a matter of honor for duelists to appear, few wanted to kill somebody—they usually aimed to miss. If a duelist was particularly incensed at his opponent, he might aim to inflict a non-vital wound.

Walker fought four duels in his life. He always fired first and always missed. Two of his opponents also missed, and one shot him in the foot. Hicks was a different kind of opponent: He always aimed to kill. He had already killed four men. As usual, Walker fired first and missed. Hicks took careful aim. He hit Walker in the arm, missing the bone or any arteries. The editor didn't even change his expression. Then he said, "I am still alive, Mr. Hicks. Perhaps you would like to fire again."[11] The seconds (the friends of the duelers) hurriedly stopped the duel.

Walker's conduct in the duel further increased his popularity. Henry Watkins, a California attorney, offered him a partnership. Walker was growing bored with journalism. As a lawyer he could take direct action against corruption and evil. He accepted the partnership with a condition that shows how much he had changed: He would return to the law only as a courtroom advocate—no research, no briefs. Stephen Field, later a justice of the U.S. Supreme Court, called the 27-year-old Walker "a brilliant speaker who could sway judges and juries alike with his rhetoric and reason."[12]

In San Francisco, Walker became acquainted with Count Gaston Raoul Raousset-Boulbon, a French nobleman who had taken a group of unlucky forty-niners, mostly French citizens, on an expedition to Mexico. Raousset had told Mexican officials he would clear the Apaches out of the northern portion of the Mexican state of Sonora if he could get the right to mine gold and silver in the area.[13] The Mexicans agreed, but after Raousset's expedition was in Sonora, President Santa Anna cancelled the agreement. There was fighting, and Raousset returned to San Francisco.

Walker and his law partner thought Raousset had a great idea, though. They approached some San Francisco bankers, who offered backing. Walker suggested to Raousset that they go back to Mexico together. Raousset politely declined. He would return again, he said, but not with any Americans, because the Mexicans hated Americans.[14]

Walker then formed an independent regiment, promoted himself to colonel, and began recruiting "soldiers." His regiment would go to Sonora to save the women and children living there from the savage Apaches, he said. He tried to negotiate a deal with the Mexican authorities like the one made by Raousset, but he failed. Walker resolved to go to Mexico, with or without the authorities' cooperation. He purchased weapons and a ship. The federal government seized the ship and all it contained, but Walker bought more weapons and another ship. In October, 1853, he sneaked the ship out of San Francisco with an "army" of 45 men, including a young American sailor named Fred Ward, destined to make a name for himself on the other side of the Pacific.

Not even Walker thought he could conquer Sonora with 45 men. So, he landed at La Paz, capital of the state of Baja California Sur. The peninsula of Baja California contains two states that in 1850 were almost unpopulated. Further, Baja California, or Lower California as it was known in the United States at that time, was almost completely isolated from mainland Mexico. Walker's men arrested the governor and put him in La Paz's one-cell jail. Walker proclaimed the formation of the Republic of Lower California, appointed himself president, and named a cabinet consisting of his associates in San Francisco. The Mexicans ignored him. Frustrated, he put the governor on his ship and sailed to Ensenada, then the capital of Baja California Norte, a slightly more populous state. He put the governor of the northern state on his ship, too, and took over a small fort in the harbor of Ensenada.

The Mexican government sent 250 men to get rid of the "Republic of Lower California." As the Mexicans sailed into the harbor, Walker fired the two cannons in the fort. The Mexicans turned around and sailed out. But as he was congratulating his men on their victory, his own ship sailed out of the harbor. The governors had bribed the captain and crew of the ship and sailed away, taking all of Walker's food and supplies.

Walker's law partner, Henry Watkins, arrived a few days later with 230 men and a load of rifles and ammunition. Unfortunately, he brought no food. When Watkins went back to get food, Walker raided the camp of a Mexican bandit named Melendrez for food. He knew that if he confiscated corn and cows from the local people, they'd turn against him.[15]

Things went from bad to worse. A Mexican gunboat appeared off Ensenada harbor to prevent any more reinforcements from arriving. Then a U.S. warship sailed into the harbor with a message for Walker. The United States had agreed to purchase the strip of northern Sonora where gold and silver were rumored to be. With the Gadsden Purchase, (named for the U.S. minister to Mexico, James Gadsden, who had negotiated it), Walker's chance to get exclusive mining rights disappeared. Gadsden told Mexican officials that his country would consider Walker an outlaw. The San Francisco bankers lost all interest in Walker. Ironically, Walker's activities probably made the Gadsden Purchase possible. At first, Mexican officials rejected Gadsden's offer of $10 million for the silver-rich strip of northern Sonora. Walker's expedition, however, persuaded them that the United States might use filibusters to seize the area by force, so they agreed to the sale.

Walker released any of his men who wanted to go home. They could take a share of the food, but they had to leave the rifles and ammunition. More than half of them left, including Fred Ward.[16] Walker gathered together a handful of ranchers he found in the area and "persuaded" them to swear allegiance to the Republic of Lower California and to donate cattle to feed his army. Then, he announced the annexation of Sonora. Driving the cattle before him, Walker and the 130 men he had left set out for the Colorado River, at the border of Sonora. They crossed the river, but the cattle drowned. Half of the army then left Walker and marched north, back across the U.S. border. Walker refused to leave the men he had stationed at San Vicente in Baja California, so he and the men still with him retraced their steps.

Before long, Walker's men were starving and barefoot. The filibusters were harassed by Melendrez's bandits and Indians as they trudged through roadless desert and mountains. Many were killed outright. Others, wounded and unable to keep up with the rest, were tortured to death by the Indians. When they reached San Vicente, they found that Melendrez had massacred the tiny garrison. Walker and his troops headed for the American border.

As the gringos approached the border, Melendrez sent a message offering all the Americans except Walker safe conduct. Walker's men refused to abandon their leader.[17] Walker's band was down to 34 men at this time. When they were within three miles of the U.S. border, near a "country house" called Tia Juana (later the city of Tijuana) Melendrez ordered a charge. The "Yanquis" fled into a field of boulders. The Mexicans were almost upon them when a dozen riflemen popped up from behind the boulders and emptied a saddle with each shot.[18] Melendrez and his men fled from the ambush, and Walker's troops crossed the border safely.

Walker was tried for violation of the Neutrality Act. His testimony was so moving it took the jury eight and a half minutes to declare him not guilty.[19]

Nicaragua

Walker was dabbling in politics and writing for the *Sacramento Democratic State Journal* when a young man named Byron Cole offered him the editorship of a newspaper he had just purchased, the *San Francisco Commercial Advertiser*. Cole was impressed with both Walker's intelligence and his record as a filibuster.

Cole was familiar with Central America. He had traveled across Nicaragua on his way to California, and he owned a share of a mining company in Honduras. He told Walker Central America needed someone like him.

Central America had been, of course, part of the vast Spanish empire. When Mexico achieved its independence in 1821 under Emperor Augustin it included the Captain Generalcy of Central America—all of modern Central America but Panama, which was part of New Granada (now Colombia). When Antonio Lopez de Santa Anna overthrew Augustin, the Central American provinces became free and formed the Federation of Central America. The Federation resembled the United States under the Articles of Confederation. But the Federation never evolved into anything like the United States, and it broke up in 1838.

Central America was not totally independent. In the 17th century, Britain had established its colony of Belize. While the provinces of the Federation quarreled and the later republics warred, Britain extended its holdings. In spite of its apologists, the British Empire was not acquired in "a fit of absentmindedness." It was acquired by staying alert and taking advantage of every opportunity. The British extended the boundaries of Belize, then announced a protectorate over the Miskito Indians. The Miskitos, descendants of aborigines and runaway slaves from all over the Caribbean, inhabited the Caribbean coast of Honduras, Nicaragua, and Costa Rica—the so-called Mosquito coast. The British established a king of "Mosquitia," a country recognized by no nation but the United Kingdom. They then took over the Nicaraguan city of San Juan del Norte, renamed it Greytown, and made it the capital of Mosquitia. Theoretically, Mosquitia was independent. But when its king sold a vast tract of land, including both banks of the San Juan River, to English and American traders for a large quantity of rum and whiskey, the British snatched him off his throne and declared the sales invalid.

Politically, these republics were much alike. They were poor, and the economy was agricultural and feudal. Their only manufactured product was rum, and the only revenue their governments got was from taxes on imports. Each contained two parties, the Liberals and the Conservatives. The parties were partly regional: in Nicaragua the Liberals were centered on the northern city of Leon and the Conservatives on the southern city of Granada. They were partly ideological: the Conservatives supported the Catholic Church and were pro-British. The Liberals were anti-clerical and anti-British. The leaders of both parties were immensely rich and their followers were abysmally poor. They were also usually engaged in civil war. The people of Central America had no notion of nationalism. A political leader in one country had no qualms about calling on a leader of the same party in another country for aid.

That was why Cole was so interested in Nicaragua. When he hired Walker, Honduras was ruled by a Liberal, Trinidad Cabanas. But if the Conservatives overthrew him, they would revoke the charters of all American companies and give them to the British. The Liberals were the "out" party in Nicaragua. If he and Walker could bring the Liberals to power in Nicaragua, it would strengthen the Liberals in neighboring Honduras.

That was Cole's personal interest in Nicaragua. But the tiny republic (population of 250,000) was important to other people for another reason—the California gold rush.

The slowest way to get to California from the eastern United States was overland—walking beside an ox-drawn wagon for thousands of miles. A somewhat faster way involved taking a ship around Cape Horn. The fastest way was taking a ship to the Caribbean coast of Central America, crossing the narrow strip of land and then taking another ship up the Pacific. Panama was the narrowest point, but it was mountainous. Until a railroad was eventually built, travelers were backpacked over the Cordillera by human porters.[20] Crossing Nicaragua made the trip to California even faster and more comfortable. The traveler landed at Greytown, took a steamboat up the San Juan River, switched to a larger lake steamer to cross Lake Nicaragua, landed at La Virgen (the filibusters called it Virgin Bay) and rode a mule or a coach to San Juan del Sur, where he took a ship for San Francisco.

A canal through Nicaragua would make the trip even faster, and a canal looked more feasible there than through mountainous Panama. It would require only widening and dredging the San Juan River, dredging a channel in Lake Nicaragua and digging through the comparatively level 12 miles between La Virgen and San Juan del Sur. Cornelius Vanderbilt, the American shipping magnate, got permission from Nicaragua to dig a canal. In the meantime, he operated the route through Nicaragua—called "the Transit"—with his chartered Accessory Transit Company.

The United States, for obvious reasons, wanted a canal through Nicaragua. Britain, for slightly less obvious reasons, did not.[21] A canal would put the big ports in the eastern United States thousands of miles closer to China than Britain was. The Americans were already cutting deeply into Britain's trade with the Celestial Kingdom.

The situation brought Britain and the United States to the brink of war. Neither country wanted a war. The U.S. Army and Navy were dwarfed by Britain's. On the other hand, the potential U.S. strength relative to Britain was vastly greater than it had been in 1812-15, when the United States had fought Britain to a draw.[22] Britain and France were also drawing close to a major war with Russia. The result was the Clayton-Bulwer treaty. The two countries agreed to jointly finance and build a canal. It looked like a great American diplomatic victory, but when Vanderbilt tried to get British financing for the canal, there was none to be had. Britain had stymied the building of the canal.

Walker's conquest of Nicaragua

An expedition to Nicaragua appealed to Walker's long-standing hatred of the British. He had been outraged when, shortly after he joined the *New Orleans Crescent*, British marines repelled a Nicaraguan attempt to retake Greytown and forced the republic to sign a humiliating peace. It was a blatant affront to the Monroe Doctrine, but his country had done nothing about it.

As Cole explained the political situation in Nicaragua, Walker was also consumed by a desire to bring the blessings of true democracy to the oppressed peons of that country—and all of Central America. Walker told Cole he would gladly lead an expedition.

Cole traveled to Nicaragua and came back with a contract signed by Francisco de Castellon, the Liberal leader. It authorized Walker to bring in a party of North American colonists, who would become Nicaraguan citizens and be given tracts of land. Of course, no Liberal leader had the authority to grant any of Nicaragua's land, and nobody suspected that William Walker was leading a group of would-be coffee planters. Secretary of War Jefferson Davis, however, had hopes that Walker's expedition might result in one or more slave states being admitted to the Union. Davis was not as concerned about Walker and Nicaragua as about Cuba. The annexation of Cuba, where slavery was still practiced, was an objective of all the Southern extremists. The U.S. Neutrality Act seriously hampered attempts to "liberate" Cuba, so Davis was obviously not interested in enforcing the act. He ordered the army not to oppose the filibuster. Walker, mindful of his experience in Mexico, chose his men carefully.[23] But he couldn't afford to take all he would have liked.

Although everyone cheered Walker, few were willing to risk investing in his enterprise. He mortgaged all his own assets to hire troops. As a result, his army was limited to 58 men. Just as he was about to sail, Walker's creditors put a lien on his ship. He squared things with the creditors, but the sheriff of San Francisco County demanded $300 for his expenses. A deputy sheriff boarded the ship. The sheriff really didn't understand William Walker. Walker gave the deputy a choice: have champagne with the filibusters and go ashore or leave with them in handcuffs. The deputy chose champagne.

In Nicaragua, Castellon wanted Walker to stay in Leon. Walker had other plans: He would seize control of the Transit. That was not only Nicaragua's main economic asset, it was a place where he might recruit additional troops from among the gold-seekers. Castellon reluctantly loaned him 100 rebel soldiers, and Walker moved against Rivas, key to the western end of the Transit. When Walker got to Rivas, he found approximately 500 Nicaraguan Conservatives, commanded by a Honduran general, Santos Guardiola. Guardiola was nicknamed "the Butcher" because of his cruelty—notorious even in Central America where killing prisoners was standard operating procedure. The commander of the Liberal army, a General Muñoz, was miffed that Walker had refused to serve under him and had tipped off the enemy.[24] The Nicaraguans in Walker's army refused to advance.

Walker led his 58 men right into the city. The Americans took cover behind trees, rocks and adobe walls as they advanced, firing each time they stopped. They had been chosen for their marksmanship, and they all had percussion rifles of the latest type and all carried modern revolvers.[25] In contrast, the government troops had obsolete smoothbore "Brown Bess" flintlock muskets sold as surplus by the British army—weapons from the era of George Washington and Thomas Gage. It was difficult to hit a man beyond 50 yards with a Brown Bess, almost impossible beyond 80 yards. None had revolvers. It was the disparity of weapons in battles such as this that gave rise to the legend that "one American is worth 10 (ethnic slur of your choice)."

There were, however, just too many government troops. Because the Nicaraguans in Walker's army gave the Americans no support, the government troops were able to surround them. Then the government forces got reinforcements, bringing their number to near 600.[26] Walker's men had to barricade themselves in a large house. Five wounded men couldn't make it inside. The government troops bayoneted the wounded men and burned both the living and dead on a log fire.[27] The government forces brought up a small cannon and began bombarding the house. Walker waited until nightfall, then he and his men broke out of Rivas. Walker's men had killed some 200 of the enemy, but they now numbered only 45.[28]

Walker was cheered when two beachcombers joined his force at San Juan. But the minuscule size of his army didn't deter him from ordering the execution of two Americans who had joined his men in Rivas. The reason: They had set fire to civilian homes.

Before the expedition began, Walker had told his men that drunkenness would be punished by discharge; cowardice, looting, or molesting women, by death.

Defeat, as usual, did not deter William Walker. More volunteers from the United States joined him. Acting on the advice of one of his new volunteers, a Prussian soldier of fortune named Bruno von Natzmer, he sought the cooperation of the Catholic clergy. The priests and Walker hit it off immediately: both hated drunkenness, prostitution, gambling, and thievery. The filibuster and the clerics became so close that Walker eventually converted to Catholicism. With the help of the clergy and a prominent citizen, an Indian named Jose Valle, he began recruiting Nicaraguans who were disgusted with both the Conservatives and the Liberals. Castellon ordered Walker to disband his Nicaraguan troops and return to Leon. Walker ignored him and struck again at the Transit.

With 165 Americans and 125 Nicaraguans, he occupied La Virgen on Lake Nicaragua. After they had dug in, some 600 troops under Guardiola attacked.[29] Guardiola's first wave "went down like grass before a scythe," an American witness reported.[30] The fight lasted three hours, and the government forces finally fled, leaving 65 dead and 100 wounded on the field. Two of Walker's Nicaraguans had been killed and one American was wounded.[31] The next day, 40 more Americans joined Walker's army. The Conservative president had died of cholera the same day Walker's troops repulsed the Conservative forces at La Virgen.

There was confusion among the government forces, but the government generals agreed on one thing: they had to get rid of the Yanqui filibuster and his growing forces. They expected that his next objective would be Rivas—the next government stronghold between Walker and the national capital, Granada. They concentrated almost all their forces at Rivas. Walker loaded his men on a steamer and took them up the lake. With all lights out and engines running slowly, they bypassed Rivas and landed at Granada before dawn. They quickly overwhelmed the skeleton garrison. Walker had no casualties.

For all intents and purposes, the war was over. Conservative General Ponciano Corral tried to hold out in Fort San Carlos on the Transit, but he had no base. A party of Americans intending to join Walker's army fired on Corral's forces from a lake steamer but were driven off. When the steamer returned carrying only civilians, the Conservative troops fired on it again, killing a large number of noncombatants, including women and children. In response, Walker arrested a Conservative politician who had been helping Corral hold out, and had him shot. He sent word to Corral that he would kill more hostages in response to further atrocities. Corral asked Walker to come to him and discuss peace. Walker demanded that Corral come to Granada. Corral came. Walker let Corral practically dictate the peace pact forming a provisional government. Corral seemed to think he had triumphed, shouting after the signing, "we have beaten them with their own game-cock."[32] He was quickly disillusioned. Patricio Rivas, a moderate Conservative who was in awe of Walker, became provisional president. The cabinet contained a mixture of Liberals and Conservatives. Corral became minister of war, but Walker was commander of the armed forces.

The first act of the new government was to put the army on a peace footing. All soldiers who wanted discharges got them. As Walker expected, all conscripted soldiers applied for discharges. The only armed forces left were Walker's "American Phalanx" and the Nicaraguan volunteers he had enlisted. Corral found that he had no power.

Corral wrote to the new dictator of Honduras, Santos Guardiola, "the Butcher." Guardiola had, as Cole feared, deposed Cabanas and begun ousting American interests and turning resources over to the British. Corral asked for aid for a Conservative coup d'etat Corral would lead. The letter fell into the hands of Valle, who gave it to Walker. Walker confronted Corral with the letter at a cabinet meeting. Corral admitted he had written the letter. A court-martial sentenced him to death.

Corral was popular among the Granada Conservatives, and his execution caused a great outcry. It also brought condemnation of Walker from American historians a century and a half later: Walker has been accused of being an imperialist even though he would not allow Nicaragua to be annexed by the United States—and died as a citizen of Nicaragua.

But Corral was clearly guilty of treason—and he was no humanitarian. Like all other Central American generals at the time, he "treated" wounded prisoners by killing them.

Nicaragua's conquest of Walker

Walker's first act on capturing Granada was to release all political prisoners. His Liberal followers wanted to immediately change the constitution, kill all Conservative leaders, and confiscate their property. Walker refused. It was time, he said, for Nicaragua to unite. Although the provisional government contained members of both parties, nobody in Nicaragua had any doubt about who held the real power—William Walker—but Walker refused to be president. Walker had adopted a traditional Central American role—the military strongman—but he would not adopt the lifestyle of a Central American dictator. Power attracted Walker, but not money. He took only the salary of a colonel in the Nicaraguan army, although he held the rank of general, and he wore ordinary civilian clothes instead of a fancy uniform. He lived in a single room in the building of the ministry of war.

Walker fell in love with Nicaragua. He loved the hills, the jungles, and the sparkling beaches. He loved the people and their culture. He was frequently seen with a young woman, Yrena Ohoran, a member of a leading Granada family whose founder had spelled his name O'Horan. It was the first time Walker had shown any interest in a woman since the death of Ellen Martin. He even started his own newspaper, *El Nicaraguense*. Walker saw himself as the "regenerator" of Nicaragua.

One of his most popular moves was to eliminate conscription into the army. As practiced in Central America, conscription was sudden, brutal, and infinitely oppressive.[33] It was more unpopular than taxes or forced labor on the haciendas. There was a legend among the Nicaraguan Indians that someday that oppressed people would be liberated by a hero who could be recognized by his gray eyes. The Indians believed that Walker was *"El Predestinado de los Ojos Grises,"* the Gray-eyed Man of Destiny. Newspapers in the United States picked up the sobriquet.

Walker hoped to unite all Central America as an independent republic. He knew, though, that he'd have to go slowly. Maximo Jerez, a Liberal firebrand, was disappointed. He had hoped for sweeping changes with Walker's victory. Then he proposed that Walker write to all the Liberal leaders in Central America and lead them in a vast crusade to overthrow the pro-British Conservatives in the whole region. But Walker knew that his few hundred Americans and Nicaraguan volunteers would have no chance against the combined armies of all the other republics. He had to recruit more troops.

He had enough trouble dealing with just one of the other republics—Costa Rica. The Costa Ricans invaded Nicaragua soon after Walker's victory. Costa Rica had a boundary dispute with Nicaragua, it had Conservative leadership, and it was heavily influenced by Britain. A British officer, Captain John Cauty, was reorganizing its army.[34] It had another motive, too, that will be examined later.

The Costa Ricans struck while there was a cholera epidemic in Nicaragua. Most of Walker's army was sick, and the general himself had been laid low by fever. He approved moving the government from Granada to Leon. Granada was too close to Costa Rica. And President Rivas wanted to be closer to the northern border so he could improve relations with the northern republics. To deal with the threat in the south, Walker sent a battalion of new recruits who had not contracted cholera—a French company, a German company, a Nicaraguan company, and an American company—to stop the Costa Ricans. He put this polyglot force of 1,600 under a German named Louis Schlesinger, who was an accomplished linguist but a poor commander.[35]

Schlesinger walked into an ambush and fled at almost the first shot. The army was routed and about 100 men killed or captured. (Those captured were later killed.) Walker got up from his sick bed and led the 500 Americans who were able to walk against the 4,000 Costa Ricans who were threatening the Transit.

Then he got an urgent message from Rivas in Leon: Come to Leon because Honduras was about to invade. Walker turned around marched north. Before he reached Leon, he learned that Rivas had panicked: There had been no Honduran troop movements. He turned south again, but by that time the Costa Ricans had occupied Rivas and La Virgen. He attacked the 3,000 Costa Ricans in Rivas. Walker's attack surprised them, and he pushed into the town from four directions. Walker intended to capture General Jose Mora, but the Costa Rican commander got away.[36] Walker's forces killed some 200 of the enemy and wounded twice as many, but he had lost 58 dead, 62 wounded, and 13 missing.[37] His force was too small to continue after such a loss. Walker withdrew from the city. The Costa Ricans had won another victory—of sorts.

The Costa Rican public had been led to believe that their army, newly reorganized by Captain Cauty and equipped with new British rifles, would sweep over Nicaragua.[38] The first victory seemed to confirm that belief. Then the casualty reports from Rivas came in. The Costa Rican population was more than disappointed: it moved to the brink of revolution. The worst was yet to come. The troops in Rivas had been infected with cholera and were dying like flies.[39] General Jose Joaquin Mora, brother of President Juan Rafael Mora, left his troops and went home. His second-in-command, Jose Maria Canas, looked over the situation and decided to follow. He wrote to Walker that he was leaving 1,500 sick and wounded and begged him to be merciful.[40] Of the 4,000 troops who invaded Nicaragua, no more than 500 made it home.[41] The Costa Rican soldiers carried the cholera home, and all desire for more war vanished in Costa Rica.

Meanwhile, Walker did something that left all Central America dumbstruck: He had his own surgeon treat the sick and wounded Costa Ricans left at Rivas. And when they recovered, he let them go home.

While Walker was busy fighting in southern Nicaragua, the politicians in the north held an election. There were three candidates—Rivas, Maximo Jerez, and Mariano Salazar. Only people around Leon could vote: the rest of the country was in too much turmoil. Salazar won by a small margin. The people around Granada were infuriated. They demanded a new election. And they also demanded a new candidate—William Walker.[42] All three candidates opposed a new election, and they vigorously opposed being forced to run against Walker, who not only commanded the army but was unquestionably the most popular man in Nicaragua.

In Leon, Rivas's cabinet was under pressure from the northern republics. Rivas told Walker that he should reduce the size of the American contingent to 200 men to appease the other republics. Walker refused to discharge any soldiers before they were paid, and demanded a new, country-wide election. All but one cabinet member opposed a new election, but he was backed by Walker. A date was set for a new election.

Walker rode back to Granada. As soon as he left the city, Salazar galloped through the streets of Leon shouting that Walker was planning to arrest Rivas, kill all government officers, and make himself dictator. A riot broke out in Leon. Bruno von Natzmer, with a small detachment of troops, was besieged in the cathedral by a mob. Walker sent word to Natzmer to return to Granada.

The election was held as scheduled. According to *El Nicaraguense*, Walker's newspaper, 23,236 of the 35,000 eligible voters in the country cast ballots. Walker got 15,835 votes, Jerez, 4,447, Salazar 2,087 and Rivas, 867. The election was undoubtedly crooked, but probably no more than any other Central American election at the time. And no election could be considered "the will of the people" when only 35,000 out of 250,000 citizens were allowed to vote.

In his inaugural address, Walker stressed Nicaragua's need to assert and guard its independence. It was a warning to those who expected him to bring a new state into the United States.

Salazar, who had led the opposition to Walker, soon had reason to regret it. Walker seized a ship he owned because it was illegally trading with Costa Rica and illegally flying the United States flag.[43] The ship was renamed *Granada* and became Walker's entire navy. Walker put a young Missourian, Callender I. Fayssoux, in command of *Granada*.

Salazar, Rivas, and Jerez starting building up armies in the Leon area. All Nicaraguans should unite to get rid of the gringo, they said. Nationalism, a completely new concept to Central America, was starting to appear. The rebel leaders were not so nationalist, though, that they shunned outside help. They asked leaders of the other republics to help them drive out Walker.[44] To meet the threat, Walker began desperately trying to raise money to hire troops and buy weapons. He had trouble, though, because early in his career, he had offended one of the richest men in the world, Cornelius Vanderbilt.

Shaking hands with the Devil

Vanderbilt had risen from a poor ferryman with an fifth-grade education to being the greatest ship owner in the United States. He was called "the Commodore" at first as a joke, later seriously. He had far more power than any admiral in the world.

Vanderbilt owned, among other things, all the steamships shuttling between the eastern United States and Nicaragua, and he owned the Accessory Transit Company (ATC), which took gold-seekers across Nicaragua. Before Walker's expedition, Vanderbilt had resigned as president of the ATC. He sold much of his ATC stock at a tremendous profit and appointed Charles Morgan and Cornelius Garrison to manage the company. He continued as agent for the Transit company at a handsome salary. But Morgan and Garrison were cut from the same cloth as Vanderbilt.[45] They acquired control of ATC and canceled the Commodore's contract while he was traveling in Europe. Vanderbilt vowed to ruin them.

Vanderbilt began acquiring ATC stock. Garrison and Morgan could see the handwriting on the wall and moved to checkmate the Commodore. Garrison was mayor of San Francisco and an acquaintance of both Walker and Edmund Randolph. He sent Randolph to Walker with a message.

Randolph pointed out to Walker that ATC had promised the Nicaraguan government 10 percent of the profits plus $10,000 a year. The ATC had never paid a penny. The company had ferried a lot of volunteers for Walker's army across the country free, but it had paid no cash.[46] Walker's oldest friend pointed out that the Nicaraguan government would be within its rights to cancel the charter with ATC. Indeed, it had a duty to the people of Nicaragua to do so. It could then charter a new company, one in which Vanderbilt would have no say—a company which would continue to ferry recruits and would also pay its debts. Garrison and Morgan, he said, would be glad to run such a company. Walker agreed and had Rivas sign the appropriate decrees.

Morgan and Garrison knew about the decrees before Vanderbilt or anyone else. They sold their stock in ATC short. Vanderbilt gobbled up what looked like a bargain in ATC stock. Then the news from Nicaragua arrived—the value of ATC stock dropped like a stone. Morgan and Garrison made a tremendous profit, and Vanderbilt took a bath.

Vanderbilt exploded. He sued Walker, Garrison, and Morgan. He unsuccessfully tried to get the U.S. State Department to intervene. He stopped all ships to Nicaragua and rerouted them to Panama. And he let it be known on Wall Street that he would consider buying Nicaraguan bonds to be an unfriendly act.

Cornelius Vanderbilt, who used his great wealth to frustrate the plans of William Walker. (Library of Congress)

Much later, when the Leon faction broke with Walker, Vanderbilt sent them money and guns. He promised more money and guns to other Central American countries if they would help to oust Walker. Walker's enemies were using Vanderbilt's wealth to build up their military strength while Walker had run out of money.

When Walker's situation was beginning to look hopeless, Mephistopheles stepped onto the stage. This demon was Pierre Soule, a French-born Louisianan, duelist, diplomat, and professional Southern fire-eater. Soule told Walker that even if the northern capitalists refused to finance him, there was plenty of money in the South. Walker was a Southerner, of course, but his anti-slavery background made other Southerners suspect that he wasn't their friend.

President Walker began issuing decrees. One prescribed forced labor for any unemployed vagrants. A second required persons who defaulted on their debts to work off their indebtedness. In other words, it legalized peonage. The decree evoked much criticism in the 20th century, but the fact is that peonage was already in force in Nicaragua. Walker apparently hoped that these decrees would indicate to Southerners that his heart was in the right place.

Another decree confiscated the estates of those Nicaraguans who had helped Costa Rica in the late invasion. Walker could have redistributed the land to some of the landless peasants. Nothing would have "regenerated" Nicaragua more than land re-form. But Walker needed money. The land would be sold to the highest bidder. Walker hoped many of the buyers would be North American, so he made English a second official language of Nicaragua. That decree was not as radical as it sounds. English was already the first, and in many cases the only, language of the Miskito Indians of the Caribbean coast.

The decree that caused the greatest outcry, both at the time and later, was nullify-ing the constitution of the Federation of Central America. The Federation had been defunct for 18 years. Liberals had been advocating constitutional reform for years, but when Walker did it, they screamed that he was legalizing slavery. The constitution had made slavery illegal.

Walker's decree did not reestablish slavery. All it did was legally kill a federation that actually had been dead for many years. No Nicaraguans could be enslaved. Ar-ticle 2 of the decree read, "Nothing herein contained shall affect the rights heretofore vested under the acts and decrees hereby repealed."[47] And Walker did want to estab-lish a new, fairer constitution. But he also wanted Southern U.S. investors to *think* he was legalizing slavery.[48] Walker was far too intelligent not to know that reintroducing slavery to Nicaragua was impossible. Where would the slaves come from? Poor and miserable as they were, the citizens of Nicaragua were free. There was no way he could make them slaves. He could not import slaves from Africa or anywhere else. International law prohibited the slave trade. U.S. Navy ships—ships of a country where slavery was practiced—stopped slave ships on the high seas and arrested their crews.

The decree did, however, give Walker's political rivals a great talking point. And it let future historians defame him for more than a century. William Walker was not only the worst sort of Yankee imperialist, he was a slaver. And the only person respon-sible for the situation was Walker himself. He did not, incidentally, get much help from the slave-holding interests in the South. And he needed help.

The Commodore vs. the General

In Costa Rica, there is a statue showing the five Central American republics, rep-resented by young women, driving William Walker away. It greatly exaggerates the role of the five republics. Walker's most dangerous opponent was not one of the re-publics or all of them together. It was one man—Cornelius Vanderbilt.

Vanderbilt did not content himself with blocking Nicaragua bonds, filing suits, petitioning the government, and rerouting his ships to Panama.[49] The rerouting stopped all recruits and supplies to Walker for six weeks, until Garrison and Morgan could send their own steamers.

Vanderbilt wanted a final solution to the Walker problem. The Commodore also prodded the British government (which needed little prodding) to do something about

Walker. The British stationed a fleet of warships at Greytown to intercept men or supplies coming to Walker and encouraged their client state, Costa Rica, to invade Nicaragua. They also gave the Costa Ricans 2,000 new rifles. The invasion was timed to coincide with Vanderbilt's boycott of Nicaragua so Walker could receive no outside help. The Costa Rica invasion was, as we've seen, defeated by Walker and cholera, but a state of war continued between the two countries.

Then the Leon faction broke with Walker. Vanderbilt and the British combined to aid them. In September, 1856, armies from Guatemala, Honduras, and El Salvador swarmed over the Nicaragua border and massed at Leon. There were more than 2,000 troops in the allied armies, not counting the followers of Rivas, Jerez, and Salazar. Simultaneously, the British sent 13 warships, manned by 2,500 sailors and marines, to Greytown. Walker had 600 men and was short of supplies.[50] At first, the northern allies spread over the countryside in small groups. Walker could not tell where they were concentrating. One of his companies misjudged enemy strength at a place called San Jacinto and suffered a sharp repulse.

The Allies concentrated some 2,300 men at Masaya, a town on the way to Granada held by 250 of Walker's men.[51] Walker ordered the garrison to withdraw to Granada, instead of reinforcing Masaya. Then, after the enemy had settled down in the fortifications of Masaya, he attacked them. This operation was the flip side of his brilliant capture of Granada the previous year. Walker and his troops had fought their way to the center of the Masaya when they heard that a Guatemalan column had outflanked them and taken Granada. Walker fell back and found the Guatemalans firmly in control of his capital. He attacked and drove them out of the city.

Then George Law took his revenge on Vanderbilt. (Law owned the steamship line plying the U.S.-Panama route.) He sent Walker several thousand rifles, a quantity of artillery, and ammunition. Most important, he sent an experienced soldier of fortune named Charles Frederick Henningsen, a British subject who had fought in Spain, Russia, and Hungary and authored several much-praised books on military strategy.

Henningsen had just started to train Walker's troops when Costa Rica decided to renew the war. It sent 3,000 troops across the border to seize the Transit. Walker took his troops from Granada and, after a lightning march, hit the Costa Ricans at San Juan del Sur. The Costa Ricans were routed and scattered into the jungle. Walker detached 250 men to guard the Transit and was back in Granada the next night.

With only 300 men, he moved against the entrenched allies at Masaya. He was outnumbered 10 to one, but he counted on the artillery Henningsen had brought to even the odds. Unfortunately, the fuses for the artillery shells were too short. The shells burst harmlessly in the air. Still, Walker, Henningsen, and their men were able, by tunneling through house walls, to drive to within 30 yards of the central plaza in Masaya. But once again, their losses were too heavy to let them continue. Walker had lost more than 100, about a third of his force.[52] Walker fell back to Granada. The allies were too badly cut up to follow.

In very short order, Granada turned into a pest hole. A large part of Walker's army had been wounded, and because of their extreme fatigue and the primitive conditions of the hospitals, cholera had broken out. It quickly spread. The medical staff estimated that if Walker continued to stay in Granada, every American would be dead within six weeks.[53] But if Walker left Granada, the enemy would occupy it again. With both the administrative and commercial centers of the country in enemy hands, the war would be over, as it had been when Walker took Granada after his midnight trip across the lake.

Walker evacuated all the civilians, his sick and wounded, and most of the army. He left Henningsen in Granada with a detachment. Henningsen's orders: destroy the city. Henningsen and his men began burning and blowing up all the buildings in Granada. When the allies realized what was happening, they rushed to Granada to take it from Henningsen's skeleton force. In days of bitter street fighting, Henningsen fought them off while he continued to destroy the city. Granada was wiped out when Walker sent a column to break the siege. Henningsen and all of his remaining men joined Walker at Rivas. Before he left, Henningsen thrust a lance into the ground. On it was a sign: *"Aquí Fue Granada."* Granada Was Here.

Meanwhile, Fayssoux, commanding the sloop *Granada*, mounting two guns, had encountered a British-built brig flying the Costa Rican flag. The Costa Rican ship was twice the size of *Granada* and carried four larger guns. A crowd of spectators on the beach watched the two-hour naval battle. It was growing dark when the spectators saw a tremendous flash and the firing seemed to stop. Everyone expected to see the Costa Ricans returning triumphant. The Costa Ricans returned, but as prisoners aboard *Granada*. Fayssoux had blown up the enemy brig.

Walker's situation no longer looked hopeless. Rivas was strongly fortified; he held the Transit, and several hundred recruits had been able to evade the British and were on the way to help him. The northern allies seemed to have had enough of war. They had suffered heavy casualties and were torn by dissension between the Salvadorians, the Hondurans, the Guatemalans, and the Nicaraguan rebels. The Costa Ricans, too, were reluctant to move after their defeat.

At this point, Vanderbilt sent in his secret weapon—a filibuster of his own, Sylvanius Spencer. Spencer, who had been an engineer on the Transit, went to Costa Rica, bringing thousands of new Minie rifles and a British government agent named William W. C. Webster.[54] Webster was to coordinate Spencer's operations with those of Captain John Cauty, who was now the de facto commander of the Costa Rican army.

Spencer, leading a picked force of well-armed Costa Ricans in canoes and on rafts, surprised Walker's small garrison at Hipp's Point, at the junction of the San Juan and Serapiqui rivers. Then he and his men paddled down the river to Greytown and seized four steamers. They took the steamers back up the river to the junction of the San Carlos River, where they joined more than 1,000 Costa Ricans, nominally under

Jose Joaquin Mora (and actually commanded by John Cauty) also armed with the latest Minie rifles.

The Costa Ricans captured two more river steamers. Spencer took one up to the lake and captured the lake steamer *Virgen* by hiding his troops on the river boat until he brought his craft alongside the larger steamer. Then using *Virgen* as an aquatic Trojan horse, he captured Fort San Carlos. The second lake steamer, *San Carlos*, got the recognition signal from the fort of the same name. Not knowing it had been captured by the Costa Ricans, it entered the river and was trapped between La Virgen and the fort. In the meantime, Cauty had taken a key fort on the eastern shore of Lake Nicaragua. Then he and Spencer occupied La Virgen before Walker even knew about the Costa Rican offensive. Spencer and Cauty had taken the whole Transit. Spencer went back to New York, where Vanderbilt gave him $50,000. Hiring Spencer was one of the best deals the Commodore ever made. Walker himself said of the erstwhile engineer, "The fortune which proverbially favors the brave certainly aided Spencer much in his operations."[55]

Cauty's British compatriots entered Greytown and stopped a force of 400 Americans, who had come to help Walker recapture some steamers. And on the Pacific coast, a British fleet bottled up San Juan del Sur. The northern allies cautiously completed the circle around Rivas. Walker was trapped.

His enemies contented themselves with sniping and artillery fire. General Mora said he would starve out Walker. After a while, he rescinded his "no quarter" order. Any Americans who surrendered would be treated well and sent back to the United States, he told Walker's troops through leaflets. Desertions became a problem for Walker until he called all his troops together and told them that anyone who wanted to was free to go. Five men took advantage of the offer. After this, desertions stopped. Walker led 400 of his men on a desperate attack on 2,000 Guatemalans.[56] The northerners were hurt, but he couldn't break out. The Guatemalans, filled with hubris, sent 2,000 men against Walker. Walker's fire cut down 700 of them. He had nine casualties.[57] That was the last battle of the siege.

Walker and his men were running of out food and supplies. Walker didn't know it, but his enemies were also having troubles. Cholera had broken out among the besiegers. Vanderbilt knew of the allies' troubles, however. If something weren't done, Walker might again triumph. He put pressure on Washington to do something about the "situation in Central America." Washington sent Commander Charles H. Davis, skipper of the sloop-of-war *St. Mary's* to negotiate Walker's surrender. Mora was happy to negotiate. He told Davis that his losses from cholera were so great that in another 20 days he would have to end the war.[58] Walker held out until Mora promised good treatment for the Nicaraguans, as well as the Americans, in his army. On May 1, 1857, Walker addressed his troops for the last time. Then he and his chief officers boarded *St. Mary's*. The rest of the army went to Greytown and boarded the U.S. frigate *Wabash* for the trip home.

Hail the conquered hero

Walker landed in New Orleans, and the city went wild. Walker's admirers literally besieged him at his hotel. When he attended the opera, the show stopped for 10 minutes while the audience gave him a standing ovation. Two nights later, he spoke for two hours at an open-air mass rally. When he went to visit his sister in Kentucky, he got equally enthusiastic welcomes in Louisville and in neighboring Cincinnati. At that stronghold of Yankee capitalism, New York, he led a parade that was not equalled until Commodore George Dewey's triumph after the Spanish-American war. At all his public appearances, Walker maintained that if Davis had not arrived, he would still be president of Nicaragua.[59] He held that he was the only legitimate president of Nicaragua, and he had to return and take his rightful place.[60]

A few days before his New York appearance, Walker went to Washington for a private conference with President James Buchanan. Buchanan, an old diplomat, had the knack of never seeming to disagree with anything anyone else said. Walker, in his obsession with regaining the presidency of Nicaragua, thought the president was endorsing his plans to return.

On November 14, 1857, Walker and 270 filibusters sailed from Mobile on the steamship *Fashion*. Buchanan ordered the navy to intercept them. But while the sloop-of-war *Saratoga* waited for them at Greytown, Walker dropped a party under Frank Anderson off farther up the coast. Anderson captured Castillo Viejo, three river steamers and a lake steamer from the Costa Ricans without losing a man. Walker and the rest of his men landed at Greytown pretending to be agents of Commodore Vanderbilt. Then they set up a camp on the shore and waited for Anderson to come down the river. At that point, Commodore Hiram Paulding trained the guns of the frigate *Wabash* on Walker's camp, landed marines, and ordered Walker to surrender. Outnumbered and vastly outgunned (*Wabash* and *Saratoga* had been joined by another American and two British warships) Walker surrendered.

Back home, he protested that Paulding's actions violated international law.[61] The treatment of Walker was the subject of several days' debate in Congress. In the end, Paulding was reprimanded and temporarily suspended from command, but Walker got no encouragement for further adventures. Nevertheless, only about a year later, Walker sent an advance party of 120 filibusters to Central America. They were shipwrecked off Honduras and ignominiously returned to the United States on a British warship.

Walker settled down to write *The War in Nicaragua*. Even his enemies praised his accuracy and objectivity (he always referred to himself in the third person) when describing the war. When he got off the facts, though, Walker launched into pure propaganda. He used all his highly developed persuasive skill to argue the desirability of slavery in hot climates. It's doubtful that Walker had really changed so radically in his feelings about the "peculiar institution." He probably cared very little about it one way or the other. At this point in his life, Walker had only one thought: he was the legitimate president of Nicaragua, and he had to return. If he had to advocate slavery to gain the necessary support, he'd advocate slavery. The book reflects Walker's monomania. It's heavy reading. All the wit and irony of his early editorials is gone. The only traces of his old style are in his lyrical descriptions of the Nicaraguan landscape.

The last cast

In April, 1860, Callender Fayssoux told Walker that an Englishman living on Ruatan, an island off Honduras that Britain had taken, had given him a message. The British government was going to give Ruatan back to Honduras in return for trade concessions. Ever since the Walker wars, the Central Americans had been growing restless. Gaining trade concessions while giving up lots of territory struck John Bull as a good bargain. But the British settlers, planned to seize the government buildings and declare their independence, rather than being ruled by Honduras. They wanted Walker to help them.

Walker couldn't have been happier. With Ruatan at war with Honduras, Walker could join Trinidad Cabanas, the Liberal leader, and return Cabanas to power. Then he could, with the help of the Liberal and American recruits, return to Nicaragua. He got two ships, filled one with filibusters and the other with supplies and headed for Ruatan. Ideally, they would arrive just after the British left.

Unfortunately, there were hitches. First, the British government learned about the scheme: the Ruatan settlers had talked too much. Second, the British captured the supply ship. Third, the British didn't leave Ruatan.

Walker and his men waited for the supply ship on the island of Cozumel. When he learned what had happened to the supply ship, and it became apparent that the British were going to wait until his supplies ran out, he decided to invade Honduras and try to link up with Cabanas.

He landed at Truxillo (now spelled Trujillo), stormed the fort, chased the Honduran authorities out, and declared Truxillo a free port. A British warship, *Icarus*, commanded by a Captain Norvell Salmon, appeared and demanded $3,000 which he said was kept at the custom house for a British inspector. He also demanded that Walker and his men surrender and lay down their arms.

Instead, Walker's troops destroyed the guns of the fort, burned all the munitions they couldn't carry, and set out to find Cabanas. They were attacked by Honduran troops and beat them off, but they could get no information as to the whereabouts of Cabanas. Finally, acting on information from some friendly Indians, they found an abandoned camp. They also found Honduran troops waiting in ambush. They fought the Hondurans for nine days. Many of the men were wounded, including Walker, who had a fever. There were barely a dozen men holding off a Honduran army.[62] Then two British boats came up the river. Captain Salmon got out and demanded that they surrender.

"To whom do I surrender?" Walker asked.

"To an officer of Her Majesty's government," Salmon replied, adding, "And you may thank me, too, that you have a whole bone in your body and that your men leave here alive."

Walker wanted to be absolutely sure he and his men would not wind up in the hands of "Butcher" Guardiola. He asked again: "Do I understand you to say, sir, that my surrender would be to a member of Her Majesty's government?"

"Yes, to me."

"Under these circumstances, I surrender to you, Captain," Walker said.[63]

But when they were aboard *Icarus*, Salmon informed Walker that while the rank and file of his army would be returned to the United States, he would be turned over to the Hondurans. He gave no explanation for his lie at the surrender. He said, though, that if Walker would ask him as an American citizen, he would intercede for him.[64]

"The President of Nicaragua is a Nicaraguan citizen," Walker said, and turned his back on the Englishman.[65]

The Hondurans held Walker six days—long enough to get instructions from Guardiola. The instructions were, of course, "shoot him." Walker confessed to a priest and received Holy Communion, then was taken out the next morning and shot in front of the fort he had stormed a few days before.

On April 12, 1861, Confederate guns opened fire on Fort Sumter. The ensuing carnage made everyone in the United States forget about William Walker. When he is remembered at all, it is as a champion of slavery.

In Central America, generations of politicians and writers have combined to picture Walker as an imperialist who combined the worst features of Attila the Hun and Genghis Khan. They ignore his real legacy. Before Walker, all of Central America was ruled by a handful of landowners and warlords utterly devoid of ordinary patriotism. A conservative Nicaraguan leader would call for help from a conservative Honduran or Guatemalan leader against his own people without a second thought.

Both Walker's insistence on Nicaraguan independence and his enemies' revolt against him changed that. Walker midwifed nationalism in Central America. By the end of the American Civil War, that nationalism had reduced British domination of Central America to the tiny and impoverished colony called British Honduras (today Belize) which had been founded by English pirates in the 17th century.

2

The Yankee God of War: Frederick Townsend Ward

A business proposal

The year 1860 did not look like a good one to Wu Hsu, the taotai of Shanghai. Wu was the second-ranking official in the province of Kiangsu, but most of the province was in enemy hands. Soochow, the capital, had been taken by the Taiping rebels. Hsueh Huan, the governor, was living there in Shanghai, which merely added to Wu's many troubles.

Shanghai was one of the five "treaty ports" the British had forced the Imperial government to open in 1842 after the First Opium War. There were now thousands of Westerners living in the city and following their own laws. The concessions the British had won in the First Opium War didn't satisfy them, so in 1856 they manufactured an incident to justify the Second Opium War.[1] Now they were invading China again with the French. While the Europeans were marching on Peking, the Taiping rebels, who had been besieged in Nanking, were able to break out and renew their offensive. One huge Taiping army was moving on Shanghai, and the city was already crowded with refugees fleeing the rebels.

Wu and Hsueh, the governor, had tried to get the British, French, and Americans to provide a military force to defend Shanghai, where they had so much invested.[2] The foreigners, though, intended to remain neutral. They were convinced they could do business with the Taipings at least as well as with the Manchu dynasty in Peking. Probably better for the foreigners—the Taipings worshipped the same Jesus the Westerners did.

Wu, then, was in a receptive frame of mind on that sunny May day when a young American came to him with a proposition he might otherwise have laughed at. Wu's old friend and business associate, the banker Yang Fang, introduced the young man, Frederick Ward. Ward was currently first mate on the armed river steamer of the Shanghai Pirate Suppression Bureau. The SPSB was an enterprise Wu had begun in order to facilitate commerce on the Yangtze. River pirates—another by-product of the accursed Opium War—had become such a plague they threatened to choke off the trade that was Shanghai's lifeblood.[3] Yang said Ward had fought wars in Mexico and Russia. Ward, who had the confident air of an old campaigner, asserted that a force of Westerners, armed and trained in the Western manner, could beat many times their number of Taipings. If the Shanghai authorities could provide money for weapons and salaries, Ward promised to recruit, train, and lead the men. He would retake towns and cities from the Taipings if the government would pay a bounty for each town. The size of each bounty would depend on the size and importance of the town. The salaries would be high: for enlisted men, $50 a month; for officers, $200 a month; for Ward, $500 a month. In addition to their salaries, Ward's troops could keep any plunder they got from the towns. The bounties for each town would be negotiated before the mercenaries attacked.

Wu did some quick calculations. The Taiping army approaching his city was commanded by Li Xiucheng, known as the Chung Wang (the Faithful King—all leading Taipings were called kings), the most formidable of the rebel leaders. No Imperial army had been able to resist him. When the Taipings captured a city, the usual result was wholesale slaughter.[4] (Before it ended, the Taiping Rebellion would extinguish 20 million human lives, making it the bloodiest war in history until World War II.) The proposition of this foreign devil Ward was expensive. But it was better to be temporarily poor than permanently dead. Wu agreed. So did Hsueh.

The Foreign Devil

Frederick Townsend Ward, born in Salem, Massachusetts, should have been a sailor. His father was a ship owner engaged in the China trade, as was his grandfather. Young Fred went to sea as third mate on a windjammer at the age of 15. But, being naturally rebellious, Ward had no desire to follow the family tradition. He wanted to be a soldier. Not a soldier in the U.S. Army, however. He had no desire to spend long, boring months in a frontier outpost. He wanted action. He was on a ship sailing up the west coast of Mexico when he heard of William Walker's planned expedition. He joined Walker's army in San Francisco but parted from the Gray-Eyed Man of Destiny in Baja California. The cause was said to be "personality conflicts."[5]

Ward stayed in Mexico for a while and tried to run a business exporting scrap metal to the United States. Today, that doesn't sound like a very promising profession (and it probably wasn't then, either). Ward went back to California and shipped out as first mate on a China clipper. Back in the United States, Ward used family connections to get a lieutenant's commission in the French Army, then thought in the Crimean War. He saw some fighting, but he didn't last much longer with the French than he did with Walker. According to a biographer, "he quarreled with his superior officer and was allowed to resign."[6] In 1857, Ward was back in China, working as first mate on a coastal steamer. He returned to the States a couple years later, tried working in an office, got bored, and took another clipper to China.

This time, he found work more congenial to his belligerent spirit, as an officer on the anti-pirate patrol boat. Ward's boss, an American who called himself "Admiral" Gough, introduced him to Yang Fang, who paid the pirate suppressors for Wu. Ward's energy and intelligence impressed Yang, who took him to meet Wu.

Thus the 28-year-old sailor began a career too fantastic for fiction. It involved fighting an even more fantastic enemy.

The Heavenly Kingdom

In 1836, Hong Huoxiu, a 22-year-old village school teacher who was in Canton to take the civil service examinations, met a foreigner with a Cantonese interpreter.[7] They gave him a book in Chinese about the Supreme God of Heaven and his son, Jesus Christ. Hong failed the examination, but the disappointed teacher kept the book. The book, *Good Words for Exhorting the Age*, was by Liang Afa, a Chinese who had been converted by an American Protestant missionary. Hong studied it along with his Confucian books as he prepared for the next year's examinations. He found parallels between traditional Chinese teaching and the beliefs of the Christians.[8] As he studied, Hong looked around him. He saw violent crime; sadistic executions; tyrannical, corrupt rulers; oppressive landlords; and a land beset by foreign enemies (the First Opium War had begun) and ruled by usurpers (the Manchu dynasty, established by Tatar conquerors 200 years before). He saw everything opposed to the heavenly peace (Taiping) desired by the strange Supreme God of Heaven who was the subject of his book.

Not surprisingly, given his study of conflicting scriptures, Hong failed the examination the second time. Deeply disappointed, he seemed to lose all energy, and was barely able to return home. At home, he became sick and eventually lost consciousness.

While he was unconscious, Hong believed that he was taken up to heaven and met the Supreme God and his son, Jesus. And he learned that he, himself, was God's second son, the younger brother of Jesus. God told Hong that China had been taken over by devils, the Manchus, and he would have to return to earth to fight them. Hong's name must be changed, God told him. Instead of Hong Huoxiu, he would be Hong Xiuquon (Xiuquon means "Complete Fire").

When Hong regained consciousness, he remembered the dream. He changed his name to Hong Xiuquon. But he could not understand the meaning of the dream. What had the Father wanted him to do? He turned to Liang's book, seeking an answer. He began writing and teaching about the Supreme God of Heaven in his south China village, claiming that the Taoists, Confucians, and Manchus had corrupted the original teaching of God. He made converts and moved to other villages. Many people were attracted to the new religion. Others were attracted to anything opposed to the Manchu dynasty. Among Hong's converts were pirates, bandits, and members of anti-Manchu secret societies.

Local landlords, local officials, and the Imperial government itself became worried by the growth of the religion of Taiping, or as Hong called it, the "Bai Shangdi Hui," (the "God Worshipping Society"). Taipings were persecuted. Hong decided to fight back. He organized his followers like an army. Four men were commanded by a corporal, five corporals by a sergeant, four sergeants by a lieutenant, up through captains and colonels, to generals, each of whom would command a division with a full strength of 13,155.[9] The top generals, Hong's closest associates, were called king ("wang" in Chinese). Hong himself was the Tien Wang, the Heavenly King.

Much like Mao Zedong a century later, the Tien Wang led his people on a long march to the north, beating off enemies and capturing cities along the way. At last, they captured Nanking, once the Imperial capital. The Tien Wang made it the capital of what was to become the Heavenly Kingdom after the Taipings had subdued the "devils."

Hong sent his forces marching north, south, east, and west. The Manchus, however, did not give in easily. They gradually pressed the Taipings back into Nanking. Then the Second Opium War began, and the Imperialists had to divert forces to meet the Europeans.

Long before that, the Tien Wang had dropped out of active participation in military affairs. He was preoccupied with other things. Until the Heavenly Kingdom was achieved, the Taipings were forbidden to drink alcohol, smoke opium, or have sex. Even married couples who slept together were beheaded. Such rules did not, however, apply to God's second son. Hong's palace was filled with mistresses, and the Heavenly King was usually besotted with drugs or drink. He was, in fact, mad—and growing madder each year. Much of the credit for breaking the siege belongs to a young farm hand who joined the Taipings well after their capture of Nanking. Li Xiucheng rose rapidly through the ranks because of his intelligence and valor. Now he was the Chung Wang, one of the Taipings' top generals, and leading the assault on Shanghai.

Raising an army

Ward didn't have any trouble finding troops. He chose an old friend, Henry Burgevine of South Carolina, to be second in command. Then he recruited the reckless, usually penniless, adventurers Shanghai had in abundance. Most were American, but they included Danes, Frenchmen, Englishmen, Swiss, and Prussians. He purchased their weapons himself. At the time, you could buy any weapons—from pocket pistols to cannons—in Shanghai. The city was full of gun-runners trying to unload obsolete weapons to either Taipings or Imperialists at exorbitant prices. Ward, unlike most Chinese buyers, knew modern weapons. He favored the Sharps breech-loader, which, although not a repeater, was the best military rifle in the world. For sidearms, he got Colt's revolvers, concentrating on the 1851 navy model—the famous "navy Colt" that became the favorite weapon of Wild Bill Hickock.[10]

Frederick Townsend Ward—portrait painted by an unknown Chinese artist. Ward probably sat for this shortly before his death in 1862. (Photo courtesy of Essex Institute, Salem, Mass.)

He established a training camp for what became known as the Shanghai Foreign Arms Corps, the Chinese Foreign Legion, or simply the "Ward Corps."

Wu, Hsueh, and Yang waited impatiently while Ward trained his 100 troops. In June, they demanded that Ward support the Imperial army in its attempt to retake two towns from the rebels. The counterattack was successful, but the rebels then captured Sung-chiang, a walled city only a few miles from Ward's camp. Wu ordered Ward to drive them out. Ward said he had no artillery and he hadn't time to train his men in siege tactics. The Chinese backers demanded action. No action, no money.

To make up for his lack of artillery, Ward planned to use surprise. He led his troops up to the walls of Sung-chiang in the dead of the night. Unfortunately, the American and European bar flies who made up his army had been celebrating their victory beforehand. They made so much noise they woke up the sleeping Taipings who blasted them with everything they had. The Taipings didn't have much in the way of guns, but they had enough. The Foreign Arms Corps was bloodily repulsed. Back as his base, Ward paid off the survivors, most of whom then disappeared back into the Shanghai underworld. The western merchants and diplomats who ruled Shanghai's foreign settlements were delighted. They were afraid Ward would antagonize the Taipings, who looked like the eventual winners, making it impossible for them to continue in business.

Ward, however, was far from finished. He immediately began recruiting a new army. Instead of hiring more western adventurers, he turned to Shanghai's large Filipino population. The "Manilamen" were found in the crews of every ship in Far Eastern waters. Captains were eager to hire them because they were intelligent, hard-working, and brave. The bravest Filipino Ward found was a 23-year-old native of Manila named Vicente Macanaya.[11] Macanaya became Ward's chief lieutenant after his friend, Burgevine, and was soon known to all Westerners in China as "Vincente," a corruption of his first name. Ward soon had 80 Filipinos in the Foreign Arms Corps. All of them spoke Spanish, a language Ward was familiar with. Word spread through the Filipino community. More and more joined the Ward Corps.

Once again, Wu and Yang began pressing Ward to attack Sung-chiang. This time, Ward would not be rushed. He obtained artillery—12-pounders and six-pounders—and was drilling his men on how to move the weighty pieces through the water-logged province of Kiangsu. To teach the Filipino sailors how to handle cannons, he recruited Westerners with artillery experience, many of them military deserters. Most of the deserters came from the British Army, which had the most men in the area. In addition to cannons, Ward bought more rifles—as many Sharps as he could get—and revolvers for his expanding army. For his blade-loving Filipinos, he also bought a load of bolo knives. But in battle, Ward himself carried nothing but a rattan walking stick. That was part of his mystique: He was the fearless leader who would charge unarmed into the hottest fire fight.

And those fights were hot. Ward would be wounded no fewer than 15 times while campaigning in China. There was a practical reason, for his battlefield behavior. If he were not distracted by defending himself, he could concentrate on the action around him and give whatever orders were necessary.

Before his second attack on Sung-chiang, Ward left most of his western officers in camp. They could drink to their hearts' content, and their carousing would make the enemy spies think nothing was going to happen. He put some 200 Filipino troops on a river steamer headed for Ch'ing-p'u rather than Sung-chiang. But after the steamer was well underway, Ward and his men left it in small boats and landed outside Sung-chiang. They moved through darkness and heavy fog right up to the walled city's moat. Then, on July 16, 1860 at 11 p.m., Ward's cannons opened up and blew down Sung-chiang's east gate. While some of his men put scaling ladders against the walls, Ward led the charge through the gate.

Inside the gateway arch, though, Ward found his way blocked by a second gate. He retreated through heavy Taiping fire then and returned with a small party carrying 20 50-pound sacks of gunpowder. The put the powder against the gate, lit a fuse and ran back. There was a tremendous explosion. Ward led his men back into the gateway. But the explosion had made only a small hole in the second gate—a hole just big enough for one man to crawl through. Ward hesitated only an instant.

"Come on, boys, we're going in!" he yelled.[12] And, armed with his walking stick, he dived through the hole. Burgevine, Macanaya, and the rest of the troops followed. Ward and his Filipinos fought their way to the top of the wall and turned the Taipings' cannons around. While they shot down the defenders with their own artillery, Ward's men fired a signal rocket to let Imperial troops outside know that the gate was open. The Imperial troops didn't move, leaving Ward's 200 facing thousands of defenders. Cannister shot (tin cans filled with musket balls that turned a cannon into a gigantic shotgun) from the cannons and bullets from the Sharps rifles, however, were too much for the Taiping garrison. They streamed out of the city by daybreak.

The victory was costly. Sixty-two of Ward's men were killed and another hundred, including Ward, were wounded. But the loot—in both military supplies and precious metals—was enormous.

Wu Hsu, Yang Fang, and Hsueh Huan were delighted. The Western merchants, though, were livid. Ward was a dangerous filibuster who would surely bring the wrath of the Taipings on all Westerners in China. The British were particularly incensed. Ward was luring British soldiers and sailors to his "gang" with salaries far higher than they'd ever earn in Her Majesty's service.

Changing fortunes of war

Ward's success at Sung-chiang was a surprise for the Taipings. They had never before seen a demonstration of the superiority of western weapons and tactics. They were better prepared the next time.

The most obvious objective of Ward's Foreign Arms Corps was capturing Ch'ing-p'u, the fortified city at which Ward had feinted before the attack on Sung-chiang. To garrison that city, the Chung Wang detailed one of his best-armed units—all the men had muskets instead of bows, spears, and swords. Commanding it was one of his western mercenaries, an Englishman named Savage.

Once again, Ward tried a surprise assault. He and Macanaya led the storming party, while Burgevine commanded the second wave, which was to rush through the breech the first wave opened. It looked as if Ward's men would catch all the Taipings asleep. There was not a sound from the city, even when they placed scaling ladders against its wall and climbed to the parapet.

Then, as they assembled on top of the wall, a storm of fire erupted from towers on the wall and houses in the city. Savage and his men had been waiting for this moment. The men on the wall were mowed down. Taiping fighters swarmed up the wall and hurled boulders at the Filipinos still climbing the ladders. Ward was hit with musket balls five times in a matter of seconds. Vicente Macanaya caught him as he was about to fall off the wall and carried him back to the ground. Ward's most serious wound was in the jaw, which left him unable to speak. But he remained conscious and, bleeding profusely, wrote out his orders and gave them to Macanaya. Vicente himself scorned the enemy's bullets and went on "firing like fury whilst his companions were dropping on all sides of him, killed by the unerring aim of the rebels on the walls."[13]

The *North China Herald*, a British paper, exulted: "This notorious man [Ward] has been brought down to Shanghai, not as hoped, dead, but severely wounded."[14]

Ward was disabled but not out of action. He purchased more artillery, including two powerful 18-pounders, and returned to Ch'ing-p'u to conduct a siege. But the Chung Wang came up with a large force and drove the besiegers back to their recently-captured base, Sung-chiang. Ward was still seriously wounded. Burgevine, afraid that he would die if he didn't get better medical attention, had him secretly lowered from the walls of Sung-chiang onto a riverboat and taken to Shanghai. He arrived there shortly before the Chung Wang and his Taiping army.

The Taiping general gave orders to his men to spare the Christian churches and not to harm the Westerners in Shanghai. The Westerners were not so sure the rebels would spare them. They organized an armed force—volunteers and regular military—to defend the Western concession areas. Among those involved was the ailing Ward. Following their general's orders, the Taiping troops did not fire on Westerners, even when the "foreign devils" were shooting them down. A week later, the Chung Wang left Shanghai. The Tien Wang had ordered him to leave Kiangsu province and help the other Taiping forces against Zeng Guofan, the most talented Imperial general, who was surrounding Anking with a powerful army from the province of Hunan. Zeng Guofan, noting Ward's success with western weapons, had starting rearming his own troops. Ward, too, left Shanghai. He went to Paris for treatment of his wounds.

Meanwhile, the British and French had captured Peking and then sacked and burned the Emperor's Summer Palace. They got what they had wanted from the Imperial government, and now they were becoming more hostile to the Taipings. One important obstacle to good relations with the rebels was opium. The narcotic was the most important product in the Western trade with China. The Imperialists had lost a war over preventing its importation, but the Taipings opposed opium in another way: They eliminated demand by beheading addicts.

To neutralize a filibuster

Hostility to the Taipings didn't make the British any more friendly to Ward. British Admiral Sir James Hope ordered a subordinate, Commander Henry Hire, to arrest all British deserters and anyone who was recruiting them. Hire approached Wu, who told him he didn't know of any British subjects in the Foreign Arms Corps. Furthermore, he had disbanded the Foreign Arms Corps in September. He didn't know where Ward was. In fact, he thought Ward had been killed. Hire knew better. He knew Ward had recently returned to Shanghai. But he didn't know where Ward was, and he didn't know what to do with him if he found him. Ward was not a British subject.

Hire reported that he "waited on the American Flag Officer asking his assistance toward the detention of Ward, to which he unhesitatingly replied that [Ward] was not an American Subject, or entitled to protection as such. I then requested him to give me that in writing, which he did."[15] Ward had, in fact, recently applied for Chinese citizenship. As a Chinese citizen, he could not be accused of violating U.S. neutrality laws. As Ward was not under U.S. protection, and as Hire could not believe he had become Chinese, the commander could see no international problems in arresting Ward. He ordered a search for the filibuster. Ward, who was not hiding, was arrested and taken to Hire's ship. Hire interrogated him about his nationality, but Ward claimed citizenship of no country. A Shanghai attorney told Hire he must turn Ward over the "proper Chinese authorities." The "proper Chinese authorities" were Wu and Hsueh, who promptly released the soldier of fortune.

The frustrated British again arrested Ward and confined him on a British ship. But Vicente Macanaya got a message to his commander. That night, Ward dived through a porthole and came up beside a boat operated by Macanaya. Before the British knew what happened, Fred Ward had disappeared into the night.

If Ward chose to remain in hiding, the task of finding him seemed hopeless. In a dispatch to Lord Russell, the British foreign minister, Frederick Bruce, the British minister to China, wrote concerning British mercenaries on both sides:

> *It will be seen that British subjects in both instances form but a fraction of the hired forces. The enlisting agent on the part of the Government seems to be a man called Ward, an ex-Californian filibuster; and on that of the Taipings, a man called Peacock. Both are of United States origin, but Ward, it appears, does not now claim to be an American citizen. The law of the United States is, I believe, very severe against enlistment in the Chinese service; but it appears that the authorities have great difficulty in putting the law into operation. Ward, it appears, besides the Foreign Legion, has undertaken to drill a body of Chinese in the employment of the Imperial Government. I look upon it as perfectly hopeless to prevent foreigners entering the service of these parties as long as the pay is sufficient to attract them, and as long as the Chinese think that they will be of use in military operations.*[16]

At the same time, relations between the British and the Taipings were deteriorating rapidly. A British officer tried to approach the Taiping-held city of Ch'ing-p'u under a flag of truce. The Taipings fired on him. A few days later, the same officer, Captain Roderick Dew, was successful in meeting Taiping leadership. He had come to warn the rebels not to attack the treaty port of Ningpo. Dew was escorted through a conquered village to Taiping headquarters. The village, he saw, had been utterly destroyed an all the inhabitants who had not fled had been massacred. The Taipings didn't agree not to attack Ningpo. After Dew returned, his superior, Admiral Hope, wrote to London recommending military intervention.

British diplomats and journalists began describing a Taiping victory as an utter disaster for China. At the same time, they saw no hope that the Imperial forces alone could put down the rebellion. The only effective Imperial force seemed to be the Ward Corps. As a result, Hope put out the word that he would like to meet with Ward. The meeting took place in mid-1861. The admiral, it seems, promised to stop harassing the filibuster, and Ward to stop enticing British servicemen. Ward's promise was easy to make. He had already decided to recruit from a new pool.

Ward's new army

When he began fighting in China, Ward doubted that Chinese could ever be efficient soldiers. That prejudice was shaken by the Taipings at Ch'ing-p'u. It was destroyed by a Frenchman, Captain Adrien Tardif de Moidrey of the French Navy. Tardif de Moidrey, inspired by Ward's operations, conceived the idea of a Chinese artillery force with French officers. He received covert support from his admiral, who put him on the sick list so he wouldn't be required to do anything for the French Navy, and from Wu and Hsueh, who financed the unit. The Franco-Chinese artillery gave a good account of itself in several skirmishes.

Ward, in turn, was inspired by Tardif de Moidrey. Why not use Chinese soldiers? If Filipinos, who had no modern military experience or tradition, could be taught to fight in the Western manner, why couldn't the Chinese? And there were infinitely more Chinese in China than Filipinos, Americans, or Europeans. Wu and Hsueh loved the idea of a Westernized Chinese army. They loved it for patriotic reasons...and also for economic reasons: Chinese privates would fight for eight or nine dollars a month instead of the $50 that went to Americans and Europeans. At their urging, the Imperial government in Peking adopted the new Ward Corps and commissioned Ward a colonel in the Imperial Army. Although the Ward Corps—which eventually numbered some 7,000 men—was a regular Chinese Army unit, it was utterly independent. Ward took orders from no one and obeyed no policy but his own.

Ward obtained modern weapons for his troops and designed Western style uniforms. They drilled in the Western manner. Taiping sympathizers jeered at them as "imitation foreign devils," but potential recruits lined up, eager to join Ward—or as the Chinese pronounced his name "Hwa."[17] In his new army, Ward retained a bodyguard of 200 Filipinos, commanded, of course, by Vicente Macanaya. The officers of the main body were Americans and Europeans at first. As time went on, however, Ward began promoting Chinese to be officers.

Chinese tactics, as practiced by the Imperialists before Ward appeared, were based on intimidation. There was a great deal of shouting, marching, and attempting to make forces look larger than they were. Guns were used more for making noise than killing enemy soldiers. Even bows and arrows looked more formidable than they were. The arrows were huge—more like spears—and the bows had immensely heavy pulls. When shot, however, their range was disappointing.[18] Ward changed all that.

Ward's men would fire their rifles only when ordered to. And they would rely heavily on modern artillery and steamships. Kiangsu was swampy and laced with rivers and canals. It was faster to move by water than by road. Water transport had long been used by both sides for transporting troops. One of the reasons the Chung Wang wanted Shanghai was to seize the river steamers based there. But Ward introduced a new idea. He mounted cannons on the steamers and used them as mobile batteries. He used ship-to-shore bombardment to support his ground forces. A short time later, U.S. Army-Navy task forces were to independently develop similar tactics in the Western theater of the American Civil War.

Ward devised a strategy to go with his new weapons and tactics. His force was small, but his main concern was with Shanghai and Kiangsu. He convinced Wu and Hsueh, as well as the British and French, that the forces in Shanghai could clear the rebels out of all points within a 30-mile radius around the city and hold that territory indefinitely. To use his troops most efficiently, Ward turned his force into a "flying column"—a highly mobile force that would strike any vulnerable points in the Taiping lines around Shanghai.

The Taipings, too, had improved their armed forces' training and equipment, particularly in the forces led by the Chung Wang. Like the Imperial general, Zeng Guofan, the Chung Wang was learning from Ward. The Taiping armies had included a number of Westerners since the beginning. Some saw the "God Worshipping Society" as fellow Christians, which they really weren't; some saw the Manchus as tyrannical oppressors, which they really were; some just saw a chance for high adventure. The Chung Wang placed those who had demonstrated military ability, like the Englishman, Savage; and the American, Peacock, in positions where they could train and command troops.

The Chung Wang returns

At the end of 1861, the Chung Wang again moved east. In spite of all his efforts, Zeng Guofan had taken Anking. The Imperial general had improved his army at least as much as the Chung Wang had improved his. As the Chung Wang saw it now, the Taiping cause depended on taking at least one of the treaty ports so the rebels could trade with the West. He captured Ningpo. And, he said, he would also take Shanghai, no matter who was defending it.

The British and French were not yet ready to commit regular forces to defend Shanghai and the remaining treaty ports. The Americans, of course, already had their hands full with the American Civil War. The Ward Corps suddenly became important. Admiral Hope completed his transition. Once Ward's most prominent Western enemy, he was now the filibuster's biggest supporter.

Ward, however, was wary. Britain had been making overtures to the Confederates—a group Ward hated as traitors. Then an American warship stopped the British ship *Trent* and arrested two Confederate agents. Britain threatened war.

"I was an American before I was a Chinaman, and these Englishmen will find it out," Ward remarked to an American friend.[19] If war came, Ward planned to use his Chinese troops, as well as a large number of Chinese pirates he had come to know, against British ships and military forces.

The *Trent* crisis passed, however, and Ward became reconciled to the British enough to join Hope on a scouting expedition. The filibuster and the admiral, posing as Western sportsmen, hiked into the interior and noted details of Taiping fortification.

The Ever-Victorious Army

After six months of training, Ward deemed his corps ready to take the field in January, 1862. The Taipings had taken and entrenched an advanced position near Wu-sung, where they could close the mouth of the Huang-po River and cut off Shanghai's harbor. The rebels had just settled into their trenches when they saw a new enemy advancing—Chinese troops wearing Western-style green uniforms and green turbans. These new troops carried American Sharps rifles, Prussian Dreyse rifles (breech-loading, bolt-action "needle guns") and British Enfield rifles. Before them, they carried a red and green standard bearing the Chinese character "Hwa." Although they outnumbered the newcomers, the Taipings were outclassed by the accurate fire and discipline of the Ward Corps and were driven out of their trenches.

A week later, Ward took 500 of his men and hit the walled city of Kwang-fu-lin with his patented surprise storm. He captured one entrance and brought up his artillery. Although the Taiping garrison was reported to number 20,000, they fled precipitously. The first week of February Ward and his corps took Ying-ch'i-pin in another surprise attack. In this battle, Ward sustained five wounds, including the loss of a finger. That did not stop the Ward Corps. On the night of February 5th, Burgevine and 600 men sneaked up to the Taiping trenches at T'ien-ma-shan and took them in a wild rush. As usual, the more numerous enemy fled in panic, with the "imitation foreign devils" following and shooting them down by the hundreds.

In Peking, the Imperial authorities gave the Ward Corps a new name—"The Ever Victorious Army." Ward was promoted to general and to successively higher grades of mandarin. He married a Chinese wife—Yang Fang's daughter—in a Confucian ceremony. Ward had been using his money from the captured city bounties and his share of the plunder to join Yang in several business enterprises. He wore his mandarin robes for the wedding but seldom after that. He also refused to grow a queue. As always, Ward followed no orders but his own.

The Chung Wang decided to eliminate the Ever Victorious Army. He moved against Ward's base, Sung-chiang. Ward set up hidden artillery batteries around the city. He waited until the Taipings were close, then opened up with cannister shot. The Chung Wang lost 2,300 men in the first few minutes, and his troops fled in panic. Ward captured between 700 and 800 Taiping soldiers and a large number of river boats loaded with munitions and other supplies.

Immediately after the battle, Hsueh asked Ward to take the Taiping base, Kau-ch'iao. Ward, reorganizing the defenses of Sung-chiang, could spare only 600 men. He was joined for the first time by British and French troops, including a French artillery battery and a British rocket detachment. For political reasons, the European troops would provide fire support, but Ward's Chinese infantry would lead the assault. The Ward Corps assault was so effective that the Taipings were in full retreat before the European troops could join the fight. Ward's losses were 10 killed and 40 wounded. Ward's men looted the city, as their contract allowed, but Ward did not allow them to kill Taiping prisoners or civilians, and he stopped an attempted massacre by Imperial troops the next day. From prisoners, Ward learned that the Chung Wang had been expected in the town the next day. He had planned to use it as a staging point for his assault on Shanghai.

Ward had been wounded again in the attack, but a week later he was back in the field leading 700 members of the Ever Victorious Army against Hsiao-t'ang. With him were Admiral Hope and seven British naval craft, 35 British artillerymen and 350 British sailors and marines acting as infantry. They were joined by 300 French troops. At first, it looked as if the Taiping trenches had been abandoned. But as the allies advanced, some 5,000 Taipings cut loose with small arms and artillery. The allies charged. Ward's men outran the British marines and got in the Taiping trenches first. The Taipings finally fled, leaving 1,000 dead on the field. Ward was wounded seven more times.

Inspired by Ward's success, the local Imperial commander attempted to take the offensive. His army was trapped at the town of Ssu-ching. In spite of multiple wounds, Ward took a thousand soldiers of the Ward Corps, his artillery, and a flotilla of his gunboats to the rescue. No Europeans were involved in this battle. Hsueh Huan reported to the Imperial government that Ward himself was the first man to break into the Taiping fortifications, where he "gunned down two rebel officers in yellow clothes (indicating high rank) and seized a yellow silk flag with a dragon design."[20] The panicked Taipings swarmed over a bridge, which collapsed under their weight. A Taiping powder magazine exploded the midst of Ward's troops, causing a number of casualties, but they went on to capture 12 large boats and more than a hundred smaller craft.

Ward's victories, particularly the last, in which no Europeans were involved, had a couple of curious effects. They showed the Imperial government that it needn't implore the European powers to intervene. Western-trained Chinese troops could put down the rebellion unassisted if there were enough of them. That pleased the Imperial authorities. It also showed the Europeans that if the Chinese adopted military reforms, they would no longer be able to play the cock-of-the-walk role they had become accustomed to.

That did not please the Europeans. It pleased them even less that Ward had so thoroughly adopted Chinese ways, and thusly, he could not be trusted. On the other hand, the Chinese authorities were not pleased that Ward refused to shave half his head and wear a pigtail. He was resisting Chinese ways. He could not be trusted. Therefore, they would not let him expand his army enough to handle the rebellion without help. In the end, Peking approved the use of foreign regulars against the Taipings, although Zeng Guofan, the most successful Imperial general, forbade their use in the interior.

On April 3, 1862, 1,450 British troops and 300 French joined Ward's forces for an attack on Wang-chia-ssu. The Europeans were to attack from the north and west. The Ever Victorious Army was to hold a position in the south and cut off the rebel retreat. The Europeans opened fire with artillery and rifles, and after a while, the Taipings abandoned their trenches and retreated to the south. Ward's men, however, were not where they had been expected. Only a few had arrived. While these, according to the *North China Herald*, did "considerable execution," most of the rebels reached safety in the complex of strongpoints that constituted the Chung Wang's new system of defense in depth. Most of Ward's army had been delayed by mud. Their artillery had become so bogged down that when the Ward troops finally arrived, they did so without cannons.

Most of the allied troops retired, disappointed, to Chi-pao, their jumping-off point. Ward, however, was burning to restore the reputation of his corps. The next day, he, accompanied by Admiral Hope, attacked the new Taiping position at Lung-chu-an without waiting for the artillery. He led his 1,500 men, unsupported by artillery, against 8,000 entrenched Taipings. The odds were too great even for the Ever Victorious Army. Ward and his men were repulsed and Hope was wounded.

With Hope out of action, General Sir Charles Stavely, an arrogant and narrow-minded Brit quite different from Hope, was the ranking British officer. Stavely decided to keep his men at Chi-pao while Ward and the French, accompanied by British marines, had another go at the Taipings. As before, the Europeans helped furnish fire support while Ward's Chinese infantry moved up under cover to the Lung-chu-an fortifications. When they were within 100 yards of them, the Ever Victorious Army stood up with a yell and dashed at the enemy. The Taipings fled. The Ward Corps destroyed all the enemy fortifications and returned to its base.

Less than two weeks later, the Ward Corps reprised its role at Lung-chu-an at Chou-p'u, the Taipings' strongest position on the strategic Pootung Peninsula. Again, the British and French artillery provided fire support, and Ward's infantry did the assaulting. The 5,000 Taiping defenders suffered 600 deaths before they were driven off, according to Augustus Lindley, a Briton serving with the Taipings.[21] Ward's casualties, thanks in part to the heavy artillery support, were light. The loot in Chou-p'u was heavy.

Ward had learned his lesson. To assault the Chung Wang's new field fortifications, he must always have powerful artillery. He used his share of the loot and the bounty on the city to buy more steamships and turn them into gunboats. And he bought many more field pieces. He also got welcome support from the Imperial government. The Anhwei Army, led by Zeng Guofan's protege, Li Honzhang, far different from the worthless "Green Banner" troops who had previously represented Peking, started moving into Kiangsu Province. And in mid-April, the French and British military commanders formally adopted Ward's 30-mile radius strategy.

But Stavely, without coordinating anything with his allies, decided to attack the Taipings at Nan-hsiang. Stavely was convinced that the Taipings would flee as soon as they saw British regulars advancing.

He received a shock. The Taipings did not flee before the British regular infantry, artillery, and naval craft. The British regulars fled. Stavely was grateful that Ward was not present to witness the rout. Ward was busy advancing on the key stronghold of Chia-ting, where the Ever Victorious Army, supported by the French and British, was to play the major role. Ward advanced with 1,400 infantry, five heavily armed steamers, and 30 smaller gun boats. He had 53 artillery pieces, including enormous 8-inch howitzers and 32-pound guns, along with a battery of rockets. Before Chia-ting, he joined a detachment of Green Banner troops and almost 3,000 British and French, including Stavely's defeated force.

Ward and the Europeans bombarded Chia-ting's walls for two hours. When the Taipings began to withdraw, the Ward Corps and the Europeans attacked, with the Ever Victorious Army winning the race to the enemy fortifications. But when they had taken the wall, Ward forbade his men to enter the city. He knew that the Europeans would not limit themselves—as the Ever Victorious Army did—to taking munitions, precious metals, and jewels. They would pillage and burn as they had in Peking. Ward did not want to sully the reputation of his army and lose the goodwill of the people of Kiangsu.

A few days later, the British and French navies, aided by a Chinese pirate fleet under a certain A-pak, retook Ningpo. Ward sent a detachment of the Ever Victorious Army under Major J.D. Morton to help garrison the town. Two days later, Ward joined French and British forces to retake Ch'ing-p'u along with 1,800 men, a fleet of steamers and gunboats and masses of artillery. The Taipings fled before an infantry assault could begin. Once again, Ward did not permit his men to plunder the town, although he received an enormous bounty for its capture.

Two more cities quickly fell to Ward and his allies: Nan-ch'iao was captured May 16; Che-lin, May 20. At the first, French Admiral August Leopold-Protet was killed. His men went wild when they entered the city and shot down Taipings who were trying to surrender. The aftermath of the second capture was worse. That time, the French, now joined by the British, tried to massacre everyone, women and children included.[22]

The Chung Wang strikes back

The capture of Che-lin completed the perimeter of the 30-mile-radius circle around Shanghai. General Stavely, having experienced the thrill of conquest, didn't want to stop there. After ordering his troops to burn Che-lin to the ground, he told them to "prepare to advance on the next rebel town."[23]

At this point, the Chung Wang called a halt to Western expansion. With an army estimated at more than 50,000 men, he retook Kuang-fu-lin and surrounded Ch'ing-p'u, where a portion of the Ever Victorious Army was stationed. He then moved on Chia-ting, with its British garrison, and Ward's main base, Sung-chiang. Stavely hit the panic button. He wrote to Bruce, the British minister, that he could do nothing to help Major Edward Forester, Ward's man in Ch'ing-p'u, because of the pressure on Chia-ting. Then he withdrew the British garrison in Chia-ting and ordered all his forces back inside Shanghai. The Chung Wang retook Chia-ting and surrounded Sung-chiang.

Ward and the Ever Victorious Army were in mortal danger. That didn't bother Stavely. Stavely wanted to replace Ward as a trainer of Imperial troops. He had already arranged with Li Hongzhang, now the governor of Kiangsu, to train 2,000 Chinese soldiers. Li signed the agreement to humor Stavely—if anything happened to the Ward Corps, he would need the British—but he found many reasons to delay sending him any troops to train. Li feared—correctly—than Stavely wanted to develop a native force that responded only to British orders. Such a force would let Stavely take over China for the British as Clive had taken over India. Li didn't even trust Ward, although the Yankee sailor was a Chinese citizen. For a long time, he made no attempt to relieve the Ever Victorious Army trapped in Sung-chiang and Ch'ing-p'u.

The Chung Wang seemed to have had a fixation on Shanghai. If his main objective was simply to secure a treaty port, he could have more easily retaken Ningpo. He knew that Shanghai, defended by the Europeans, Li Hongzhang's Anhwei Army, and the Ward Corps would be a tough nut to crack. However, he was willing to spend men, supplies, and time that were needed elsewhere. While the Chung Wang was trying to crack Shanghai's defensive perimeter, Zeng Guofan and his Hunan Army were closing in on Nanking, the Taiping capital. In spite of Western legend, the Ever Victorious Army (under "Chinese" Gordon) certainly did not put down the Taiping Rebellion. However, Ward's defeats of the Chung Wang outside Shanghai undoubtedly hastened its end.

Stavely's withdrawal infuriated Admiral Hope, who sent ships and supplies up the Huang-pu River to Sung-chiang. Ward repulsed assault after assault on Sung-chiang, but he couldn't break the Chung Wang's encircling lines. In Ch'ing-p'u, Forester was in the same situation. Neither garrison could link up with the other.

The Chung Wang sent Ward a letter, demanding his surrender. "Had you not invaded my territories, I should not have troubled you; the people would have remained undisturbed. Would this not have been better for both sides?" the rebel leader wrote.[24] Ward didn't bother to reply. The Chung Wang sent a similar note to Forester in Ch'ing-p'u. Forester replied:

You say that if I do not give you the city to-day or to-morrow you will attack it and kill us, and I write to tell you it is impossible for me to do so. My master, Ward, having given me charge of this city, with plenty of troops, guns, stores, munitions of war, etc., I am bound to hold it, whatever numbers come against it, and prevent your taking it; and I have given all my officers orders to do their best to do so, as I dare not give it up on my own responsibility. I regret you do not approve of us foreigners stopping here, but if you want us, you must come and take the city.[25]

The next month, Li Hongzhang began to regret his inaction. He wrote admiringly of Ward, who, he said in a letter to Zeng Guofan, "valiantly defends Sung-chiang and Ch'ing-p'u."[26] He ordered counterattacks on the Taipings. At the same time, Morton took his troops in Ningpo back to the Shanghai area and began trying to break the siege of Sung-chiang. Then, Hope sent boats and marines to help Ward, who broke the siege and pushed on to Ch'ing-p'u.

One June 10, Ward rescued Forester and his garrison at Ch'ing-p'u . But for some reason that has never been discovered, Forester dashed back into the city.[27] He was captured, tortured, held for weeks in captivity, but finally released for a ransom paid by Li Hongzhang.

The Chung Wang withdrew to Soochow, apparently out of pure frustration. He did not return to Nanking to try to push back Zeng Guofan and his Hunanese.

The last campaigns

Ward reorganized the Ever Victorious Army and joined Li Hongzhang in clearing the last Taipings out of the Pootung Peninsula. Li wrote to Zeng Guofan asking that the Ever Victorious Army be allowed to join in the taking of Nanking. Zeng was reluctant to do so. He didn't trust any foreigners, even those who had become Chinese citizens and Imperial generals.

Actually, there was still work to be done around Shanghai. The Chung Wang had not given up on the city. In mid-July he sent a column to retake the Pootung Peninsula. The Taipings fought their way past Li Hongzhang's troops but were stopped by Ward's Ever Victorious Army and driven back to Chin-shan-wei. Ward quickly conferred with Li and drew up a plan for taking Chin-shan-wei. Ward's and Li's troops surrounded the city, then Ward's artillery began a heavy bombardment. Finally, Chinese soldiers of the Ever Victorious Army and the Anhwei Army charged through breaches in the walls and took the town.

Meanwhile Ward had continued increasing his "navy" of gunboats. He and Li thought it might be used to assault one of Nanking's watergates. To convince Zeng, Li asked Ward to use the boats to take the river port of Liu-ho, a base for both Taipings and pirates. Ward's gunboats bombarded the town, then he led his infantry into the fortifications. The Ward Corps released hundreds of prisoners, captured ships and destroyed the enemy fortifications completely.

Zeng noted the performance of the Ever Victorious Army, but suggested it "try out its guns" some more by recapturing Ch'ing-p'u. Once again, Ward's river steamers began the bombardment. The naval guns were joined by the Ever Victorious Army's land artillery directed by a Colonel Sartoli, an Italian artillery expert who had served with Garibaldi. Sartoli soon opened a wide breach in the walls and Ward and his troops charged through. The first man through the breach was Vicente Macanaya, followed closely by Ward. Unfortunately, Sartoli left his guns to join the charge. He was killed.

At Ch'ing-p'u, Ward had certainly demonstrated the power of his guns. But in the end, Zeng refused to let the Salem native take part in the capture of Nanking. Denied a role in what would be the decisive campaign of the war, Ward turned his attention to Ningpo. Before he could move any men south, however, the Chung Wang made one last desperate attempt to take Shanghai. He again besieged Ch'ing-p'u. This time, there was no prolonged siege. The combined forces of the Ever Victorious Army and the Anhwei army defeated the Taipings and pushed them back to their starting point. Shanghai was safe. The next task was to guarantee the safety of Ningpo in Chekiang Province. Li wrote to Zeng that Ward was the ideal man for the job:

> Ward is indeed brave in action, and he possesses all sorts of foreign weapons. Recently I, Hongzhang, have devoted all my attention to making friends with him, in order to get the friendship of various nations through that one individual.[28]

Ward's strategy at Ningpo was the same as for Shanghai: establish a perimeter with a 30-mile radius around the city. On September 20, 1862, Ward was reconnoitering his latest objective, the city of Tz'u-ch'i. Suddenly he put his hand on his abdomen and said, "I've been hit."[29] A British naval officer standing nearby helped him to a gunboat. The ship headed for Ningpo at full steam, but Ward died on the way. He was two months short of his 31st birthday.

A stolen reputation

Ward was gone, but his spirit remained (at least, so the non-Taiping Chinese believed). They erected a memorial mound over his grave in Sung-chiang and dedicated a Confucian temple to his spirit. There, for years afterward, Chinese leaders came to offer sacrifices to the spirit of the foreign-born soldier who had shown China how to maintain its independence. Ward was not worshipped as a god, but he became Confucianism's nearest thing to a saint. Thousands visited his temple to ask for his help.

Immediately after Ward's death, the Ever Victorious Army sorely needed help. General Stavely attempted to have the Army brought under British control. The idea was repulsive to its troops. The veterans, wrote Charles Schmidt, one of Ward's officers, "do not want any regular Military Foreign Generals, however necessary the latter may be supposed to be. Do not intrude! We want men of Ward's and Vincente's [sic] stamp." Vicente Macanaya was undoubtedly the best qualified man to command the Ever Victorious Army. But, Schmidt was forced to admit, Macanaya's "being a Manila man puts the damper on his chances of election to the position of Commander under the present Sung-chiang dynasty."[30]

In the end, the command went to Henry Burgevine, not so much because he was Ward's second-in-command as because he, like Ward, had become a Chinese citizen. Burgevine was brave enough, but he was by no means Ward's intellectual peer. He was also rash, hot-tempered, and frequently drunk. And he did not have Ward's ability to get money from Yang. The old banker was, after all, Ward's father-in-law. Before long, the Ever Victorious Army was lacking supplies, ammunition, and pay for the officers. Burgevine finally exploded. He burst into Yang Fang's office, beat the old man up, and left with 40,000 silver dollars.

No sin could have been worse in the Confucian universe. Burgevine had not only attacked an elder, but a *mandarin*. When Burgevine sobered up and realized his position, he deserted and joined the Taipings.

Command devolved upon Burgevine's chief of staff, a British marine captain named John Holland. Holland had been nominated for the job by Admiral Hope. The nomination was undoubtedly the greatest mistake Hope ever made. The new commander's first act was to change the army's "American-style" uniforms to what looked like British uniforms minus the red coats. Holland knew more about uniforms than about military tactics. On February 14, 1863, he met the Taipings at T'ai-ts'ang. According to *Friend of China*, a local English-language periodical, "It took the troops four days to reach T'ai-ts'ang;—it took them—less muskets, blankets, provisions, munitions of war, ordnance—everything—to the tune of over a hundred thousand dollars—eight hours only to get back! Such a skedaddle was never seen."[31]

Finally, the Chinese authorities accepted Stavely's choice—his young brother-in-law Charles George Gordon, a captain of engineers—and waived the requirement that the commander be a Chinese citizen.

Gordon, fortunately, was no Stavely. He was, in fact, an eccentric's eccentric: an unchurched mystic whose deep desire to be a martyr was to lead to his wholly unnecessary death in the Sudan many years later. He was not a Ward, either. He lacked the Yankee's originality and his ability to not only get along with, but to inspire, anyone— bankers and peasants, mandarins and pirates, European regulars and American adventurers. Gordon, though hardly a typical British officer, had the typical British officer's contempt for those who were not regular officers and for all who were not white. He had, though, the good sense to copy Ward's tactics, especially the use of gunboats. He even adopted Ward's personal armament, the rattan walking stick. But while the Ever Victorious Army again performed competently, it was without the old enthusiasm, according to all who fought under both the Ward and the Gordon regimes.

Gordon had one talent Ward lacked. He was perhaps the greatest military self-promoter since Julius Caesar and before Douglas MacArthur. When, at the end of his career, he made his suicidal choice to remain in Khartoum with a handful of Egyptian soldiers surrounded by hostile hordes of Mahdists, practically all of his country's foreign policy centered on rescuing him.

America, beset by the Civil War, little noted nor long remembered Frederick Townsend Ward. In China, during World War II, the Japanese knocked down his temple. When the Communists took over, they dug up his bones and paved over his grave. But England not only remembered Gordon—it attributed all Ward's accomplishments to him. According to Lytton Strachey in *Eminent Victorians*, Gordon originated the gunboat tactics of the Ever Victorious Army. Strachey even marvels at Gordon's personal armament—a rattan stick. For Strachey, the Ever Victorious Army practically *was* Gordon:

> [T]he Ever Victorious Army was defeated more often than not. Its first European [sic] leader had been killed....It was in these circumstances that command of the Ever Victorious Army was offered to Gordon....In eighteen months, he told Li Hung Chang, the business would be finished; and he was as good as his word.[32]

The business was finished in 18 months because the Chinese government disbanded the Ever Victorious Army. The Taiping Rebellion went on. Some months after Gordon left China, the mad Tien Wang took poison. His followers, including the Chung Wang, surrendered and, following time-honored custom, all of his officers were executed, usually with appalling cruelty.

— ⊏⊐ —

Two modern British historians, John Keegan and Andrew Wheatcroft, who should know better, say of Gordon that he "commanded a Chinese 'Ever Victorious' army raised by the Europeans of Shanghai to protect themselves against the Taiping rebels. Gordon's transformation of this rabble into a genuinely effective force, and his pacification of the region he conquered with it made his name a household one."[33] The amazing thing about this is that so much misinformation can be packed into so few words.

For the last hundred years "Chinese" Gordon has been remembered as the man who ended the Taiping Rebellion. It will probably be so for the next thousand.

But though the British called him "Chinese," the Chinese built no temples to honor Gordon. That temple in Sung-chiang was erected for the veneration of America's most thoroughly forgotten military hero, Frederick Townsend Ward.

Part 2

Guerrillas in the Rearguard

3

The Different Drummer: John Singleton Mosby

The general and the private

Young, handsome, dashing General James Ewell Brown Stuart liked pretty girls. And pretty girls liked Jeb Stuart. Those facts led to a chain of circumstances resulting in thousands of Union troops being tied up during some of the most crucial campaigns of the American Civil War. And that prolonged the war for at least six months.

Early in 1862, two young women had been visiting Stuart in Fairfax, Virginia. The general, commander of the Army of Northern Virginia's cavalry, knowing the war was about to get hotter, wanted a trooper to drive the ladies to a safer area. The man he got was a private named John Singleton Mosby. Mosby, a 28-year-old former lawyer, was short, slight, stooped, homely, and happily married. Mosby had argued against secession before the war, but when it occurred and he understood that his home state would be invaded, he joined the army. He was, his first company commander said, "an indifferent soldier."[1] He hated army routine and pointless regulations. It might be said that Mosby marched to a different drummer. It would be more accurate to say he *was* the different drummer. John Mosby never marched to anyone else's tune if he could help it. Mosby enjoyed the assignment not because he had any interest in Stuart's friends but because it was a break in the monotony of camp life.

Mosby endured the good-natured jibes of his comrades as he drove off sandwiched between two Southern belles. He completed his mission and returned the buggy to Stuart's headquarters. To his surprise, Stuart told him to stay that night at the house he shared with two other generals, G.W. Smith and Joseph Johnston, commander of the Department of Northern Virginia. The private sat practically tongue-tied through dinner with the three generals. Breakfast the next morning began as a repetition of the torture. But after a while, Stuart and Johnston managed to draw out the bashful private. His conversation apparently impressed them. Soon after he returned to camp, he was promoted to regimental adjutant, a commissioned officer with rank and pay just below that of captain.

The conversation apparently impressed Mosby, too. He learned that generals were just people. Stuart, the West Pointer, the Supreme Cavalryman, was only 10 months older than Mosby—another young man with his own hopes, dreams, and quirks. It was the beginning of a friendship.

Mosby did not hold his commission long. The largely ceremonial job of adjutant bored him to tears. About the only amusement he got was annoying pompous fellow officers, particularly one named Fitzhugh Lee, nephew of Confederate President Jefferson Davis's military advisor, General Robert E. Lee. In March, Mosby saw a chance to break the monotony.

Union General George B. McClellan began embarking troops for what was to become the Peninsular Campaign. Johnston, worried about his right flank and rear, abandoned Manassas, ordered precious supplies to be burned, and fell back toward Richmond. Union cavalry began pressing the retreating Confederates and skirmishing with Stuart's cavalry. Nobody in the Southern army knew if McClellan was really planning to land troops in the Tidewater area and move on Richmond from the east or if that was just a feint. Mosby went to Stuart and volunteered to learn the size of the Union force pursuing them. Stuart gave Mosby his approval, along with three privates. Mosby and his men rode completely around the Union cavalry and reported to Stuart that the Yankees were not leading McClellan's advance. They were a comparatively small body of cavalry and had no communications with Washington.

Stuart was elated. He counterattacked, captured many prisoners, and drove the Yankees back. He recommended Mosby for promotion. Mosby's circumnavigation of an enemy force was the first such cavalry operation in the Civil War. It would later become almost a standard maneuver. But by that time, Mosby would be most at home behind enemy lines.

The next month, the Confederate Congress took a look at all promotions and came up with a new policy: all units would elect their officers. Fitzhugh Lee was elected commander of Mosby's regiment. The prospect of working directly for the pompous and regulation-bound Lee appalled Mosby. He resigned his position as adjutant and with it, his commission. Stuart invited the new private to join his couriers and told him he wouldn't be long without a commission.

In the meantime, McClellan landed on the peninsula between the York and the James rivers. He began inching his way toward Richmond with more than 100,000 men. Johnston attempted to stop him at Seven Pines, but was wounded. With McClellan at the gates of Richmond, Robert E. Lee took command of the Army of Northern Virginia.

Stuart still had not been able to get Private Mosby another commission, but he maintained friendly relations with the intrepid soldier. One morning, at a private breakfast, Stuart asked Mosby what he thought of the chances for a cavalry probe of McClellan's right flank. That was the area where General Thomas J. Jackson, leading a new army, planned to attack the Yankees. Mosby volunteered to reconnoiter. He took four men and returned a few days later to tell Stuart that McClellan's line

John Singleton Mosby in the uniform of a Confederate colonel. Mosby, the master of "Mosby's Confederacy," rose from private to colonel during the Civil War. (Library of Congress)

was so porous a large body of cavalry could sneak through it and do great damage in the rear. Stuart took 1,200 horsemen and ravaged the Union rear, riding completely around McClellan's army and returning loaded with everything from weapons to wine. One man was killed. Another, a German immigrant, was captured because he was, Mosby said "too full of Rhine wine" liberated by the raiders to ride.[2]

Using information Stuart had obtained, Lee and Stonewall Jackson hit McClellan in a two-pronged offensive. McClellan outnumbered the two Confederate armies combined, but he thought he was facing overwhelming odds. In the fighting that followed, McClellan suffered 15,000 casualties; the Confederates, 21,000.[3] But the Union general, seeing what he thought were hundreds of thousands of enemies, retired. His troops fought a number of rear guard actions, inflicting more casualties than they took, but McClellan kept calling for more troops and moving back. President Abraham Lincoln replaced him as head of the Army of the Potomac with John Pope, leaving McClellan only the troops on the Peninsula. Pope would lead another force to Richmond from the north.

When the fighting in eastern Virginia died down, Mosby grew restless. Stuart sent him to Jackson, who was campaigning farther west, with a letter of recommendation.

Mosby never arrived. He was captured by a Union patrol and sent to Washington. The horrible death camps for Civil War prisoners were still in the future. Mosby was able to write home and was courteously treated. Mosby spent only 10 days in captivity before he was exchanged.

On the way to the exchange point, he noticed a number of Federal transport ships filled with soldiers. Were they going to reinforce McClellan or Pope? He learned, from a Confederate sympathizer, that they were going to Pope. As soon as he was inside Confederate lines, he went directly to Lee. The once-bashful private no longer felt awed by generals. He told Lee what he had learned. Lee immediately ordered Jackson to strike Pope before the reinforcements arrived. Then he moved his own troops out of Richmond and marched against Pope. McClellan, not knowing that Richmond was virtually unguarded, evacuated. His army was sent to join Pope at Manassas. Jackson and Lee met Pope and McClellan again near the site of the first battle in northern Virginia. In the fighting that followed, Mosby was slightly wounded. Lee outmaneuvered Pope and sent the Yankees reeling back toward Washington.

Lincoln fired Pope and replaced him with McClellan as Lee invaded the North. McClellan met Lee at Antietam Creek in Maryland and fought the bloodiest single day of the war. Lee's bruised army retired south, but McClellan, overcautious as always, did not pursue him. The frustrated Lincoln again replaced McClellan, this time with Ambrose Burnside. Burnside then proceeded to make Pope look good by ordering a foolish frontal attack on strong Confederate positions at Fredricksburg.

After that bloodletting, infantry action subsided. Stuart decided to take another excursion into the enemy's rear areas. He swept around the Federal lines and came within a dozen miles of Washington, capturing supply wagons and raiding depots. At one point, he sent a telegram to the Federal quartermaster general complaining about the quality of his mules. To evade Union troops, he went north, instead of south, stopping at Middleburg in Loudoun County, Virginia, about 40 miles due west of Washington. The night before the Confederate cavalry left for Fredricksburg, Mosby asked Stuart to let him remain here behind the Union lines with a squad of troopers. He said he thought he could do some good.

That turned out to be quite an understatement.

Guerrilla warfare

Left behind with nine men, Mosby began a new kind of war. In April, 1862, the Confederate Congress had passed the Partisan Ranger Act. It was the land-bound equivalent of the traditional "letters of marque and reprisal" issued to sea captains to make them privateers. Privateers raided enemy shipping, but the letters theoretically prevented them from being treated as pirates. Theoretically, partisan rangers would not be considered bandits.

Partisans would not be paid by the government, but they were allowed to keep what they captured. Mosby and his nine original men were regulars, not partisans, but they would operate as partisans and would enlist new recruits as partisans.[4] Mosby didn't mind giving up his Confederate pay as long as he could operate as he saw fit. He did want a promotion, though. For some time, the most feared guerrilla force in northern Virginia was led by a private.

Mosby began by raiding sutlers' wagons and surprising and capturing isolated outposts. (Sutlers were civilian army provisioners.) He soon began picking up recruits. The Confederacy conscripted all white men between 18 and 35. Mosby did not knowingly take such men. Many of his recruits came from Maryland, which had never joined the Confederacy. Others were men who were too old, too young, or had been rejected by the draft. Membership in Mosby's army was constantly changing, because many of his troops were regular Confederate soldiers who had been wounded and joined the guerrillas while they were recuperating. One notable recruit was "Yankee" Ames, who had been a sergeant in the Fifth New York Cavalry until he decided to change sides. Some of Mosby's troopers might have been eligible to be drafted into the Confederate army, but there was no way for that to happen in Union-controlled territory. Inevitably, though, Mosby picked up some men who *really* were bandits. As a result, his force was denounced not only by Federals, but by some regular Confederate officers.

Confederate regulars were irked by the partisans' way of life. The regulars claimed the partisans were getting rich by stealing supplies from the Yankees and selling them in the blockaded South. The partisans did not live in camps, they stayed in the private homes of Confederate sympathizers. They were scattered throughout the territory that came to be called "Mosby's Confederacy," because the guerrilla chief functioned as a judge and governor as well as a cavalry officer. Civilians in the territory turned to Mosby instead of Yankee-sponsored civil officials.

Before an operation, Mosby would call together as many of his hidden troopers as he needed. They were not, as a Union soldier wrote, local farmers who "have taken the oath of allegiance to the Union a few times" and who at night "arm themselves with anything that comes handy—pistols, sabers, carbines, shotguns, etc. and being mounted and in citizen clothes proceed to lay in wait for some poor devil of a blue jacket."[5] Mosby's men were usually not residents of the area, they had not taken any oath of allegiance to the Union, and they wore Confederate uniforms. They were certainly not armed with anything they could pick up—Mosby had armed his men carefully. Most of them had Spencer repeating carbines, the world's most advanced military rifle at the time.[6] All of them had two revolvers with loaded spare cylinders for a quick reload. The revolver was the principal arm of Mosby's cavalry. At the time, most of the world's regular cavalry, including that of the United States Army, relied on sabers for close quarters fighting.[7]

Guerrillas were a problem for the Union army. Orders issued from Washington called for captured guerrillas to be hanged without trial and for the arrest of all able-bodied men of military age in areas where guerrillas operated. Officers in the field, however, found the orders repugnant. They were not about to hang prisoners of war or arrest civilians. *Most* officers, that is. One, British-born Colonel Percy Wyndham, proposed to deal with guerrillas the European way. He sent an ultimatum to Middleburg, Virginia, where he believed (correctly) Mosby had his headquarters: Either turn in the guerrillas or see your town burned to the ground. The Middleburg town fathers asked Mosby to move his forces elsewhere. Mosby said he would not be blackmailed, and Stuart backed him up. Then he struck back at Wyndham.

Mosby and his men sneaked past the Federal outposts and went right into the headquarters of Wyndham's regiment. Wyndham was away in Washington, but Mosby's raiders wakened his superior officer, Brigadier General Edwin Stoughton, and captured him, along with 100 Federal officers and enlisted men. After that demonstration, Mosby could do no wrong in the eyes of the citizens of Middleburg. Nor was there any attempt to burn Middleburg. The order to hang guerrillas also continued to be ignored. Many months later, though, six of Mosby's men were captured by troops commanded by George Armstrong Custer. Custer, whose recklessness and cruelty were later demonstrated during the wars against the Plains Indians, had them executed.[8] In retaliation, Mosby ordered six of Custer's men to be hanged. The hangings stopped.[9]

There was no letup in the Yankee search for Mosby and his guerrillas, though. Mosby's wife had moved from their home in southwestern Virginia to Fauquier County, where she stayed as a guest of James Hathaway, whose house was located between Middleburg and Salem. One night, a Federal patrol came to Hathaway's house while Mosby was in bed with his wife. The Rebel leader had just time enough to crawl out of a window and hide in a tree next to the house.

Mosby's capture of Stoughton brought him a promotion to captain. He was ordered to enroll a company (which he had already done). The company would be Confederate regular cavalry. A couple of weeks later, he was promoted to major. In January of 1864, he became a lieutenant colonel. In December of the same year, he became a colonel. After Mosby officially became a company commander, he was ordered to hold an election for junior officers. Mosby remembered the election that made Fitz Lee commander of his regiment. He let his men vote on candidates for company officers, candidates he appointed. There was only one candidate for each position. As new companies were added to Mosby's Rangers, new elections followed the same procedure.

The promotions were testimonials to Mosby's value to the Confederacy, but they didn't affect his operations. His ranger force grew steadily, but irregularly. Altogether, as many as 1,800 men may have served under Mosby, but he never had more than 800 at one time. That small force, however, kept thousands of Union troops away from the battle fronts, chasing fruitlessly through fields and woods after guerrillas who fought only on their own terms.

Mosby's tactics

The weaponry available in the Civil War caused a major change in cavalry tactics. Ever since Gustavus Adolphus in the 17th century, the cavalry's principal tactic had been charging on horseback with the sword. William Washington, who commanded the Third Continental Cavalry in the Revolution, called the sword "the most destructive and almost the only necessary weapon a Dragoon carries."[10]

The general use of rifles changed that. A smoothbore musket had an effective range of about 80 yards. An infantryman had a chance to get off one shot at charging horsemen before they were on him, slashing with their sabers. The foot soldier's chief defense was his bayonet. Horses could not break through a solid line of bayonets. Cavalry could, however, wreak havoc among scattered infantry.

In the Revolution, the rifle was a specialist's weapon.[11] The regular infantry carried smoothbore muzzle-loaders. But rifles became general issue about the middle of the 19th century. The infantry weapon's effective range grew from the smoothbore's 80 yards to the rifle's more than 800 yards—half a mile. A rifleman had many chances to fire at charging cavalry. That was especially true as an increasing portion of the infantry now carried breech-loading single-shots or repeaters, both with much higher rates of fire than muzzle-loaders. And a man on a horse makes a big target.

It didn't take long for Civil War soldiers to adapt to the new conditions. More and more, the cavalry fought dismounted. In most fights, the cavalry were really mounted infantry. And in the West, some infantry outfits, like Wilder's "Lightning Brigade" of the Federal army, got horses and became mounted infantry.[12] When cavalry faced only other cavalry, however, there was still mounted action. But here, too, weaponry had wrought change.

In earlier wars, a cavalryman carried a smooth-bore, muzzle-loading carbine or a pair of smooth-bore, muzzle-loading pistols. Neither—especially the pistols—had even the range of the infantryman's musket. As a result, said "Light Horse Harry" Lee, Robert E. Lee's Revolutionary father, "the fire of cavalry is at best innocent."[13] When horseman met horseman, then, the sword decided the day.

That was before Colonel Colt's revolver. A revolver could fire six shots before the old "horse pistol" could get off two. It could be quickly reloaded with a spare cylinder. And all revolvers were rifled: they had many times the effective range of the old infantry musket. Revolvers first showed their potential in fights between the Texas Rangers—the national police force of the Republic of Texas—and the Comanches. Such fighting, though, was beneath the notice of the world's professional soldiers. As late as 1870, the U.S. Army's Small Arms and Accoutrements Board reported that "The Remington (single shot) is the only single-barrel pistol submitted. It is an excellent weapon..."[14] The British lancers did not replace their single-shot muzzle-loading pistols with revolvers until 1872.

Use of revolvers by Civil War cavalry eventually became general, regardless of the theories of military planners in Washington and Richmond. But Mosby recognized the weapon's potential from the first. His knowledge of what the revolver could do was both theoretical and practical. He had been expelled from the University of Virginia for shooting another student with a revolver and spent time in jail before he was pardoned.[15] The frail Mosby didn't consider shooting a big, muscular bully anything to be ashamed of. His different drum was beating well before the war.

On April 1, 1863, Mosby and 69 troopers were surprised by 150 horsemen of the First Vermont Cavalry, led by Captain Henry C. Flint.

"As Capt. Flint dashed forward at the head of his squadron, their sabers flashing in the rays of the morning sun," Mosby recalled later, "I felt like my final hour had come."[16] Mosby's men quickly mounted and charged with their revolvers. Flint was one of the first men killed. In the melee, revolvers completely outclassed sabers. Some of the Rebels held their reins in their teeth while they fired revolvers with both hands. Mosby's losses were heavy, but the Vermonters lost far more. In a short time, the Yankees were fleeing headlong. One dismounted Vermonter called out to Mosby, "You have played us a nice April Fool, boys."[17] That fight brought Mosby his promotion to major two weeks after becoming a captain.

Mosby's men were not such formidable fighters just because they had revolvers. They practiced with the weapons. They had plenty of ammunition, which they had captured from the Federal government. A favorite drill was to ride past a tree at full gallop while firing three shots into it. According to John Alexander, one of Mosby's Rangers:

> This deadly aptness with the revolver not only reacted on our men and gave them nerve and self-confidence, but it increased their efficiency and formidability to a degree that one can scarcely appreciate....It is one thing to shoot for the purpose of making smoke and noise, or automatically in volleys; it is an awfully different thing to shoot to kill. Believe me, a calm, cool "dead shot" behind a Colt's revolver or a Spencer repeating rifle has more moral force than a Gatling gun.[18]

Alexander would not have agreed with the current military theory that aimed fire is not important. In 1948, the U.S. Army's Operations Research Office (ORO) began a study of World War II casualties, and as Edward C. Ezell puts it, "ORO's investigations revealed that aimed rifle fire does not seem to have been any more important in creating casualties than randomly fired shots."[19] Ezell does not list all the data ORO processed, but the data obviously did not include the results of centuries of combat between competent and incompetent marksmen.

Unlike regular cavalry, Mosby's men almost always fought mounted. They made none of those long charges across open country—either mounted or dismounted—that made the Civil War so bloody. Mosby always tried to surprise his enemy. His men sneaked through woods on little-known trails, attacked at night or burst from cover at the last moment. They were always mounted. Mosby thought the strength of cavalry, especially guerrilla cavalry, was its mobility. A cavalryman without a horse was half-armed. Mobility made possible one of Mosby's favorite tactics, the feigned retreat. A small force of guerrillas pursued by a larger body of Federals often led their pursuers right to Mosby's main force, which would charge from a hidden position, revolvers blazing. The results were often amazing. At Chantilly, Mosby's counter-charge with 50 men routed a federal force of 200. Bluff was a major Mosby tactic, and the longer he operated, the more effective it was.

...And his strategy

Mosby was not merely a partisan harassing the occupying forces at random. (There were plenty of those in the South.) Mosby was different. He had a plan.

Soon after he began operations, Mosby came to Stuart with his plan. The Union forces had set up a defensive chain of cavalry outposts at half-mile intervals between Dranesville on the upper Potomac and Alexandria on the lower Potomac. By attacking these outposts, he could force the Yankees to either contract their line, freeing more Confederate territory from Federal occupation or forcing the Union forces to divert more men from the fighting front. Stuart not only approved the plan, he loaned Mosby some troopers from Fitzhugh Lee's regiment for a time. Mosby succeeded in both objectives.

Raiding Union supply wagons and trains was another part of his strategy. Federal operations were delayed for lack of supplies, and Federal troops had to be diverted to guard the supply lines. Diverting troops also hampered Union operations, but it didn't do much to protect the supply lines. The Federal troops were necessarily strung out all along the supply routes, while Mosby could concentrate at any point he chose. From raiding isolated sutlers' wagons, Mosby advanced to attacking trains—sometimes using artillery—and destroying railroads. At one point, he captured the monthly pay of the Army of the Shenandoah. But as Mosby noted in a report to Stuart:

> *The military value of the species of warfare I have waged is not measured by the number of prisoners and material of war captured from the enemy, but by the heavy detail it has already compelled him to make, and which I hope to make him increase...and to that extent diminishing his aggressive strength.*[20]

And, of course, one of Mosby's prime objectives was the collection of intelligence. That became especially important as the war entered a new phase.

New faces from the West

After Burnside's debacle, the Army of the Potomac got a new commander, a boastful coward who somehow acquired the name "Fighting Joe" Hooker. Late in April, 1863,

Mosby learned that Hooker was on the move and sent word to Stuart. Then he set out to divert the Yankees by attacking their rear. On the way, he discovered a party of Federal cavalry, relaxed, scattered, and unaware that any enemy was nearby. He attacked them and was involved in a fight when another party of Union horsemen appeared. They surprised the surprisers, and Mosby was routed for the first time in his career.

It wasn't a serious loss for Mosby, but it was the first of a series of increasingly severe setbacks for the Confederacy in the East. The next day, after Lee's masterpiece at Chancellorsville, Stonewall Jackson was shot. Stuart took command of Jackson's corps and led it ably through what remained of the fighting, but Jackson, Lee's "right arm," died two weeks later.

The Federals began retreating north, and Mosby, towing a mountain howitzer, stepped up his attacks on the railroad bringing the Northerners supplies and reinforcements. He used his cannon to smash a locomotive. The Rebels took all the supplies they could carry and burned the train. Then drums and bugles were heard all along the railroad, and Federal troops began assembling. Mosby's men found their way blocked by some of the Fifth New York cavalry. After a sharp fight, they lost their cannon and scattered into the woods.

Stuart, too, was having troubles. The reorganized Federal cavalry under Alfred Pleasanton was able to break through his screen and discover Lee's route to the north. Pleasanton's cavalry could not, however, stop Stuart from learning about Federal troop movements. Stuart had Mosby.

Mosby took two dozen of his best men and rode right into the Union army. He later recalled:

> Along the pike a continuous stream of [Union] troops, with all the impedimenta of war, poured along....I rode out into the column of Union troops as they passed along. As it was dark, they had no suspicion who we were, although we were all dressed in full Confederate uniform.[21]

Mosby saw three horses held by a man in front of a house. He concluded that the horse-holder was an orderly and that they were officers' horses. He questioned the orderly, who thought Mosby was a Union officer, and Mosby learned that he was correct. He captured the officers and the papers they were carrying—papers that revealed Federal plans. Mosby and his men then took the captives back through the stream of Union soldiers, keeping them covered with revolvers held in their coat pockets. After that, the guerrilla leader began shuttling between Stuart's headquarters and Hooker's army, bringing back intelligence and, frequently, prisoners.

Stuart planned to meet Mosby for another ride around the Federal army, but he found his way blocked by Hancock's retreating Union corps. He changed his direction and rode into Maryland, never connecting with Mosby.

Meanwhile, Lee, perhaps feeling invincible after Chancelorsville, marched into disaster at Gettysburg.

Major General George Meade, the Union commander at Gettysburg, followed Lee cautiously, to the extreme annoyance of Lincoln. Once again, the Gray Fox escaped. Lincoln let the victor at Gettysburg retain command of the Army of the Potomac, but he began looking for a new commander-in-chief. He found one early the next year, a plain-spoken, cigar-chomping general named Ulysses S. Grant. Grant came from the West, where, in contrast to the seesaw fighting in the East, Union forces were usually successful. Grant brought another new man with him, a short, ungainly Irishman named Philip H. Sheridan, and put him in command of the cavalry.

The beginning of the end

Although action by the main armies in the East slackened off late in 1863, Mosby's Rangers shifted into high gear. Mosby's private army expanded rapidly, and the guerrilla chief stepped up his attacks on the enemy's communications. In August of 1863, he was wounded while attempting to drive off the horses of a Federal cavalry regiment. He was smuggled through the lines to his parents' home near Lynchburg. But by late September, he was back in the field. He led a raid into Alexandria, across the Potomac from Washington, and captured the military aide of the Federally-appointed governor of Virginia.

The new year did not open auspiciously for Mosby. He joined one of Stuart's scouts for a raid on the headquarters of the Federal Maryland cavalry regiment which had been scouring the countryside for guerrillas. The scout, Frank Stringfellow, alerted the Federals with a premature attack, and Mosby's 100-man raiding party was so roughly handled the Rangers attempted nothing new for a month.

Grant took command early in March of 1864. The Confederates expected the Federals to begin an offensive as soon as the weather grew warm. They relied on Mosby, now the eyes and ears of the Army of Northern Virginia, to keep them informed of Yankee movements. The Rebels were ready when Grant attacked. But Grant was not like other Union generals. He didn't stop attacking, no matter how heavy his losses. Little Phil Sheridan was equally pugnacious. He led 10,000 horsemen around the Confederate army in the kind of sweep Stuart was noted for, ripping up railroads and destroying Confederate supply depots. His object: to bring Stuart out to fight. He succeeded. The Southern and Northern *beaux sabreurs*—the courtly, plumed Stuart and the blunt, carelessly dressed Sheridan, both in their early 30s—met at a place called Yellow Tavern. It was a black day for the Confederacy. Stuart was mortally wounded and his men driven off. The Confederate cavalry was never the same again. In his memoirs, Mosby says, "After General Lee lost Stuart he had no cavalry corps and no Chief of Cavalry. No one was there who could bend the bow of Ulysses."[22]

Grant's meat-grinder offensive was starting to take its toll on the Army of Northern Virginia. Lee's army was melting away because of casualties and also because of desertions. In contrast, Mosby's Rangers continued to expand. The Confederate regulars were right: The partisans did have a better life than the regulars.

Lee still had a few tricks up his sleeve. He sent Jubal Early up the Shenandoah Valley to threaten Washington from the west. The vanguard of Early's force was Mosby's Rangers, now at peak strength and towing field guns. Early put Federal officials in Washington into a panic, but Grant had the answer. He sent Sheridan, as much Grant's right arm as Jackson had been Lee's, to take over the Army of the Shenandoah. Sheridan took command August 7. Mosby strove mightily to delay the offensive he knew the new commander would launch. On August 13, he attacked a 525-wagon supply train that included hundreds of head of horses, mules and cattle. He took 300 prisoners and a thousand head of livestock after burning a week's rations for 2,200 Federal soldiers. Sheridan stepped up his anti-guerrilla patrols. In mid-September, Mosby was seriously wounded and again taken to his parents' home.

With his guerrilla problem in remission, Sheridan moved against Early. He drove Early out of Winchester with the loss of a quarter of his army. Four days later, he routed Early's army at Fisher's Hill, south of Strasburg. Early's troops scattered into the mountains.

Grant asked Sheridan to send him his Sixth and Nineteenth Corps to help him press his attack on the Confederate lines at Petersburg, the Confederate strongpoint guarding Richmond from the south. Sheridan, though, pleaded the difficulty of sending men over the mountains. It was, he said, already difficult to keep his army supplied. Guerrilla raids had resumed. Mosby, hobbling around on crutches, was directing them. To ease Sheridan's supply problem, Grant ordered the reopening of the Manassas Gap railroad, a short cut through the mountains. Mosby saw that reopening the railroad would not only ease Sheridan's supply problem, it would let Sheridan easily shift troops to help Grant. He concentrated on keeping it closed. His efforts were so successful that on October 4, General Henry W. Halleck, the Federal chief of staff, suggested to Grant that "Sheridan's cavalry should be required to accomplish this object (driving Mosby's men away from the railroad) before it is sent elsewhere. The two small regiments under General Augur have been so often cut up by Mosby's band that they are cowed and useless for that purpose."[23]

Meanwhile, Early had reorganized his army and received reinforcements. On the night of October 18-19, while Sheridan was away in Winchester, Early silently moved up to the Federal army at Cedar Creek and fell on the unsuspecting Yankees. Sheridan, hearing guns, got on his horse and dashed to the army. He found it in retreat—almost in a rout. Sheridan then performed the war's greatest example of personal leadership. He turned his troops around and annihilated Early's army.

The end

Now Sheridan was able to give his full attention to Mosby. The guerrilla had permanently squashed the plans to reopen the Manassas Gap railroad. In so doing, he later estimated, he had lengthened the life of the Confederacy by six months. So far, Mosby had been unbeatable. But Sheridan saw where he was vulnerable.

Mosby's troopers had "lived on the land." Every year, they collected a "grain tax" from the farmers of "Mosby's Confederacy." Sheridan's strategy was simple: deprive them of the land to live on. He sent troops into the heart of Mosby's Confederacy and up and down the Shenandoah Valley. Their orders: molest no civilians, and burn no homes. But burn barns, destroy crops, confiscate food, and run off or kill livestock. The troops were thorough. They turned the most fertile areas of Virginia into a desert. Mosby tried to stop the destruction, but ultimately, he had to shift his operations to less strategic areas.

Mosby was still by no means impotent. The reputation of this skinny little man who waged a war of his own was that of a giant, among both Federals and Confederates. Mosby wanted a new surgeon for his force, an old friend named Aristides Monteiro. He went directly to Robert E. Lee to request the transfer. Lee said that was not in his power. Mosby would have to see the army medical director, Dr. Lafayette Guild. Mosby and Dr. Monteiro went to see Dr. Guild. Guild merely murmured that such a change was "impossible."

"This infamous red tape!" Mosby shouted. "I won't submit to it! You do what I ask, sir, or you will have an order to that effect tomorrow morning from the Secretary of War."

Guild asked Monteiro who this impudent officer thought he was. Monteiro told him it was Colonel John Singleton Mosby. Guild turned pale, apologized to Mosby and assured him Monteiro would be transferred. Mosby thanked the medical director with "a ghastly grin" and galloped off.[24]

On December 20, back in Mosby's Confederacy after his trip to Richmond, Mosby was dining at the home of a friend when a large party of Federal cavalry stopped in front of the house. Some Union officers entered, and Mosby managed to hide the insignia of rank on his coat. He knew that if they knew they had a colonel, the bluecoats would guard him carefully—even if they didn't know they had the most wanted man in Virginia. Suddenly shooting erupted from the back yard. Mosby yelled, "I'm shot!" hoping to add to the confusion. There was a stampede of civilians, Confederates and Federals. Somebody knocked over a table and put out the lamp. In the darkness, Mosby took off the coat and hid it. Then he began to feel weak. He really had been shot. He was lying on the floor in a pool of blood when the lamp was relit and the commander of the Union troops entered the house. Asked who he was, he replied weakly, "Lieutenant Johnston, Sixth Virginia Cavalry." The Union officer looked at his wound and decided the little lieutenant wouldn't live another 24 hours. The Yankees left without him.[25]

Again, Mosby was carried to his parents' house. It was a while before the Union forces learned who "Lieutenant Johnston" really was. Some civilians saw him as he passed through Charlottesville. They told Union troops that he was spitting blood and appeared close to death.

On the last day of 1864, Sheridan wired another officer from Winchester, "I have no news today, except the death of Mosby. He died from his wounds at Charlottesville."

Sheridan was wrong—Mosby recovered. On January 20, 1865, he was in Richmond, being honored by the Confederate Senate. On February 2, he was conferring with Lee. Marse Robert hoped that Mosby would soon be back in the saddle, giving the Yankees around Petersburg the same medicine he had given them in the north.

By March, the weather was warming up, and Mosby was preparing for new battles. So was Sheridan. The Yankee general had returned from the Shenandoah Valley and resumed command of all Union cavalry. Grant added two infantry divisions to his corps.

Lee was also ready. He knew he could not hold Petersburg. He planned to withdraw and link up with Joe Johnston, currently retreating before William T. Sherman in the Carolinas. He sent George Pickett with his division and the divisions of Fitzhugh Lee and B. Johnson to guard the junction at Five Forks and prevent the Yankees from blocking the way to the south.

On the night of March 31, Pickett's men drove off some Federal cavalry, and Pickett apparently thought the Yankees could give no more trouble. He invited Fitz Lee and his other ranking officers to a shad bake. April 1, while Pickett and his generals were savoring fresh fish, Sheridan's dismounted troopers with their 16-shot Henry repeaters suddenly appeared in front of and behind Pickett's position. Then Yankee infantry hit his flank. Pickett's corps collapsed. Sheridan captured 4,500 Rebels.

Lee sent a message to President Davis telling him it was no longer possible to hold Richmond. Then he moved his army west instead of south.

On April 9, near Appomatox, Mosby's friend William Blackford was amazed when a Union officer, "a short, heavily built, coarse-looking man" rode into the Confederate camp and asked to speak to General John B. Gordon.[26] He was astounded when the Yankee introduced himself as General Philip Sheridan.

Gordon sent a courier to Lee. It was all over. Grant and Sheridan had blocked all escape routes. That afternoon, Lee surrendered.

Peacetime

The war wasn't quite over for Mosby. He was not included in the blanket parole of all Lee's troops, but he got confusing messages indicating that he might be. He disbanded Mosby's Rangers, because the Union officers threatened to continue their devastation of Virginia if he didn't. He returned to civilian life, but was arrested and released several times. There was even a rumor that he was involved in the assassination of Abraham Lincoln.

His wife, Pauline, tried to do something about the constant harassment. She went to Washington to see an old family friend, President Andrew Johnson. But Johnson gave her no satisfaction. Pauline Mosby didn't give up. She called on the commander-in-chief of the U.S. Army. General Grant listened sympathetically, then issued an order. The harassment of Mosby stopped, and the ex-guerrilla was restored to full citizenship.

Before the next presidential election, Grant was nominated for president by the Republicans. The Democrats nominated Horatio Seymour, a New York governor who had been as close to being a Copperhead as one could while staying out of jail. (A "copperhead" was a Northerner who sympathized with the South during the Civil War.) Mosby not only voted for Grant, he campaigned for him ferociously. Grant actually carried Virginia, although most of those most opposed to him were still disenfranchised. Mosby's stand was hardly one that would make him popular with his friends and neighbors. Mosby, though, had never cared what anyone else thought. He felt he owed Grant support. And besides, he felt more comfortable with a soldier than with a politician.

His wife had met Grant, but Mosby did not until the president was into his second term. The two old soldiers hit it off immediately. Mosby quickly became part of Grant's "inner circle" a strange amalgam of real soldiers, like Sheridan and "Cump" Sherman, political soldiers, shady politicians, and shadier millionaires. As a friend of Grant, Mosby was able to do favors for friends in Virginia. But as more native white Virginians resumed voting, Mosby became a pariah. He couldn't practice law in his home town of Warrenton. That didn't faze Mosby. When Grant's term neared its end, Mosby joined the former Yankee generalissimo in supporting Rutherford B. Hayes. Gradually, though, Mosby grew tired of the South. Pauline had died in 1876, and his children were scattered around the country. There was little to tie him to a region in which he was so unpopular. In 1877, somebody tried to assassinate him. At Grant's request, Hayes appointed him U.S. consul in Hong Kong.

In the British crown colony, Mosby quickly alienated the British and American communities. He angered the British by befriending the governor, Sir John Pope-Hennessy, an Irish Catholic aristocrat who actively sided with the Chinese inhabitants against the British ruling class. He annoyed not only the Americans in Hong Kong but the entire State Department hierarchy by exposing the corrupt practices of American consuls in the Far East. He kept up a continuous correspondence with Washington about abuses in the consular service, but it was not until the administration of Chester A. Arthur, a machine politician turned reformer, that he got action.

At one point, when China was quarreling with France over what is now Vietnam, Fred Ward's old friend Li Hongzhang, now the most powerful man in China, offered Mosby command of a Chinese army. Mosby later wrote, "I decided to decline....I had never admired the soldiers of fortune who go around poking their noses into other persons' quarrels."[27]

On returning from China, he joined the legal staff of the Southern Pacific Railroad. Later, Theodore Roosevelt appointed him to prosecute cattle barons using unlawful fencing to discourage homesteaders—a job on which he made as many enemies as he'd had in the South or in China. He worked in the Department of Justice until 1910, when, at age 76, he was told he was too old. He lived on, crippled, blind in one eye, honest and cantankerous as ever until Memorial Day 1916.

Disdained for years in his native region, forgotten for more years, John Singleton Mosby is again starting to be considered a regional hero in northern Virginia. At the very least, a tavern there has been named after the teetotaling Mosby. As a daring and imaginative soldier, as a martyr in the cause of post-Civil War reunification, and as a brave and unshakably honest civil servant, he deserves more than that.

4

Treachery in the Badlands: Captain Jack

A routine assignment

There were 40 cavalrymen in the party under Captain James Jackson, and they were accompanied by a dozen civilians.[1] Jackson's orders were to move the party of Modocs camped on the Lost River back to their reservation "peaceably if you can, forcibly if you must."[2] It didn't look like a difficult task. There were 16 Modoc warriors in this camp, including their chief, Kintpuash, known to the whites as Captain Jack, and 16 more in the camp across the Lost River.[3] At the camp sites, the Lost River was a deep, sluggish stream 100 yards wide that could be crossed only by boat. The civilians had split off from the troopers before they got near the camps and crossed the river at a ford. They came up behind the Modoc camp on the other side of the Lost River. The civilians planned to forestall any Indian attempt to escape the soldiers.

As the troopers approached, an Indian fishing in the river saw them and ran into the village screaming "Soldiers! Soldiers!" A Modoc warrior called Scarfaced Charley came out of his tent holding a rifle. He fired a shot.

"He told me after the surrender that it was an accidental discharge. I believed him," Major F.A. Boutelle later recalled.[4] Boutelle, then a lieutenant, was second in command of the troopers.

Captain Jackson attempted to summon Captain Jack, but the chief did not appear.[5] Scarfaced Charley had withdrawn to a far corner of the camp, where he was talking excitedly to other warriors.

"He had one rifle in his hand, which he waved defiantly, and three or four lay on the ground at his feet," according to Boutelle, who later became a friend of the scarfaced warrior.[6]

Jackson ordered Boutelle to take some men and arrest Scarfaced Charley and the men with him. Charley heard the order and raised his rifle. At the same moment, Boutelle drew his revolver. Both men fired simultaneously. Both missed. Then firing became intense. Captain Jack came out of his tent and directed the Modoc forces. A number of soldiers were hit; so were some Indian men and more Indian women and children. The Indian warriors withdrew from the camp, leaving the women and children behind. Jackson sent the military dead and wounded to the nearby Cawley ranch. As he was arranging this, some civilians appeared and requested protection from the hostile Indians. The captain moved his troops to the Cawley ranch, leaving Boutelle and 10 troopers to hold the camp. Some Modocs returned to attack Boutelle's party but were repulsed. The women and children left with the warriors and the soldiers burned what was left of the camp.

Meanwhile, the Indians in the camp across the river heard the firing and decided to flee. The civilians attempted to stop them, but the Modocs, under a sub-chief nicknamed Hooker Jim, because he had once worked for a man named Hooker, killed several of them and drove the rest off. That band then began raiding white settlements and killed 17 whites in their retreat. Boutelle later recalled that the civilians on the other side of the river had attacked the Indians without provocation.

"The citizens who attacked the Indian camp on the left bank of the Lost River were there without orders or authority, and had no more right for their attack than if it had been made on Broadway, New York," he wrote. He indignantly refuted statements that Jack's band had committed atrocities. "In contrast with the actions of this civilized party (the civilians across the river) may be noticed the actions of some of Jack's people who saw two cowboys, whom they knew, approaching their assemblage. They went out to meet them, telling of the occurrences of a few hours previous, and advising them to go away while they were at war with the soldiers, as they did not want to hurt them."[7]

Captain Jack's band did not attack white settlements. They headed directly for their tribal stronghold, what they called their "rock fortress" and is today the Lava Beds National Monument in California.

It was November 29, 1872, and the Modoc War, one of the strangest of all American Indian wars, had begun.

The Modocs

The Modocs were related to other California Indians, collectively called "the Diggers," because they lived to a large extent on edible roots.[8] The Diggers were peaceful people. The Spanish had no trouble subduing them and turning most of them into virtual serfs.

American-Indian activists and Anglo-Californians have long cursed the Spanish for what they did to the Indians. Until recently, they forgot what the gold-seekers from the eastern states did. They committed genocide. Patricia Nelson Limerick, a professor of history at the University of Colorado, says, "I would hesitate to use the word genocide in the rest of the West, because you need a state policy. But in California, you had that. The governor and the legislature were determined to get the Indians out. There was not only brutality, but a formal, stated, worked-out agenda."[9] The state paid millions of dollars in bounties to individuals and militia groups to hunt down and kill Indians. Thousands of Indian children were sold as slaves, although California was a free state.

"No one remembers the Chilulas, Chimarikos, Urebures, Nipewais, Alonas, or a hundred other bands whose bones have been sealed under a million miles of freeways, parking lots, and slabs of tract housing," Dee Brown writes in *Bury My Heart at Wounded Knee*.[10] The California Indians were almost completely wiped out.

The Modocs were one of the few tribes that survived. The reason they did was because they lived off the beaten path. Their ancestral home was around Tule Lake, which is bisected by the California-Oregon border. Even today, the northern end of California is sparsely populated. When the gold rush began, an occasional wagon train wandered into Modoc country. At these initial contacts, Indians were abused and killed. But they were not overwhelmed, like the other Diggers. After the first appearance of the whites, the Modocs were able to prepare for new invaders.

In September 1852, the Modocs under their chief, Schonchin, ambushed a wagon train in a narrow pass on the edge of Tule Lake. They killed 62 immigrants. Only one man and two girls (ages 12 and 14) escaped. Armed white settlers tried to exact revenge, but the Modocs eluded them in the mountains. Finally, the whites invited the Indians to a peace conference. Schonchin was ill and unable to attend, but 46 sub-chiefs and important warriors came to the feast. The food had been poisoned with strychnine. Fortunately for the Indians, the strychnine was too weak to kill them. Unfortunately for them, the whites had another plan. When the meal began and the Indians didn't keel over as expected, the leader of the settlers whipped out a concealed revolver and shot the nearest Indians. The rest of the settlers followed suit. The Modocs, understanding that all participants would be unarmed, had brought no weapons. Only five Modocs escaped, one of them Schonchin John, the chief's younger brother.

In 1864, the Modocs signed a treaty which called for them to move to a reservation where the "Great White Father" would see to it that they had food and shelter. In 1864, the federal government had more important things on its mind—like preserving the Union—so it didn't ratify the treaty until 1869. When the treaty went into effect, the Modocs lived up to their part of the bargain: they moved. But the "Great White Father's" representatives forgot their obligations. The reservation was already occupied by the much more numerous Klamath tribe, hereditary enemies of the Modocs. The Klamaths destroyed the Modocs' crops and stole their livestock. The Modocs moved to another part of the reservation. The Klamaths followed and continued harassing them. The federal government provided neither protection nor food.

Finally Kintpuash, Schonchin's son, led some of his people back to their ancestral homes. The young chief saw that the future of his people depended on them maintaining good relations with the whites. He adopted the whites' agriculture, weapons and clothing. He was fond of blue coats with brass buttons, the type worn by steamship captains. Before long, the whites were calling him "Captain Jack." Most of the Modocs spoke some English, but none of the settlers spoke Modoc, so the whites gave many of the Indians nicknames, especially those who worked on their ranches or with whom they traded.

"I have always told the white men when they came to my country that if they wanted a home to live there, they could have it," Kintpuash said. "I never asked them for any pay for living there as my people lived. I liked to have them come there and live. I liked to be with white people."[11]

All was not sweetness and light, however. In times of drought, when the deer were scarce, the Modocs sometimes took cows instead. The settlers admitted that the Modocs were not violent. But, they said they were dirty, drunken, and they scared the white women. They asked the government to move them. So the government sent Captain Anderson on his ill-fated mission.

The Lava Beds

Captain Jack's "Rock Fortress" is a unique area. The product of what must have been a horrendous volcanic eruption millions of years ago, it is hundreds of square miles of decaying lava. If the Pacific surf on the rocky coast of California were instantly solidified, it would resemble the Lava Beds. The undulating, porous rock was pitted with caves and intersected with wide, deep fissures. Many of the caves formed tunnels from one ravine to another. Soil had filtered into the spaces between the "waves" and desert plants had sprung up. There were springs of fresh water around, but these were known only to the Modocs and the wildlife of the Lava Beds.

Captain Jack's band had been in the Lava Beds for a full day before it was reunited with Hooker Jim's. Jim told how he and his men had killed a number of settlers in Oregon before coming to the Lava Beds. Jack was not pleased.

"What did you kill those people for?" he demanded. "I never wanted you to kill my friends."[12]

A few days later, another band of Modocs joined Captain Jack. The chief now had 50 fighting men and a larger number of women and children in his band.

There was little action during December. But Jack knew the soldiers would be coming in force. On January 13, the Modocs' sentries saw army scouts approaching and drove them away with heavy rifle fire. Three days later, 225 regular soldiers and 104 militiamen from Oregon and California took up positions around the Modoc camp. Outnumbered more than six-and-a-half to one, Jack wanted to surrender. There was no way his little force could hold out against the U.S. Army. Hooker Jim, who knew he would probably be hanged for the murder of the settlers, violently opposed surrender. Jack called for a vote. Of the 51 warriors, only 14 wanted to surrender, while 37 voted to fight to the death.

Kintpuash, known to the whites as Captain Jack, stands at right after his capture. With him is one of his warriors, known to the whites as Boston Charlie. (Library of Congress)

In the army camp, the soldiers, too, were eager to fight. "A more enthusiastic, jolly set of regulars and volunteers I have never had the honor to command," wrote Colonel Frank Wheaton.[13] His men were joking that they'd have "Modoc steak" for breakfast.[14]

On the morning of January 17, the Modocs heard bugles, and shells began exploding in their camp. Jack led out his warriors, who were wearing sagebrush on their heads. They ran crouching through the crevices and crawled through the tunnels. They'd pop up at intervals to fire, but they kept moving all the time to make the soldiers think there were far more of them than there were. By midday, the soldiers were spread out in a line more than a mile long. The soldiers saw the smoke from the Modocs' rifles, but they hardly ever saw an Indian. They fired volley after volley at the lava ridges, but they didn't kill a single Modoc.

Brigadier General David Perry, a troop commander during the Modoc War, later wrote, "During all this day's fighting, I did not see an Indian, and I don't recall that anyone else did, though they called to us frequently, applying to us all sorts of derisive epithets. It was at this point that our greatest number of casualties occurred. I was wounded about 4 p.m., having raised myself upon my left elbow to look at a man who had just been killed. A shot at my head missed that, passed through my left arm and into my side."[15]

By nightfall, the soldiers withdrew to the shores of Tule Lake. Their casualties: nine killed and 30 wounded. Colonel Wheaton reported that to drive the Modocs out of the Lava Beds, he'd need a thousand men with howitzers and guns as well as mortars.

Peace talks

Another month passed while the army began concentrating troops around Tule Lake. Eventually, there were more than a thousand soldiers to oppose the 51 Modoc warriors. General Edward S. Canby, the senior officer in northern California, took personal command of the force. Canby was an unusual soldier. He sympathized with the Indians and frequently took their side against the civilian Indian agents. He organized a peace commission to solve the Modoc problem.

On February 28, Captain Jack's cousin, a woman named Winema, came to the Modoc camp. Winema, who now called herself Toby Riddle, was married to a white man named Frank Riddle. She arrived with Riddle and two other white men, Alfred B. Meacham, superintendent of Indian affairs in Washington and Oregon and an old friend of the Modocs, and L.S. Dyar, an Indian agent. Winema told Jack the white men were envoys from an army peace commission. Meacham said the soldiers did not want any more killing. If the Indians went back to the reservation all would be well. Jack wanted to know what would happen to Hooker Jim and his followers. He understood that the state of Oregon had charged them with murder. Meacham said that if the Indians surrendered, Hooker Jim and his band would not be tried under Oregon law. Instead, they would be sent to a reservation in one of the warm places, Arizona or the Indian Territory (now Oklahoma).

Jack told Meacham and his companions, "Go back and tell the commissioners that I am willing to hear them in council and see what they have got to offer me and my people. Tell them to come to see me or send for me. I will go and see them if they will protect me from my enemies while I am holding these peace councils."[16]

The next day, Hooker Jim and his followers appeared at the Fairchild ranch, where Canby had set up his headquarters. They told the general they were surrendering under the terms Meacham had given them. Canby was astounded and delighted. He telegraphed General William T. Sherman, now commander-in-chief of the army, informing him of the end of the Modoc War and asking where he should transport his prisoners of war.

He was so happy, he neglected to put Jim and his men under arrest or do anything to limit their movements. The Indians wandered around the ranch. A civilian from Oregon recognized them. He called Hooker Jim a murderer and said the governor of

Oregon would see that he and all his band were hanged. Jim and his men mounted their horses and galloped back to the Lava Beds. Hooker Jim warned Captain Jack not to go the ranch to meet the peace commission. He said the white men could not be trusted.

Back in the army camp, Canby got orders from Washington to withdraw the amnesty to Hooker Jim's band. Political pressure from Oregon was too much for the military authorities.

The peace commission reiterated its demand for Hooker Jim and his men. Captain Jack replied:

> *Let everything be wiped out, washed out, and let there be no more blood. I have got a bad heart about those murderers. I have got but a few men, and I don't see how I can give them up. Will they (the white men) give up their people who murdered my people while they were alseep? I never asked for the people who murdered my people....I can see how I could give up my horse to be hanged; but I can't see how I could give up my men to be hanged. I could give up my horse to be hanged and wouldn't cry about it, but if I gave up my men I would have to cry about it."[17]*

Canby continued trying to negotiate, although from Washington, Sherman advised him to attack, "so that no other reservation for them will be necessary except graves among their chosen Lava Beds."[18]

On March 21, Canby rode into Jack's camp personally. He told the chief that if he took his people out of the Lava Beds they would be given food, clothing and many presents. Jack said his people would rather have them remove the soldiers. They wanted only to be left alone.

Instead of removing the soldiers, Canby brought up more. Jack sent a message to the peace commission asking to meet them half way between the lines. On April 2, Canby, Meacham, Wenema and Frank Riddle, Dyar, and a minister, the Reverend Eleazar Thomas, met Captain Jack, Hooker Jim, and other leading Modocs. The Indians had brought their wives along to show that their intentions were peaceful. Jack greeted Meacham as a friend, but he complained to Canby about the general's bringing up more soldiers. He said there could be no peace until the troops were withdrawn and the soldiers agreed to treat Hooker Jim and his men the same as the other Modocs. The meeting broke up.

Two days later, Jack sent a message to Meacham, asking to meet him and John Fairchild, a friend who owned a nearby ranch. He asked Meacham not to bring Canby, who talked too much of his love for the Indians, or Rev. Thomas, who represented a religion opposed to the Modocs' beliefs. At the meeting, Jack asked to be allowed to stay on Lost River.

"I can take care of my people," he said. "I do not ask anybody to help me. We can make a living for ourselves. Let us have the same chance other men have."

Meacham countered that the Lost River was in Oregon, where Jim's warriors had killed the settlers. "The blood would always come up between you and the white men," he said.

Jack agreed. In that case, he proposed, let his Modocs stay in the Lava Beds. They were badlands that no whites would want. "I can live here," he said. "Take away your soldiers, and we can settle everything."

Meacham said there was still the matter of Hooker Jim and his warriors. They would have to be tried in a court of law.

"Who would try them?" Jack asked. "White men or Indians?"

"White men."

"Then will you give up the men who killed the Indian women and children on Lost River, to be tried by the Modocs?"

"The white man's law rules the country," Meacham said. "The Indian law is dead."

"The white man's laws are good for the white men, but they are made so as to leave the Indians out," Jack said. "No, my friend, I cannot give up my young men to be hung. I know they did wrong. Their blood was bad....They did not begin; the white man began first....No, I cannot give up my young men; take away the soldiers and all the trouble will stop."

"The soldiers cannot be taken away while you are in the Lava Beds."

Jack grabbed Meacham's arm. "Tell me, my friend, what am I to do. I do not want to fight."

"The only way now to peace is to come out of the rocks. No peace can be made while you stay in the Lava Beds."

"You ask me to come out and put myself in your power. I cannot do it. I am afraid—no, I am not afraid, but my people are....I am the voice of my people....I am a Modoc. I am not afraid to die. I can show him how a Modoc can die."[19]

Treachery in council

Canby decided to give the Modocs one more chance. He sent Winema to Jack with a message: any Modoc who wanted to leave the Lava Beds peacefully could return with her. Jack called a council, but Hooker Jim and his followers said they would kill any Modoc who surrendered. Winema returned alone, but she told her husband that Jim and his faction were planning to kill any peace negotiators. Riddle passed the warning on to Canby, but the general still wanted to give peace a chance.

In the Modoc camp, the angry talk was getting angrier. Schonchin John, who barely escaped death from white treachery years before, said the peace commissioners were merely stalling for time until they had enough soldiers to overwhelm the Modocs and kill every last one. A Modoc named Black Jim said they should kill the peace commissioners at the next council. Captain Jack tried to reason with Hooker Jim's growing faction. He was shouted down.

"If you are our chief," Black Jim said, "promise us that you will kill Canby the next time you meet him."

"I cannot, and I will not."

"You will kill Canby," Hooker Jim said, "or you will be killed by your own men."

"Why do you want to force me to do a coward's act?"

"It is not a coward's act," Hooker Jim said. "It will be brave to kill Canby in the presence of all those soldiers."[20]

Some of Hooker Jim's men put a woman's shawl on Jack, called him a coward and renounced him as a chief. Jack asked all of those who wanted him to kill Canby to stand up. All but about a dozen stood. Finally, he said that if Canby did not agree to his terms, he would kill the general.

At the next council, April 11, 1873, Captain Jack demanded that the troops be withdrawn. Canby could not promise that. Jack drew a pistol and shot Canby dead. Immediately, other Indians produced concealed weapons and fired at the commissioners. A Modoc nicknamed Boston Charley shot and killed Eleazar Thomas, the minister. Winema saved Meacham's life by knocking Schonchin John's revolver aside, but the Indian affairs superintendent was wounded several times by other Indians. Boston Charley was about to scalp him when Winema yelled, "Soldiers are coming!" The Indians fled back to the Lava Beds. Winema, her husband and L.S. Dyar fled in the other direction. The soldiers rescued Meacham, who was unable to move.

Treachery in the field

The council in which Canby and Thomas were killed took place between the army and the Modoc camps. The troops couldn't see what happened, but they heard shots. While the council was under way, another party of Modocs approached the troops. Two officers, Lieutenants Walter Sherwood and W. H. Boyle, approached them. The Indians opened fire, killing Sherwood, but missing Boyle. Hooker Jim's plan had been to kill the army officers as well as the peace commissioners, expecting a forced troop withdrawal.

Needless to say, the troops did not withdraw—they attacked immediately. The fighting was a rerun of the earlier battle in the Lava Beds. This time, though, the soldiers had heavy artillery and outnumbered the Indians more than 200 to one. They subjected the Modoc camp to intense bombardment and charged the lava ridges with what seemed to the Modocs an endless number of men. On April 17, after a week of heavy fighting, they entered the Modoc camp. Nobody was there. The Modocs had filtered through the lava maze and were still at large among the rocks.

On April 21, a troop of cavalry with 15 friendly Indian scouts, commanded by Captain Evan Thomas, was trying to locate the Modocs. Thomas threw out a screen of skirmishers in front of his force and on both sides of it. The soldiers no longer joked about "Modoc steaks." Although the 85 men in Thomas's command amounted to twice the number of Captain Jack's effective warriors, the soldiers proceeded with the utmost caution. The skirmishers were continually shrinking back toward the main body.

The soldiers were eating lunch when they heard a shot from a ravine where two scouts were stationed. That was followed by a volley, and a number of soldiers were hit. The rest took cover, then charged a sand hill from where the enemy fire seemed to be coming. They reached the crest of the hill, but saw no Indians. But they did see that hill was commanded by a higher hill. The Indians on the second hill opened fire. The first hill became a death trap. Fire seemed to be coming from all sides, but none of the soldiers so far had even seen a Modoc. Every officer except the surgeon was killed, and half the troops fled in panic. Twenty-two cavalry troopers were killed and 18 were wounded. The Modoc attackers numbered only 22, and none of them had been hit.[21]

Fighting went on and on. Sniping, ambushes, and brief skirmishes were constant. The soldiers couldn't corner the Indians, but they were slowly wearing down Captain Jack's forces. General Jefferson C. Davis, now in command of the troops, reorganized his forces, whose morale had been shattered. He began a series of carefully planned advances through the lava. Troops would occupy a section of lava, fortify it and move on. Davis was gradually tightening a cordon around the Modocs.

Relations between Captain Jack and Hooker Jim continued to worsen. Hooker Jim and his hardcore followers split off from Jack's people. Jack now had no more than 37 warriors to fight off more than a thousand troops.[22]

On May 10, Captain Jack led 33 warriors in an attack on two troops of cavalry and a battery of artillery—a force that outnumbered his at least five to one. He stampeded the soldiers' horses and mules, but the troops counterattacked and drove the Modocs away. They killed one Indian, but more important, they captured Jack's pack animals, which were carrying most of the Modocs' food and ammunition.

On May 22, the soldiers captured Hooker Jim and his people. Hooker Jim immediately agreed to help the Bluecoats find Captain Jack.

Five days later, Hooker Jim and three members of his band found Jack and his starving band. Hooker Jim told Jack he had come to take his surrender. The soldiers would give the Modocs plenty to eat, and would give them justice, he said. Jack looked at Jim with intense contempt. He replied:

> *You are no better than the coyotes that run in the valleys. You come here riding soldiers' horses, armed with government guns. You intend to buy your liberty and freedom by running me to earth and delivering me to the soldiers. You realize that life is sweet, but you did not think so when you forced me to promise to kill that man, Canby. I knew life was sweet all the*

time; that is the reason I did not want to fight the white people. I thought we would stand side by side if we did fight, and die fighting. I see now that I am the only one to forfeit my life by killing Canby, perhaps one or two others. You and all the others that gave themselves up are getting along fine, and plenty to eat, you say. Oh you bird-hearted men![23]

Although almost beside himself with rage, Captain Jack let Hooker Jim and his companions return to the army unmolested.

Hooker Jim and his men now guided the soldiers in the pursuit of Captain Jack. They knew the location of all the springs, and they knew all the routes through the wilderness. Thirst and starvation depleted Jack's band far more than the soldiers. Members began deserting him. On June 1st, the soldiers trapped Captain Jack and the three warriors who remained with him.

"Jack's legs gave out," the chief said as he handed his rifle to an officer. "I am ready to die."[24]

The white man's justice

General Davis prepared to hang Jack immediately, but Washington demanded that he and other Indians accused of murder be tried. No one would be tried for the murders of the settlers by Hooker Jim's band. Hooker Jim and two of his faction were not charged with murder of the peace commission because they had given state's evidence. Captain Jack, Schonchin John, Black Jim, and Boston Charley were tried by a military tribunal and condemned to death. They were not represented by counsel, and soldiers were constructing a gallows while the trial was going on.

Jack and the three other Modocs were hanged October 3, 1873. Hooker Jim and the rest of the Modocs captured in the Lava Beds area were sent to the Indian Territory.

Before he died, Captain Jack told the military court that condemned him, "You white people conquered me not; my own men did."[25] It was a truthful statement. In the Modoc War, 12 Indian warriors were killed. Of them, four were executed and one committed suicide. A larger, but unknown, number of women and children were killed. Of the whites, 86 were killed and 82 were wounded. All of them were men and the overwhelming majority were soldiers.[26] In the Lava Beds, 51 Indian warriors held off 1,200 U.S. Army troops for over six months and cost the U.S. Government more than half a million dollars.[27] Perhaps that's why Captain Jack's name does not come up as frequently as that of Sitting Bull, whose warriors outnumbered Custer's at least five to one.

Part 3

The White Man's Burden

5

"Damn, Damn, Damn the Filipino": Frederick Funston

Reluctant warriors

Brigadier General Frederick Funston loved the writings of Rudyard Kipling. He thought the latest piece by the English author particularly appropriate:

> *Take up the white man's burden—*
> *Send forth the best ye breed—*
> *Go bind your sons to exile*
> *To serve your captives' need;*
> *To wait in heavy harness,*
> *On fluttering folk and wild—*
> *Your new-caught sullen peoples*
> *Half devil and half child.*

Funston had fought in the last Cuban guerrilla war against Spain. Now he was on the other end of a guerrilla war in the Philippines. "A nasty little war," he called it.[1] His soldiers did not take as "benevolent" a view of their "new-caught sullen peoples" as Mr. Kipling. They had their own verse, a marching song:

Damn, damn, damn the Filipino—
Pock-marked khakiak ladron*!*
Underneath the starry flag,
We'll civilize him with a Krag,
And then go back to our beloved home.

By way of explanation, "*ladron*" is Spanish for thief, and "Krag" is the name of the then-current U.S. service rifle.

Funston, like his men, had never wanted to be in the Philippines. The story of how they came to be there—and what they did—is one of the least glorious chapters of our national history.

Birth of an empire

It began with an island 8,000 miles from the Philippines—Cuba. The idea of ousting Spain from Cuba had been around almost as long as the United States. "These islands (Cuba and Puerto Rico)...are natural appendages to the North American continent," John Quincy Adams wrote in 1823, "and one of them, Cuba...has become an object of transcendent importance to the political and commercial interests of our Union."[2]

In William Walker's day, most of the impetus for annexing Cuba came from the slave states. In Walker's time, slavery was still legal in both Cuba and the United States. If Cuba were annexed and made a state, the slave states would have more clout in Congress. The Civil War eliminated that motive, but new reasons appeared.

In 1890, the U.S. Census Bureau declared that our internal frontier was closed. That year ended with the finale of 300 years of Indian wars—the massacre at Wounded Knee. From now on, any expansion would have to be beyond our borders. At the same time, a new reason for expansion appeared: U.S. industry and agriculture had outgrown the domestic market. We were producing more than we could consume. Failure to allow for that situation caused a depression that started in 1893 and continued through much of the decade. That reason for expansion appealed to many on both ends of the economic spectrum—the owners of industry and the laid-off workers.

To most, expansion meant continued expansion of the United States in the Americas. That was an old story—the Louisiana Purchase, the Mexican War, the purchase of Alaska. The people of Cuba were unhappy. Wouldn't they rather be one of the United States than a colony of Spain? And how about Puerto Rico and the other Spanish colonies? The idea of the United States itself having colonies was a strange one to most people, but it was becoming less strange as time went on. All other great powers had colonies. The United States was a great power. Where were its colonies? Colonies were not only desirable, they were necessary.

Horace N. Fisher, a writer and financial analyst, put it this way: "Even now, our domestic consumption can not take more than 75-percent of our manufactured products....Hence the necessity for great foreign markets for such surplus, with the alternative of the curtailment of production or of wages."[3] In that era of high protective tariffs, "foreign markets" to most people meant colonies. Africa had been almost totally divided up among the European powers. It looked as if China would be next, and the United States had no presence on the far side of the Pacific.

There was another school of expansionists, or "imperialists" in the jargon of the times. That was composed of those who, like Frederick Jackson Turner, believed that the frontier had shaped the national character. Many of them also believed that without a struggle against untamed nature and untamed barbarians, the country would lose "manliness." Their chief spokesman was a young politician named Theodore Roosevelt. Soon after he was appointed assistant secretary of the navy, Roosevelt expressed his philosophy at the Naval War College: "All the great masterful races have been fighting races...No triumph of peace is quite so great as the supreme triumphs of war...the diplomat is the servant, not the master, of the soldier."[4] Roosevelt's contemporary, German Kaiser Wilhelm II, could not have topped that.

Allied to Roosevelt's clique, and strongly influencing them, were the strategists, particularly navy Captain Alfred Thayer Mahan, whose *The Influence of Sea Power on History* is to navies what Carl von Clausewitz's *On War* is to armies. Mahan stressed the need for bases and coaling stations to maintain sea power in the modern age. In the sailing era, ships could stay at sea indefinitely and travel anywhere on the globe. But in the late 19th century, they had to be able to refuel. When he was writing, the United States lacked coaling stations abroad.

A major difference between the "blood and iron" imperialists (like Roosevelt) and the economic imperialists is that many of the latter, particularly the wealthy ones, would prefer to acquire colonies without war. One of the leaders of this group was Mark Hanna, chairman of the Republican National Committee.

There was a third group: anti-imperialists who were eager for war. A whole generation had grown up since the Civil War. They celebrated heroes and glorious victories, but never knew the agonies that accompanied them. This new generation shared Roosevelt's belief in the messianic mission of the United States. Expansion is more than colonies, Roosevelt had said. It is "the extension of American influence and power, the extension of liberty and order, and the bringing nearer by gigantic strides of the day when peace shall come to the whole earth."[5] These anti-imperialists looked not to annex Cuba, but to liberate it.

Getting rid of colonial powers in the Americas was always a popular cause, and Spain was a particularly unpopular colonial power. There was some prejudice: generations of Protestant Americans had grown up with tales of Spanish iniquity from the Armada to the Inquisition, even Spanish treatment of the Indians—in spite of Wounded Knee and similar occurrences.[6] But there were a lot of reasons for hostility toward

Spain, too. Spanish rule in Cuba was autocratic and harsh. Americans had, for years, been engaged in filibustering expeditions to help Cuban rebels. In 1839, the steamer *Virginius*, flying the American flag, was stopped by a Spanish warship in international waters. It had been carrying what the Spanish authorities believed (correctly) were Cuban rebel recruits and munitions intended for the rebels. Taken to Cuba, the ship's captain, crew, and passengers, 53 men in all, were executed. The captain and most of the crew were American citizens. The *Virginius* affair left a very sour taste in American mouths.

In 1895, a new revolt against Spain began. It was an extremely brutal affair on both sides, but the American public heard only about the Spanish atrocities. Putting down the revolt was too much for the stomach of the Spanish captain general (governor) Arsenio Martinez de Campos, a man who had crushed the last revolt, known in Cuba as the Ten Years War. He wrote to his friend, the Spanish prime minister, that only the most oppressive measures could end the revolt. "Perhaps I may arrive at such measures, but only as a last resort, and I do not think that I have the qualities for such a policy. In Spain, only Weyler has them."[7]

The prime minister accepted Martinez's resignation and appointed General Valeriano Weyler y Nicolau, a native of Majorca who had recently crushed a revolt in the Philippines. Weyler was one of the two men who made war with Spain almost inevitable.

The other was the new President of the United States, William McKinley. McKinley, an amiable soul, had the knack of appearing to let others push him in the direction he chose to go. He invented the "front porch campaign" later used successfully by Warren G. Harding. Seldom stirring from his Ohio homestead, he delivered anti-boss cliches to delegations coming to visit him while power brokers twisted arms behind the scenes. Thousands of employees across the land heard that if the Democrats won, they'd have no jobs.

"Gentlemen," McKinley said when voting results showed that he had defeated Democrats' "silver-tongued orator," William Jennings Bryan, the "the Almighty has given us victory." According to one story, Mark Hanna, applauding with the rest of the audience, whispered to Matt Quay, boss of the notorious Pennsylvania Republican machine, "The Almighty? What the hell does he think *we* did?"

Hanna and his friends did not want war; war interrupts commerce. But they wanted colonies. Roosevelt, Henry Cabot Lodge, and the clique of increasingly powerful war hawks wanted both. A majority of the American public wanted war...but with no colonies. A minority wanted neither.

How could anyone keep all those factions happy—especially amiable and apparently spineless William McKinley? McKinley may not be the most manipulative, duplicitous, and hypocritical president in history—the competition for that title is intense—but he is a strong contender.[8]

"We want no wars of conquest; we must avoid the temptation of territorial aggression," McKinley said in his inaugural address.[9] But for his first 10 months in office, the

Cavalry troopers prepare to set out on an anti-guerrilla patrol in the Philippines. Funston found cavalry essential for such patrols. (National Archives)

new president seemed to be building up a case for U.S. intervention in Cuba. His general counsel in Cuba was the rabidly anti-Spanish Fitzhugh Lee, John Mosby's onetime commanding officer. His secretary of state was the equally anti-Spanish John Sherman, "Cump's" older brother. When Fitz Lee reported that a high percentage of inmates in Weyler's concentration camps were American citizens, McKinley made no attempt to investigate that fantastic claim. He just asked Congress to appropriate $50,000 for their relief, thus giving Lee's story wide publicity.

McKinley continually pressed the Spanish to make reforms—get rid of Weyler, do something to relieve the people held in the concentration camps, and give the Cubans autonomy. And gradually, the Spanish did. But when they did, the president said it wasn't enough. The American public expected that if we intervened in Cuba, the whole island would greet us as liberators. Actually, there was a good deal of anti-American feeling in Cuba, particularly among the *Peninsulares* (people who had been born in Spain).

There were anti-American riots in Havana. McKinley ordered the battleship *Maine* to Havana for a "friendly visit." Even Fitz Lee asked him to delay the visit so it wouldn't provoke more riots. There was no delay.

"After warning the Spanish ambassador that an anti-American outburst in Cuba would compel him to send in troops," wrote historian Walter Karp, "the President ordered the warship to Havana to provoke an anti-American outburst."[10]

The explosion that sank the U.S.S. *Maine* remains a mystery.[11] Most students of the tragedy think the cause was a spontaneous fire in the ship's coal bunkers that ignited a magazine. Certainly, no party had more to lose from the explosion than the Spanish government. But emotion—not logic—ruled the public response. Of all the possible causes—accident, or sabotage by the Cuban rebels, by renegade Spaniards, by the Spanish government—the Spanish government was "obviously" the most responsible because it was hated. Roosevelt flew into a rage when Lieutenant Philip Alger, the navy's leading ordnance expert, said he knew of no submerged mine that could cause the damage suffered by the *Maine*.

McKinley maintained he was keeping an open mind, while he let the public hysteria build up. He waited to act until, not surprisingly, the commission he appointed found that the explosion was caused by a submerged mine. Then he sent an ultimatum to Spain: It must not only abandon the concentration camps, it must reach an immediate armistice with the rebels; it must lay down its arms; and it must accept the "friendly offices" of the United States in reaching an agreement with the Cuban rebels.

The Spanish stalled for time. McKinley became more demanding. Eventually, the Spanish agreed to everything. McKinley then said it was too late. Two days after the Spanish completely capitulated, McKinley asked Congress to let him intervene. In his message to Congress, he specifically did not ask for recognition of the Republic of Cuba, the government the rebels had set up in the eastern end of the island. That would preclude annexation.

But for once, McKinley let things get slightly out of control. The faction for liberation—rather than annexation—had gotten too strong. Senator Henry M. Teller of Colorado slipped in an amendment to the bill authorizing intervention: the United States might not exercise "sovereignty, jurisdiction, or control" over Cuba. The amendment didn't mention anything about Puerto Rico, Guam, or the Philippines, because nobody was interested in those territories. If this situation were allowed to stand, the Hanna faction would get a war, which they did not want, and they would not get colonies, which they wanted.

In April, 1898, few Americans had ever heard of the Philippines. The few that did, however, included McKinley, Roosevelt, and the clique of warhawks around Roosevelt, including Henry Cabot Lodge and Commodore George Dewey. Roosevelt, as assistant secretary of the navy, had managed to get Dewey assigned to command the U.S. Navy's Asiatic Squadron. If war came, Dewey was to go at once to the Philippines, where an insurrection against Spain was already in progress. To Roosevelt, possession of the Philippines was absolutely essential to give America a place in the Far East.

At the beginning of 1898, their "American cousins" were still rather a joke to the British. The Americans were even less than that to most Europeans. World opinion changed radically before the end of the year.

Dewey sank all the Spanish ships in Manila Bay without losing a man; Sampson sank most of the rest of Spain's navy—all its ships in Cuba—off Santiago with the loss of only one seaman.[12] The United States was now generally accepted as one of the great powers. McKinley did not intend to waste that upgrade in status. Right after Dewey's triumph, McKinley scribbled a memorandum to himself: "While we are conducting war and until its conclusion we must keep all we get; when the war is over we must keep what we want."[13] Taking advantage of war fever, he signed an order annexing the Republic of Hawaii, completing a deal that had been in progress for a decade.[14]

When war came, Roosevelt resigned from the administration. He formed the Rough Riders volunteer cavalry regiment along with Dr. Leonard Wood, another of his clique. Before he left for Cuba, Lodge wrote to him, "They mean to send at least 20,000 men to the Philippines....Unless I am utterly and profoundly mistaken the administration is now fully committed to the large policy that we both desire."[15] Even the knowledgeable Lodge didn't know that McKinley was committed to that "large policy" before anyone else.

But it looked as if neither Lodge, nor McKinley nor anyone else knew much *about* the Philippines. The American public and press were utterly clueless. Cartoons in imperialist and anti-imperialist newspapers alike portrayed the Filipinos as grass-skirted savages, usually with the enormous lips and pie-eyes used to portray blacks in that era.[16] In the Philippines, there were a few tribes like the Igorots who wore loin cloths and hunted with bows and arrows, but they were no more representative of the Philippine population than the contemporary Apaches and Sioux were of the U.S. population.[17] That ignorance was understandable in a population that knew only that the islands were in the "South Seas," that vague domain of cannibals and hula dancers. But the president of the United States knew that the islands, like Cuba, had been exposed to three centuries of European civilization. McKinley knew about the insurrection, but he still called the first batch of 20,000 soldiers an "army of occupation." He acted as if Spain held unchallenged sway over the 7,000 islands, and Dewey's fleet action was all the fighting that would occur.

The Insurrectos

Actually, almost all of the Philippine Islands were under the control of insurrectionists. Spanish garrisons held Manila and a number of towns. But they were under siege by rebel armies loyal to Emilio Aguinaldo, exiled to Hong Kong. The rebels held 9,000 Spanish prisoners of war under conditions that would have won the Geneva Convention's seal of approval. This latest insurrection had been going on since 1896. There was a lull when Aguinaldo went into exile December 27, 1897.[18] The destruction of the Spanish fleet gave the rebels new life, and in a short time they controlled every province on Luzon, the main island. Dewey transported Aguinaldo from Hong Kong back to the Philippines. The American admiral treated "Don Emilio," as he called him, with the utmost courtesy and led him to believe there would be an alliance with the United States.[19]

The rebels, called *Insurrectos* by the Spanish—a name adopted by the Americans— had already elected Aguinaldo president. Under his leadership they adopted a constitution and a declaration of independence, both modeled on those of the United States. Aguinaldo and his followers were profoundly shocked, then, when American troops appeared. They had already proved that they could handle the Spanish; they didn't need help, el presidente protested. It got worse. The Americans began by demanding a place in the siege lines around Manila, then they demanded that the Filipinos let them assault Manila alone.

Aguinaldo's army was certainly not composed of grass-skirted savages. Brigadier General Thomas Anderson, who arrived with the first U.S. troops, reported on the insurgents: "They are not ignorant, savage tribes, but have a civilization of their own; and although insignificant in appearance are fierce fighters, and for a tropical people they are industrious."[20] Aguinaldo's troops had uniforms, officers, and a full military hierarchy. Some of them had repeating Mausers—far better weapons than the single-shot, black powder Springfields most of the Americans carried.[21] But not all had Mausers, or even the single-shot Remingtons that were secondary Spanish weapons. They had hardly any artillery, and those few other guns were ancient muzzle-loaders. Half of the insurrectos had little besides their *bolos* (Philippine Spanish for large work knives, similar to the machetes used in Cuba). Aguinaldo had to admit that the U.S. Army was better prepared to assault Manila, but he didn't like being left out of what should be the crowning feat of the rebel's war.

The Spanish resolved the impasse. They agreed to surrender to the Americans alone after a short demonstration.

Friction between the Americans and Filipinos had been growing ever since the U.S. troops landed. The Americans called the Filipinos "niggers" and treated them like a conquered people instead of allies. Americans searched Filipino houses without warrants, knocked down any Filipino who showed "disrespect" for them at check-points, showed no respect *at all* for Filipina women they searched. Filipinos were shot simply because they looked hostile. "We have to kill one or two every night," one private wrote home.[22]

This was going on while the Insurrectos thought the United States was still an ally. On November 29, 1898, Spain agreed to sell the Philippines to the United States for $20 million. McKinley said the decision to annex the Philippines did not come easily.

> *I walked the floor of the White House night after night after night until midnight; and I am not ashamed to tell you, gentlemen, that I went down on my knees and prayed to Almighty God for light and guidance more than one night.*
>
> *And one night it came to me this way—I don't know how it was but it came: (1) that we could not give them back to Spain—that would be cowardly and dishonorable; (2) that we could not turn them over to France or Germany—our commercial rivals in the Orient—that would be bad business and discreditable; (3) that we could not leave them to themselves— they were unfit for self-government—and they would soon have anarchy*

*and misrule over there worse than Spain's was; and (4) there was nothing
left for us to do but to take them all, and to educate the Filipinos, and uplift
and civilize and Christianize them...[23]*

At the time McKinley was passing along this wisdom he had received from on
high that we did not have the Philippines to "give" to Spain or any other country—we
didn't even have Manila. He did not explain why Filipinos were less fit for self-government than Cubans. Admiral Dewey himself had reported, "In my opinion, these
people are far superior in their intelligence and more capable of self-government than
the natives of Cuba, and I am familiar with both races."[24] The capital of the land
McKinley was going to "civilize" had electric street cars and electric lights—something most American cities still lacked. And the Philippines were the only predomi-
nantly Christian country in the Far East—81 percent Christian, 14 percent Muslim,
and most of the remaining 5 percent Animist.[25] For perspective, the United States in
1998 was 85-percent Christian.[26]

When they heard of the treaty, some Insurrectos wanted to declare war on the
United States. Aguinaldo, however, thought the U.S. Senate might reject the treaty.

But on the night of February 4, 1899, 36 hours before the Senate was scheduled to
vote on the treaty, a group of drunken Filipinos approached a U.S. Army checkpoint.
The sentry, Private William Grayson, called "Halt!" One of the Filipinos mimicked
him, calling, "Halto."

"Well, I thought the best thing to do was shoot him," Grayson testified later. Another
sentry shot a second Filipino, and Grayson shot a third. Then the sentries ran back, calling
to their comrades, "Line up fellows; the niggers are in here all through these yards."[27]

Firing erupted all down the American line. Some Filipinos fired back. American
artillery opened up. The Americans charged the Filipinos. The fighting ended with
3,000 Filipinos and 60 Americans dead. The next day, Aguinaldo proposed to General
Elwell S. Otis, the American commander, that they establish a neutral zone between
the two armies to eliminate friction.

Otis replied that "the fighting having begun, must go on to the grim end."[28]

What McKinley called the "benevolent assimilation" of the Philippines had
begun.

In U.S. history books the fighting is usually called the "Philippine Insurrection."
There certainly had been an insurrection against Spain. But when the Americans began fighting the Filipinos, the Insurrectos controlled 99.9 percent of the country. To
call that an insurrection against the United States is stretching things a bit. The ten-
dency now is to call it the "Philippine War." Actually, as we'll see, it was the *first*
Philippine War. It was immediately followed by a second, quite different, war against
the Moros of the southern islands.

Secretary of War Elihu Root gave the official U.S. version of how the fighting
started—the only version the rest of the world would hear for a year and a half:

> *"On the night of February 4th, two days before the U.S. Senate approved the treaty, an army of Tagalogs, a tribe inhabiting the central part of Luzon, under the leadership of Aguinaldo, a Chinese half-breed, attacked, in vastly superior numbers, our little army in possession of Manila, and after a desperate and bloody fight was repulsed in every direction."*[29]

Root managed to cram a staggering amount of untruth in that single sentence. There was no organized attack. The Filipinos did not fire first. And while there were 80,000 Insurrectos, they were spread over the 7,000 islands—only about 30,000 of them were even on Luzon. No more than half of the Insurrectos had rifles and few of those knew how to aim a rifle.[30] The 16,000 Americans were all in Manila.

Further, the Tagalogs (tah-GAH-logs) were hardly a "tribe," which implies some sort of organization, however primitive. They were the major linguistic group in Luzon, and today, Tagalog is the basis of Pilipino, one of the two national languages of the Philippines (the other is English). Emilio Aguinaldo y Famy had no Chinese blood. His was a middle-class Tagalog family; his father, a lawyer and politician. Why Root called him "a Chinese half-breed" is unknown. ("Half-breed," of course, was derogatory.) "Chinese" may have been used because Root considered pure Filipinos incapable of organizing anything.[31]

The United States quickly shipped 100,000 troops to the Philippines. Among the troops already was the 20th Kansas Volunteer Infantry Regiment, and its leader, Colonel Frederick W. Funston.

Funston

In appearance, Fred Funston was the antithesis of his father, a 6-foot 2-inch congressman from Kansas known as "Foghorn Funston, the farmer's friend." Young Fred was five-ft. two-in. tall and so uncoordinated he was never even mediocre at any sport. But Fred wanted a life of adventure, and he was not going to be held back by a small body. He did push-ups and lifted weights to build up his arms. He was never much of a boxer, but he packed such a punch he usually won the many fights he got into.

After high school, he tried to enter West Point. But even though his father was a congressman, he couldn't pass the entrance examination. Instead, he went to Kansas University. One of his closest friends there was William Allen White, who was later the famous editor of the *Emporia Gazette*.

At his enrollment, a clerk misspelled his name as "Timston," leading his classmates to nickname him "Timmy." Funston was an avid reader, got top marks in English composition, and excelled in biology. He was, however, more interested in camping, climbing mountains in Colorado, drinking, or anything else except classes. He dropped out before graduation and worked for a time as a newspaper reporter in Kansas City, Missouri and Fort Smith, Arkansas.

Disgusted with his last paper's politics, he quit and became a ticket collector on the Atcheson, Topeka and Santa Fe. While Fred was growing up, the cattle drives from Texas to Kansas began. Wild cowboys were shooting up Kansas towns while Wild Bill Hickock, Luke Short, Wyatt Earp, and their associates were shooting down cowboys in those towns. Kansas had not calmed down noticeably when Funston took his railroad job.

One time he asked a cowboy for his ticket.

"I ride on this," the puncher said, showing a revolver. "That's good, that's good," Funston said.

A few minutes later, the cowboy heard the ticket-taker's voice behind him. "I've come to punch your ticket." The passenger looked around and found himself staring at the muzzle of a cocked rifle held by Fred Funston. He hastily coughed up the cash needed.[32]

Another time, a drunken cowboy amused himself by lying in the aisle and shooting holes in the ceiling of the car. Funston stopped the train, picked the cowboy up, and threw him off—literally.

In spite of incidents like this, there wasn't enough adventure in railroading to satisfy Fred Funston. He quit that job and signed up as a field biologist for the U.S. Department of Agriculture. The new job took him from Death Valley, where he almost died of thirst and to Alaska, where he almost froze to death.

On a trip to New York, Funston learned about the revolt in Cuba. He developed a desire to be a filibuster.

Cuba

Filibustering was dangerous before the would-be soldier ever got to Cuba. The Cleveland administration was enforcing U.S. neutrality laws zealously. The Spanish government had legions of spies, including agents of Pinkerton's International Detective Agency.

The Cuban rebels were wary, but eventually decided that Funston was sincere. He learned that they had a great need for artillerymen. He knew absolutely nothing about cannons, but he found an arms broker who was willing to teach him. He learned to aim, clean, and disassemble a Hotchkiss breech-loading 12-pounder.[33] Eventually, he was invited to join some rebel sympathizers on Long Island for artillery practice. The featured attraction was the Sims-Dudley Dynamite Gun, a turn-of-the-century wonder weapon.[34] The dynamite gun made such a mighty blast when its shell hit the water, the gunners feared the authorities would be alerted and the artillery practice might be cut short.

Finally, through the good offices of an American railroad and shipping magnate, Funston was smuggled into Cuba, along with a Hotchkiss 12-pounder, small arms, and four other would-be gunners. The filibusters were met by General Maximo Gomez himself, the military chief of the rebels. Gomez asked Funston how much he knew about artillery.

"My knowledge is limited," the American replied.

"Well, you can't know less than the last American who came here and said he knew everything. You will be in charge of this gun."[35] Funston became an instant captain. As it turned out, Funston was the only one in Gomez's army who knew *anything* about artillery. Before long, he was the rebels' chief of artillery with the rank of colonel.

Funston quickly learned the nitty-gritty of guerrilla war. This latest revolt had been touched off by the U.S. depression of 1893 and the subsequent Wilson-Gorman Tariff Act of 1894. Cuba's economy was built on the export of sugar to the United States, and the new tariff made that difficult. Unemployment soared. Unhappy Cubans petitioned Gomez, who had been a leader in the Ten Years War, to return to Cuba from his native Santo Domingo and lead a new revolt. Gomez returned and brought a new strategy with him.

The Dominican general knew the rebels could never beat the Spanish regulars in the field. So, instead of fighting the Spanish army, he made war on the Cuban economy. The idea was to make it so unprofitable for Spain to hold on to Cuba that the Spanish would give up and go home. Or, the disorder would prompt the intervention of a foreign power, which would most likely be the United States.

On July 1, 1895, he ordered his troops to burn the sugar cane fields. The unemployed farm workers would then flock to the cities. The rebels would prevent food from reaching the cities from the countryside. In theory, if the Spanish authorities found the Cuban economy in shambles and themselves unable to aid masses of starving people, they would capitulate. By the end of summer, eastern Cuba was pretty well devastated. Gomez and his second-in-command, the black general, Antonio Maceo, moved into the richer, more populous western part of the island. In September, Gomez told the western planters that if they processed their sugar cane, they would be treated as supporters of Spain and killed.

Martinez, the Spanish captain general, tried to bottle up the rebels in the eastern part of the island with a fortified line, but Gomez and Maceo could not be held back, even after Martinez added a second line. Weyler, who replaced him, strengthened the fortified lines and invented a new strategy, *reconcentraccion*. The Majorcan general recognized that guerrillas require the support of the general population. He proposed to remove the general population. With no people in rural areas to provide food and shelter, the guerrilla army would wither away. Weyler, therefore, began removing the rural population from vast areas and confining them in camps near military posts—the world's first concentration camps. On paper, Weyler made provisions for food to be delivered to camp dwellers and land to be made available for them to farm. However, little food ever arrived, no land was given for farming, and shelter was often in abandoned warehouses and ruined buildings—often buildings with no roofs. According to a *Spanish* estimate, "at least a third of the rural population, that is to say, more than 400,000 human beings" died in those camps.[36]

Weyler instituted martial law and executed anyone suspected of supporting the rebels. At first, he ordered sugar planters to bring their crops for processing to locations where the military could guarantee security. Later, when he learned Gomez was taxing sugar producers, he forbade the grinding of sugar cane in the next season. The result of all this was that the Cuban peasant was being ground down by both the government and the rebels. Hundreds of thousands of people who supported neither side were killed.

Soon after Funston arrived, the rebels began to feel the effects of Weyler's policies. There was little food but sugar cane, much of it growing wild. Life as a guerrilla was constant wandering, with occasional ambushes and infrequent sieges of Spanish positions mixed in.

Funston had little chance to practice modern artillery tactics: He had no equipment to allow accurate indirect fire. He moved his few guns close to his targets and aimed them like rifles. The technique required more daring than science, but Funston had bravery in abundance. Even firing the devastating dynamite gun took daring. The weapon was never generally adopted because its shell was prone to explode in the barrel instead of where it was aimed, taking out the gunner instead of the target. Because set-piece battles were rare, Funston fought almost as often as a cavalryman or an artilleryman. He quickly learned something that Gomez and his lieutenant, Calixto Garcia, apparently never learned in their long military careers: cavalry cannot charge infantry in position with any hope of success. More important to his later career, he also improved his Spanish and learned the importance of intelligence in guerrilla operations. He also learned to be wary of the most dangerous foe in the tropics—disease.

Funston's daring got him wounded repeatedly, and the tropics gave him repeated bouts of malaria. Finally when he was incapacitated by both wounds and disease, his commander, Calixto Garcia, gave him leave to return to the United States to recuperate. He promised to return when fit for service. On the way to the coast, however, he was captured by Spanish troops. He readily admitted he had been fighting for the rebels, but he said he had deserted them and was trying to return home. The Spanish were suspicious, but Fitzhugh Lee came to Funston's rescue, and he was sent home.

Before he recovered, the United States declared war on Spain.

The Philippines

The recuperating Funston had gone on the lecture circuit, both to support himself and to spread the word about Cuba. He found himself something of a hero, especially in Kansas. When war came, heroes were in demand.

The United States began the war with a growing navy of moderate size, both well-equipped and well-trained. It had a minuscule army, trained and equipped only for fighting Indian tribes.

U.S. Artillery in action against the troops of Emilio Aguinaldo. (National Archives)

McKinley called on the states to provide volunteer units to supplement the regular army.[37] Kansas was asked for three regiments. The governor, John W. Leedy, appointed his state's leading war hero a colonel and gave him command of the 20th Kansas Volunteer Infantry Regiment.

Funston's qualifications included a knowledge of Cuba, of warfare in tropical conditions, and of the Spanish.[38] But he knew almost nothing about training troops, regular infantry tactics or even modern artillery tactics. The army did send him to Florida to brief the officers of the force that would be going to Cuba. The regular officers, however, tended to ignore a mere volunteer, especially one without a full uniform or even a sword.[39] Funston himself was bitterly disappointed when he learned that his new regiment would not be going to Cuba. Instead, it was sent to California and would be part of the "army of occupation" in the Philippines. He could expect no fighting—only garrison duty in a tropical backwater.

After his thankless briefing assignment, Funston, with a new sword presented to him by the citizens of Kansas, joined the 20th in camp outside San Francisco. A number of the regiment's officers and NCOs had served in the regular army, and Funston learned from them such military minutiae as the details of close-order drill. He imparted those details to his men with a vulgar vocabulary drawn from both English and Spanish. The men liked "Colonel Freddy," though, because he was no impersonal martinet. He was less popular with regular officers. Among other things, he slouched in the saddle like a cowboy instead of sitting up like a soldier. And he still limped from the wounds he'd received in Cuba.

While waiting for orders, the 33-year-old colonel met 24-year-old Eda Blankart. He married her after a whirlwind courtship of seven weeks and, having been told when he would be shipping out, got her passage on a ship taking army wives to the Philippines. The Funstons had barely settled into their new home when the fighting broke out.

The first few hours of fighting the Filipinos made the Americans overconfident. The fighting quickly settled down to something grimmer and more brutal than anything their compatriots experienced in Cuba. The Filipinos were poorly armed and rotten shots. However, they were excellent at building field fortifications, adept at cover and concealment, brave, and deadly with their bolos at close quarters. Funston's regiment held the center of the American force that was to push up the railroad running north from Manila to the Lingayen Gulf.

At the time, orthodox infantry tactics called for troops to fire a volley, rush forward a short distance and fire another volley. Funston quickly found that it was more effective if the troops advanced at a walk, firing at will, then charged with the bayonet for the last few yards. His troops' old .45-70 caliber rifles were accurate at well over 1,000 yards, but the big lead bullet's velocity was so low it described a high arc getting to a target at that range. Consequently, unless the shooter could calculate the range precisely, the slug would probably miss. His troops were farmers, cowboys, clerks, and teamsters—not professional soldiers. Range estimation was not among their skills. Funston didn't let his men fire until they were within 200 yards of the enemy, when the trajectory was so flat no range calculation was necessary. They would move up to that range by taking advantage of all cover or by rushes in small groups if there were no cover. Funston's revised tactics were so effective the 20th Kansas usually finished each advance in front the regiments on either side.

His men captured several disassembled locomotives as they moved north. General Otis ordered them to be towed back to Manila for repair and refitting, but one of Funston's Kansans had been a railroader. He directed the assembly of one engine, which then powered what Funston's men dubbed "Freddy's Fast Express." The FFE brought supplies from Manila. The Americans also used that locomotive and the others captured by Funston to push armored railroad cars containing such armament as two Gatling guns, two Colt automatic machine guns, and a breech-loading three-inch cannon or two three-inch breech-loaders or two Hotchkiss revolving cannons (weapons resembling king-size Gatling guns).

The biggest impediment to the American advance was unbridged rivers. It would have been worse if an English railroad engineer had not persuaded the Insurrectos that it would be better not to destroy bridges completely. Because of its position on the railroad, the 20th Kansas was the spearhead of every crossing. Funston's standard operating procedure was to look for a ford and outflank the Insurrecto bridgehead. Sometimes that was impossible. At the Marilao River, he got his men across on a raft out of sight of the defenders. At the Bagbag River, machine gun and artillery fire from an armored car, plus the rifle fire from the 20th Kansas drove most of the defenders from their trenches. It was not known, however, whether there were still a few Filipinos in the trenches across the river. Funston selected a dozen volunteers then led them across the ruined bridge, picking their way from girder to girder. Finally, there was nothing but open water. Funston and his men jumped in and swam to the other side. By that time, any enemy troops there had retreated.

The next crossing was a key one. The Rio Grande de la Pampagna is the biggest river in Luzon. The bridge over it, leading to the town of Calumpit, had been the longest in the Philippines. Insurrecto General Antonio Luna built his main defense line behind the river. "Calumpit will be the sepulcher of the Americans," Aguinaldo had been advised.[40]

Funston's regiment and the 1st Montana Volunteer Infantry were to make the crossing. As always, Funston took the lead. The Kansans had recently received some of the new Krag repeating rifles, which had a flatter trajectory and consequently longer effective range than the Springfields. Even this additional firepower could not budge the Filipinos from their trenches across the river. Funston asked his division commander, Major General Arthur MacArthur, for permission to sneak across the ruined bridge at night and attack the Insurrectos at daybreak. At the same time, the rest of the troops would fire as fast as possible, yell and cause a commotion to make the Filipinos think the whole army was crossing. MacArthur finally gave his permission. Funston and his volunteers carried long boards to lay across gaps in the bridge. But when they got to the bridge, they learned that there were gaps far too wide for any boards. The river was deep and swift—too deep and swift for most men to swim.

Funston took a larger party and went scouting downstream. On April 27, 1899, they found a raft the Insurrectos had not completely burned. Two strong swimmers volunteered to take the end of a rope across the river while the rest of the troops gave them covering fire. With the Kansas and Montana riflemen, along with a field gun, blasting away over their heads, the two men, Edward White and W.B. Tremblay, stripped and towed the rope across. MacArthur brought up the rest of the division and laid a barrage of fire on the Filipino position. Tremblay and White reached the opposite shore, but Filipino Insurrectos were still in the trench right above them. The two naked, unarmed men threw mud balls into the Filipino trench. The Insurrectos, believing the Americans were using some devilish new explosive, fled. Tremblay and White then tied the rope to a tree. Funston crossed with the first raftload of men, pulled hand over hand along the rope. When he had 120 Krag-armed riflemen across, Funston moved against the flank of the Filipino bridgehead, knocking out a Maxim machine gun and driving off the Insurrectos. Enemy fire having been eliminated, the rest of MacArthur's division was able to cross.

After that crossing, General Luna asked Aguinaldo to give up the classic warfare the Filipinos had been waging and revert to the guerrilla war they had used against the Spanish. Aguinaldo decided to continue regular warfare for a while, but he was shaken. Funston's performance earned him the Medal of Honor, the nation's highest award, and promotion to brigadier general of volunteers. Soon after the crossing, Funston was wounded. When he returned to the front, he was commanding both the 20th Kansas and the 1st Montana. At the end of June, both regiments got orders to return to the United States. They had enlisted for the Spanish American War, and that war was over. All were to be mustered out, including General Funston. Back home, though, Funston got a message from the War Department asking him to stay on as a brigadier general of volunteers and return to the Philippines. He agreed.

However, there was trouble while he was home. Some regulars were miffed at the honors and publicity given to a ragtag volunteer who had never had any formal military training. They told lies about him: that he had told his men to kill prisoners and that one of his friends had actually been seen murdering a prisoner. They spread other lies about him: that he had looted Catholic churches.

Investigations showed that no one had ever heard Funston order the killing of prisoners, that he had, in fact, expressly forbidden such action. One "witness" to the murder said his name had been used without his permission and that he had never seen such a crime. Another was found to have been many miles from the alleged scene. There were no witnesses, because there was no such murder. As to the alleged looting, that story originated with a woman Funston had *stopped* from carrying off articles from a ruined church.

Funston made good copy: He was not only colorful, he was outspoken. However, much of what he said did little to boost his stock with the authorities. He criticized the army for not enlisting native troops and for lack of communications with the Philippine population. He was right, and he was to prove it, but criticism by mavericks like Funston has never been popular in the army.

Unfortunately, much of what Funston told reporters was much less sensible—some of it was nonsense. He predicted the war would be over in six months. In talking about Philippine independence, he said:

> The word independent...is to them a word, and not much more. It means with them simply a license to raise hell, and if they get control they would raise a fine crop of it. They are, as a rule, an illiterate, semi-savage people, who are waging war, not against tyranny, but against Anglo-Saxon order and decency.[41]

Aguinaldo, he said, was a "cold-blooded murderer" presiding over "a drunken uncontrollable mob" with "minds like children."[42] This was the same man who had praised the courage of Filipino soldiers and criticized the army for ignoring Philippine citizens. He was no racist. He had fought in a Cuban army where not only many of the soldiers, but many of the officers and the second-ranking general were black. The trouble was a habit he had picked up in his student days. His old classmate, William Allen White later wrote:

> Funston, who was rising in the army, was still talking too much. Kellogg and I guessed why: Funston, who to us was still "Timmy," still could not

carry his liquor. Roosevelt sent me to Timmy to tell him he must quit talking or the President would have to rebuke him publicly. When I told him my message, Timmy looked at me and grinned: "Oh, Billy, look not upon the gin rickey when it is red, and giveth color in the cup, for it playeth hell and repeat with poor Timmy."[43]

Counterinsurgency

When Funston returned to the Philippines, he found a new kind of war. Aguinaldo, leading the main Insurrecto army, had narrowly escaped capture. He then followed Luna's advice. He ordered the troops to get rid of their uniforms, go back to their villages, and wage guerrilla warfare. Command of the Insurrectos was radically decentralized, but *el presidente* maintained overall control through couriers. Instead of commanding a brigade advancing in battle order, Funston found himself in charge of a military district in central Luzon.

The war itself was as brutal and barbaric as any of the century's Indian wars; almost as brutal as the guerrilla war Funston remembered in Cuba. The Filipinos had doffed chivalry along with their uniforms. Peaceful-looking peasants would suddenly draw hidden bolos and hack up unsuspecting Americans. The Americans, in turn, used torture liberally to get information. Suspects were repeatedly hanged by the neck until they passed out, lowered and revived, then hanged again.[44] The "water cure" was a favorite method of persuasion. The captive's mouth was forced open and water poured down his throat. His body became painfully distended. When he was near the point of death, his captors forced the water out of his body with kicks. In addition, whole villages were burned in reprisal for attacks on American troops.

Funston's first task was to restore order among his troops. He had elements of six regiments in his command, all of them with headquarters elsewhere. The men were sick and exhausted; the supply system was in disarray. One unit had 12 percent of its men in a hospital; others had been living on water buffalo and rice or hardtack and bacon. The guerrillas were cutting his telegraph lines, attacking small parties, and preparing for a major assault. At the same time, headquarters was pressing him to set up schools and a system of civil government.

Funston ignored the army's "pacification" program, which included such measures as setting up native police forces and prohibiting the sale of hard liquor. The program was designed by officers who had no previous knowledge of guerrilla operations. Funston got the supply lines straightened out, improved sanitation, and took other measures to avoid tropical disease. Then he established camps in guerrilla-infested territory and conducted extensive patrolling. On March 18, 1900, one patrol surprised and routed some 700 guerrillas who were massing to attack U.S. installations.

When he took over the district, "General Loudmouth," as his rivals were calling him, talked tough. His job, he told reporters, was "exterminating the Goo Goos."[45] But in Brian McAllister Linn's *The U.S. Army and Counterinsurgency in the Philippine War, 1899-1902*, a study conducted under a grant from the U.S. Military History Institute, the author says of Funston, "Although a vocal advocate of repression, his actual conduct was characterized by lenient surrender terms, rewards for collaboration, and personal friendship."[46] Funston protested mistreatment of Filipino civilians by soldiers in other military districts although his superior officer, Major General Lloyd Wheaton, thought that officers who reported American misconduct were soft on guerrillas.

Funston spoke Spanish, the second language of most Filipinos, and he understood the Philippine social structure. Most Filipinos deferred to the *principales*—important people who filled all the leadership positions in the guerrilla movement—in these areas. Funston actively courted the principales in his command area; he befriended former guerrillas, and he used native auxiliary troops extensively. Most important, he established a secret service. His military district, the Fourth, had unequaled intelligence of enemy operations. Funston had been in the district only a few months when, acting on his intelligence, American patrols captured the entire provincial leadership of the Insurrectos. Aguinaldo sent one of his top officers, Brigadier General Urbano Lacuna, into the district to reorganize the guerrillas. Funston, however, had already obtained so much support from the native leadership that Lacuna received almost no cooperation. In desperation, he resorted to terrorism to compel cooperation. He only succeeded in driving the villagers closer to the Americans.

Aguinaldo

Funston's intelligence service ultimately led to the coup that all but ended the Philippine War. On Feb. 4, 1901, Funston got a message that one of his officers had captured a courier from Aguinaldo along with the messages he was carrying. Funston ordered the officer to send both the courier and his messages to headquarters "with all possible speed."

It turned out that the courier, Cecilio Segismundo, had been traveling with a party that was ambushed by an American patrol. Segismundo was able to escape into the jungle. After wandering for some time, he came to a village. He sought help from the mayor of the town. (However, the mayor was one of Funston's converts.) He persuaded Segismundo to give himself up. The courier surrendered at the nearest American post and was sent to Funston. He agreed to take the oath of loyalty to the United States. Under questioning, he revealed that Aguinaldo was staying at Palanan, an isolated village in the Sierra Madre range of eastern Luzon. There were sentries overlooking all approaches to the village, and the aborigine Negritos who hunted in the otherwise uninhabited mountains informed the Insurrecto headquarters of any strangers long before they got near Palanan. Segismundo had no idea what was in the messages he carried.

Funston sent for one of his aides, Lazaro Sergovia y Gutierrez. Sergovia was a brilliant Spaniard who had earned a bachelor of arts degree at the age of 15. He'd wanted to continue his education, but he had no money. So he joined the Spanish army. He was sent to the Philippines and joined a regiment that was mostly Filipino. When the war with America ended, he found that he could not take his Filipina wife back to Spain, so he joined Aguinaldo's army.

It didn't take Sergovia long to see which way the war was going. As soon as he could, he surrendered to Funston personally. Funston was no man to let brains like Sergovia's go to waste. He made the Spaniard a member of his staff—a strange collection of U.S. officers, native scouts, reformed bandits, and former Insurrectos.

Sergovia could read Tagalog, the language of the messages. Most of them were just letters to home from lonely soldiers. But some were signed "Pastor" or "Colon de Magdalo," nom de guerres used by Aguinaldo. The interesting parts of these letters were not in plain Tagalog but in a cipher using numbers and punctuation marks. Funston and Sergovia worked all night to break the cipher. When they were finished, Funston had a plan.

One letter had been to Aguinaldo's cousin. In it, *el presidente* told his kinsman to take over command in central Luzon and send him reinforcements. "Send me about 400 men at the first opportunity with a good commander; if you cannot send them all at once, send them in parties," Aguinaldo had written. "The bearer can serve as a guide to them until their arrival here; he is a person to be trusted."[47] Funston planned to send Aguinaldo more troops, but not Insurrecto troops. He talked over the plan with Sergovia and a few other trusted members of his staff. Earlier, Funston had raided the headquarters of the Insurrecto chief in his district, Urbano Lacuna, and captured documents and Insurrecto stationery. They could write a letter over Lacuna's forged signature saying that following instructions from Aguinaldo's cousin, he was sending a party of men and more would follow.

The men would be the U.S. Army's Macabebe Scouts.

The Macabebes were a minority community with a long history of hostility toward the Tagalogs.[48] They had been the mainstay of the native contingent of the Spanish army, and they had enlisted with equal enthusiasm in the American army. They would go to Aguinaldo disguised as Insurrectos, supposedly under the orders of three Tagalog officers of Aguinaldo's army who had surrendered and taken the loyalty oath to the United State. Commander of the column was theoretically Lt. Col. Hilario Talplacido. Actually, the commander, after Funston, was Lazaro Sergovia, disguised as a captain in the Insurrecto army. Segismundo, of course, would guide the troops. The false Insurrectos were to tell Aguinaldo that they had a fight with American troops and captured five prisoners, which they were bringing with them.

One of the prisoners would be Funston.

Funston had to get permission from his old division commander, Maj. Gen. Arthur MacArthur, now overall military commander in the Philippines. MacArthur gave his permission most reluctantly. MacArthur's farewell as Funston embarked was not exactly encouraging.

The American team that captured Aguinaldo. Left to right: Harry Newton, Burton J. Mitchell, Oliver Hazzard, Frederick Funston, and Russell Hazzard. (Courtesy Kansas State Historical Society.)

"Funston, this is a desperate undertaking. I fear I shall never see you again."[49]

A navy gunboat landed Funston's party on the coast near the town of Casiguran. The Macabebes had been instructed to speak only Tagalog; Talplacido and the other Tagalogs were to speak as little as possible. Sergovia did most of the talking with the local people, and he was able to persuade them that they really were Insurrectos bringing prisoners to Aguinaldo. Then they set out on foot for Palinan—a journey only one white man, a Spanish priest, had ever made. As they marched, Funston and Sergovia conducted a correspondence, letters transmitted by runners, with Insurrecto headquarters. When they ran out of food, they requested supplies from Palinan. At one point the Insurrectos sent a column to collect the prisoners, but Sergovia tricked them and was able to bring his "captives" into the Palinan area.

Aguinaldo had drawn up an honor guard to welcome the reinforcements. Sergovia gave a signal, and the "reinforcements" opened fire at the honor guard.

Aguinaldo thought the firing was a salute.

"Stop that foolishness! Don't waste ammunition!" he called from his office.

At that moment, Sergovia dashed into the office, pistol in hand, and arrested Aguinaldo and his staff. He was immediately joined by Funston.

Almost the end

In spite of screams from the United States to hang Aguinaldo, MacArthur treated his prisoner as a high-ranking prisoner of war. Aguinaldo saw that there was no hope in ousting the Americans and surrendered, calling on his subordinates to surrender, too, and end a useless war. Most of them did.

For his effort, Funston was commissioned a brigadier general in the regular army. He was no longer a mere volunteer and could not be mustered out. As the war was winding down, Funston had an attack of appendicitis and was hospitalized. Surgery was followed by infection, which doctors said could not be cleared up in the climate of the Philippines. The general and his wife returned to the United States.

While Funston was laid up, the war broke out again in the Luzon province of Batangas and on the island of Samar. Once again, "peaceful" peasants drew hidden bolos and hacked up unsuspecting American troops. With Funston in the United States, his methods of fighting guerrillas were ignored. On Samar, Brig. Gen. Jacob "Hell Roaring Jake" Smith became a precursor of Lt. William Calley of My Lai infamy. Smith ordered his men to turn the island into a "howling wilderness."

> "I want all persons killed who are capable of bearing arms in hostilities against the United States," he ordered a subordinate.
>
> "I would like to know the limit of age to respect, sir," the subordinate asked.
>
> "10 years."
>
> "Persons of ten years and older are those designated as being capable of bearing arms?"
>
> "Yes."[50]

His men carried out the orders.

Smith was eventually court-martialed. Lieutenant Calley's sentence, called a "slap on the wrist," was like a savage beating compared to what Smith got. He was retired early.

No court martial, but honors, went to Brig. Gen. J. Franklin Bell, the U.S. commander in Batangas. He revived Spanish Gen. Valeriano Weyler's concentration camp idea. "Within a comparatively few weeks after this policy was inaugurated the guerrilla warfare...ended," according to a War Department report.[51]

Theodore Roosevelt, who had been McKinley's vice president during his second term, was catapulted into the White House when McKinley died from an assassin's bullet September 14, 1901. Roosevelt declared the Philippine War over July 4, 1902. It really wasn't. Violence continued to break out in the northern islands for years, gradually blending in with a new Philippine War—this one against the Muslims (called "Moros," Spanish for "Moors") of the southern islands. The Moro war reached a climax when troops under Roosevelt's old friend, Leonard Wood, slaughtered 900 Moro men, women, and children in the crater of an extinct volcano. That war officially ended in 1913, when troops under John J. Pershing defeated the forces of the Sultan of Sulu on Bagsak Mountain on the island of Jolo.

Hero's return

All this brutality renewed Stateside protests against the Philippine War. Fred Funston, whose actions—not his words—showed him to be the most humanitarian and effective of the American generals, became the prime target of the protesters. In traditional style, he responded to an intemperate attack by a senator with an intemperate rebuttal. Roosevelt, who was as intemperate as anyone in public life before he became president, decided that Funston was politically incorrect. He sent William Allen White to tell Funston to keep quiet. And even though "Timmy" complied, Roosevelt still found it expedient to publicly rebuke him. That ended a long relationship of mutual admiration between the two men.[52]

Roosevelt was followed by Taft, who as head of the civilian authority in the Philippines had quarreled constantly with Funston's mentor, MacArthur. In disfavor with two presidents and resented by much of the army establishment as an outsider, the man who, at 34, was the youngest general in the army, watched scores of men with less ability get promoted ahead of him. That happened even though he became a hero again—at least a local one—after the San Francisco earthquake of 1906. Acting on his own authority, Funston sent troops into the burning city to fight the fires and restore order. Finally, after Taft left office, Funston was promoted to major general. The U.S. entry into World War I was approaching. Funston was heavy favorite to lead any American troops sent to Europe. But on Feb. 19, 1917, while attending a dinner in San Antonio, Frederick Funston dropped dead at the age of 51.

With the exception of a few individuals like Arthur MacArthur, Funston was never much liked by the regular army. Some of the regular army prejudice against the maverick Funston apparently remains to this day. In his study of American counterinsurgency, Linn downplays the importance of Funston's capture of Aguinaldo and also contends that Funston had an easier task than commanders of other military districts, because "Many of the accepted methods of guerrilla resistance: the shadow governments, Katipunans [secret nationalist societies], assassination, and so on were never able to seriously challenge the American control."[53] They were never able to because Funston had actually achieved that oft-stated goal of counterinsurgency forces—"winning the hearts and minds of the people." Because of that prejudice, and the fact that Funston was the hero of what is arguably this country's most disreputable and one of its most unpopular wars, the boozy, brilliant, intrepid "General Loudmouth" has been largely forgotten.

In the Philippines, though, his legacy lived on. By enlisting Filipino soldiers, consulting Filipino leaders, and by treating Filipinos as rational adults rather than children needing guidance, Funston planted the seeds of democracy in the islands. This made a big difference in the subsequent histories of the Philippines and two neighboring colonies, French Indochina and the Dutch East Indies.

6

The African Ghost:
Paul von Lettow-Vorbeck

Travelers

On the last night of 1913, the German liner *Admiral* was steaming down the Red Sea. The passengers, mostly German and English people bound for East Africa, were about to drink a New Year's Eve toast to the brotherhood of the white race. A thin German army officer with close-cropped hair and an eye patch got two glasses of champagne from the bar and gave one to a pretty, dark-haired young Danish woman. Since the steamer *Admiral* had left Naples two weeks before, this pair had spent much of their waking time together. It was, however, a distinctly chaste flirtation.

The woman, Karen Dinesen, nicknamed Tanne, was on her way to join her fiance in British East Africa. The man, Paul von Lettow-Vorbeck, had reluctantly left his fiancee in Germany when he was transferred to German East Africa. He planned to bring her to the colony as soon as he got settled.

There was a mutual attraction in spite of the age difference (he was 44, and she was 28). Language was another obstacle. Her German was poor; his Danish, nonexistent. They spoke mostly in English. Her fiance, she told him, was a Swede, Baron Bror von Blixen-Finecke. They had acquired a farm in British East Africa, where there was already a thriving Swedish colony.

He had been in Africa before, he told her. He had lost the sight in one eye in the Maji-Maji rebellion in German Southwest Africa. Now

119

he was to command all the Kaiser's troops in German East Africa. He was only a lieu-tenant colonel, but there weren't many troops to command.

The prospects for any commander of German troops in Africa were not bright. All of the colonial powers maintained armies in Africa only to keep order. In each colony there were no more than a few score European officers and a few hundred black sol-diers, called *askaris* (from the Arabic word for *soldier*). If war came, the enormous British Navy could prevent supplies or reinforcements coming to any enemy power in Africa. At the same time, Britain could pour in overwhelming manpower from its globe-girdling empire, as it had done during the Boer War at the turn of the century. If war came, Tanne Dinesen wrote home, Von Lettow-Vorbeck's role would be to "wage war passively in East Africa."[1]

Like all the passengers on the ship, both hoped war would never come. Von Lettow-Vorbeck said he wanted to find some good brood mares for his cavalry. Dinesen, a member of the Danish landed gentry who fancied herself a horse expert, said she knew of some excellent horses near Nairobi; she would buy some for him. Von Lettow-Vorbeck promised to send her a Persian carpet. He also gave her a signed picture of himself. It might help her if she were traveling in German East Africa, he said.

While the passengers on the German liner were nervously toasting peace and friend-ship, another old African hand was planning for the next war. Richard Meinertzhagen, a tall, muscular Englishman, was in Mesopotamia observing work on the Berlin-to-Baghdad Railway, a pet project of the Kaiser. Meinertzhagen, posing as a tourist, was an intelligence officer with the Indian Army. In case of war with Turkey, the Indian Army, a quasi-independent branch of the British Army, planned to invade Mesopotamia and add it to the Indian Raj. Meinertzhagen was a big game hunter and naturalist making a name for himself as an ornithologist. He fondly remembered commanding native troops in Africa. He hated India and wished he were back in Africa.

The night *Admiral* pulled into Mombasa, von Lettow-Vorbeck, Karen Dinesen and Bror von Blixen dined together. They talked about taking a safari together that August. The next morning, the Blixens were married and von Lettow-Vorbeck left for Dar es Salaam to report to his new superior, Governor Doctor Heinrich Schnee.

German East Africa

As colonial governors went in 1914, Heinrich Schnee was one of the most enlight-ened. The colony had a thousand schools for blacks. Literacy in German East Africa was higher than in any country on the continent. Schnee developed an institute of tropical biology and agriculture. Coffee plantations flourished. So did the native farm-ers, who were pretty much left alone. German colonists still lorded it over the Afri-cans, but not to the extent the English did in neighboring British East Africa.

"Where the natives are concerned, the English are remarkably narrow-minded; it never occurs to them to regard them as human beings," Karen Blixen wrote home.[2] Most

English colonists assumed that Africans were an inferior race, capable of only the most menial tasks. They would always need, the colonists thought, Europeans to guide them. Schnee, on the other hand, saw Africans as people with the potential to develop their talents to the same extent as Europeans. On this matter, Schnee and von Lettow-Vorbeck saw eye-to-eye.

Where they differed was over the threat of war. No matter what happened in Europe, Schnee wanted peace in Africa. He believed the words of the General Act of Berlin of 1885—an international conference at which all African colonial powers declared that in case of war in Europe, all African colonies would remain neutral, if everyone agreed. Schnee saw that the only two who had to agree were the Germans and the British. The French

Major General Paul Emil von Lettow-Vorbeck as he appeared in 1918 wearing his glass eye. (Courtesy AKG London)

did not border his colony and the Belgians and Portuguese were unlikely to initiate any fighting. Schnee held a number of consultations with Norman King, the British consul. London was encouraging but noncommittal. Finally, after conferring with his superiors in Britain, Consul King said while London would put nothing in writing, it was inclined to honor German East Africa's neutrality if the German colony remained strictly neutral.

Schnee's main concern was German East Africa. Von Lettow-Vorbeck's, however, was Germany. If war broke out in Europe, he believed his duty was to draw as many British troops as possible away from the decisive European theater.

As soon as he arrived at his new post, von Lettow-Vorbeck began trying to make his askaris into an effective fighting force. He bombarded Berlin with requests for new equipment, especially new rifles. The askaris used the Mauser 71, a single-shot black powder rifle adopted in 1871. Germany had adopted three rifles after that, in 1884, 1888, and 1898, but none of them reached Africa.[3] The old rifle, which produced a dense cloud of white smoke with each shot, was quite effective against tribesmen armed with spears and bows. Nothing more, German authorities felt, was needed in Africa. Von Lettow-Vorbeck got some new supplies, but few rifles. The Great General Staff knew the German Army would need as many rifles as possible in Europe.

Von Lettow-Vorbeck did improve the uniforms, training and discipline. He was a Prussian, after all. But hardly a stereotypical Prussian.

Early in 1914, a young German officer, bored to death with watching askaris drill on a dusty parade field, left his post to get a beer in town. As he walked along the dirt track, he met a middle-aged man, probably a settler, chewing a stick of sugar cane. The two began talking. The lieutenant talked about the boring routine of camp life and said he just had to take a break.

"I hope the new commander, von Lettow-Vorbeck, doesn't hear about it," he said. "They say he's a real bastard."

The two turned a corner and saw two officers, both outranking the lieutenant. The officers snapped to and saluted the older man. The lieutenant suddenly realized who the "settler" was. He turned pale.

"What you said," von Lettow-Vorbeck told him, "was said to a comrade. No comrade would inform the commander, certainly."[4]

British East Africa

British East Africa (later Kenya) was just north of the German colony. Mount Kilimanjaro, Africa's highest peak, sat squarely upon the border. Years before, Queen Victoria redrew the border to give her grandson, the future Kaiser Wilhelm II, Kilimanjaro as a birthday present. The little boy cried—he had hoped for a pony.

Sir Conway Belfield, governor of the colony, was no more enthusiastic about war than his German counterpart, Schnee.

Several months after the war was underway, Belfield said in a speech: "I wish to take this opportunity to make it abundantly clear that this colony has no interest in the present war except in so far as its unfortunate geographical position places it in such close proximity to German East Africa."[5]

Belfield was even less prepared for war than Schnee. The colony's military force, the King's African Rifles (KAR), were no better equipped than their German counterparts—and more poorly trained and disciplined.[6] The British settlers did not want the KAR to be too effective. As Judith Thurman, a biographer of Isak Dinesen, puts it, "They were afraid to arm the natives with weapons that could be turned against them; and they were afraid that the Africans—who were soldiers of great prowess, stamina, and courage—would lose respect for their white superiors."[7] When the settlers organized a militia, it was as much to guard against a black revolt as against a German invasion. Karen Blixen wrote to her mother that "In the event of a native uprising it (her farm house) has been chosen as *headquarters* and assembly point for all the *farmers* in the district."

The settlers were not, in fact, worried about the war. As soon as war was declared, there was a rush of war fever. "Bands of settlers," wrote a witness, "cantered into

Nairobi on horses and mules and formed themselves into mini-regiments of irregular cavalry. Their weapons were fowling pieces and elephant guns, their uniforms tattered bush jackets and broad-brimmed tera hats with fish-eagle feathers protruding from leopard-skin puggarrees."[8] But the war fever soon wore off, and the "troops" went back to their farms.

The settlers knew the Germans could not win. They knew that Britain controlled the sea, and that an army would come from India that would squash the Germans like a bug. Their complacency annoyed the new settler, Karen Blixen. "One cannot help—despite ancient hatred of the Germans—reacting against the incredible boastfulness of the English," she wrote to her mother.[9]

War

On June 28, 1914, Archduke Franz Ferdinand was assassinated in Sarajevo. Governor Schnee ordered von Lettow-Vorbeck to move his troops out of Dar es Salaam to make it an open city.

Many of the German settlers hoped Schnee's bid to make the colony neutral would succeed. Many others, though, were spoiling for a fight. Many of the "German" settlers were actually Afrikaners who had fled their South African homeland after the British conquest. But one of the biggest war hawks was an Englishman.

Thomas von Prinz had once been Thomas Prince, son of an English father and a German mother. He had gone to British schools until he was 15. Then his parents died, and he went to live with relatives in Germany. After he graduated from Germany's Ritter Akadamie he tried to get a commission in the British Army. He was turned down. So he attended the German military academy at Kassel, where he met von Lettow-Vorbeck. He took part in Germany's colonial wars in Africa, where the Africans gave him a nickname—Bwana Sakharani, "the Gentleman Who is Drunk with Fighting" or "Lord Berserker"—and the Germans gave him a *von*. He Germanized his name to Prinz and became a superpatriot. Although retired from the army, he raised a black and white volunteer force and placed it at von Lettow-Vorbeck's disposal.

Schnee's plan for a neutral German East Africa was undone by the German cruiser *Konigsberg*. Just before war was declared, *Konigsberg* left Dar es Salaam to go commerce raiding in the Indian Ocean. On August 6, less than a week after the opening of the war, Konigsberg captured the British steamer *City of Winchester*. The British began seriously hunting *Konigsberg*. Somehow, the British Foreign Office had not told the navy about King's discussions with Schnee. Two British cruisers entered Dar es Salaam harbor. When they couldn't find the German cruiser, they shelled the radio tower. The governor fled inland to Morogoro. In spite of his efforts, war had come to German East Africa.

Von Lettow-Vorbeck now took over. He ordered von Prinz to take his troops to the Kilimanjaro area to raid British outposts, cut all telegraph and telephone lines, and disable the Uganda Railway. That would induce the British to send troops to East Africa. Von Prinz immediately took the British railroad station at Taveta, driving off the British troops stationed at the town. Then he began mining the railroad, tearing up track and cutting communications wires.

The British were coming, but it took them a while. Meanwhile, the Germans were raiding in all directions. That was a good trick, considering that von Lettow-Vorbeck had only 216 German officers and 2,540 black askaris at the beginning of the war. He sent German officers and askari NCOs around the colony to recruit new askaris. He enlisted large numbers of civilian settlers as auxiliaries, called on reserves, and latched on to any volunteer talent like Tom von Prinz.

Von Lettow-Vorbeck's highest ranking volunteer was Kurt Wahle, a retired major general in the army of Saxony. Wahle was in Africa visiting his son when the war broke out. He came to Lettow, and although he greatly outranked the lieutenant colonel, offered to serve under him. Von Lettow-Vorbeck put him in charge of transportation. In a few weeks, the general vastly improved the efficiency and security of the German supply routes. Next, von Lettow-Vorbeck gave Wahle 600 men and launched him at Kisumu, a port city on Lake Victoria which was the terminus of Britain's Uganda Railway. The British sent a steamboat full of troops to stop Wahle, but the German armed tug *Muanza* drove it off. The British then attacked overland with the South African Mounted Rifles. The Afrikaner mounted infantry had repeating rifles that used smokeless powder. The German askaris' single-shot black powder Mausers were definitely outclassed. Wahle lost a quarter of his officers in that battle. Von Lettow-Vorbeck's main aim, though, was not to win battles but to siphon enemy strength from France.

What would really attract British troops would be a German strike at a major target like Mombasa. Moving overland through the rough country around Mombasa would be difficult, but von Lettow-Vorbeck had another idea. He would attack from the sea. The British, secure in their belief that they owned the sea, would be surprised. Von Lettow-Vorbeck contacted the commander of *Konigsberg*, Captain Max Looff. The German cruiser had returned to German East Africa and was hiding in the vast delta of the Rufiji River, emerging only to strike at targets of opportunity. With *Konigsberg's* support, he hoped to land at Mombasa and give the British lion's tail a mighty twist.

Unfortunately, Looff had already aroused the lion. *Konigsberg* had crept out of the Rufiji and had sunk the British cruiser *Pegasus* and a smaller craft in Zanzibar harbor. The British now had a small fleet blockading the mouths of the Rufiji. Looff couldn't come out. He was drawing off British naval strength, but the British had more than enough of that to spare.

In London, Lord Kitchener, although one of the most overrated soldiers in English history, was not foolish enough to take troops from France to deal with a minor annoyance in East Africa.[10] But the settlers in Africa were complaining, and the newspapers told of the threat to the colony by the "ruthless" and "ferocious" von Lettow-Vorbeck.

Kitchener agreed to transferring a partially-trained battalion of the North Lancashire Regiment and 10,000 distinctly third-rate troops from India to East Africa.

"They constitute the worst in India," Richard Meinertzhagen wrote in his diary, "and I tremble to think what may happen if we meet with serious opposition."[11] Captain Meinertzhagen was the intelligence officer for the Indian expedition.

Von Lettow-Vorbeck's intelligence service was pretty good. He used a network of black agents who regularly crossed the border. He knew the Indians were coming, he knew about when they'd arrive, but he didn't know where they'd strike. The British plan was for one army to hit the Germans in the Kilimanjaro area, where von Lettow-Vorbeck's strength was concentrated. The second army would make an amphibious landing at Tanga in northern German East Africa, the colony's second largest port. Tanga was the Indian Ocean terminus of one of the colony's two east-west railroads. The other terminus was Moshi, von Lettow-Vorbeck's headquarters near Kilimanjaro. The British knew that most of the German troops would be found between those two points. They were to be crushed in the Indian nutcracker.

Tanga

British intelligence officers in Africa had assured the commander of the Tanga landing force that Tanga was unoccupied. Meinertzhagen pointed out, however, that because of the railroad, von Lettow-Vorbeck could have troops there in short order. He was ignored.

The commander of the King's African Rifles offered his unit as pre-landing scouts. They were African and knew the territory. Major General Arthur Aitken, commander of the landing force, said the service of the KAR would be unnecessary. His "magnificent" Indian troops would have no trouble beating a bunch of blacks. He said he intended to "thrash the Germans before Christmas."[12]

Captain F.W. Caulfield, commander of the landing force's naval escort, heard about the agreement between Schnee and King. He didn't hear that it had ended. He insisted on sending a ship into Tanga harbor with a white flag to inform the Germans that all deals were off. So von Lettow-Vorbeck learned (if he hadn't known already from reading British newspapers) that Tanga was a target. There was a further delay while the British swept the harbor for non-existent mines. Although they didn't find any, Caulfield remained suspicious. He persuaded Aitken to land about a mile from the town, out of sight behind a headland. It was 9:30 p.m., November 2, almost 24 hours after they first appeared —before the first British troops, a mere two companies, landed. They found themselves in a swamp swarming with crocodiles and poisonous snakes. They had landed in the worst possible spot.

The British landed troops all through the night. At dawn, they attacked, reaching the outskirts of Tanga. Von Lettow-Vorbeck was still moving troops down the rickety railroad from Moshi, but his handful of askaris brought the Indians to a standstill.

More British troops landed and tried to outflank the German askaris. The brush was too thick for them to see anything. The German askaris didn't have to see anything: they just hosed down the brush with machine guns. Some British attempted to rush the machine guns. They were all wiped out. British officers tried to get the Indians to resume their advance, but they refused to move. The German askaris counterattacked. The Indians couldn't see them in the dense brush, but they could hear them. They broke and ran. Brigadier Michael Tighe reported to Aitken that his 2,000 Indians were outnumbered by "2,500 German rifles." Meinertzhagen, who had been present through all the action, said, "From what I saw it was more like 250 with four machine guns."[13] Meinertzhagen was right. The British force lost 300, mostly officers and NCOs.[14]

Von Lettow-Vorbeck got his last troops into Tanga at 3 a.m. November 4. He bicycled into town to look over the situation and even passed through the British-held sector. At the telegraph office he found a message from Schnee forbidding him to fight in Tanga. He ignored it. From that point on, he, not Schnee, would be the top German authority in German East Africa. He had about 1,000 men in Tanga, askaris and von Prinz's settlers. Aitken had about 8,000.

The British didn't resume the attack until noon. By that time, most of the Indians had already emptied their canteens. By 3 p.m., they had advanced only 600 yards. British troops were dropping from heat exhaustion.

The German machine gunners had set up interlocking fields of fire. Members of the one company of askaris with the modern Mauser 98 rifles were sniping from tree tops.

The fighting was house-to-house. Meinertzhagen, an intelligence officer who had to see for himself, was ducking in and out of houses when he saw a thin German with an eye patch and fired at him. He missed. The German fired back. He missed, too. Later, von Lettow-Vorbeck noted in his memoirs, "This was my first social contact with my friend Meinertzhagen."[15]

The German askaris began to push back the fading Indians. The English of the Lancashire battalion were also forced back. During their retreat, the "Lancs" passed through a grove full of wild beehives. Annoyed by the commotion, the "African killer bees" of modern horror stories attacked them. The English soldiers were convinced that the Germans had wired the beehives to trigger the attack. They hadn't: attacking the troops was the bees' own idea. But as von Lettow-Vorbeck's reputation grew among his enemies, the bee attack became part of the legend of his evil genius.

By the dawn of November 6, von Lettow-Vorbeck was in firm control of Tanga. The British evacuated after sending Meinertzhagen to the Germans with a white flag to arrange a truce. The attackers lost 800 killed, 500 wounded, and hundreds more missing. Lettow captured 16 machine guns, hundreds of rifles, and 6,000 rounds of ammunition, along with other supplies. His own losses were trifling, except for the death of his old friend, Tom von Prinz.[16]

When the British appeared off Tanga, von Lettow-Vorbeck had sent messages to all his units in the Kilimanjaro area to come to Tanga as soon as possible. The message didn't reach the troops at Longido, commanded by a major named Kraut. (A little later, Lettow's enemies would field a general named Brits.) That was a lucky break for the Germans. The second prong of the British offensive ran right into Kraut's force while Aitken's men were landing at Tanga. Kraut had one company of settlers and three companies of askaris—86 Germans and 600 Africans. The British had 1,500 men, mostly from the Indian Army. The Indians fought bravely, charging the German machine guns, but the firing stampeded the mules that were carrying their supplies. With the mules gone, the soldiers had only the water in their canteens. That night, the Indians withdrew. The first British offensive was dead.

The British generals, of course, greatly overestimated the size of the forces opposing them. Kitchener accepted their figures, but he wasn't mollified. He sacked Aitken and replaced him with Brigadier Richard Wapshare. With his new assignment, he gave Wapshare a new order: no more offensives. Wapshare didn't object. In his diary, Meinertzhagen wrote that the mention of von Lettow-Vorbeck's name "sends him [Wapshare] off into a shivering fit of apprehension."[17]

Raids and counter raids

"There's always somebody who doesn't get the word," they say in the U.S. Army. That must have been true in the British and German forces. Rear Admiral Herbert King-Hall, commanding the British cruiser squadron at the Cape of Good Hope, thought that Governor Schnee's neutrality policy was still in effect. So did the German civil authorities at Dar es Salaam. When King-Hall appeared off the German port, they ran up the white flag. The British admiral sent some ships into the harbor to make sure the Germans were not engaged in hostile actions—such as harboring the cruiser *Konigsberg*.

But von Lettow-Vorbeck had sent General Wahle to take over defense of the harbor. Wahle ordered his subordinate, a Captain Kornatzky, to fire on the British. The outraged King-Hall responded by bombarding Dar es Salaam with the 12-inch guns of the battleship *Goliath*. That ended any pro-peace sentiment among the people of Dar es Salaam.

Von Lettow-Vorbeck resumed the raids on the Uganda Railway. The British introduced armored trains, but armored trains were of no use when the enemy mined the track and disappeared. Their trains began pushing loaded flatcars ahead of the locomotives to set off the mines. The Germans responded with delayed-action fuses. The British pushed across the border and took the German town of Jasin. Lettow counterattacked. Jasin was no pushover. The troops holding it restored the honor of the Indian Army. Jasin increased von Lettow-Vorbeck's doubts about victories. That victory cost him his aide, Captain Alexander von Hammerstein, and five other regular officers who could not be replaced. The town itself meant nothing.

Von Lettow-Vorbeck reorganized his army, called the Schutztruppe (guard force). The largest unit would be a platoon of some 30 rifles and two machine guns. Each platoon would support patrols of no more than three or four men. Before, he had enlisted native carriers to carry supplies for the askaris. Now soldiers going into action would carry their own food and ammunition. Carriers would accompany the troops during large-scale movements, but most of the time, it would be a knapsack war for the German forces.

Von Lettow-Vorbeck's patrols stole horses from British posts, cut telegraph wires and blew up trains. One of the trains they blew up was carrying Brigadier Michael Tighe, who had replaced Wapshare and Meinertzhagen. Both jumped out unhurt, but the German troops were long gone.

Meinertzhagen organized his own patrols to gather intelligence, using askaris from his old outfit, the King's African Rifles. On one such patrol, he and another Briton, J.J. Drought, and 14 askaris surprised a German platoon. They took nine prisoners and killed 15 enemies, including the German count who led the platoon. On another, he sneaked into a German camp alone and estimated that there were 1,400 sleeping enemies all around him. Challenged by a guard, he spoke in Swahili and pretended to be a German officer until he got close enough to bayonet the sentry. He reached safety only by swimming a crocodile-infested river.

Not all of Meinertzhagen's feats involved blood and guts. He stopped German raids at one area by posting a sign declaring that the only waterhole was poisoned and surrounding it with freshly-killed birds and animals.

Tighe begged London to let him take at least one offensive action. He was given permission to take Bukoba, a German port and radio station on Lake Victoria. The British had received some reinforcements—the Second Rhodesian Regiment and the 25th Battalion of the Royal Fusiliers. Both were primarily staffed with British African settlers. The Fusilier battalion contained Americans and other foreigners, but most of its troops were homegrown. Among them were two famous big game hunters, Frederick Courtney Selous and Pieter Pretorius, destined to play important parts in the East African campaign.

Neither the Fusiliers nor any other unit covered itself with glory at Bukoba. The campaign began well enough. The 2,000 British troops completely surprised the fewer than 1,000 German askaris when they landed. The British expected to make a quick knockout. They made no provision for food and shelter for the troops, who, as a result, spent a frigid, hungry night on the battlefield. The next day, they took Bukoba. The Germans lost 15 men; the British, seven killed and 25 wounded. The British captured a disabled German field piece and 60 useless black-powder rifles.[18] The British troops celebrated this rather minor victory with a drunken orgy of pillage, rape, and murder. One soldier's loot included a parrot who, appropriately, could say only "Ach, du Schwein!"

In July, von Lettow-Vorbeck occupied a high point called Mbuyuni which commanded the road running through the Taveta Gap in the mountains around Kilimanjaro. The British made a frontal attack with two battalions and sent another battalion out as a flanker. The German askaris mowed down troops in the frontal assault. The attackers fell back and called back the flankers. British casualties amounted to 10 percent of their force, but they announced a "successful operation." The operation was so successful it encouraged Lettow to strike again. He took a second hill, Kasigaw, which provided security for his patrols along a 30 mile stretch of the Uganda Railway.

Von Lettow-Vorbeck grew stronger steadily. New recruits joined his forces after each victory.

Guerrilla logistics

While von Lettow-Vorbeck and his men were holding their own, the other German colonies in Africa had fallen to the British like overripe fruit. The reason was they received no guns, ammunition, food, medicine or other supplies from Germany. Von Lettow-Vorbeck received little enough. If he relied on Berlin's interest in East Africa, he would have received nothing at all. But the cruiser *Konigsberg* was in the Rufiji delta. Captain Looff had radioed Berlin that he found a stream in the delta the British had not covered. If he had coal, he could steam out of the swamp and raid British shipping. Berlin sent a freighter, disguised as a Danish ship, loaded with coal. As an afterthought, the navy added weapons and supplies for von Lettow-Vorbeck.

The blockade runner almost made it to Tanga. The British found it, though, and the captain, a Danish-speaking German named Carl Christiansen, ran it aground. The British shelled it, starting a fire, opening gaps in its hull, and totally disabling the ship. Lettow's troops, however, unloaded 1,800 new Mauser 98 smokeless powder repeating rifles, 4,500,000 rounds of ammunition, several field pieces, several dozen machine guns, ammunition for the field guns and the cruiser's guns, medicine, food, clothing, and tents. About the only cargo not salvaged was the coal. It had been soaked in sea water and was useless. Looff would never get a chance to move *Konigsberg* out of the Rufiji swamps.

The British made sure of that while von Lettow-Vorbeck was seizing hills in the Kilimanjaro area. The Rufiji delta was a labyrinth of creeks and mangrove swamps as big as the state of New Jersey. Looff could stay out of range of the British ships at sea and he could move to another location if spotted from the air. But he couldn't hide from Pieter Pretorious, an Afrikaner ivory poacher. He knew every foot of the Rufiji swamps. Small, dark, fluent in Arabic and German—as well as Afrikaans and English—he could pass for either an Arab or a German settler. He was a German settler on safari when he located the big cruiser. One of his scouts, posing as a porter on the safari, even got a job as a temporary crew member on the ship. Pretorius knew where Looff was at all times. Then he set to work mapping the channels through which the British could send monitors—shallow-draft craft mounting enormous guns—to destroy the German ship.

The monitors arrived and ended *Konigsberg's* threat to British shipping. That did not, however, hurt von Lettow-Vorbeck. He gained 320 new fighting men and all the ship's guns (including 10 105-mm cannons, which were mounted on makeshift gun carriages, hundreds of modern rifles, and more machine guns).

Max Looff, as a navy captain, outranked the army lieutenant colonel. Governor Schnee thought about having the sailor replace the obnoxious von Lettow, but Looff was not enthusiastic. Von Lettow-Vorbeck had 14,000 soldiers who would march through hell for him, and if he didn't want to be replaced, he wouldn't be. Von Lettow-Vorbeck did not want to risk any more interference from the governor, though. He asked Looff to take over defense of Dar es Salaam and sent Schnee to join him.

The supplies from Germany helped greatly, but von Lettow-Vorbeck's troops were becoming almost self-sufficient. They developed fuel for motor vehicles from coconut. They made ersatz tires from rope covered with raw latex from rubber trees. Von Lettow-Vorbeck's people built a gunpowder factory, a brewery and even a whiskey distillery. They distilled salt from wild plants and ate other plants. They got some of their food from native villages and shot game for much of the rest. Women made homespun uniforms, which were colored khaki with a homemade dye; shoemakers made shoes from buffalo hide. Farmers made soap and candles. Von Lettow-Vorbeck captured enough horses from the British to field a new company of cavalry. The Amani Biological Institute, one of the world's leading research centers on tropical diseases, made a quinine substitute.

At first, Schnee cooperated fully in all logistical matters. Later, although he readily helped in anything that would benefit the general population, he dragged his feet on projects that would help only the army. He didn't seriously hurt von Lettow-Vorbeck's efforts, but he was a constant annoyance.

All the supplies the German forces obtained, including those captured from the enemy, allowed von Lettow-Vorbeck to greatly expand his army. By the summer of 1915, he had 3,000 Europeans and 11,000 African askaris in his forces.[19]

He was going to need them.

Smuts

By the end of 1915, a largely Afrikaner army from the Union of South Africa had conquered German Southwest Africa. The only reason it took them that long was that the South African prime minister, General Louis Botha, first had to put down a revolt by his colleague in the Boer War, General Christiaan de Wet. South Africa then offered Britain 20,000 troops to conquer German East Africa. The South Africans hoped to annex German East Africa as well as German Southwest Africa to their Union.[20]

Botha's duties as prime minister kept him too busy to allow him to go to East Africa. He delegated command of the South African army to his deputy, Jan Christiaan Smuts. An English general, Horace Smith-Dorrien, was supposed to command the entire British force, but he became ill en route to Africa, and Smuts got overall command. They called him "Slim Janie," but not because of his physique. "Slim" in Afrikaans means sly or tricky. In the Boer War he had proved to be a talented guerrilla leader. And unlike the British and the Indians, he was as African as any askari in Von Lettow-Vorbeck's Schutztruppe.

Smuts's Africa, though, was largely *veldt*—thousands of square miles of rolling grassland, ideal for cavalry and mounted infantry. German East Africa was more varied—malarial swamps, mountains, desert, and *bundu* (wide, thick expanses of scrub thorn trees as easy to ride through as barbed wire). And when Smuts was a guerrilla, he was so from necessity. He was leading numerically inferior irregulars against a huge regular army. Now he had the huge regular army, and he was going to wage war by the book. But Smuts's biggest handicap was his Afrikaner racism. His opponents were black—"damned kaffirs" he called them. "I'll drive them with a whip," he told Meinertzhagen.[21] The past failures of the British didn't impress him. Their troops were only "Indian coolies."

When the first group of South Africans got to East Africa, they and the British decided to drive the Germans off Mt. Oldorobo and give it to Smuts as a present on his arrival. Von Lettow-Vorbeck learned of their plan and reinforced the post with a group under the reliable Major Kraut. Even so, the 6,000 British attackers outnumbered Kraut's troops five to one. The British opened with a tremendous artillery barrage on the German trenches, then charged. The trenches were empty. The German troops were hidden in the brush far behind them. Their machine guns cut down the dumbfounded British as they stared at the "fortifications" they'd captured. The British fell back to think about things. Nine days later, February 12, 1916, they came back. Rhodesians, Indians, and English attacked from the front, South Africans from the flank. It was like the Western Front in Europe—men versus machine guns. As always, the men lost. Then Von Lettow-Vorbeck's "kaffirs" charged the South Africans with bayonets and drove them back to the British lines where they were rescued by "coolies" from Baluchistan.

Smuts chalked up the defeat to the British tactical error of direct attacks on machine guns. When he moved against the Germans again, a frontal attack was designed only to hold them in place while Brigadier Jacobus van Deventer delivered a strong flank attack. Van Deventer was not to do the job alone. Smuts sent Brigadier James Stewart on a wide sweep around the German forces to encircle them. But Stewart couldn't hide his movements from Lettow's scouts. German askari snipers harried them all the way, destroyed bridges, blocked roads, and set up ambushes. Stewart's men laid telephone line as they marched, but giraffes cut his communications. The ungainly but immensely powerful beasts simply walked through the line strung on trees and broke the wire. Stewart arrived at his blocking position four days late. By then, the Germans were gone. Von Lettow-Vorbeck knew exactly what Smuts had planned and fell back.

Smuts sent bombing planes against the new German positions. He expected to terrify the simple savages in the Schutztruppe. But the simple savages had shot down a plane before. They knew it was not a magic beast but a machine, and not a particularly dangerous machine.

The German askaris were still in position on a line of hills when the British advanced March 10. The British struggled through head-high thorn bushes while the German rifles and machine guns cut them down. They were forced to dig in before they got halfway up the slope. At night, the South Africans launched a charge. German machine guns, with interlocking fields of fire, laid them in heaps. The Germans counterattacked. Then their fire ceased. The British again advanced, and the Germans were nowhere to be found. This was Lettow's kind of war: he let the British have useless land at the cost of heavy casualties while he suffered few casualties himself.

It wasn't Smuts's kind of war. The South African general was besides himself with rage. He blamed his British subordinates for allowing von Lettow-Vorbeck to escape his traps and sent back three British generals. Smuts' troops outnumbered von Lettow-Vorbeck's more than three to one. He was developing an obsession: destroy von Lettow-Vorbeck. He had reached the German northern railroad. He would push down it southeast to Tanga, expecting that von Lettow-Vorbeck would oppose him with his main force, which could be encircled. Then Smuts would march south into the interior and wipe out any remaining German forces.

The rainy season was beginning—the period in East Africa when almost all activity comes to a screeching halt. Rain was not going to stop Smuts, though. He struck east, along the railroad to Tanga.

The rainy season

The campaign that followed made Smuts a hero in England. He pushed the Germans down the railroad and took Tanga. Then he pushed them south and took the southern railroad. His forces took the whole coastline, including Dar es Salaam. It was like a triumphal march.

It was probably the most grisly triumphal march in history.

Smuts' basic plan never varied: Advance directly against the enemy while sending out flankers on a wide sweep to encircle him. Von Lettow-Vorbeck's responses varied, but the result was always the same: the Germans inflicted heavy casualties and disappeared.

Von Lettow-Vorbeck mounted one of the *Konigsberg* guns on a railroad car. Whenever they had time, the Germans tore up the tracks between them and the British, burned the railroad ties and heated the tracks over the fire until they could be twisted and rendered useless. They burned all bridges. They made stands wherever terrain made it impossible to flank their position. For instance, they stopped the

British between two branches of the flooded Pagani River. Each flank was covered by crocodile-infested water, and thick thorn bush filled the ground between the water and the rails. Smuts sent van Deventer on a wide sweep, but the South African brigadier got lost. When the British resumed their attack, the Germans were gone.

Von Lettow-Vorbeck took his main body away from the railroad and marched south to Kondoa-Irangi, leaving Kraut to defend the railroad. Smuts sent van Deventer after von Lettow-Vorbeck as the rest of the British pushed on to Tanga.

Van Deventer's columns encountered the usual German opposition: constant sniping and ambushes. The German askaris had porters carry their Maxim machine guns. The porters learned to set up a gun in seconds and remove it equally fast. The Germans would pick a site a little ahead of a British column, plan fields of fire, and camouflage themselves. When the British appeared, they'd mow them down with a short, violent burst of fire and retreat along hidden paths. At times they used land mines manufactured from the explosives in the shells for *Konigsberg* to slow down any pursuit.

Worse than the Germans and their askaris was Africa itself. The mud bogged down and ultimately destroyed all vehicles. Following von Lettow-Vorbeck took the British through tsetse-fly country. Their horses and mules died by the thousands from *nagana,* an African disease carried by the tsetse fly.[22] Men contracted sleeping sickness from the same fly, as well as malaria spread by mosquitos. There were also leeches and jiggers, which were ultimately worse than the rhinos, leopards, crocodiles, hyenas, and lions. The British uniform, with shorts, short sleeves and open collars, made them more susceptible to insect attacks. Further, the German askaris, being native to the region, had a certain immunity to the diseases.

By May 9th, near the end of the rainy season, van Deventer's force was nearly exhausted. They had lost almost all their horses and mules and most of the men were too sick to fight. Von Lettow-Vorbeck gathered about 3,000 men and prepared to attack the British. That night, a German scouting party under Lieutenant Colonel von Bock, got into a firefight. Von Bock was killed. His second-in-command, Captain Kornatzky (Wahle's second-in-command at Dar es Salaam) decided to attack van Deventer's whole force with his scouts instead of retreating.

The Germans ran into a hornets' nest, and von Lettow-Vorbeck had to come up to extricate his men. In the darkness, Meinertzhagen, who was traveling with van Deventer, was attacked by an enemy with a knobkerrie (an African war club). He took the club away from his attacker and killed him with it. The next day, he learned that his attacker was Kornatzky. "My God," he wrote in his diary, "I should have liked to have caught old Lettow instead of poor Kornatzky."[23] Meinertzhagen was becoming as obsessed as Smuts. He kept the knobkerrie with him all through the war.

Von Lettow-Vorbeck's losses were not serious by normal standards, but he had lost German officers he could not replace. He considered attacking van Deventer again. A proper attack could wipe out the South African's column. However, the Germans would suffer casualties for no good reason: Sickness, insects, and animals had already rendered van Deventer almost impotent. The Afrikaner had reached Kondoa-Irangi, but of his original 10,000 men, only 1,500 were able to walk. All his animals were dead. The Germans had lost only 100 men in the whole campaign.[24] On the railroad, Kraut was moving back slowly, ambushing the pursuers as he went. Smuts's flanking columns were slowed by roads blocked by fallen trees and boulders, destroyed bridges and swollen rivers. His telephone lines were destroyed by giraffes and elephants, his troops terrorized by lions and leopards. Again and again, Kraut managed to escape encirclement. Finally, he headed south to join the *Kommandeur.*

Von Lettow-Vorbeck's situation was still serious. The rains had ended. Smuts took Tanga. He had more than 80,000 troops, because the British were, as he hoped, sending more soldiers to East Africa.[25] The Belgians were now moving into German East Africa from the west; another British column was moving up from the south from Nyasaland. Even the Portuguese were moving in.

Lettow performed like the conductor of an orchestra. He struck here and there, keeping all his enemies in play with raids, retreats and ambushes. The Portuguese weren't much of a problem. Besides the Belgians (in the era when King Leopold ran the Congo Free State as his private possession) the Portuguese were the most oppressive colonialists in Africa. Their askaris had been conscripted and hated the service. They saw battle as a chance to escape into the bush.

The modern Belgian native troops, on the other hand, had excellent morale. However, the British government did not encourage them to penetrate deeply into German East Africa. The British wanted the colony for themselves: They didn't want to share it with an ally.[26] The British column from Nyasaland was weak. Smuts was the main enemy.

Smuts was the hero of the British public, the man who was "outwitting" the "old fox," von Lettow-Vorbeck. Smuts was the man before whom the Germans "fled." But as the old fox eluded trap after trap, he, too, was beginning to take on hero status. Karen Blixen was proud to be his friend. Characters based on him appeared in the stories for which Blixen, as "Isak Dinesen" was gaining fame. When Meinertzhagen returned to England, he found that the King and Queen were more interested in von Lettow-Vorbeck than anyone else in Africa.

In some ways the war in East Africa was like some exotic conflict from another age. When Smuts learned that the German government had awarded von Lettow-Vorbeck the "pour le merite," Germany's highest honor, he sent word to his opponent under a flag of truce. Later, the British did the same when von Lettow-Vorbeck was promoted to major general, making him unquestionably the highest-ranking German in Africa.

Smuts and von Lettow-Vorbeck were alike in their penchant for visiting the front lines. One day, as he was doing some personal reconnaissance, he saw a small man with a neat red goatee out in front of the British position in easy rifle range. He recognized him as Jan Christiaan Smuts. He didn't fire, because, he later confessed, that didn't seem sporting.

Frederick Courteney Selous had another view of "sporting." On January 4, 1917, the 66-year-old professional hunter, author, and naturalist was in the Rufiji swamps, not far from where his comrade, Pieter Pretorius, had discovered the *Konigsberg*. Selous was hunting, too. He was after even bigger game than a warship. He was after the most dangerous game in Africa: Paul Emil von Lettow-Vorbeck. Camouflaged in a tree, with his old gunbearer camouflaged nearby, Captain Selous (only two years before, he had been broken from lance corporal to private in the Royal Fusiliers) watched German officers and askaris pass all around him. He'd take one life, and it would save so many other lives. Soon, he was sure, he'd see General von Lettow-Vorbeck. He never did—a German sniper saw Selous first.

Ships through the jungle, ships through the sky

Von Lettow-Vorbeck had moved away from the Lake Victoria shore, but he still had forces on Lake Tanganyika. Water-borne transportation was important to his style of mobile defense. At the end of 1915, the Belgians began building a 1,500-ton steamer on their Tanganyika shore. That would eliminate German control of the lake. The Germans sent a boat to destroy the Belgian craft while it was under construction. What the Germans didn't know was that the British had sent two fast motorboats, 40-feet long and seven-feet wide, to Lake Tanganyika from Capetown. British Commander G. Spicer Simpson took them by rail to Livingston, Rhodesia. Then, he watched an army of workers cut down the Congo jungle and build 200 bridges so he could complete the 2,300 mile trek by hauling the boats by steam tractor to the water. It took Simpson and his boats 11 minutes to capture the German craft. The Allies took control of Lake Tanganyika.

Von Lettow-Vorbeck had been holding off Germany's enemies in Africa for three years. He was keeping more than 150,000 enemy troops away from Europe. He was one of Germany's leading heroes. Berlin finally decided something should be done to help him.

"Something" was the biggest dirigible in the world, the L-59. It was to carry supplies to East Africa, over the heads of the blockading British. The airship, 750-feet long, was loaded with 50 tons of supplies, including 30 machine guns, 311,900 boxes of ammunition, 61 bags of medical supplies, two sewing machines and a case of cognac. It was to locate von Lettow-Vorbeck's headquarters, land and then be cannibalized. Any extra fuel could power his vehicles and other engines, the airship's engines would drive his generators, the envelope could be used for uniforms and tents, the leather catwalk could be turned into shoes, the girders used for buildings and the gas cell containers for sleeping bags.

The Zeppelin, under Lieutenant Commander Ludwig Bockholt, took off from Bulgaria and headed due south, passing over Egypt and the Sudan, which were both British-held. It was almost to Kilimanjaro when the radio operator received a message in the German naval code:

> ABANDON UNDERTAKING AND RETURN STOP ENEMY HAS OCCU-
> PIED GREAT PART OF MAKONDE HIGHLANDS AND IS ALREADY AT
> KITAUGARI STOP.[27]

The origin of the message remains a mystery to this day. The most probable explanation is that the British, who had previously broken a German naval code, had done it again and sent the message.

Bockholt, bitterly disappointed, turned his ship around and sailed home. When he arrived in Bulgaria, he had flown 4,225 miles nonstop. That was in 1917, when a flight of 200 miles was considered remarkable. It would be many years before any kind of aircraft would make a comparable flight.

The day the airship turned back, von Lettow-Vorbeck, was invading enemy territory.

New worlds to conquer

At the end of 1916, Smuts reviewed the results of his triumphal march. The North Lancashire battalion had come to Africa with 900 men. Now it had 345—and that *included* replacements. The 25th Fusiliers enrollment had dropped from 1,200 to 200; the 9th South African Infantry, from 1,135 to 120. All his transport animals had died and all his motor vehicles, including his armored cars, had broken down, most of them permanently. Virtually every one of the Indian troops was sick. Mental stress had taken a toll on his officers. Meinertzhagen, a giant of physical strength, started to crack up and had to be shipped back to England. (After almost a year there, he recovered enough to go to Egypt. As a member of Allenby's staff, he set the stage for the British breakthrough at Beersheba—the only Allied stroke of strategic genius in the war.)[28]

Von Lettow-Vorbeck had accomplished all of that, plus tying up more than 150,000 Allied troops with a force that never numbered more than 14,000.[29] Nevertheless, Smuts told London that the war in East Africa "may now be said to be over." That impressed Prime Minister Botha and the British so much that Smuts was appointed to represent South Africa at the Imperial Conference in London. When von Lettow-Vorbeck heard the news, he sent a message to Smuts, congratulating him on the manner in which he had waged the war.

Major General Reginald Hoskins replaced Smuts. When Hoskins arrived, he found the British forces in total disarray. Their transport system was totally destroyed. At the start of the war, the British used 7,500 native porters—now they needed 135,000.[30] The new porters were not hired: they were pressed into service. When Hoskins couldn't report a final victory in the war Smuts declared to be over, he was replaced. Van Deventer took over command.

Von Lettow-Vorbeck had moved his headquarters into the Rufiji swamp. The swamp was a formidable obstacle to an attacker who didn't know the territory. However, the Germans found elephant and buffalo meat delicious, crocodile meat surprisingly good, and hippo meat edible. Again and again, the British tried to encircle Lettow's detachments. Again and again, they failed, taking heavy losses in the process.

Von Lettow-Vorbeck also discovered a new source of intelligence: army ants. Before the rainy season began, the insects would leave their nests in the low ground and march to high ground where they would be safe from floods. The ants began to move in January 1917. When they were gone, he moved his forces out of the swamp up to a plateau in the southern part of the colony. Lettow moved his troops when the ants did and was safe from the floods. When the rains began, the Germans were separated from their enemies by a plain 90 miles wide, entirely under water.

When the rains ended, van Deventer adopted a new strategy. He divided his army into many columns and converged on all German-occupied territory. There would be an encirclement on a grand scale. The first big clash came in October. Brigadier Percival Beves, with 6,000 men, engaged General Wahle, with 2,000. Von Lettow-Vorbeck came up to join Wahle. The British continued attacking. Beves eventually retreated, having lost between 1,500 and 2,000 men. Fourteen Germans and 81 Africans were killed, 55 Germans and 367 Africans wounded. Lettow gained a field piece, nine machine guns and 300,000 cartridges.[31]

After that, von Lettow-Vorbeck again reorganized the Schutztruppe. The British had begun raiding the villages that supplied the army. Lettow could no longer maintain a large army. He set up a field hospital and left all his sick and wounded in it. He knew they'd be well cared for by the British. Most of his other troops and carriers he released to go to their homes. He cut the force to 200 Germans, 1,700 Africans, and 3,000 carriers. Each carrier would go home as soon as the supplies he was toting were exhausted. All the supplies the new Schutztruppe could not carry were destroyed, including the last 105-mm gun from *Konigsberg*.

With this cutback force, von Lettow-Vorbeck invaded the Portuguese colony of Mozambique. He crossed the border the same day the L-59 turned around. The British said they'd won a major victory by driving von Lettow-Vorbeck out of German East Africa. He didn't care—he attacked 1,500 Portuguese soldiers in a fort, drove them away and resupplied his troops. The Germans moved into country where game was scarce, so Lettow divided his forces into three columns. To confuse the Portuguese and British, they began moving in different directions.

Van Deventer detailed part of his forces to line the border to prevent Lettow's return. He sent another part into Mozambique to pursue him. The pursuers didn't fare well. Von Lettow-Vorbeck captured a Portuguese supply depot at Alto Moloque; he captured two field pieces, a river steamer and a load of medicine at Kokosani; then he attacked a British-Portuguese ammunition dump, killing 209 defenders and capturing 540. He picked up 10 machine guns, 350 rifles, and more ammunition than his troops could carry there. By July, 1918, the Schutztruppe was completely self-sufficient. The next month, the Germans captured two more field guns, a load of rifles, and 100,000 cartridges.

At one point, a British column encircled Lettow's group and almost captured the general himself. But Lettow turned the tables and captured the British commander. British askaris and porters were deserting and asking von Lettow-Vorbeck to take them into his army.

Von Lettow-Vorbeck's columns, with their confusing movements, were edging back toward German East Africa. On September 28, they recrossed the border. But borders meant nothing to Lettow. His only interest was keeping his force alive and the British in play. In October, he invaded Northern Rhodesia. On November 11, 1918 von Lettow-Vorbeck's troops were taking control of the Rhodesian town of Kasama, a place well stocked with supplies. On November 13, von Lettow-Vorbeck was trying to decide on a new target when his men captured a British courier. The courier carried a startling message:

> *Send the following to General von Lettow-Vorbeck under white flag. The prime minister of England has announced that an armistice was signed at 5 hours on Nov 11th. I am ordering my troops to cease hostilities forth-with unless attacked and of course conclude that you will do the same. Conditions of armistice will be forwarded to you immediately [after] I re-ceive them. Meanwhile, I suggest that you remain in your present vicinity in order to facilitate communications. General van Deventer.[32]*

Peace, war, and peace

The first thing von Lettow-Vorbeck did when he returned to Germany was marry Margarethe Wallrath, the fiancee he'd left four years before. Then, he joined a group of other generals who, incensed by Germany's disarmament, tried to overthrow the Weimar Republic. He was court-martialed, deprived of his rank, and imprisoned. Released from jail, Germany's only victorious general found he was still popular. He was elected to the Reichstag.

Back home, he renewed old friendships. One old friend was Karen Blixen—now the famous writer, Isak Dinesen. She had left her husband and returned to Denmark. He also made a new friendship with an old enemy. Richard Meinertzhagen had retired from the army and gained fame as an ornithologist. While in Germany to visit another ornithologist, Meinertzhagen called on von Lettow-Vorbeck, a soldier he had always wanted to meet. The two became fast friends.

In 1929, Meinertzhagen invited von Lettow-Vorbeck to come to England and meet another old enemy, Jan Smuts. With Smuts was Winston Churchill. The four men dis-cussed Germany and the rising power of the Nazis. Soon after the meeting, von Lettow-Vorbeck resigned from the Reichstag.

Of all the strange characters in East Africa during the war, Meinertzhagen was one of the strangest. He was a fanatical—even bloodthirsty—hater of Germans. In his *Seven Pillars of Wisdom*, Meinertzhagen's friend, T.E. Lawrence, mentioned him as one of his supporters on Allenby's staff:

> *This ally was Meinertzhagen, a student of migrating birds drifted into soldiering, whose hot immoral hatred of the enemy expressed itself as readily in trickery as in violence.... Meinertzhagen knew no half measures. He was logical, an idealist of the deepest, and so possessed by his convictions that he was willing to harness evil to the chariot of good. He was a strategist, a geographer, and a silent laughing masterful man; who took as blithe a pleasure in deceiving his enemy (or his friend) by some unscrupulous jest as in spattering the brains of a cornered mob of Germans one by one with his African knob-kerri. His instincts were abetted by an immensely powerful body and a savage brain, which chose the best way to its purpose, unhampered by doubt or habit.*[33]

Meinertzhagen protested to Lawrence about this description. In his *Army Diary*, he writes that Lawrence's "remarks were intended to be most flattering, though in fact they amount to almost a gross libel.. .. My brain and nature are not entirely 'savage,' nor did it give me real pleasure to knock Germans on the head."[34] But any reader of Meinertzhagen's own diaries would have to agree with Lawrence.

Nevertheless, in the post-war years, this enemy of all things German became a leading member of the Anglo/German Association. As such, he got to know a number of leading Nazis, including Joachim von Ribbentrop, the German foreign minister, who invited him to visit Hitler. What Ribbentrop apparently did not know was that Meinertzhagen was also an ardent Zionist, a friend of Chaim Weizmann.[35]

The meeting with Hitler, on October 17, 1934, began amicably, although the Führer greeted Meinertzhagen with the Nazi salute and "Heil Hitler," at which Meinertzhagen responded by raising his hand and saying, "Heil Meinertzhagen." In his diary, the Englishman noted, "Nobody smiled." During the conversation, Meinertzhagen suggested that von Lettow-Vorbeck would make a good ambassador to Britain. Hitler seemed eager to associate himself with the popular war hero. He slapped his thigh and said that was a capital idea. But then Meinertzhagen tried to persuade Hitler to stop his persecution of the Jews. The dictator threw a tantrum, and the conference ended. Von Lettow-Vorbeck did not become an ambassador. From that point on, the general, without a pension and unable to get a decent job, supported himself by gardening and carving fancy pipes.

During World War II, Meinertzhagen returned to army intelligence. British intelligence kept track of von Lettow-Vorbeck through Isak Dinesen. When the German generals planned to kill Hitler, they asked for help from British and American intelligence. They were told they must first get a commitment from von Lettow-Vorbeck. Approached by the conspirators, the old general refused to help. "No," he said, "the old Germany is lost and will not find its soul again until we pay the full price."[36]

Paul Emil von Lettow-Vorbeck died in 1964 at the age of 95. Isak Dinesen died two years earlier; Richard Meinertzhagen, three years later. All had been born in another age—an age of kings and colonies, an age of white "bwanas" ordering around primitive tribesmen they thought could never be fully human. In his now-forgotten war, von Lettow-Vorbeck, by showing that black Africans could be soldiers as good or better than Caucasians, whether Indian or European, took a giant step toward relieving the white man of his "burden."

Part 4

Britannia's Wayward Sons

7

The Pen and the Sword: Erskine Childers

Rendezvous at sea

At 7 p.m., with the sun still high in the sky, a sleek ketch glided up to a big tug anchored near the Roetigen Lightship at the mouth of the Scheldt.

"That's the second Mexican boat, yes?" the tug's captain asked his passenger. The passenger said it was.

The ketch's crew, four men and two women, were all on deck. The women were a surprise. The tug captain had never seen women on a gun-running boat before, but maybe they did things differently in Mexico.

The passenger called to the sailboat captain, "Conor's loaded and off now, with 600 rifles and 20,000 rounds. He's left you 900 and 29,000 rounds."

"*Kelpie's* no smaller than *Asgard*," the ketch's captain answered. "But we'll fit them aboard somehow."[1]

The tug's captain thought it odd that Mexicans should be speaking English, a language he understood. But he suspected that the passenger and the passenger's friends were not really Mexican.

He was right. The passenger was an Irish journalist, Darrell Figgis. The captain of the ketch was a member of the Anglo-Irish "ascendancy," Erskine Childers. One of the women was his American-born wife, Molly. Though a cripple, Molly demanded to go on this expedition. The other woman was Mary Spring Rice, who had organized the entire gun-running conspiracy and could not be denied a place on the boat. One of the other men was an Englishman, Gordon Shephard, a friend of Childers, and the others were two Irish fishermen, Patrick McGinley and Charles Duggan. The first "Mexican" boat had been captained by Conor O'Brien, another well-to-do Irishman.

A few weeks before, Childers and Figgis had gone to Germany to arrange the purchase of 1,500 Mauser 71 rifles, the same single-shot black powder rifles von Lettow-Vorbeck's troops had. Germany was getting rid of the obsolete weapons by selling them to all comers. Among the customers were Michael and Moritz Magnus, international arms dealers. The British government had put an embargo on all arms shipments to Ireland, and the Magnus brothers didn't want to be accused of smuggling. There was no problem shipping rifles to Mexico. That country was in the middle of the Mexican Revolution, and all parties were buying anything that would shoot. The Irish gun-runners and the German tug crew began stuffing rifles and ammunition into every nook and cranny of the ketch *Asgard*.

It was July 12, 1914. Just two weeks earlier, the heir to the Austrian-Hungarian Empire had been murdered in an obscure Balkan city. Few worried about that in Ireland. In Ireland, the Orange Order was celebrating King William's Day, the anniversary of the Battle of the Boyne, which established Protestant ascendancy on that island. The celebration this year was more raucous than usual: the Ulster Protestants now had 3,000 more rifles to discourage England from granting home rule to Ireland.

Those rifles had been landed at the town of Larne in April. It was done at night, but quite openly, with members of the Ulster Volunteer Force, a private army formed to oppose home rule, guarding the dock to prevent interference. There would have been no interference from the authorities. High military and civil officials in Britain and Ireland encouraged the formation and arming of the Ulster Volunteers. In March, during the so-called "Curragh Mutiny," British army officers refused to reinforce the guards of military armories in Ulster. The British government backed down.

The Ulster Volunteer Force was an arm of the minority Unionist party in Ireland, the faction that wanted political union with Britain at all costs—even if it meant fighting the British Army. A bill for Home Rule for Ireland had already passed Parliament when Sir Edward Carson, a Dublin Protestant of Italian ancestry, notified the government that his Ulster Volunteer Force was prepared to fight to the death to prevent the implementation of home rule.

"Home Rule means Rome rule," Protestant crowds chanted in Ulster. Randolph Churchill, Winston's father, added, "Ulster will fight, and Ulster will be right." The government postponed the implementation of Home Rule.

To counter the Unionists, two other Irish factions—the Home Rulers, who favored Canadian-style autonomy, and the Republicans, who wanted full independence—formed the Irish Volunteers.[2] The Volunteers had few weapons.

When the Unionists got their big arms shipment, the Home Rulers and Republicans were outraged. One of the most outraged was the Hon. Mary Spring Rice, 34-year-old daughter of an Anglo-Irish peer. She began contacting like-minded people. One was Sir Roger Casement, an Ulsterman who had gained an international reputation by exposing the crimes against humanity committed in the Congo by King Leopold of Belgium. Another was Conor O'Brien, Spring Rice's cousin and a prominent journalist. Yet another was Alice Stopford Green, widow of a famous historian, Richard Green. Still another was Michael O'Rahilly, called The O'Rahilly because he was chief of an ancient clan in County Kerry. The O'Rahilly was one of the founders of the Irish Volunteers. Another Volunteer was Bulmer Hobson, who was also a member of the secret Irish Republican Brotherhood.[3] In view of the religious spin Carson had put on the struggle against Home Rule, it's worth noting that all of this group except The O'Rahilly were Protestant.

Erskine Childers, foreground in raincoat, arrives at the port of Howth with a load of rifles in his yacht. Members of the Irish Volunteers, some in uniform, wait for the rifles. Childers' wife, Molly, who accompanied him on the gun-running expedition, stands behind him. (Courtesy Trinity College, Dublin.)

The Volunteers planned to have young Figgis purchase rifles in Europe, but there were two problems: paying for the weapons and transporting them to Ireland. O'Rahilly managed to get $5,000 from Clan na Gael, an Irish-American organization. Spring Rice and the others received contributions from Liberal Party Home-Rulers in Ireland and England. That took care of financing, but transportation remained a problem. O'Brien owned a yacht, but it wasn't big enough to carry the whole load. Besides, Spring Rice said, her cousin was hot-headed and inclined to panic. He could not command the expedition. Mary Spring Rice said she knew only one person who could handle the assignment. His name was Erskine Childers.

A romantic fussbudget

Childers had been born in London, but he'd been raised in Ireland, his mother's birthplace. After graduating from Cambridge, he had become a clerk of the House of Commons in Parliament. He loved the minutiae of Westminster, the process of turning complex ideas into formal bills. He was, in fact, a fussbudget. Frank O'Connor, who was later to help him publish a Republican newspaper, said of Childers: "Apart from his accent, which would have identified him anywhere, there was something peculiarly English about him; something that nowadays reminds me of some old parson or public school teacher I have known, conscientious to a fault and overburdened with minor cares."[4]

Yet, this was the man O'Connor also described as "one of the great romantic figures of the period."[5] Childers was the "bureaucrat compleat," with the imagination of a 14-year-old boy. During the darkest days of the Irish Civil War, when he and Childers were being chased from pillar to post by the Free State army, O'Connor, whose reading tastes ran to Dostoevsky, was amazed to see his boss devouring (for the hundredth time) James Fennimore Cooper's *The Deer Slayer*. The difference between Erskine Childers and a day-dreaming schoolboy was that Childers had the means and the will to make his dreams a reality.

Childers had a yacht of his own and a love of solo sailing. He began taking one-man trips into the blue before he was out of the university. By graduation, he was familiar with every cove, fjord, and sandbar on the continental coasts of the stormy North and Baltic seas. A few years after he had begun his parliamentary duties, the Boer War broke out in South Africa. After the succession of British defeats called "Black Week," Childers returned to London from vacation and joined the horse artillery of the City Imperial Volunteers. As a driver, mounted on one of the four horses pulling a quick-firing gun, Childers delighted in combat.

But the war quickly became much more than a glorious adventure for him. Childers came to admire the enemy, particularly Christiaan de Wet, the Afrikaner guerrilla chief, and to deplore the crushing of the independent Afrikaner states. He observed everything and recorded his observations in hundreds of letters home. His adoring sisters circulated the letters to friends. One of the friends was a publisher, Reginald Smith. Smith met the returning Childers as he got off the troopship and got him to collect the letters in book form. *In the Ranks of the CIV* came out in 1901 and made Childers a popular author.

He enjoyed publishing so much he wrote another book. This one drew on his experience as a small boat navigator. It was a spy novel, *The Riddle of the Sands*. It sold 2.5 million copies (and is still in print). *Riddle* was more than a classic of espionage and seafaring—it concerned a German plan to invade Britain from the islands and inlets of Frisia. It had two effects on British policy: It stimulated naval construction to keep the British Navy superior to the German High Seas Fleet, and it caused Britain to move its Home Fleet base south from Scapa Flow to be closer to the Frisian coast.

Childers' Boer War outfit, the Honorable Artillery Company (HAC), was invited to visit Boston in 1903 by that city's militia company, the Ancient and Honorable Artillery. While there, he met the beautiful but crippled Mary Osgood, nicknamed Molly. They were married a little more than three months later. In Molly Osgood Childers, the Anglo-Irish gentleman found a wife whose strength of mind and will more than made up for any weakness in her body.[6] Among other things, she saw to it that Erskine Childers no longer had to sail alone.

While clerking for Parliament, Childers continued writing. He wrote most of a more formal Boer War history, *The HAC in South Africa*.[7] He was then commissioned to write Volume Five of the *Times History of the War in South Africa*. The volume contained some frank criticism of British strategy and tactics.

Childers resigned from the Parliament staff in 1910 to devote his energies to the Liberal Party and to military analysis. One result was *War and the Arme Blanche*, another, *The German Influence on British Cavalry*. Both books were highly critical of British and European cavalry tactics. Both relied heavily on the experience of cavalry in the Boer War and the U.S. Civil War. They stressed that the saber—the *arme blanche*—beloved by all European cavalry officers, was hopelessly obsolete. The rifle, and especially the modern high-velocity repeating rifle, had made the cavalry charge impossible. And if circumstances forced troopers to fight while mounted, the pistol or revolver was infinitely more effective than the sword.[8] These conclusions, reached in the 20th century, may seem somewhat less than revolutionary. But they were. For most British and other European cavalry officers, the cavalry tactics of Napoleon and Wellington could not be improved upon. The idea of using cavalry as mounted infantry was so radical Childers arranged to have Field Marshal Earl Roberts, Britain's leading military hero, endorse his views.

As a Liberal politician and as an Anglo-Irish gentleman, Childers became more and more interested in Irish Home Rule. His parents had died when he was a child, and he had lived with his mother's family, the Bartons, in a "big house" in County Wicklow. His uncle, Charles Barton, was no Home Ruler. He considered his fellow Wicklow squire, Charles Stewart Parnell, little more than a traitor, and rejoiced when "the uncrowned king of Ireland" fell from power. But Erskine Childers and his cousin, Robert Barton, moved steadily toward the political left. Childers still thought Ireland's best bet lay in an autonomous relationship with England. But he knew that achieving even that might require violence. As a matter of fact, he knew that by sailing his ketch, overloaded with a highly illegal cargo of guns and ammunition and therefore both slow and unstable, he was risking his neck right now.

The trip home

To help his customers, the tug's captain offered to tow *Asgard* to within a short distance of Dover, where he was going to take Figgis. When Childers and his crew left the tow, the weather continued to be good, which was fortunate—the ketch had no auxiliary engine.

Suddenly, British warships appeared on all sides of them. After a moment, *Asgard's* crew realized the ships were not after them. It was a fleet review. Molly Childers stood in the stern of her boat holding a lantern so the big, fast warships wouldn't run down the ketch inadvertently. *Asgard* pulled into Milford Haven in Wales to drop off Shephard. Childers' friend was an aviator with the Royal Flying Corps, and his leave was about to run out.

As the gun-runners set out across the Irish Sea, the weather turned nasty. Then it turned ferocious. They were in the worst storm on the Irish Sea in 32 years.[9] Childers sent all hands below as enormous waves broke over the sailboat. The boat heeled over so far Molly Childers became convinced her children would be orphaned. Childers stayed at the wheel while the boat rolled and pitched. Then he heard a pop. To him, it sounded like an exploding bomb. Some tackle had broken. He lashed the wheel in place and made his way across the heaving, frequently submerged deck, crawling from handhold to handhold. At last he reached the main mast, climbed it as it swung wildly from side to side and repaired the damage. He returned to the wheel the same way he'd come and kept his boat on course until dawn.

He arrived at Howth, a fishing town just outside of Dublin, right on schedule. Figgis was supposed to meet him in a motorboat, but there was no sign of the young journalist. It turned out that Figgis could not get up the coast in the storm.

Childers took his boat in anyway. As he was about to dock, O'Rahilly, Hobson, and the Dublin brigade of the Volunteers suddenly appeared. All of Dublin—and most of the Volunteers themselves—thought they were simply on a routine route march until they were told to take the rifles.[10]

The rifles O'Brien took had been transferred from his *Kelpie* to a motor yacht belonging to Sir Thomas Myles, a Limerick physician and another Home Ruler, off the coast of Wales. A few days later, Myles landed them secretly at the town of Kilkoole.

Childers, though, had no time to get further involved in Irish politics. World War I had broken out. Winston Churchill, first lord of the admiralty, had sent out an urgent call for Childers to come to the Royal Navy's intelligence office. Churchill had a scheme for an amphibious landing in northwest Europe to outflank the German Army's thrust into Belgium and France. And Childers probably knew more about that coast than any man alive.

Churchill's scheme came to naught, but Childers got a commission in the navy as an intelligence officer. He was sent to the seaplane tender *Engadine*. Being at sea was not enough action for Childers. He pestered his commanding officer to be allowed to personally observe the enemy from a seaplane, and he eventually got his wish. As an aerial observer, he spotted Zeppelin hangers on the North Sea coast and located Turkish batteries in the Dardanelles. He was forced down in the Egyptian desert while photographing Turkish positions in Sinai and received the Distinguished Service Cross for valor. Then somebody in the admiralty decided that a man in his late 40s should not be risking his life in a flimsy biplane. Childers was transferred to shore duty. After three unhappy months of complaining while he analyzed reports, Childers got back to combat duty, this time as commander of a motor torpedo boat squadron trying to ambush German ships off the Belgian coast. The navy saw small boat navigation as Childers' greatest strength, but to Childers nothing could compare with the thrill of flying. With the creation of the Royal Air Force (RAF), Lieutenant Commander Childers of the Royal Navy became Major Childers of the RAF. That made him one of the few men to have seen combat with all three British armed forces.

The "Irish question"

While Childers was fighting World War I, Ireland had exploded. In 1916, the Volunteers and labor leader James Connolly's Citizen Army, using the rifles Childers had landed at Howth, staged an uprising in Dublin.[11] Roger Casement was to bring thousands of captured Russian rifles and machine guns to Ireland from Germany. It was supposed to be a national uprising. But Casement was arrested after landing in Ireland from a German submarine, and the German freighter (disguised as a Norwegian ship) was scuttled with the weapons. The Dublin rebels fought alone.[12] It was a hopeless fight. The O'Rahilly was killed in combat, shot down while charging a British barricade. Most of the other rebel leaders were secretly executed after they surrendered. The only Volunteer commandant not killed was Eamon de Valera. The reason: de Valera, son of a Spanish father and Irish mother, had been born in New York and was an American citizen.

The executions, the attempt to cover up British atrocities during the uprising, the wholesale arrests of Irishmen (many of whom were loyalists), and the imposition of martial law had an effect that was the opposite of what the British intended.

When the British troops marched their rebel prisoners through the streets of Dublin, citizens of the city threw garbage at the Republicans. But then the executions began. The murders of civilians by British soldiers, especially the murder of Francis Sheehy-Skeffington, a prominent eccentric, leaked out. The British tried to cover up the murders, then pardoned the murderers. Martial law was the last straw.

In Irish politics, Sinn Fein had always been considered the lunatic fringe. The name in Irish means "We Ourselves." The party followed Arthur Griffith, who advocated creation of a parallel government and court system. The Irish people could then support their own institutions and boycott those of Britain. The system, Griffith said, had been used by the Hungarians to gain autonomy in what was now the Austro-Hungarian Empire. Griffith had preached the Sinn Fein gospel for years without any noticeable effect. However, Sinn Fein began winning elections. Eventually, all the Irish members of Parliament were Sinn Feiners except a handful from Ulster and Trinity College in Dublin. The Irish MPs refused to go to London. They set up a national parliament, the "Dáil Eireann," a national court system, and proclaimed Ireland a republic.

Erskine Childers's reactions to the Easter Rising and what followed, mirrored those of the Irish people. His first reaction was that the rising was madness. That quickly changed to disgust with the government when he first learned of the executions. Disgust grew and became outrage, particularly after the execution of Casement, whom he knew. He had not yet become as radical as his cousin, Robert Barton, who resigned his commission in the army when ordered to Dublin to implement martial law. (Barton became an instant Republican, vowing to fight for full independence.)

Herbert Asquith, the British prime minister, made a half-hearted attempt to revive Home Rule. In 1917, he appointed a convention representing all elements in Ireland to work out a constitution for an autonomous Ireland. Childers, author, war hero, and Liberal politician, was appointed an assistant secretary to the convention. The convention was an exercise in futility. The Carsonites simply refused to consider any degree of separation from London. The convention finally ended. Childers abandoned the verbal conflict and went back to aerial combat. The convention had one effect: It turned Childers into a Republican.

In 1918, he caught influenza and he returned home, more dead than alive. As soon as he recovered, he made his way to the nearest Republican headquarters and offered his services.

The Black and Tans

Irish politics, as Childers knew them, had changed completely. He had been a Liberal Home Ruler, almost a dilettante, before his gun-running expedition. Of the few Republicans he knew then, O'Rahilly was dead and Hobson had been shunted aside as insufficiently militant.

Childers made two important new friends. One was Eamon de Valera, the only surviving commandant of the 1916 Rising and then president of the Dáil Eireann. That subtle intellectual admired Childers's much more straightforward intelligence. The other was the bluff, hearty, and charismatic Michael Collins who was impressed by Childers's idealism and charmed by the manners of Erskine and Molly. When Childers joined the Republican movement, Collins gave him a Colt .25 caliber automatic pistol for his protection.[13] Childers always treasured the pistol—not because he felt the need for protection, but because it was a gift from Collins. Childers also made an important enemy—Arthur Griffith. How that came to be is an involved story.

When Childers offered his services to the Republicans, there was some confusion as to where to put him. He had been a combat aviator, but the Irish Republic had no air force. He had naval experience, but the republic had no navy. He had a reputation as cavalry expert, but the Irish Republican Army had no cavalry. It didn't even have artillery, so Childers's experience as a lowly gunner was useless. But Childers also had a reputation as a writer, and he had high-level contacts in England. The Republic had to get its story out to the world beyond Ireland. Childers was assigned to propaganda.

This new assignment brought him in contact with Arthur Griffith. Griffith was minister of home affairs. One of his responsibilities was propaganda. Among his subordinates was Desmond Fitzgerald, a poet and minister of propaganda. Childers reported to Fitzgerald, and after Fitzgerald was arrested, replaced him. Childers, with a keen sense of words, got his own title changed from minister of propaganda to director of publicity. Griffith, a former newspaper editor, was at first delighted with Childers's work as editor of the *Irish Bulletin*. But then he began to find his subordinate's mannerisms annoying. He came to think Childers was putting on airs— acting superior to the common herd. Griffith was distressed by what he considered Childers's fanatical insistence on accuracy—checking and double-checking every fact before publication. He became so distressed he conceived the strange idea that Childers might be a double agent. Hadn't British Intelligence snatched him out of Ireland right after the Howth landing? Wasn't he an intelligence officer during the war? Why would an author and military expert of Childers's stature abandon a great career in England to join an impoverished revolutionary movement in Ireland? Such suspicions were born and nurtured by the fussy "old parson" side of the dashing warrior.

In spite of his personality conflict with Griffith and his own desire for more action, Childers made his greatest contribution to Irish independence as propaganda chief. ("I had thought I was going off to a bloody combat," he once remarked to Frank O'Connor, "and instead I found myself in Mick Sullivan's feather bed in Kilnamartyr."[14]) This was all due to the Black and Tan War.

The British government, under a new prime minister, David Lloyd George, sought to treat the Dáil Eireann and all its works as a criminal conspiracy. Putting it down was a job for the police, not the army. Lloyd George loaded Ireland with troops, but they were primarily there in case of pitched battles. The work of hunting down and eliminating the "conspirators" was to be done by the Royal Irish Constabulary (RIC).

The trouble was that there weren't enough police. RIC members, mostly Irishmen, found that they were being shunned by former friends and neighbors. They began leaving the force in droves. To replace them, the British government recruited large numbers of Englishmen. There were so many recruits the government ran out of police uniforms. So the new recruits appeared wearing elements of the dark green, almost black, police uniform and khaki army uniform. Some wit called them the Black and Tans—the name of a famous pack of Limerick fox hounds. The implication was that the new "police officers" were dogs. It was not an unfair judgment.

Irish legend has it that the Black and Tans had been released from British jails to serve on the force. This wasn't true. They weren't released from jail, although many, perhaps most, of them should have been sent there. They were jobless—in some cases homeless, veterans of the first World War. Few people endured the years of mind-boggling slaughter in the trenches without being changed. The Black and Tans had changed more than most. They had become callous. They burned the house of anyone even suspected of involvement in the Republican movement. If one of their number were killed in a fight, their custom was to ride through the nearest village, shooting civilians indiscriminately. At times, they wiped out whole villages—shooting men, women, and children and burning all the buildings. Torture was standard operating procedure for obtaining information.

On June 16, 1920, a Lieutenant Colonel Smyth commanding the Black and Tans in the province of Munster, told his men, "The more you shoot the better I will like it, and I assure you no policeman will get into trouble for shooting any man."[15]

The "Tans" were not able to cow the Irish. Irish Republican Army guerrilla leaders, such as Tom Barry, ambushed Black and Tan truck convoys. IRA intelligence agents under Michael Collins infiltrated Dublin Castle, the seat of British rule.[16] Collins' agents killed all the RIC detectives in Dublin trying to track down Republicans. There were other detectives who only pretended to look for Republicans. They were working for Collins. The British sent in a new crop of agents, nicknamed the Cairo Gang, from the cafe where they hung out, to arrest or murder (preferably the latter) Republicans. The gang killed a few of Collins's men. Then Collins learned the names of the Cairo Gang members. On the morning of November 21, 1920, his agents killed them all. The Black and Tans retaliated by sending troops and an armored car into a football stadium during a game and firing into the crowd.

Irish resistance infuriated some members of the British government. Winston Churchill, then secretary for Ireland, thought the government should follow the example of the Russian Communists. "Look at the tribunals which the Russian Government has devised," he said. "You should get three or four judges whose scope should be universal and they should move quickly over the country and do summary justice."[17]

The Black and Tans needed help, Churchill thought. He proposed "a special force of 8,000 men" to make up for their deficiencies.[18] This force, called the Auxiliary Division of Police, was composed of British officers mustered out of the army at the end of the war. Much like the Black and Tans, they were jobless and frustrated. But they were more frustrated than the "Tans." They had once held the power of life and death over dozens—in some cases, hundreds—of men. They took out their frustrations on the Irish. One of their most notable achievements was burning the city of Cork after an ambush in which two of their men had been killed. British authorities blamed the burning on the IRA, but the "Auxies" did not try to hide their responsibility.[19] They wore burnt corks in their Glengarry bonnets so there would be no mistake.

The pen is mightier...

Irish patriots like to think that the IRA outfought the British and forced them to sue for peace. The idea is absurd. The IRA consisted of a few thousand men with no ships, planes, tanks, armored cars, artillery, almost no machine guns, and not enough rifles to go around. Britain had one of the world's largest and best equipped military establishments.

Frank O'Connor said, "Though the Volunteers ambushed lorries and attacked barracks, and the military instituted vast roundups, thousands of men on both sides never fired a shot in anger at them; the real fighters were postmen, telephone operators, hotel porters, cipher experts; the only real weapon, the revolver."[20]

O'Connor was referring to the intelligence war—the ruthless, clandestine war Michael Collins was winning against the British. Collins's objective was to keep the British from finding, killing or imprisoning Republican leaders. But that was strictly a defensive operation. It could prevent the British from destroying the Republic's government, but it couldn't win the war.

There was another war that O'Connor and Childers waged, using a more potent weapon than the revolver: the typewriter.

Lloyd George always referred to his Irish opponents as "murder gangs." According to the British government, the Black and Tans and the Auxiliaries were embattled police trying desperately to restore order. The British press printed what the military authorities told them because there was no other source. What they wrote reinforced all the ancient English prejudices about the Irish: the Irish were feckless, incapable of ruling themselves; they were always in rebellion or on the verge of rebellion, but they could never agree among themselves; only strong military rule could keep order in Ireland. Republicans needed to let the people of the world—and the people of Britain—know what was really happening in Ireland.

The Dáil's first attempt to tell the world the Irish side of the story was not a success. It sent three delegates to the Versailles peace conference—de Valera, Griffith, and Count Plunkett, a Republican nobleman and father of Joseph Mary Plunkett, one of the 1916 martyrs.

Childers went along as Griffith's assistant. But the big powers did not want to hear about Ireland. Woodrow Wilson, who had made the freedom of small nations an aim of the "Great War," found it was easier to be a prophet than a statesman. Harold Nicolson, who was there, said, "[Wilson] was able, like all very religious men, to attribute unto God the things that were Caesar's....Early in January, he immersed himself within the Ark of the Covenant. No one thereafter, least of all Mr. Lansing [the U.S. secretary of state] was able to get him out."[21] Asked why he couldn't see the Dáil delegates, Wilson said, "You have touched on the great metaphysical tragedy of today. When I gave utterance to those words I said them without the knowledge that nationalities existed which are coming to us day after day."[22]

An American president who'd never heard of the Irish?

The Dáil delegates came back to Ireland, and Childers went back to the *Irish Bulletin*. The *Bulletin* began as a few mimeographed sheets distributed to Dublin newspapers and to reporters for the foreign press. It came out five days a week, and Friday's edition featured "The Weekly Summary of Acts of Aggression Committed in Ireland by the Military and Police of the Usurping English Government." The summary listed all the murders, woundings, floggings, burnings, lynchings, and other atrocities perpetrated by the Crown forces. It also described killings and other acts attributed to the Republican forces. Within a year, it had picked up 600 readers in Ireland, England, Europe, and the United States. Dublin Castle tried desperately to find the paper's plant and staff. Once the Auxiliaries actually raided the plant and confiscated the equipment, but the staff escaped before they arrived. Altogether, Childers operated out of 11 different locations. The *Bulletin* began to be widely quoted. Senator Robert LaFollette, the famous Wisconsin Progressive, delivered a series of speeches in favor of Irish independence, using material that had been gathered by Childers. The editor of the *London Daily News* requested Childers to write a series of eight articles on "Military Rule in Ireland." The articles were reprinted in a pamphlet and distributed by the thousands in Britain and the United States. They detailed incident after incident of murder, brutality, and blatant disregard for civil rights and common decency. "All this in your name," Childers reminded British readers.[23] Another pamphlet with a wide circulation in England was titled *Who Burnt Cork City?* It created a sensation in Britain. Although the Auxiliaries openly boasted of their arson, the facts had been hidden from the British public.

Members of the Establishment in England began to speak out against the atrocities of the Black and Tans. They included former Prime Minister Asquith, G.K. Chesterton, G.B. Shaw, H.G. Wells, Lord Bryce, Lord Grey, Lady Frances Balfour, Lady Robert Cecil, Gen. Sir Hubert Gough, Maj. Gen. Sir Frederick Maurice and the Archbishop of Canterbury. Even Lloyd George's cabinet secretary and right hand man, Tom Jones, finally told Bonar Law, a hard-line Unionist, "that I felt intensely about the Irish business and that the ghastly things that were being done were enough to drive one to join the Republican Army."[24]

Childers's efforts created a new element to revolutionary warfare, one that was to have world-wide impact and bear fruit generations later. He demonstrated that a small, weak nation could gain its independence through low-level warfare, if it combined that fighting with intensive propaganda aimed at the world at large. One after another, nations in Asia and Africa followed Ireland's lead in their struggles for independence.

While Erskine Childers was publishing an underground newspaper, Molly Childers, who was fluent in French, was conducting a salon for Irish, English, and foreign dignitaries. The invalid beauty exerted all her charm in the cause of Irish independence.

Arthur Griffith had complained about Childers holding such an important job while not a member of the Dáil. In May of 1921, Childers was elected to the Dáil as a member from Wicklow. The British hunt for him intensified. Eventually, they caught him and his assistant, Frank Gallagher. But to their chagrin, the Castle authorities were forced to release both men a few hours later. The reason was that Lloyd George was secretly trying to start negotiations with the Irish leaders, and Childers was a key player in the process.

As a result of Childers's efforts, the pressure on Lloyd George to end the horrors in Ireland had become immense. Even King George V was complaining. To the prime minister's rescue came Jan Christiaan Smuts, who thought Britain and Ireland could be reconciled, as Britain and South Africa had been. The South African had begun corresponding with Childers and de Valera seeking some common ground. Then he wrote a speech for the King on a visit to Ireland.

"I speak from a full heart when I pray that my coming to Ireland today may prove to be the first step toward the end of strife among her people, whatever their race or creed," the monarch said. "May this historical gathering be the prelude of the way in which the Irish people, North and South, under one Parliament or two as the Parliaments may themselves decide, shall work together in common love of Ireland."[25]

Three days later, Lloyd George proposed a truce and peace talks.[26] Irish prisoners were released, including Robert Barton, who was the republic's minister of economic affairs. On July 5, 1921, Smuts came to Ireland as an emissary of Lloyd George to convince the Irish leaders of the desirability of reaching a compromise. "We argued most fiercely all morning, all afternoon, until late at night," Smuts reported. "And I found the men most difficult to convince were de Valera and Childers."[27] On July 14, 1921, de Valera went to London for a preliminary meeting. He took a number of Irish leaders, among them Childers, Robert Barton, Arthur Griffith (then vice president of the Dáil), Count Plunkett, and Austin Stack (minister of home affairs). Griffith, a pacifist and long-time advocate of autonomy under the British crown, was the most amenable. De Valera and Childers objected violently to the exclusion of six northeastern counties of the nine counties of Ulster from the proposed Irish dominion.[28] Further, as Republicans, they objected to taking any oath of loyalty to the British monarch.

The Free State

De Valera took the British proposals back to the Dáil. They were unanimously rejected. Stack and Cathal Brugha, minister of defense, were so opposed they wanted to break off any more talks with the British government.[29] The Dáil did not want to go that far. De Valera wanted some form of association with the British Empire—such association would make it easier to bring the missing six counties back into the fold.

He did not want to swear an oath of loyalty to the British crown, however. He knew that would never be accepted by such extreme Republicans as Brugha (and probably Childers). He proposed an "external association" with the Empire. To Lloyd George, that was unthinkable, although today it is the status of India, Pakistan, South Africa—and may soon be that of Australia.

When it came to choosing a delegation for further talks in London, de Valera excluded himself. There were several reasons:

1. He felt he would be needed in Dublin to restrain such bellicose hard-liners as Brugha and Stack.

2. By staying remote from the fray, he could act as a brake on the delegates. Although they were called plenipotentiaries, they were supposed to check with him before agreeing to anything.

3. The delegation was headed by Arthur Griffith, a skilled negotiator, and his deputy was Michael Collins, who could charm a marble statue. Sean McEoin, later a high ranking Free Stater, said, "Mr. de Valera knew that he personally could not get any more than he had already been offered by Lloyd George in London....He thought that Collins with his personality and Griffith with his sagacity might do better—and, indeed, they did."[30]

In addition to Griffith and Collins, the delegates included Barton and two lawyers, Gavin Duffy and Eamonn Duggan. Childers was secretary to the delegation.

Britain had originally proposed that the 26 southern and western counties would have local self government. They would not, however, have any armed forces, nor any say in foreign relations. Nor could they levy tariffs and taxes and manage their own budget. All harbors and estuaries would be under the control of the British Navy. The Irish delegation eliminated most of those restrictions. The 26 counties would control their own finances and have their own armed forces. They would be largely in control of their foreign relations. Britain would, however, have some naval bases in Ireland.

But officials of the new Irish Free State would have to take an oath of allegiance to the Crown.

Both sides negotiated long and hard. Griffith, as always, was most amenable to British suggestions. Collins and Duggan were much less so. Barton and Duffy fought tooth and nail for a Republic. Childers, although only the secretary, was as intransigent in London as Brugha was in Dublin. Griffith's hostility to Childers became pathological. He refused to speak whenever Childers was present. He even accused Childers of starting World War I by writing *The Riddle of the Sands*.[31] Finally, Lloyd George demanded that the Irish sign the final agreement now "or face instant and terrible war." Griffith had already agreed to sign. Collins knew the IRA was low on arms and ammunition. He finally decided to sign. Duffy and Duggan followed him. Barton signed at the last minute. Nobody had checked the final decision with de Valera. Childers was despondent. He knew that Lloyd George had not asked for peace out of the goodness of his heart. The British public was *demanding* peace. The "instant and terrible war" was just another of the "Welsh Wizzard's" bluffs.

War

Debate in the Dáil was furious. De Valera, who could not accept the treaty, resigned from the Dáil. Arthur Griffith was elected president in his place. Childers asked Griffith what his policies would be.

"I will not reply to any Englishman in this Dáil," Griffith answered the member from Wicklow.

"My nationality is a matter for myself and my constituents who sent me here," Childers said.

"Your constituents did not know what your nationality was."

"They have known me since my boyhood days."

"I will not reply to any damned Englishman in this assembly."[32]

In the end, the Dáil voted for the treaty 64 to 57. Ironically, the pro-treaty faction gained its edge because many members of the Dáil belonged to that supposed stronghold of Republicanism, the Irish Republican Brotherhood. The IRB recognized its current chief, Michael Collins, as the rightful president of Ireland. It followed Collins wherever he chose to go. Griffith was not a member of the IRB (a republic being against his principles) but he had sided with Collins. De Valera, Childers, and Brugha were not IRB members. They were considered "the enemy."

In the end, the Republicans—Childers, de Valera, Brugha, Stack, and the rest—walked out of the Dáil.

"Deserters all! We will now call on the Irish people to rally to us. Deserters all!" Collins yelled at them.

"Up the Republic!" the Republicans replied.

"Foreigners—Americans—English!" Collins shouted at de Valera, Childers, and Brugha, who like Childers, had an English father. (Cathal Brugha was originally Charles Burgess.)

"Lloyd Georgeites!" screamed Countess Constance Markievicz, a combat veteran of 1916.[33]

The shouting match was a result of the extreme tensions built up by the debate. A few hours earlier, Barton had seen Childers and Collins arguing in a corridor.

"Does this mean we're going to part?" Collins finally asked.

"I'm afraid so," said Childers.

Then "Collins crushed his fists into his eyes, and all at once Barton saw the flood of tears as he tossed his head in misery."[34]

Most of the army hierarchy agreed to support the Free State. But the IRA had never been a monolithic organization. It was more like a collection of regional bands commanded by independent warlords. Many of those warlords said they had sworn an oath to the Republic and they were bound to fight for a republic.

De Valera joined them, but not as a leader. He said he was merely a private. No privates in any army have ever had such prestige, but the IRA executive board felt free to ignore him when his advice was inconvenient. Rory O'Connor became commander in chief of the Irish Republican Army, which opposed the Free State Army. Childers followed his friend and idol de Valera and became a staff captain with responsibility for propaganda.

On the Free State side, Arthur Griffith remained president of the Dáil, but Michael Collins became chairman of the provisional government under the treaty with Britain. In other words, he was chief of state and chief of government.

For a while, Republican and Free State troops jockeyed for territory. Then O'Connor acted. He seized the Four Courts buildings in the heart of Dublin. Collins tried frantically to get the Republicans to surrender or at least evacuate the Four Courts. Churchill was threatening to send in British troops to restore order.

Finally, Collins borrowed artillery from the British and began to shell the Four Courts. O'Connor and his men left the building and filtered away through the Dublin streets. At the end, only Cathal Brugha remained. In 1916, Brugha had suffered wounds that would have killed two other men, but he survived. At one point during the shelling, Brugha appeared in the street waving a white flag. But he wasn't surrendering. He just wanted to warn the Free State commandant that firemen were in danger from mines the Republicans had distributed around the Four Courts. At last, when the Courts were a mass of flames, Brugha ran into the street, firing at the Staters with a Mauser automatic in each hand. A machine gun burst cut him down and ended the career of as steadfast and brave a man as ever fought for Irish freedom.

Childers, meanwhile, was publishing an underground newspaper, *An Phoblacht*, for the IRA. Assisting him were Sean Hendrick and Frank O'Connor, later to become a world-famous writer. Childers worked night and day, covering combat at the front, interviewing wounded, printing the paper and arranging for its delivery. He and his team kept moving as Free State troops tried to hunt them down. In some ways it was like the Black and Tan War. In others it was not. The audience was different—the Irish people were sick of war. They wanted the killing and burning to stop, and they didn't care what oaths their officials took. The Republicans began losing ground. The Free Staters, supplied by the British, were gaining popular support as well.

On August 12, 1922, Arthur Griffith had a massive stroke and died within minutes.

"Death can hush the bitterest controversy that ever rent a nation," Childers wrote in his propaganda sheet, "and it is in that spirit that we endeavor to write these few lines. Deep and impassable as is the gulf that has divided us from Arthur Griffith, we join in mourning the death of a great Irishman."[35]

Ten days later, Michael Collins, who had taken over command of the Free State Army, was killed in an IRA ambush. O'Connor recalled rejoicing with Hendrick "and it was only later I remembered how Childers slunk away to his table silently, lit a cigarette and wrote a leading article in praise of Collins."[36]

"Like a gallant soldier he took the risk of that perilous passage through hostile territory—and like a gallant soldier, he fell on the field of battle," Childers wrote. "His boyant energy, his organising powers, immense industry, acute and subtle intelligence....charm and gift of oratory....he flung without stint into the Republican cause for five years."[37]

Irish Republican delegation entering 10 Downing Street, October, 1921. Erskine Childers is in the center, just right of John Chartres (carrying the roll of paper). (Military Archives of Ireland)

Collins was dead. Griffith was dead. It was time for the new men—the organizers—who usually take over when the revolutionary firebrands leave the scene. In Mexico, Villa and Zapata were followed by Calles, who set up the one-party system that ruled Mexico for almost seven decades. In Russia, Lenin and Trotsky were followed by Stalin. In Ireland, the rising organizer was a young man named Kevin O'Higgins, the minister of home affairs.

"It is necessary to remember that the country had come through a revolution and to remember that a weird composite of idealism, neurosis, megalomania and criminality is apt to be thrown to the surface of even the best-regulated revolution," O'Higgins later wrote explaining why he was needed.[38]

O'Higgins was a strange man. An ex-seminarian, he decided he did not have a vocation to be a Catholic priest after he was expelled from three seminaries. However, he appeared to be devoutly—even fanatically—religious. He attended Mass every day and fasted for six months before his marriage. But soon after his marriage, he became involved in a steamy affair with Lady Hazel Lavery, the American-born wife of Sir John Lavery, the Irish painter.[39] According to his friends, he was a gentle and compassionate man, but he is famous for having introduced flogging to the Irish penal code and having executed 77 Irishmen, including his one-time best friend, Rory O'Connor. The imprisoned O'Connor was not executed for a crime but in reprisal for an IRA killing. Kathleen Napoli MacKenna, an Irish socialite who knew him well, called O'Higgins "the Irish Robespierre."[40]

O'Higgins quickly zeroed in on Childers. According to O'Higgins and the Free State government, Childers was the source of all evil, the master saboteur who was blowing up bridges and railroads all over the country.

"I do know that the able Englishman who is leading those opposed to this government," O'Higgins said, again denying Childers his nationality as well as grossly exaggerating his role, "has his eye quite definitely on one objective, and that is the complete breakdown of economic and social fabric, so that this thing that is trying so hard to be an Irish nation will go down in chaos, anarchy, and futility."[41]

This was not the paranoia of old, exhausted Arthur Griffith. Someone in O'Higgins's position making a statement like this had to be either a fool or a complete cynic. O'Higgins had many enemies, and they said many harsh things about him, but nobody ever called him a fool. He wanted a scapegoat. He would make Childers into an Englishman and say that his aim was to destroy Irish society so Britain would have to come back to restore order. The statement was also the rant of a politician who had never seen combat against a soldier who had seen too much, a declaration of war by a law-and-order bureaucrat who had never been in much danger against a man who began risking his life for Ireland in 1914.[42]

Actually, Childers did nothing but try—in increasingly difficult circumstances—to publish an underground newspaper. Other IRA members didn't want him near them. He was too hot. While on the run, he lost part of his printing press in a bog. He asked to be reassigned. No commanding officer would take him. "We'd have no peace night or day if the Free Staters knew you were with us," he was told.[43]

"The newspapers continued to appear with bloodier stories of the fights and ambushes Childers himself is supposed to have led," Frank O'Connor recalled, "and Hendrick and I only laughed at them. We, who didn't even know how to redraft and slant an agency message, couldn't be expected to understand how clever men prepare the way for someone's execution....At the same time, I fancy that Childers would have been very happy with a column to lead."[44]

The last act

Finally, Childers got a message from de Valera. The former president of the Dáil was going to reconstitute the Republican government, which had been virtually dissolved by the IRA warlords. He needed Childers. Childers set out for Dublin, where de Valera was hiding. He stopped off at the Barton home, where he had spent his boyhood. Someone tipped off the Staters. Free State soldiers surrounded the house and dashed for Childers's bedroom. Childers heard the shouts and the rush of feet. He got out of bed with the pistol Collins had given him. In the hall, a squad of soldiers leveled their rifles at him. He raised the pistol, but an old servant woman, trying to shield him, ran up crying "Don't shoot Mr. Childers!" and wrapped her arms around him. Before he could free himself, another group of soldiers grabbed him from behind.

At Free State headquarters, the soldiers beat Childers in a vain attempt to get information. Then they sent him to a succession of prisons. He was tried by a military tribunal on the charge of having a gun in his possession and was sentenced to death.

Before the trial began, O'Higgins called Childers "a man who was outstandingly active and outstandingly wicked in his activities."[45] It was obvious that the verdict had already been determined. Winston Churchill, who once called O'Higgins "a figure from antiquity cast in bronze," rejoiced over Childers' capture.[46] "Such as he is, may all who hate us be."[47]

In spite of protests from Ireland, England, and the United States, Childers was shot by a firing squad November 24, 1922.

Five years later, Kevin O'Higgins was assassinated. The murder was never solved. There were too many people in Ireland with a motive.

In 1926, Eamon de Valera ran for office in spite of the required oath he had fought against so hard.[48] He became President of the Irish Free State in 1932, and immediately began dismantling all the ties to England. Sixteen years later, Ireland left the British Commonwealth of Nations.

In 1967, the yacht *Asgard* was declared a national shrine in a ceremony presided over by de Valera.

In 1973, Erskine Hamilton Childers, Erskine Childers's eldest son, was elected president of Ireland after a long career in Irish politics. He died in office in 1974.

8

Crazy Orde:
Orde Wingate

Horror in the afternoon

he colonel felt absolutely awful. His depression was worse than it had ever been before—worse than those periodic bouts of which he had written:

> *It is impossible to describe the kind of horror that engulfed me at these times. It was not the horror of any particular fate or of any one fear; nor was it concerned with general ideas of sin or suffering. It was much worse, because it was without form or limit and it swallowed up the whole of existence.*[1]

The horror of those days was not as bad as what he was feeling now. He was not only depressed—he had reason to be. He had just completed a brilliant military campaign. Using fewer than 2,000 Sudanese and Ethiopian irregulars in conjunction with untrained Ethiopian tribal warriors, he had destroyed a modern, well-equipped Italian army that outnumbered his many times. And his government acted as if he had done nothing.[2]

To complete his misery, he was running a malarial fever. He was afraid that if he checked into a military hospital, his enemies would see to it that he would end up in a staff officer pool...and never again command fighting men. Instead, he was combatting his fever with atabrine, which had been prescribed by an Egyptian doctor. Atabrine does reduce fever, but it is also a depressant—the last sort of drug that Orde Charles Wingate, should have been taking. His fever had now reached 104 degrees, and he'd run out of atabrine. He stumbled out of his Cairo hotel. Befuddled with malaria and atabrine, he couldn't find the doctor who had prescribed it. He returned to his room, trembling with fever and barely able to stand. He decided life wasn't worth living.

He picked up a bowie knife an American war correspondent had given him and plunged it into the side of his neck, hoping to hit the carotid artery. He missed the carotid. If he hadn't, he would have died almost instantly. But he did cut the jugular vein. He suddenly remembered he had not locked the door. With the knife still jammed in his neck and blood flowing all over him, he locked the door. Then he collapsed.

Fortunately, Col. Cudbert Thornhill in the room next door heard the door being locked and a body falling on the floor. He got the hotel manager to open the door. They found Wingate almost dead in a vast puddle of blood. At the army hospital, they gave him 17 pints of blood and operated on his wound. Wingate revived, but, delirious, he thought he had died and gone to Hell.

That sounded like a matter for a chaplain. But what chaplain? Wingate had been raised as a member of the Plymouth Brethren, a kind of modern Puritan sect that put heavy emphasis on the Old Testament. He had left the Brethren and was now a non-denominational Christian, like Richard Meinertzhagen and Erskine Childers. He was, however, far more conscious of God and sin than either of them. The Anglican chaplain failed to console him, as did the Church of Scotland chaplain (Wingate was Scottish). Finally, the Catholic chaplain was able to convince him that God would forgive his suicide attempt. He added that the officer's almost miraculous escape from death suggested that the Lord had work for him to do.

That thought gave Wingate heart. He would still be doing God's work; he'd continue to be a tool of the Almighty. That aim had animated him even before he went to Palestine and began fighting in the places where the ancient Israelites had battled for the Lord.

The making of an irregular

Born in India to a martinet of an army officer and a Bible-thumping mother, Wingate had studied to be an artillery officer at Woolwich. Neither studious nor outgoing, he barely managed to graduate from the academy. As a junior officer, his only interest seemed to be horses, fox hunting, and steeple-chase racing. He did have a steady girlfriend, Enid Margaret "Peggy" Jelley. She was wildly in love with him, but although they eventually became engaged, he kept putting off the marriage date.

Wingate began to grow more serious, to feel that he had a mission in life. He started thinking about a posting overseas. Influenced by his cousin Sir Reginald Wingate (also known as Rex) he began to study Arabic. Rex, had been commander of all British forces in the Anglo-Egyptian Sudan. He had been retired early for advocating Arab independence too strongly.

Wingate got a transfer to the Sudan, where he was given command of a Sudanese company. His duties primarily consisted of arresting Ethiopian smugglers, poachers and slavers. Between chronic bouts of depression, he learned to navigate on the desert using either a compass or the stars, and he learned to set ambushes to capture border criminals. Once he took a leave to try to find a lost oasis in the Libyan Desert. The expedition—Wingate, three Arab camel drivers, and several camels—didn't find the oasis, but Wingate learned a lot about survival in a hostile environment.

Ordered back to England at the end of his tour, Wingate boarded the steamer *Cathay* at Port Said. On the ship was a 16-year-old girl, Lorna Paterson, returning to England with her parents after a visit to Australia. Lorna later recalled that when she saw the 30-year-old officer, "I marched up to him and said, 'You're the man I'm going to marry.'"[3] Wingate couldn't have been hard to convince. They were married two years later.

Wingate ended his long engagement to Peggy. He later said he couldn't marry her because she always agreed with him: he had to have someone to argue with. Peggy was crushed. She never married.

Wingate developed a passion for promotion. "Only rank," he said, "gives you the power to do what you know should be done." When he failed to get appointed to staff officers school, he walked up to the general in charge of selection and pointed out that the selection committee had not considered his oasis-seeking expedition nor the report he wrote on it. All the nearby officers were dumbfounded, expecting lightning to strike that presumptuous captain. The general, however, told Wingate that although there were no vacancies in the school, he would be considered for a staff position as soon as one appeared.

In short order, Wingate was offered a staff position in Palestine. He'd be the intelligence officer for the Fifth Division.

The promised land

Palestine in 1936 was in turmoil. Britain governed it under a mandate from the League of Nations. Until the end of World War I, Palestine had been part of the Turkish Empire. During the war, the British had made promises to anyone who might help them. The Arabs who fought with T.E. Lawrence, for instance, thought they were fighting for Arab independence. European Zionists looked forward to a Jewish nation in the Biblical Holy Land.

However, when the war ended, the British government took a new look at its often contradictory promises. Instead of an independent Arab kingdom, the Arab world north of the Arabian peninsula was split up between Britain and France. Instead of a Jewish homeland in Palestine, Britain allowed a strictly limited Jewish immigration and conspired to keep Jews out of any positions of power.

Palestine, at the time, had a semi-feudal social and economic structure. It had most of the bad features of feudalism with only a few of the good. Only a few rich men controlled almost all of the land. The Palestinian peasant, unlike the medieval serf, could be evicted from his farm or forced to sell his interest in it for a pittance. The large Arab landlords forced their peasants off the land, paying them little to nothing. Then they sold the land to Zionist immigrants for enormous profits. And the Arab peasants blamed not the Arab landlords. Instead, they blamed the Jews.

There was trouble between Jews and Arabs but it didn't become serious until the 1930s. Zionism was not particularly popular with European Jews. Living in the heart of Europe, with all the advantages the 20th century had to offer, few of them wanted to move to some desert outpost and try farming in a waterless wasteland.

Then Hitler appeared. By 1936, there were hordes of refugees clamoring to get into the Promised Land.

Wingate, a qualified Arabic translator and student of Arab culture, went to Palestine with a predisposition favorable to the Arabs. (Besides, the prevailing culture of the British army at the time was anti-Jewish.)[4] The average Briton knew no Arabs and very few Jews. However, he had his stereotypes, derived from everything from Shakespeare's Shylock to Valentino's Sheik. The Jew was a conniving, cowardly, money-grubber. The Arab, on the other hand, was a noble knight of the desert. When he got to Palestine, that average Briton, now a soldier, mixed as little as possible with either Jews or Arabs...but he kept his stereotypes.

Wingate was different. As an intelligence officer, he knew that the best information about a country comes from the people who live there. The Jews were people he understood. As many of them were Russians and Central Europeans, they were steeped in European culture, understood modern technology, and practiced democratic government in their settlements. They were doers. They had run businesses and factories, taught at universities and worked in scientific laboratories.

Furthermore, as he studied the situation, Wingate decided that the Jews were not exploiters—they were the oppressed. Finally, and most important, they were returning to the land God had promised them.

Wingate saw the task God had set for him: He would help the Jews establish a national home in Palestine. It would also help his country. A Jewish state in Palestine, he foresaw, would be far more powerful than any combination of Arab states. Allied to Britain, a Jewish state would give His Majesty's Empire a solid hold on the Near East.

Wingate's view of the situation was not popular with British staff officers. Neither was Wingate. Among the spit-and-polish, red-tabbed headquarters troops, he stood out like a skunk in a rabbit hutch. He seldom shaved and favored a ragged sweater and a sun helmet of a type that had been obsolete since World War I. It didn't help that he had peculiar dietary ideas and was continually gnawing on raw onions. But Wingate knew that natty dressing had not made the British forces any more effective.

Groups of Arab terrorists were crossing into Palestine from Trans-Jordan and Syria. They blew up pipelines and bridges and murdered Jews in kibbutzim and towns. Wingate explained why the British troops and police couldn't stop them:

> Owing to the number of roads in Palestine, to the high degree of mechanization of the troops, and to the presence of an air arm, engagements with the rebels tended to take on a very definite form. A rebel gang would carefully choose a site commanding a road with a covered line of retreat and good air cover at hand. It would then lie up and shoot up the first body of troops, police, or Jews, which it considered strong enough to engage with impunity. In the case of troops, the following would occur: The troops, invariably caught at a ground disadvantage, would jump out of their vehicles and take cover. Then, they would open fire. Meanwhile an XX call [a call for reenforcements] would be sent for aircraft, which would arrive within 20 minutes, and often sooner. On the appearance of the aircraft the gang would retire to its covered position usually among rocks and scrub, and, in spite of claims, very seldom suffered casualties from the subsequent air action.[5]

With the army and police unable to protect them, the Jews had to rely on themselves. They formed an organization, "Haganah" (from the Hebrew word for defense) that included just about all young Jewish men. But Haganah was poorly armed and completely illegal. Jews and Arabs could be executed if caught carrying weapons. The British relented to the extent of letting the kibbutzim buy a few shotguns and .22 rifles, but they were still no match for the Arab terrorists.

As an intelligence officer, Wingate knew who the suspected leaders of Haganah were. He tried to meet them. The Zionists were suspicious at first, but they soon learned that Wingate was more of an extreme Zionist than most of themselves. He became a close friend of Emmanuel Wilenski, intelligence chief of Haganah. While he was waiting for Lorna to join him, he stayed at the home of David Hacohen, another leading member of the Jewish community. Eventually, the Wingates became close to Dr. Chaim Weizmann, the world leader of Zionism, and his wife.

Special Night Squads

Wingate started studying Hebrew and visiting kibbutzim. He was distressed by what he saw. The Jewish guards waited behind their fences for the Arabs to attack. He went to Wilenski.

"I've seen what happens to your settlers when they are attacked by the Arabs," he told his friend. "Now I have a scheme by which the British Army, with the help of your people, can put down these marauders. But I need information about Arab methods and plans before I contact my headquarters. So I have come to request your help."[6]

What he wanted was some men to join him on reconnaissance patrols. The Jewish Agency told Wilenski that while it had good reports on Wingate, it didn't entirely trust him. No men would be sent.

In a fury, Wingate demanded to see Moshe Shertock, political secretary of the Jewish Agency.

"Shertock," he shouted at the political officer, "why do you spend so much time truckling to your enemies and ignoring the help of your friends?"[7] Then he walked out.

The next day, the agency sent men to join Wingate at a settlement called Hanita. One of them was a youngster named Moshe Dayan, who would later become the one-eyed commander of the Israeli Army. After a short period of training, including reconnaissance patrols around Arab villages, Wingate took his men into action. He took seven of them on a 30-mile walk through dense scrub, mostly in the dark. They arrived at 3 a.m. on the approach to an Arab village Wingate believed to be a terrorist base. He put his men in position for an ambush.

"I shall go forward and reconnoiter," he told Zvi Brenner, his second-in-command. "If I don't come back, the decisions will be in your hands, Zvi. But don't attack unless you are sure of success."[8]

The waiting men heard a couple of shots, then a fusillade. They heard screams in Arabic, then the sound of people rushing through the scrub. Brenner and Dayan, closest to the village, saw Arabs run past them, but they held their fire until they heard shots from the farthermost ambush positions. Then they joined in the shooting. The Jews killed five Arabs and captured four.

When Wingate appeared, carrying a captured rifle, he asked one Arab where they had hidden their weapons. The man said they had no weapons hidden. Wingate shoved a handful of dirt into his mouth. He repeated his question to the choking Arab. The Arab still refused to tell him.

"Shoot this man," Wingate told one of the Jewish soldiers. The soldier hesitated.

"Did you hear? Shoot him."

The Jew shot the Arab. Wingate turned to the other Arabs. "Now speak."[9] They spoke.

Wingate and his patrol found the rifles, destroyed all they couldn't carry, and took the rest and their remaining captives back to Hanita.

Hugh Foot, a British diplomat, wrote that with tactics like this, Wingate "forfeited our reputation for fair fighting."[10] (As if there were anything "fair" about murdering unarmed civilians, which was the prime terrorist tactic.)

"We had originally planned to be back at 10 o'clock that evening, but instead returned at 7 o'clock the following morning, from what turned out to be the greatest military experience we ever had," Brenner later said.[11]

There was hell to pay at British headquarters. The British army was supposed to be neutral, but Wingate had not only sided with the Jews, he had led a Jewish force against the Arabs. Even worse, he had led them right out of Palestine and into Lebanon. Wingate was called before Sir Archibald Wavell, the British commanding general in Palestine.

Wingate explained theories to the general. The Jews had far more military potential than the Arabs, he said. Jewish settlers, mixed with volunteer British soldiers could be organized as "Special Night Squads" and used to guard terrorist targets such as the pipeline running to the huge oil refinery in Haifa. What the settlers had done at Hanita could be done all through Palestine. With the Jews trained, equipped and organized by the British, Britain would need fewer troops in the Holy Land.

Wavell liked the idea. He gave Wingate permission to form the Special Night Squads.

The squads were Wingate's private army, armed, uniformed and organized as he dictated. They wore Australian broad-brimmed hats, blue police shirts, shorts and tennis shoes. Wingate demanded absolute silence on the march. Every section (the equivalent of a U.S. infantry squad) had a grenadier. Wingate contended that at night, when targets are invisible at a short distance, rifle fire loses much of its value. He stressed the use of the bayonet and the grenade. Surprise was the foundation of Wingate's tactics. The squads would usually leave their camps by truck, hop off the truck at some desolate spot, and march in another direction.

The squads guarded the pipeline, ambushed terrorists crossing the Jordan or the Syrian and Lebanese borders, and raided terrorists in their base villages. The war suddenly turned against the terrorists.

But Wavell, who was Wingate's "godfather," was replaced. The new commanding general was much less happy with the idea of sponsoring Jewish soldiers, even if they were amalgamated with British troops. Many British officers feared that someday they would be fighting the Jewish soldiers they had trained. There were even reports that Wingate had told the Jewish leaders that they had to be prepared to fight Britain and that he had given them targets.[12] As the "Arab Revolt" subsided, the Jewish element in the Special Night Squads was reduced. Eventually, Wingate was sent home and the Night Squads were disbanded.

Before he left Palestine, Wingate got one chance to show higher headquarters what his Jewish fighters could do. On October 8, 1938, Sir Edmund Ironside, chosen to be commander-in-chief of the Middle East Command, was in Palestine. A large gang of terrorists sneaked into Tiberias and massacred 19 Jews, 10 of them children. While the terrorists were killing civilians, a number of them with machine guns surrounded a nearby British battalion and bottled the soldiers up in their own fort. Most of Wingate's troops were elsewhere, but he happened to be leading two squads about 10 miles from Tiberias when he heard of the massacre. Wingate and his two squads (20 men) trapped the terrorists and killed 50 of them. The next day, he caught up with the survivors of that battle and killed 14 more.

Ironside dismissed the commander of the besieged battalion on the spot and decided that the eccentric Captain Wingate was a man to watch.

Wingate went back to England with scars from the wounds he'd received fighting the Arabs, the Distinguished Service Order, and the gratitude of the Jewish settlers. Moshe Dayan later summarized Wingate's contribution to what a decade later would become Israel:

> *I never knew him to lose an engagement. He was never worried about odds. If we were 20 and the Arabs were 200, or if we were at the bottom of a hill and they were at the top, he would say: "All right, there's a way to beat them."...In some sense, every leader of the Israeli Army even today is a disciple of Wingate. He gave us our technique, he was the inspiration of our tactics, he was our dynamic.* "[13]

Wingate, now a major, commanded an anti-aircraft battalion in Britain when World War II began. He did not give up his interest in the Jewish settlers, though. He and his wife spent most of their spare time in England working with Zionist leaders. That did not endear Wingate to the army brass. The chief of army intelligence in Palestine had written: "Orde Charles Wingate, D.S.O. is a good soldier, but so far as Palestine is concerned, he is a security risk. He cannot be trusted. He puts the interests of the Jews before those of his own country. He should not be allowed in Palestine again."[14] And, sure enough, when Wingate did return to the Middle East Command, his passport was stamped "The bearer of this passport should not be allowed to enter Palestine."[15]

Wavell now headed the Middle East Command, which included Egypt and the Sudan as well as Palestine. And what had been a backwater command had suddenly become an important war zone.

Italy had entered the war on the German side.

Ethiopia

Marshal Rudolfo Graziani, the conqueror of Ethiopia, was about to invade Egypt. The Italian Navy and Air Force had cut Britain's Mediterranean supply route to Egypt; Italian planes based in Eritrea and Ethiopia also kept British ships out of the Red Sea: all supplies to Wavell had to come to the Cape of Good Hope and be transported overland.

Wingate proposed the creation of a mobile desert army, composed of Jewish settlers in Palestine, to defend Egypt's Western Desert. Wavell had other ideas. He and his most talented field commander, Lt. Gen. Richard O'Connor, laid plans for countering Graziani with the numerically inferior and poorly supplied troops available to them. Graziani did invade Egypt, but his offensive quickly ran out of steam. Then, in a bewildering series of moves, O'Connor hit the Italians from the west, south and east simultaneously. Graziani was routed, and O'Connor invaded Libya.

Meanwhile, Wavell planned to move against Italy's other African possessions, Eretria and Ethiopia. But as in the First World War, East Africa could never be more than a sideshow. Britain, bracing for a German invasion of the home island, had no men to waste on sideshows. Wavell did not ask for massive reinforcements. He asked for one man—Wingate.

Wingate got the strange title of Chief Officer for Rebel Activities. The title demands a short back track.

The Lion of Judah

Haile Selassie, the deposed Emperor of Ethiopia, the Lion of Judah, the supposed descendant of King Solomon and the Queen of Sheba, arrived in Khartoum in July 1940. He expected that the British would quickly restore him to his throne. A large number of Ethiopian refugees had arrived in the Sudan, and the emperor asked the British commander in the Sudan, Maj. Gen. William Platt, for artillery and anti-tank guns to equip them. Platt could not help him. There were no artillery pieces or anti-tank guns in all of the Sudan. The British had only 9,000 soldiers.

In Ethiopia, the Italians had an army numbering a quarter of a million, all well equipped, along with an air force. Their commander, the Duke of Aosta, was also the civil governor. The Duke, unlike the brutal Graziani, was an enlightened administrator. Many British officials in the Sudan admired Aosta and thought the Italian conquest was not a bad thing. To them, the Ethiopians were bandits and slave raiders, and Italian rule had reduced their looting. The British officials were in no hurry to help the deposed leader of that kingdom of thieves and slavers.

Wingate thought otherwise. Before he arrived in Khartoum, he had looked through army files for anything relating to Ethiopia. He found a letter written by five Australian soldiers who had been on leave in Jerusalem. There they had met a number of Ethiopian Coptic priests and other refugees who told them about the conquest of their country. The Australians had this to say:

> *For the first time, this war begins to make sense to us. We have all read about the conquest of small countries by big ones, of the brutal aggressions of Hitler and Mussolini. But in Jerusalem, from these simple Ethiopians, we learned for the first time from the lips of the victims what conquest can mean, and what liberation can mean, too. We begin to see that we are in the Middle East for a reason, and that we have a part to play. We hope that the part we play will be concerned with the liberation of Ethiopia. Hence this letter. It is a formal notification that the undersigned are prepared to volunteer for service, in any circumstance or condition you may designate, in any operation planned for the liberation of Ethiopia. We should be honored to fight with any army pledged to bring the Emperor and his exiled followers back to their capital."* [16]

171

Wingate had discovered a new crusade.

As Haile Selassie was arriving in Khartoum, Italian troops were crossing the border and occupying the towns of Kassala and Gallabat. It looked as if Aosta was preparing to conquer the Sudan. He had, in fact, already given the Sudanese assurances of civilized treatment when the Italian offensive began. Aosta seemed to be in no hurry, which was good for Wavell. He ordered Platt to counterattack at Gallabat, and he sent Col. Daniel Sandford, and old Ethiopia hand, across the border as head of the British Mission to Ethiopia. Wavell wanted Sandford to be a kind of "Lawrence of Ethiopia," to preach rebellion against the Italians.

Platt's counterattack was roughly handled by the Italians and achieved little. William Slim, his field commander, had to retreat. Sandford showed remarkable courage on his mission behind enemy lines, but he was no Lawrence. The rebellion never got started.

Wavell arrived in Khartoum with the ubiquitous Jan C. Smuts and Anthony Eden, Britain's foreign minister and Prime Minister Winston Churchill's right-hand-man. Eden found Platt's lack of aggressiveness most unsatisfactory and told him so. However, O'Connor's offensive had been so successful Wavell transferred an Indian division to the Sudan. Wavell wanted Platt to attack the Italians in Eritrea, then move south into Ethiopia. Meanwhile, a South African army being organized in Kenya would push up from the south. There were a lot of Ethiopian refugees in Kenya, too. But British East African authorities, like the troops they had brought in from South Africa, had no faith in black soldiers. The Ethiopians were not formed into a "Patriot" army as they were in the Sudan. They were considered prisoners of war and put into labor camps. Any lessons taught by von Lettow-Vorbeck a generation before had been forgotten in Kenya.

It was at this point that Wingate arrived in Khartoum. Short, shabby, arrogant and most unmilitary-looking, he made his usual negative impression on Platt and his staff. He got Platt's grudging cooperation by shamelessly exploiting his friendship with Wavell and some VIPs back in England, as well as by pure bluff.[17] Wavell made him a lieutenant colonel (and Sandford a brigadier). Wingate made himself Haile Selassie's chief of logistics, training, and operations. He arranged to have the Ethiopian POWs in Kenya transferred to the Sudan and incorporated in Haile Selassie's army. He flew to Sandford's headquarters in the interior of Ethiopia.

The visit included one incident which says a lot about Wingate. He and his pilot were preparing for the return flight. The runway was short and ended at a deep ravine. The pilot tried to take off twice but had to brake to avoid going over the cliff. He told Wingate the plane couldn't become airborne in time with both of them aboard. He tried to explain the limitations of his aircraft.

"Don't worry me with such nonsense," Wingate said. "You understand aerodynamics. I understand the will of God. Let's take off."

They took off and missed disaster by inches. For this feat, the pilot won the Distinguished Flying Cross.[18]

Brigadier Daniel Sandford (left) and Colonel Orde Wingate (right) discuss the campaign with Ethiopian Emperor Haile Selassie. (AKG London)

Wingate was not impressed with Sandford's work. He let it be known that he didn't think much of the Lawrence technique of recruiting guerrillas.

He wrote a memo, "The Right and Wrong Methods of Dealing with a Fifth Column Population," which he sent to Wavell, Platt, and Lt. Gen. Sir Alan Cunningham, the British commander in Kenya. He demanded that his recommendations be acted on immediately "before these fools ruin everything."

The Wrong (or Lawrence) Method:

> *On entering the occupied area, the invading commander gets in touch with the local patriot leader and after an exhortation suggests that the leader can do something to help carry out the operation. The patriot at once replies that he desires nothing better but has no arms, money, or ammunition. The commander asks how much he wants. He names some impracticable figure. The commander promises a fraction, which he hands over and waits for results. These are nil....*

The Right Method:

> *The commander enters an area with a small but highly efficient column with modern equipment and armament, but none to give away. On meeting the*

> *patriot he says he has come to fight for the common cause but preserves an air of secrecy and confidence regarding the action he intends to take. The patriot asks what he can do. The commander replies: "Give me supplies which I will purchase at a fair price and pass me information."...The following night the commander carries out a successful operation. Next day comes the patriot saying: "Why didn't you tell me you intended to attack? I could have been great help to you." Says the commander: "Oh well, you have no arms and you are not a soldier. And after all why should you get killed. That is our job." Says the patriot: "But I am a soldier and have been fighting the enemy for years. Only tell me what you want me to do and I will show you we can do it." "But you have no arms or ammunition and I have none to spare." "It is true," says the patriot, "that I have very little ammunition but what I have I want to use in support of my flag." So the commander agrees: "Very well, come along with me this afternoon. I am making a reconnaissance and can probably find some useful job for your followers. But I shall judge by results and if you make a mess of it I shan't be able to use you again." Result: the patriot rushes to the fray with keenness and devotion. He regards the commander as his leader. It is a privilege to follow him.[19]*

Humility had never been one of Wingate's virtues. When a general sneered at Wingate's plan to invade Ethiopia with native troops, he replied, "You are an ignorant fool, General! It is men like you who lose wars."[20]

Inevitably, there were conflicts between Wingate and Sandford. It was decided that Wingate, now with the rank of colonel, would be in charge of military affairs and Sandford political matters. But Wingate continued to approach Haile Selassie directly and Sandford continued to issue orders to Wingate's troops.

Gideon Force

The British high command expected Platt from the north and Cunningham from the south to crush the Italians in a giant pincer. As for Haile Selassie and his "nigger army," who cared? The "little man" would probably never reach the Ethiopian highlands. If he did, he and his rabble would undoubtedly be destroyed. Good riddance. The black Emperor (tipped off by Wingate) had already written to Churchill and torpedoed the Brocklehurst Commission. Lt. Col. Courtenay Brocklehurst of the Special Operations Executive (SOF—the counterpart of the American OSS) had headed a delegation of East African movers and shakers who devised a plan to split up Ethiopia and incorporate a large part of it into the British Empire. The Emperor's letter killed that plan.

There were good reasons for supposing the Lion of Judah and his followers would get nowhere. There were no roads from Khartoum to the border crossing-point Wingate had selected. And there were few motor vehicles that could be spared for the Ethiopians. Even if they could be spared, there was no way any motor vehicle could cross the escarpment between the desert and the Ethiopian Highlands. There had been no time to train "Gideon Force," as Wingate had dubbed his army. Wingate himself called the Ethiopian troops "an ill-trained, ill-armed, ill-equipped, and demoralized rabble."[21] There were few machine guns or mortars and few of the troops knew how to use those they had. Several times, Wingate himself had to act as a mortar gunner. Most of the Ethiopians were equipped with U.S. M-1917 rifles which had been lend-leased to Britain. These were used mostly for training in Britain, because their caliber, .30-06, was not compatible with other British weapons. (Wingate, however, considered the .30-06 superior to the standard .303 cartridge and carried a .30-06 rifle himself).

On January 19, 1941, Gideon Force set out. It included 800 soldiers of the Sudanese Defense Force, 800 Ethiopian "patriots," 50 British officers, 20 British NCOs, a number of camel drivers, and 25,000 camels. It marched across the desert to the Ethiopian escarpment—a sheer, 3,000 foot-high rock wall. The escarpment was considered absolutely impassible for an army, so it wasn't guarded. Wingate discovered a steep treacherous path up the cliffs. To avoid observation from Italian airplanes, his army climbed it that night. In places, the camels had to be hauled up with ropes, but most of them—and almost all of the troops—made it to the top. On top, they found a paradise of green fields, cool streams, and wild flowers. The exiled emperor had returned to his country.

War against the will

Wingate was now ready to wage a new kind of war. He would attack the enemy's mind; he would destroy the enemy's will more than its troops. "Given a population favorable to penetration, a thousand resolute and well-armed men can paralyse, for an indefinite period, the operations of a hundred thousand," Wingate had written.[22]

There were no lines of communication. The troops would have to operate for long periods without supplies. Some emergency supplies could be air-dropped, but for the most part, they'd have to live off the country. At the same time, they would destroy the enemy's lines of communication, paralyzing an army that believed well-organized supply lines were essential to the conduct of war. They would operate in small groups over a wide area and enlist the support of local people. That would convince the enemy that Gideon Force was enormously larger than it really was.

Wingate divided his force into two main columns. They moved at night to avoid aerial observation and kept in touch by radio. Gideon Force began by isolating two Italian strong points—one containing 14,000 troops and the other 17,000. The weaker of his two columns surrounded the 14,000 Italians at Bahardar and kept them pinned down with a dizzying series of raids and ambushes. The stronger column blew up the bridge over the Nile chasm, cutting off retreat, and, with the help of local tribesmen, took one Italian outpost after another. The Italians had a large number of native troops. But Wingate ordered his forces to concentrate their fire on the white regulars and encourage the natives to desert and join the Emperor.

Gideon force seemed to be everywhere in western Ethiopia. The Italians decided they were greatly outnumbered. Garrisons began withdrawing before they were even attacked. When he entered one city, Wingate got Edmund Stevens, an Italian-speaking correspondent for *The Christian Science Monitor*, to call ahead to a string of garrisons down the line. Stevens claimed to be a physician hiding from the Ethiopian rebels who had entered the town and were wreaking havoc. To each Italian he talked to, he had the same advice: "Get out!" They did.[23]

In central Ethiopia, the Italian army was no longer functioning. There was still local fighting. At one point Wingate and his volunteer secretary, Avraham Akavia, a Jewish civilian from Palestine, were separated by an Italian force. Wingate commanded one part of the column and Akavia took command of the other. They defeated the Italians after a long battle. When they were rejoined, Wingate shouted to Akavia, "Thank God you have come back. I thought I had lost the only other Zionist in Ethiopia."[24]

Another time, Wingate's second-in-command, Lt. Col. Anthony Simonds, was hard pressed by a large Italian force. Simonds noted the direction of the wind and fired a flare pistol into the eight-foot-high elephant grass, then watched the flames rout the Italians.

Meanwhile, Platt's troops in Eritrea had run into strong opposition and were stalled. But Cunningham's force from Kenya had hardly any opposition. All the Italian forces were engaged in trying to hold off Platt and Wingate.

Wingate was organizing his troops for the advance on Addis Ababa that would install Haile Selassie in his capital when he saw an opportunity to end the war with one stroke. Most of the enemy troops opposing him had gotten jammed between his Ethiopians and Sudanese. All he needed was an air strike to make the demoralized Italians surrender. "It is no exaggeration," he said later, "that the capture of this force would have made possible an immediate and successful advance to Addis Ababa. But the appeals were ignored."[25] Without air support, there was no way his force of fewer than 2,000 could have captured more than ten times as many Italians. That was not the only instance when headquarters failed to support Gideon Force. British engineers managed to get a road over the escarpment so trucks could get to the troops in Ethiopia. Wingate was allotted several hundred trucks—only 12 reached him. The rest went to the other, far less effective, units.

Cunningham and his South Africans, facing no opposition but the desert itself, got to Addis Ababa first. He sent orders that under no circumstances would Haile Selassie be moved to the capital until he was ready to receive the Emperor. Wingate thought this was part of a plot to bring Ethiopia under British control. He had seen plans for a "transitional" British military government of Ethiopia, with the Emperor's ministers appointed by British military authorities.[26] He was sure there was a conspiracy to do Haile Selassie out of his throne and that frustrating Gideon Force was part of the conspiracy. Douglas Dodds-Parker, who acted as liaison between Wingate and headquarters in Khartoum, had this to say about Wingate:

There was no conspiracy, but Wingate lacked the manner a commander in the field needs to get what he wants. He was rude and dictatorial and insistent—and this went down very well with his men and his subordinate officers, who thought what a strong chap he was. But with his superiors, it did not work. His manner put their backs up. In wartime, as in peace, the way you get favors from people is by being powerful but charming too. That Wingate never was. I have always believed that for every good mark he made with his subordinates in the field, he lost two marks with his superiors. A less brilliant officer with better manners could have achieved more every time.[27]

Dodds-Parker was by no means unsympathetic to Wingate. When Wingate returned to Britain, his superiors asked him to discontinue *private* discussions about Ethiopia. "Later I found out that South African pressure had been brought to play down the victory of mainly non-white troops over a largely white army."[28]

The trouble with Cunningham's order about Haile Selassie was that the British military could not been seen pushing around an emperor, particularly one who had for years been hailed as a martyr in about every country except Italy and Germany. In his order, Cunningham added that if, in spite of discouragement, the Emperor insisted on returning to Addis Ababa, Wingate should inform him and take every precaution to insure Haile Selassie's safety.

Wingate told Cunningham the Lion of Judah was coming, then arranged a triumphal parade. Haile Selassie waved to his cheering subjects from an open truck, riding behind a column of Ethiopian Patriots led by Wingate on a white horse. Wingate had once told Peggy Jelley that he dreamed of someday returning a king to his throne. This was a high point in his life, even though he was coming down with malaria.

There was still fighting to be done. Wingate took Gideon Force and as many local troops as he could find to mop up the Italians. He received orders to stop the pursuit and reinforce the regular forces, but he pretended the radio messages were not understandable. Order after order crackled over the radio from Cunningham and Platt. Wingate was not about to break off the action. He was particularly concerned with a column under Col. Saverio Maraventano that had about 8,000 combat troops and 4,000 women and children. Wingate had about 1,000 troops with him, but he was able to convince the Italians that his column was much larger. The Italians were retreating, but Wingate got his troops around them and established a strong defensive position. He then maneuvered them into a trap—a box canyon where they were surrounded by cliffs on three sides.

He sent a message to Maraventano suggesting surrender. The rainy season was coming, he said, and the British troops would leave. Maraventano would have to deal with the Ethiopians alone. After further negotiations, Maraventano agreed to surrender to the British troops, provided that "I and my staff are received by a guard of honor consisting of at least a company of British soldiers."[29] The Italians marched out and left their weapons with a platoon of Sudanese soldiers. They then marched over a hill and were received by Wingate and Akavia. Maraventano asked where the other British were.

"In position," Wingate said, gesturing vaguely at the hills around them.[30] The Italians marched into captivity, not knowing they had talked to almost all of the British there were.

Wingate's "rabble" had accomplished far more in Ethiopia than Platt's troops...and infinitely more than Cunningham's. But he did not return to headquarters in triumph. Platt and Cunningham were furious with him for ignoring orders—not that they had any love for this sloppy, impertinent officer to begin with. The fever-ridden Wingate was ordered to leave for Cairo immediately. He didn't even have time to say goodbye to Haile Selassie.

Breakdown

When Wingate got to Cairo he found out that nobody knew what he had accomplished in Ethiopia. His superiors hadn't seen fit to pass on that information. Wavell himself wrote: "Of Wingate's brilliant performance in Central Abyssinia I knew little until afterwards." Wingate recommended awards for a number of his officers and a civilian award, the MBE (Member of the Order of the British Empire), for his civilian secretary, Akavia. All were presented except those to Simonds and Akavia. Both were personal friends of Wingate. Wingate himself got another bar for his DSO. He couldn't be ignored totally.

But in Cairo, he was a man without a job. Nobody wanted him. It was not that the British had no need for talented officers. Wavell had been forced to send a large part of his army to Greece, preventing any further advances in Libya. The outnumbered and outgunned troops in Greece had been defeated. Most of them were captured, including the brilliant O'Connor. The German Afrika Korps under Col. Gen. Erwin Rommel had arrived in Libya.

Wingate, his fever growing worse, met Simonds in Cairo. Both were now unemployed. Both wrote reports on their activities in Ethiopia. Simonds' was terse and factual. Wingate's was factual, but hardly terse. He detailed at length the lack of support he had received and he called his superiors "military apes" and similar complimentary names. He appended Simonds' report to his, had hundreds printed and distributed them to Wavell and every other important military person. The report (except for Wingate's personal copies) got no farther than Egypt. Middle East Command headquarters burned all it could find.

Wingate had an interview with Wavell. The commanding general tried to be sympathetic, but he was obviously displeased with the report. Wavell had other things on his mind. The politicians, having stripped him of his forces and left him helpless, were about to replace him. His replacement was Claude Auchinleck, a notoriously spit-and-polish soldier who took an instant dislike to Wingate. (He was later to revise his opinion.)

Wingate retired to his hotel room and stuck a knife in his neck.

The rise of the Rising Sun

The doctors in the military hospital discovered another reason for Wingate's suicide attempt. He had cerebral malaria, which causes insanity and death. The suicide attempt became top secret. Lorna Wingate heard only that her husband was severely ill and had been injured in a fall. The doctors were able to cure Wingate's malaria. They sent him back to England for a long rest. He would have to have a complete medical examination—physical and psychiatric—before he could return to duty.

He had plenty of enemies who hoped this would be the end of him. He also had plenty of friends. A Zionist doctor, Ben Zion Koumine, got Wingate an interview with Lord Horder, honorary physician to the King. Dr. Chaim Weizmann gave Lord Horder his personal guarantee of Wingate's mental stability. Leopold Amery, an important figure in the SOF, also vouched for him. So did Cousin Rex, Sir Reginald Wingate. Wingate got a clean bill of health and returned to active duty. Once again, there was a request for his services. Once again, it came from Sir Archibald Wavell. Once again, Wavell had been packed off to a quiet area—India, this time—only to have it explode.

Japan had entered the war. While deeply involved in China, it had bombed the U.S. fleet at Pearl Harbor, crippling the world's most powerful navy, and invaded the Philippines and Malaya. Before long, American and Filipino troops were bottled up on the Bataan Peninsula, and Japanese soldiers were threatening Singapore. On the Malay Peninsula, the Japanese were outnumbered two to one, but the British couldn't stop them. Each time the British set up a defense line, the Japanese either landed troops behind it on the Malay coast or infiltrated through the jungle and attacked from the rear. In a few weeks, the warriors from the Empire of the Sun accomplished feats far surpassing anything done by Hitler's vaunted panzers and U-boats.

Singapore and Malaya conquered, the Japanese turned on Burma. British and Indian troops from Wavell's India Command and American and Chinese troops, led by "Vinegar Joe" Stilwell, Chiang Kai-Shek's adviser, tried to stop them. Again the Japanese were outnumbered, but again, they were able to filter through the jungle and attack the Allies from the rear. To the British in India, the Japanese troops began to acquire the aura of supermen.

Wavell had hoped Wingate could establish a guerrilla campaign to slow down the Japanese invaders. The Japanese, however, had closed the Burma Road (China's main supply line) and completed the conquest of almost all of Burma before Wingate could organize anything.

At the end of 1942, Japan had four divisions in Burma. Facing it were 14 Chinese divisions in China's Yunnan Province, a Chinese-American force under Stilwell that amounted to two and a half divisions, and one British armored and three infantry divisions in India. The general who would command Japan's army in western Burma, Mutaguchi Renya, was aggressive to his fingertips, but he knew that with the numbers at his disposal and the terrain of Burma, no offensive was possible for a while. The Japanese began to set up defenses and reorganize their occupation force. Mutaguchi was to command the 15th Army, composed of three divisions in Burma plus a fourth which was to arrive. A fifth division was under the Burma Area Army headquarters in Rangoon.

Wingate saw that Burma resembled Ethiopia only in that it was difficult to travel through. The Burmese had never been pro-British and were unlikely to help British guerrillas. The Japanese were far better trained and infinitely more determined than the Italians. In Ethiopia, Wingate planned a guerrilla infiltration that would cause a revolution and oust the Italians by itself. In Burma, he believed the function of guerrillas would be to disrupt the Japanese supplies and maneuvers so they could not effectively oppose an invading regular force.

If the British in the coming campaign faced new problems, they also had new advantages. This time, the numbers were on the Allied side. Even more important, the Allies had air superiority. Further, the Japanese forces in the Far East were overextended, and their supply lines were a mess. U.S. aircraft and submarines were making the movement of troops and supplies among the various Japanese outposts extremely hazardous. Mutaguchi's men were chronically short of supplies.

Having the edge in numbers, air power, and supplies does not guarantee victory, however. In November, 1942, the British counterattacked in the Arakan area of Burma. They were repulsed. The Japanese were better jungle fighters.

The reason, Wingate knew, was that the Japanese were trained to fight in the jungle; the British were not. With men who were trained for jungle warfare, he told Wavell, he could introduce a new kind of warfare that would make the reconquest of Burma easy. The new kind of warfare was long range penetration. The Japanese had practiced short range penetration. Their troops, carrying all the supplies they would need for a few days, worked their way past the Allied front lines and attacked from the rear.

Wingate's long range penetrators, would go far behind the enemy lines. They'd attack army and corps headquarters, destroy supply dumps, roads and railroads. They would be resupplied by the air. At the time, army and RAF officers viewed each other with suspicion. Wingate's concept depended completely on close cooperation between army and air force units. He would require RAF men to train with his infantry. His guerrillas could take no artillery; dive bombers would substitute for howitzers.

Wavell gave Wingate permission to create a long range penetration force and promoted him to brigadier. Wingate wanted an all-volunteer elite force. It didn't quite work out that way. Instead of elite volunteers, he got regular units of the British Indian army.[31]

Wingate's private army got a designation—the 77th Brigade of the Indian Army—and a distinctive uniform: green, instead of khaki, worn with Australian hats. It got a badge, too, the *chinthe,* a mythical Burmese monster. "Chinthe" quickly became "Chindit," which became the common name of the long range penetration groups. Rigorous training weeded out the undesirables.

The Chindits were supposed to infiltrate the Japanese lines and create havoc in the rear while regular troops from India and China, including Stilwell's American-Chinese force, attacked. But the planned Allied offensive never came off. Wingate pleaded with Wavell to let him unleash the Chindits anyway. It would show what long range penetration could do and would be valuable training for the time when the Allies finally launched their attack. Besides, he said, the troops' training had reached a peak, and it would hurt their morale if they didn't get into action.[32] Wavell agreed. He gave Wingate three objectives:

1. Cut the rail line between Mandalay and Myitkyina.
2. Harass the Japanese around Shwebo.
3. If circumstances are favorable, cross the Irrawaddy and cut the railroad between Mandalay and Lashio.

The first Chindit expedition began in February 1943. There were two groups: the first was split into two columns; the second, under Wingate's personal command, included five columns. Altogether, there were seven columns, 3,000 men and 1,000 pack animals—mostly mules, but including some elephants. Wingate and his men crossed the Chindwin River and the Zibyu Mountains almost without incident. One column moved against the town of Indaw to distract the Japanese while two other columns demolished the Mandalay-Myitkyina railroad on a grand scale. The Japanese routed the column threatening Indaw, but most of its members returned to India safely. Two columns which had been out of radio contact for 10 days got back on the air and told Wingate they had crossed the Irrawaddy. The two columns that had cut the rail-road asked for permission to cross the river too. They'd have to do that to achieve Wavell's third objective, so Wingate approved. They crossed in spite of Japanese opposition. Wingate then crossed the Irrawaddy with his remaining two columns. Then the Chindits ran into trouble.

The columns that had cut the first railroad moved against the second, but the country across the Irrawaddy was open, not jungle. The Japanese quickly located all of the Chindit units. Wingate had to call off the attack on the Mandalay-Lashio railroad and order a retreat. Getting out of Burma was much harder than getting in. The Japanese were aroused. Wingate ordered his columns to disperse as small groups. Although Mutaguchi knew roughly where the Chindits were and every Japanese in Burma was looking for them, 2,200 of the 3,000 who entered Burma got back safely. That was after 12 weeks of marching through enemy territory without the support of any regular force or even lines of communication.[33]

The expedition did teach the Chindits several lessons. One was that every man in the next expedition should be able to swim. There were many rivers to cross in Burma, and boats were not always available. The Chindits also should have stronger air support, particularly for resupply. Training in close-quarters fighting and radio communications should be improved. And there should be some way to evacuate the wounded. But the biggest lesson was that long range penetration was feasible.

The Japanese also learned something. Mutaguchi wrote later that Wingate's expedition "brought about a great change in my strategical thinking, which hitherto had been based on the defense of Burma could be achieved by a defensive attitude, using these great forests as a barrier."[34]

Strategically, even Wingate admitted that the first Chindit expedition achieved little. But its effect on British morale was enormous. The British soldier no longer considered his Japanese counterpart a superman. Wavell was so happy he created another long range penetration group, the 14th Brigade, which would report to Wingate. The British public, depressed by an unbroken string of defeats, went wild when news of the Chindit operation reached Britain.

As he had after the Ethiopian campaign, Wingate wrote a report. It wasn't as critical as his Cairo essay, but it was critical enough to induce India Command to censor large portions of it. But somehow, an uncensored copy reached Winston Churchill. Churchill wanted to see this outspoken brigadier who had received so much publicity. He asked Wingate to visit him in London.

The Quadrant Conference

Wingate arrived just before Churchill was planning to leave for Quebec for a conference, code named "Quadrant," with President Franklin Roosevelt and the American chiefs of staff. He found Wingate's discussion of guerrilla war so fascinating he invited the officer to come with him. Wingate mentioned that he'd regret not being able to see his wife. Churchill invited her to come, too.

The conference was mostly concerned with landing American and British troops in France, but Wingate got a chance to present his theories on long range penetration in Burma. He fascinated not only Churchill and Roosevelt but both the British and American chiefs, particularly Gen. H.H. Arnold, commander of the U.S. Army Air Forces. Arnold assigned Col. Philip Cochran and Col. John Alison to raise and command an American air unit—"No. 1 Air Commando"—that would work exclusively with Wingate.[35]

Wavell had been "kicked upstairs" to be viceroy of India. His place was again taken by Claude Auchinleck, who still didn't like Wingate. Auchinleck had been opposed to any new Chindit expedition.

On August 26, the British chiefs of staff told Auchinleck to form an expanded long-range penetration force. This would include two RAF wing headquarters, the existing 77th and 14th brigades, and four new long range penetration groups. The whole unit would be called Special Force and commanded by a brand-new major general, Orde Wingate. Then it told Auchinleck that direction of the war in Burma would be taken out of his hands and given to the new Southeast Asia commander, Lord Louis Mountbatten. Wingate met Cochran, an officer as unmilitary as himself, but in a laid-back way, in England.

Then he flew back to India with his old friend, Derek Tulloch, whom he had chosen as his chief of staff. He had previously detailed Tulloch to locate commanders and staff officers for Special Force and to look over the latest weapons. Wingate wanted his men to carry the U.S. M-1 rifle and M-1 carbine, both semiautomatics. Instead of either the British Sten or the American Thompson submachine guns, they'd have the Australian Austen. They'd have Bren light machine guns, mortars, flame throwers, and anti-tank rifles. All men would carry the Gurkha kukri, a curved jungle knife. It turned out, though, that most of the foreign weapons were unavailable. Wingate apparently believed being a major general gave him enough rank to carry out his own ideas. Later when Mountbatten offered him a promotion to lieutenant general, he refused it. He remarked, according to Tulloch, "that he was too busy to worry about rank and preferred to wait for such things until after he had proved himself by the success of his operation."[36]

In India, Wingate met nothing but hostility. In a conference with Auchinleck's staff, he learned that nothing had been done to implement the Quadrant decisions, in spite of orders from Auchinleck himself. Wingate told the staff officers that he would have to explain the situation to the Prime Minister. Then he walked out.

The next day, Wingate came down with typhoid fever and had to enter a hospital. While Wingate was in the hospital, the RAF balked at participating in some of the joint training with the infantry Wingate wanted. Only after a long wrangle did the Royal Air Force agree to cooperate. In contrast, Cochran and Alison visited Wingate in the hospital to go over plans for the next long range penetration.

The Sextant Conference

Meanwhile, at a new British-American chiefs of staff conference called Sextant, the Quadrant accords began to fall apart. Chiang's cooperation with the projected offensive in Burma—which was designed primarily to help China—became doubtful. The British became less enthusiastic, although the Americans were still committed to invading Burma.[37]

Just before Mountbatten left for India, Churchill told him an amphibious invasion of Sumatra had his top priority for Southeast Asia. "Sumatra or nothing," Churchill said.[38] A short time later, the British chiefs of staff took all of Mountbatten's amphibious landing equipment. The invasion of Normandy was about to begin, and all landing gear was needed for the English Channel. With Sumatra out of the question, that left "nothing." Mountbatten was not displeased. He had come to agree with the India Command staff that the war in Europe should be settled before any major effort was made in the Far East.

Mountbatten told William Slim, who now commanded the Indian Army. He did not tell Wingate. Wingate's Special Force had been trained and equipped to act as lightly armed guerrillas in the enemy rear to support an offensive from the front. Unless the enemy were engaged in the front, the Special Force couldn't perform its special function. Mountbatten and Slim continually placed restrictions on Wingate's plans, but didn't tell him the reason. This time, he couldn't threaten to tell Churchill, because Churchill was behind the change of plans.

Stilwell knew the British were stalling and became even more furious than usual. He wanted to advance into Burma and looked for Wingate to disrupt supplies and reinforcements to the Japanese who were opposing him. The American chiefs of staff shared Stilwell's annoyance.

Finally, the situation was resolved by two men on opposite sides of the world who couldn't have had more opposing views. One was Franklin Roosevelt, who put through an irate call to Churchill and got the Prime Minister to agree to start moving in Burma. The other was Lt. Gen. Mutaguchi Renya. Since the first Chindit expedition, Mutaguchi had been fretting about the vulnerability of the Burma frontier. He decided to forestall a British attack by striking first at the Indian city of Imphal. British regular forces would be engaged whether they wanted to be or not, and the stage was set for the second Chindit operation.

Fly-Ins

Wingate sent one brigade down from the north, roughly parallel with Stilwell's advance. That would disrupt the rear of the forces opposing the Chinese-American push. The other brigades were to be flown in. The fly-ins depended on another of Wingate's revolutionary ideas—the "strongholds."

Cochran's and Alison's Air Commando had been surveying the jungle for months while they bombed Japanese installations and communications. They photographed clearings surrounded by dense jungle. These, Wingate proposed to turn into "strongholds," a term he picked up from the Old Testament line, "Turn you to the stronghold, ye prisoners of hope" (*Zechariah* 9:12). He explained the stronghold in his training notes:

> *The stronghold is a machan overlooking a kid tied up to entice the Japanese tiger.*
>
> *The stronghold is an asylum for Long Range Penetration Group wounded.*
>
> *The stronghold is a magazine of stores.*
>
> *The stronghold is a defended air strip.*
>
> *The stronghold is an administration center for loyal inhabitants.*
>
> *The stronghold is an orbit round which the columns of the Brigade circulate. It is suitably placed with reference to the main objective of the Brigade.*

The stronghold is a base for light planes operating with columns on the main objective.[39]

The stronghold was both a base and a bait. It was a garrisoned strong point that allowed supplies and reinforcements to be flown in and wounded flown out. It was also a magnet to attract Japanese forces. After they launched an attack, those attackers would be taken in the rear by the "floater columns" operating in the surrounding jungle. All strongholds would be inaccessible to wheeled transport, thus preventing the Japanese from using heavy weapons.

Wingate's troops were to fly to the stronghold sites in gliders towed by the C-47s of Air Commando. Besides men, the gliders would carry mules and artillery as heavy as the 25-pounder (88-mm) gun-howitzer. Because of a shortage of planes, two gliders were towed by each plane in the first wave. That caused difficulties in night flights, so later waves took only one glider to a plane.

An hour before the first fly-in, one of Air Commando's photographers, Maj. "Rush" Rushon, dashed up to the airstrip with a photo that showed logs laid in pattern on the landing site of one of the three projected strongholds. There was a brief panic when it seemed that the Japanese had heard of the operation and sabotaged the projected airstrip.

It was decided to go ahead with the operation, using the other two sites. It turned out the Japanese had no idea the landing sites existed. The logs had been laid out by local lumbermen. The troops quickly fortified the strongholds and sent columns out to set up roadblocks and blow up bridges.

The Chindit II fly-in was the largest airborne operation in history until that time. It was exceeded only by the landings in Normandy later that year and has not been equaled since. The planes made 579 sorties and the gliders 74 sorties. Low-flying C-47s snatched the gliders up from the strongholds and used them again. Altogether, they transported 9,052 soldiers and 1,359 tons of pack animals. They moved in 254.5 tons of stores and a Bofors 40mm anti-aircraft gun and a 25-pounder gun-howitzer. Not a single aircraft was lost.[40]

When Mutaguchi heard about the landings, he pretended to be unconcerned. Three days later, the commander of the air division supporting Mutaguchi's army told him the enemy had destroyed many of his planes on the ground. "If Wingate's forces build up, they'll create a major threat to the Myitkyina-Mandalay area and dislocate our supply system," he told Mutaguchi. The Japanese commander, however, refused to be distracted from his offensive. His staff unanimously asked him to suspend the offensive until the Chindit threat was neutralized. He refused.

He finally delegated a battalion to take care of the British guerrillas. Mutaguchi's commanding general ordered him to detach two infantry regiments and an artillery battery to do the job. For five weeks, he was unable to move forward. And he still didn't get rid of the Chindits.

Further, he had to let his dwindling airpower concentrate on the Chindits. His own troops hardly ever saw a Japanese plane.

The fighter pilots of Cochran's and Alison's Air Commando steadily whittled down the Japanese air force, destroying hundreds of planes on the ground and in the air. At the same time, they played hell with Mutaguchi's transport and lines of communications. The B-25s carried 75-mm guns, which did a lot to make up for Wingate's lack of artillery.

One trick the Air Commando pilots used was to pull down telephone lines by flying over them and hooking them with a spare set of landing gear. One pilot flew his P-51 through the wires and snapped them off. Another unconventional method of attack was dropping depth charges, which were intended to blast submarines, on Japanese troops. When the Japanese were besieging one Chindit strong point on the Myitkyina-Mandalay railroad, John Alison recalls, "We put hundreds of depth charges into the wood surrounding this position and the effectiveness of this was attested to by Japanese casualties which were counted in the area."[41]

Wingate's new strategy was working well. Churchill cabled his congratulations. The young general didn't have time to gloat, though. He was busy flying from one stronghold to another, and visiting columns in the jungle.

Final frustration

In London, on March 25, 1944, Peggy Jelley woke up from a terrible nightmare. She still heard the anguished voice of Orde Wingate, whom she had not seen since 1935. Something terrible had happened to him in her dream. She didn't remember what it was, but she had a premonition that he was in some kind of trouble.

In Aberdeen the same day, Lorna Wingate got one of those dreaded wartime calls. Maj. Gen. Orde Wingate was missing in action and presumed dead. Lorna Wingate had just given birth to a son—a boy his father would never see.

The night of March 24, Wingate had been flying back from Stronghold Broadway when the B-25 he was flying in crashed and burned. He was 41.

One of the Chindit brigade commanders took over Special Force, but he was no Orde Wingate. The Special Force was broken up. Some brigades went back to the regular Indian Army, others were given to Stilwell. In both cases, they were grossly misused. They had no armor, no heavy artillery, and little light artillery, but both Slim and Stilwell used them as regular infantry. They were wasted and eventually their survivors were withdrawn.

In spite of the way the Long Range Penetration Groups were misused after Wingate's death, they killed 5,764 Japanese and wounded more than 5,000 others. Their own casualties: 1,034 killed and 2,520 wounded.[42]

Wingate had been a rude, and sometimes violent know-it-all. He made many enemies. After he was dead, they took their revenge. According to them, he accomplished nothing in Ethiopia and the Chindit expeditions were a waste of time and lives. Wingate himself was a poseur, a charlatan, and was probably mad. To many of the few who still remember the general who impressed President and Prime Minister, he was simply "Crazy Orde."

Wingate, it must be admitted, was not a model of stability. He was subject to moods of deep depression and fits of violent rage. Once, he literally kicked one of his subordinate officers through the doorway of a taxiing airplane. He felt he was surrounded by enemies, and he was sure he knew the will of God. He may have had a touch (or more than a touch) of psychosis. But he was also the most innovative commander of World War II.

In Palestine, he convinced the British—and more important, he convinced the Jews themselves—that the Jews could be soldiers every bit as formidable as King David's troops. That led directly to the founding of Israel.

In Ethiopia, he repeated von Lettow-Vorbeck's lesson: Color has nothing to do with military efficiency.

And in Burma, he invented long range penetration and the use of airplanes to resupply troops. In the last days of the Burma campaign, the air supply system pioneered by Wingate was used by all Allied forces.

Strangely, the most just estimates of Wingate's effectiveness came not from the historians of his own country but from the fighting men who opposed him. Here is Lt. Gen. Mutaguchi Renya, said shortly before he died in 1969:

> *The advance into Burma of General Wingate's forces at the time of the Imphal campaign brought about serious failures in the strategy of the Japanese Army....*
>
> *...General Wingate's airborne campaign spread more and more widely, and the Area Army Commander picked out the 24th Mixed Independent Brigade and a part of the 2nd Division to confront Wingate's forces. The counterattack by these units on 25th and 26th March ended in failure....Further the fact that we had no alternative but to use our feeble air force against these airborne forces was a very great obstacle to the execution of the Imphal campaign....and were an important reason for its failure.*
>
> *On 26th March I heard on Delhi radio that General Wingate had been killed in an aeroplane crash. I realized what a loss this was to the British Army and said a prayer for the soul of this man in whom I had met my match.*[43]

Part 5

The Square
and the Spook

9

From the Jaws of Defeat (and Dugout Doug): Matthew B. Ridgway

Old Iron Tits

**M**atthew Bunker Ridgway is a strange addition to this collection of military mavericks. He never tried to conquer a country with a handful of bar flies, like William Walker. Unlike Fred Ward, he never became a demigod in an exotic, foreign country. He did not even enter the army near the top, like Fred Funston. Yet, here he is, sandwiched between Crazy Orde Wingate and Spooky Ed Lansdale. He is not yet as forgotten as Paul von Lettow-Vorbeck, but he's on the way to historical oblivion.

He isn't ignored because he was a maverick. Ridgway was as straight-arrow as they come—the model West Point graduate. He was a former Military Academy athletic manager who, as commander of the 82nd Airborne Division, jumped into combat in Normandy in 1944. He was square. He tried to develop a colorful image, a personal signature like Patton's ivory-handled handguns and riding breeches. He wore a parachute harness with a hand grenade and a first aid kit dangling from his chest, earning him the nickname, "Old Iron Tits."

Ridgway is not known for daring strokes of strategy. He was notorious for his meticulous attention to detail—everything from requiring appropriate silverware in the general headquarters mess to insuring that all units stay in communication, even if that means using smoke signals.[1]

There are two reasons for Ridgway's obscurity: He was commander of U.S. forces in what is now known as "America's forgotten war"; and he has been overshadowed by his predecessor, one of the most flamboyant mavericks in American history: General of the Army, Douglas MacArthur.

Dugout Doug

In any discussion of overrated generals in World War II, some names invariably come up. There was, for instance, Kliment Efremovich Voroshilov. Dispatches from Moscow always referred to him as "the famous Marshal Voroshilov," but never explained what he was famous for. He was famous because his old friend, Josef Stalin, decided he should be famous. In all truth, he was a military moron who had to be retired soon after the war started.

Then there was Bernard Law Montgomery. Unlike Voroshilov, Monty was not unsuccessful. He wasn't brilliant either, but he won battles. His success stemmed from his ability to, in effect, tell Winston Churchill to go to hell. He had replaced Claude Auchinleck, who had, like Wavell, been sent to India. Auchinleck had incurred Churchill's displeasure by his reluctance to move against Rommel and his Afrika Korps after the Germans were stopped at El Alamein in Egypt. Churchill expected a quick offensive by Montgomery.

Montgomery, however, ignored the Prime Minister and continued building up his forces until he was able to overwhelm the Germans. Montgomery seldom moved until the odds were heavily in his favor. But he won battles, which the British public found immensely appealing. And he had a signature—a beret with two regimental badges—and an ego, which made him good copy for correspondents. If Montgomery's abilities matched his ego, historians would forget about Napoleon.

But Douglas MacArthur was in a class by himself. Montgomery was a man of mediocre ability who pretended to have great talent. MacArthur was a man of immense ability and many talents—who thought he was God. His greatest ability was to convince many people that he was.

As a young officer in the Philippine troubles and in World War I, he had demonstrated plenty of personal courage, leadership, and tactical sense. He was a great orator, a persuasive talker, and he had an awesome intellect. He was also a master of office politics.[2] He became army chief of staff and commanded the troops that routed the Depression-stricken bonus marchers from Washington.

When he retired from the army, he became head of the Commonwealth of the Philippines armed forces. (The colony Fred Funston had helped to secure was moving toward independence.) Through all of this, MacArthur enjoyed the adulation of the American press, particularly the magazines of the Luce empire—*Time*, *Life*, and *Fortune*. Among his other talents, MacArthur had a genius for public relations.

In July of 1941, as the United States drew closer to World War II, MacArthur was recalled to U.S. service and placed in command of all forces in the Philippines—both U.S. and Filipino. He was in command in the Philippines on December 7, 1941, when the Japanese bombed the Pacific Fleet in Pearl Harbor and the Army Air Forces planes left on the Hawaiian airfields. He was in command the next day when, eight hours after the Pearl Harbor attack, the Japanese bombed the planes lined up on the ground at Clark Field in the Philippines.[3] For his negligence in Hawaii, Lt. Gen. Walter C. Short was sacked. For his negligence in the Philippines, MacArthur was made commander of all U.S. forces in the Southwest Pacific.[4]

General Matthew B. Ridgway, wearing the trademark parachute harness with grenade and first aid kit that earned him the nickname "Old Iron Tits." (Library of Congress)

In the Philippines, American troops nicknamed MacArthur "Dugout Doug" because while they were fighting in the jungles of Bataan he stayed in the fortress of Corregidor and then went out to Australia in a PT boat. In fairness, even MacArthur's severest critics must admit that it would not have helped the U.S. war effort if he had stayed to become a prisoner in Japan. In mid-1942, after the Japanese Navy received a setback at the Battle of the Coral Sea and a major defeat at the Battle of Midway, MacArthur instituted an island-hopping campaign through the Solomons, New Guinea, and the Philippines which eventually reached the threshold of the Japanese home islands.

Island hopping depended on local air and sea superiority. Selected islands (or, in New Guinea, outposts) were denied sea-and-airborne supplies and reinforcements, then attacked. Other islands or outposts were bypassed, left to "wither on the vine," as U.S. troops eliminated garrisons in their rear. The strategy was brilliant and successful, but it wasn't unique to MacArthur. Admiral Chester W. Nimitz, commander of U.S. forces in the Central Pacific, was doing the same thing at the same time.

MacArthur, though, would not be upstaged. As soon as the Coral Sea fight was reported, MacArthur claimed the credit, although it was strictly a naval battle. The land-based bombers, the only U.S. units under MacArthur, accomplished little. When MacArthur returned to the Philippines, movie cameras were on the beach to record him wading ashore as U.S. snipers carefully plunked bullets into the cameras' field of view.

At the end of the war, MacArthur became commander of the U.S. occupation forces in Japan. In Japan, he demonstrated his real genius—politics. He became, in effect, the uncrowned emperor of Japan, dictated its new constitution, and turned an army-dominated authoritarian state into a modern democracy.

He was there when the Korean War broke out. Soon he would make his strategic masterpiece, along with a series of increasingly disastrous mistakes.

The Land of Morning Calm

Korea, according to someone, was called "the Land of Morning Calm." All American GIs there became familiar with that name, although none could identify the source. They remembered it because it was so ironic. The GIs had other names for the country (most of them are not printable). One that was printable was "frozen Chosen," from "Chosen," the Japanese name for the peninsula, and the ferocious winters. American soldiers shipping out to Korea were told the country had a temperate climate, just like the United States. Sometimes the briefing officer offered more detail: The summer was like southern Louisiana and the winter like northern Minnesota.

Before June of 1950, Korea was not a place the American public cared much about. The U.S. Government didn't care much either. The Soviet Union, however, did care. As the Pacific War was about to end, Russian troops swarmed into Manchuria and Korea, held by a Japanese military so denuded it could not even be called a skeleton force. Korea was, under the Yalta agreement, to become an Allied trusteeship governed by the "Big Four"—the United States, the U.S.S.R., Britain, and China. The United States and the U.S.S.R. agreed to occupy Korea jointly, with their zones separated by the 38th parallel.[5] There was never an attempt to implement a trusteeship governing a united Korea.

Washington left Korea up to MacArthur. MacArthur, dealing with a multitude of issues in Japan, issued an uncharacteristically hasty "occupation" decree, as if the ancient kingdom were enemy territory instead of a liberated country. The U.S. commander in Korea, Lt. Gen. John Hodge, continued in power through the Japanese colonial government and its Gestapo-like police. Eventually Washington abolished the colonial government and ordered Hodge to implement a democratic government. By that time, Hodge had been so thoroughly attacked by Korean leftists he had aligned himself with the wealthiest and most conservative elements in South Korea.

Hodge replaced the colonial police with a new force, equipped with old Japanese rifles and surplus American jeeps. MacArthur turned down his proposal to create a 50,000-man army. The head of the U.S. Far East Command (FECOM) seemed to have a lingering idea that Korea was really part of Japan. He allowed a "constabulary" of 25,000, organized like an army but equipped with nothing heavier than mortars. After the U.S. forces withdrew from Korea in 1948, the constabulary was upgraded to a 100,000-man army, given some obsolete anti-tank guns, 2.36 inch bazookas, and 100 obsolete howitzers.

The Russian occupation was a complete contrast with the American. The Russians set up a Communist dictatorship under Kim Il Sung, who had been born in Russia, a Korean son of refugee parents. There were a lot of ethnic Koreans in Russia, descendants of people who had fled the Japanese. Many had served in the Red Army in the war against Germany. They formed the basis of a new North Korean Army, along with other refugee Koreans who had fought with Mao Zedong's Chinese Communist army. The Russians supplied the North Koreans with tanks, especially their excellent T-34, artillery, machine guns, mortars, and small arms. They trained the North Koreans in Russian tactics.

MacArthur's headquarters got reports of North Korean troops massing on the borders, but no one worried. At FECOM headquarters, the opinion was that the troop movements were just posturing. Washington certainly didn't worry. The next war, if there were such a thing, would begin—and end—with an exchange of nuclear bombs and missiles. It probably wouldn't happen, because that would mean the end of civilization, if not the human race.

One reason MacArthur didn't worry was that the United States had local air superiority and sea supremacy. In the Pacific, control of the air and sea let MacArthur isolate islands at will. Korea wasn't an island, but it was a peninsula—a narrow peninsula with very few roads.

War

On June 25, 1950, the North Korean army rolled across the border. The pitiable South Korean army had nothing that could stop a T-34 tank, and had nothing to answer the North Korean 122-mm guns and 120-mm mortars. After some brief resistance it fell back. As soon as he heard of the invasion, U.S. President Harry Truman ordered all naval and air units to guard the evacuation of American civilians from Korea.[6] The United Nations Security Council, which the Russians were boycotting, ordered North Korea to withdraw its forces behind the 38th parallel. The next day, Truman ordered U.S. naval and air forces to help the South Koreans. The same day, the U.N. Security Council voted to intervene militarily and make MacArthur commander of U.N. forces.

There were no U.N. forces in the area except four American divisions occupying Japan.[7] That, MacArthur believed at first, would be enough. He had air and sea superiority. However, he had to move quickly before the South Korean army was wiped out. The troops occupying Japan were scattered all over the country. There was no time to lose, so MacArthur began feeding units into Korea in a piecemeal fashion. The first units had no tanks or self-propelled artillery and almost no anti-tank shells for their howitzers.[8] Battalions—and even companies—found themselves facing divisions. There was no continuous line. North Korean units were able to envelop or threaten to envelop American and Republic of Korea (ROK) units that tried to stop them.

MacArthur quickly learned that no peninsula is an island. His World War II strategy of isolation didn't work. After a few successful strafing missions by U.N. planes, the North Koreans moved at night and hid in the wooded mountains during the day. Except for their armored units, most of the troops walked. They could not be stopped by anything but strong ground forces.

More troops and equipment got to Korea from Japan, and then the first non-American troops, a British unit. The U.N. troops in Korea—ROKs, Americans, British, among others—now constituted the U.S. Eighth Army, commanded by Lt. Gen. Walton "Johnny" Walker. Walker created a perimeter defense around Pusan, Korea's largest port. Reinforcements continued to pour in. Even then, it was touch-and-go. Walker had to shift units around continually to meet the threat of North Korean breakthroughs. One unit, the 27th Infantry Regiment, became known as his "fire brigade," because it was rushed from point to point to meet each threat.

Inch'on

Whenever there's fighting on a peninsula, the side that has command of the sea naturally considers landing troops behind the enemy's lines. The outnumbered Japanese in Malaya did that repeatedly, driving their British enemies back to Singapore. It isn't quite as easy as you'd think, though. The attacker must try not to land in an area held by the enemy's reserve troops, and he must have sufficient forces to damage his opponent. Small units can land a short distance behind the enemy to achieve local success. That's what the Japanese did again and again. Larger units may strike farther back and threaten much larger enemy forces.

Soon after hostilities began, MacArthur approached the Joint Chiefs of Staff with a proposal for an amphibious landing behind the North Korean lines. As former army combat historian Bevin Alexander says, "The remarkable thing about this plan is that it is what the situation practically demanded, and yet MacArthur had to fight a dogged battle with the top American military leadership, the Joint Chiefs of Staff, to get it approved."[9]

The one Allied attempt at this sort of envelopment in World War II was the landing at Anzio, in Italy. Unlike the Japanese, the American-British expedition did everything wrong. It was aiming for a major envelopment, but it wasn't far behind the German lines and it was close to Rome, a key position. It achieved surprise, but the commander, Maj. Gen. John Lucas, took the instructions of his superior, Gen. Mark

Clark, too seriously. Clark told him "don't stick your neck out." As a result, Lucas lost the advantage of surprise and the Germans surrounded his force and besieged the beachhead. Anzio just missed becoming a disaster. However, it was a vast waste of resources.

The navy didn't object to amphibious landings per se, but it didn't like MacArthur's choice of a landing site, Inch'on, Korea's second largest port. Inch'on was far from the battlefield and is adjacent to Seoul. More important, Inch'on Harbor had a narrow entrance along with enormous tides. The difference between high and low tide could be as much as 35 feet. At low tide, the water ran out of the harbor exposing mile-wide mud flats that could not be sailed over or walked upon. The navy proposed landing at Kunsan, just a short distance behind the North Korean lines.

MacArthur knew that would be too close to the enemy's main force and it could become another Anzio. Besides, Seoul was a nerve center. Korea's principal north-south communications passed through or near the city. He knew the North Koreans were trying desperately to break through the Pusan Perimeter. Almost all their forces would be there. Inch'on and Seoul would have few troops. MacArthur exerted all his powers of persuasion. The Chiefs gave in.

MacArthur left nothing to chance. He even had navy Lieutenant Eugene Clark land on an island at the mouth of the Inch'on ship channel. Clark stayed on the island for two weeks, checking on conditions in the harbor. He commandeered a motor boat for scouting. He captured 30 North Korean boats, as well as a number of North Korean policemen and soldiers. The North Koreans knew there was some guerrilla operating off the coast, but they never suspected a landing at Inch'on. When the invasion began, Clark turned on the long-dead navigational light in the channel. He was later awarded the Navy Cross.

U.N. forces made feints at landings on both the east and west coasts. Then an enormous invasion fleet appeared off Inch'on and smothered the North Koreans with a bombardment greater than they had ever experienced or even imagined. The First Marine Division, a unit cobbled together at MacArthur's insistence (he wanted specialists in amphibious landings) led the invasion, followed by the Seventh Infantry Division. The tiny North Korean garrison was overwhelmed.

Ridgway later called the landing a "5000-to-1 gamble."[10] It was actually a piece of cake. The only serious opponent was the tide, and all the overcoming that it took was the proper timing. In World War II the Allies had overcome vastly tougher conditions in both the Pacific and Normandy.

But because the Joint Chiefs had opposed it so strongly, the Inch'on landing is still described as nearly miraculous. More important, because the Joint Chiefs had opposed it so strongly, and MacArthur had proved them wrong, they now assumed that MacArthur was infallible. He had to work hard to change that opinion.

Wonsan and the Yalu

The North Korean army (the Korean Peoples Army or KPA) had taken heavy losses around Pusan. All of its 150 tanks had been destroyed—some by airplanes, some by artillery, some by American tanks, and some by the brand-new 3.5 inch "super bazooka." Its air force was gone as well. For a short time after the Inch'on landing the KPA continued fanatically trying to break through the Pusan Perimeter. Then the KPA broke. Panic-striken North Koreans began dashing northward, with Johnny Walker's Eighth Army in pursuit. There was no question that the U.N. forces could reestablish the border along the 38th parallel.

MacArthur, however, wanted to destroy the North Korean forces. He also wanted to destroy North Korea—something for which there was no U.N. mandate. To destroy the KPA, he'd have to cut it off. The peninsula was mountainous and the roads were both scarce and terrible, but the North Koreans were in no condition to defend territory.

MacArthur decided against moving overland. He'd use the Inch'on landing force, designated the X Corps and commanded by Maj. Gen. Edward "Ned" Almond, his sycophantic and arrogant chief of staff. They would land at the east coast port of Wonsan. The Joint Chiefs saw problems, but after Inch'on they were convinced "father knows best."[11]

Father, however, slipped up. Shipping the X Corps out of Inch'on used up all that port's facilities, cutting the Eighth Army off from badly needed supplies. It also took too long. Most of the KPA was north of Wonsan when the X Corps finally sailed off. By the time Almond's troops got to Wonsan, it had been taken by a ROK force.

The Red Chinese had repeatedly warned that they would not tolerate any threat to Manchuria. MacArthur, who prided himself on his knowledge of "the oriental mind," knew that they were bluffing. He ordered a hot pursuit of the fleeing North Koreans. Scattered U.N. units rushed up the roads through North Korea. Korea gets wider near Manchuria, so the units were soon widely scattered. Chinese began appearing. But even when his troops took Chinese prisoners, MacArthur refused to believe they were more than a few volunteers. His offensive, he said, would "have the boys home by Christmas."

Some U.N. units reached the Yalu River, the border between Korea and Manchuria. Then the roof fell in. Four Chinese field armies pushed between the scattered U.N. forces, enveloped some and drove the rest back precipitously.

The surreal war

The Korean War has been called our "forgotten war." It was certainly our most surreal war. It was surreal from the beginning, as it wasn't a war, but a "police action."[12] Unlike George Bush on the eve of the Gulf War, Harry Truman sought congressional support. But he didn't want a declaration of war. His administration was having enough trouble without the burden of leading the country into a war over some faraway country. The United States was acting in support of the United Nations, the quasi-world government which was supposed to eliminate war. Fortunately for Truman, the Soviet Union had walked out of the Security Council and could not veto the U.N. action. So the Korean War, which, if you except the two world wars and the Civil War, killed more Americans than all our previous wars *combined* (and also killed a million and a half people who were not Americans) wasn't a war. Fighting it was a United Nations army (which meant it was a South Korean and American army with a sprinkling of other nations). The British Commonwealth contribution eventually grew to a division. Turkey sent a brigade. France, Belgium, the Netherlands, Greece, Thailand, Ethiopia, and the Philippines sent a battalion each.

When China entered the war it got more surreal. Four Chinese field armies, their organization, equipment (including artillery), and chain of command all intact, had "volunteered" to serve Kim Il Sung in Korea. The Chinese government was not involved. China, was not at war with anyone. U.S. soldiers on leave were able to go to Hong Kong and from there visit Red China. There was a reason for all this hocus pocus, and it affected both Truman and Mao Zedong, the Chinese dictator.

The Cold War between the U.S.A. and the U.S.S.R. was at its height. Both countries had hoards of nuclear weapons and each was afraid the other would use them. Economizers in the U.S. Government had cut back the American military tremendously, but the Soviet Union was supposed to have 175 army divisions ready to roll across Western Europe. A war—even a local war in Korea—might escalate into World War III, which most people considered a synonym for mutual nuclear suicide. A war between China and the United States would greatly increase the chance of escalation.

One person who didn't worry about escalation was Douglas MacArthur.

Dugout Doug hits the panic button

On November 28, 1950, three days after the Chinese offensive, MacArthur, who had ridiculed the notion that China posed a threat, sent a message to the Joint Chiefs of Staff. It was evident, MacArthur told the Chiefs, that the present U.N. forces were "not sufficient to meet this undeclared war by the Chinese....This command has done everything humanly possible within its capabilities but is now faced with conditions beyond its control and strength."[13] MacArthur followed that cheerful report with another on December 3. Unless he got heavy reinforcements, he said, his army would be driven to a tiny beachhead. Then, "facing the entire Chinese nation," it would be destroyed by "steady attrition."[14]

On December 29, the Joint Chiefs told MacArthur, "It is not practicable to obtain significant additional forces for Korea from other members of the United Nations. We believe that Korea is not the place to fight a major war. Further, we believe that we should not commit our remaining available ground forces to action against Chinese Communist forces in Korea in face of the increased threat of general war. However, a successful resistance to Chinese-North Korean aggression at some position in Korea and a deflation of the military and political prestige of the Chinese Communists would be of great importance to our national interests, if this could be accomplished without incurring serious losses."[15]

The next day, MacArthur proposed another idea. If, he said, the government decided "to recognize the state of war which has been forced upon us by the Chinese authorities," it could blockade China; destroy its factories, transportation, ports, and other war-making facilities by naval and aerial bombardment; reinforce the Eighth Army with Chinese Nationalists; and let Chiang Kai Shek's troops raid the mainland.[16]

The infallible MacArthur apparently did not understand or care that a blockade of China would drive all of America's allies wild. And as China had an enormous inland border with the Soviet Union, a blockade would never prevent it from obtaining weapons and supplies. Further, the Allies had bombed Germany, a highly industrialized country, for four years and failed to stop its war-making potential. What would bombing a vast, agricultural country like China accomplish? Besides, no Chinese—Communist or Nationalist—were welcome in Korea. South Korean President Syngman Rhee threatened to pull his ROKs out of the line and drive any Chinese Nationalists into the sea.

The Chiefs replied to MacArthur January 9. "After careful consideration," they said, they turned down his proposals. They told him to defend Korea from successive positions, "subject to the primary consideration of the safety of your troops and your basic mission of protecting Japan."[17]

MacArthur sent a quibbling reply. A beachhead could be held for a while, but there would be losses. "Whether such losses were regarded as 'severe' or not would to a certain extent depend upon the connotation one gives to the term." As to his troops, he said, "The troops are tired from a long and difficult campaign, embittered by the shameful propaganda which has falsely condemned their courage and fighting qualities in misunderstood retrograde maneuver, and their morale will become a serious threat to their battle efficiency unless the political basis upon which they are asked to trade life for time is clearly delineated, fully understood, and so impelling that the hazards of battle are cheerfully accepted."[18]

While MacArthur was telling the Joint Chiefs that the U.N. forces could not hold out...they were doing just that. Furthermore, the Chinese were retreating. The Chinese retreat was due to the primitive logistics of their army. After a period of fighting, the Chinese ran out of supplies. They would then withdraw to reorganize and resupply. That in itself was not significant. What was significant was that the Eighth Army was about to take advantage of that pause. A new war had begun under a new Eighth Army commander—but MacArthur was not yet aware of it.

Ridgway joins the fray

Matthew Ridgway was sipping an after-dinner cocktail on December 23 when Gen. J. Lawton Collins, the army chief of staff called and told him that Johnny Walker had been killed in a traffic accident. He had been selected to replace Walker. Unknown to Ridgway, MacArthur had selected him. Ridgway flew immediately to Japan, conferred with MacArthur and went on to Korea.

As soon as possible, Ridgway toured the front lines. He found a dispirited army. "Even their gripes had to be dragged out of them," he wrote later.[19] And they had many legitimate gripes. Food was sometimes in short supply, frequently delayed. The soldiers' clothing was not adaptable to the Korean winter. And, after a second bitter retreat, the men lacked confidence in the high command. Units had been flanked because there were no supporting troops on either side of them way too often. To men in the field, that indicated that somebody who was supposed to be directing things didn't know his business. Anyone who knew about the FECOM commander's messages to the Joint Chiefs must have had even less confidence in the high command.

Ridgway ordered the field kitchens moved nearer the front lines to the troops so they would always get enough hot food and get it on time. He ordered more winter clothing, and especially gloves. He strengthened the armor and artillery components of the Eighth Army. Helicopter removal of wounded men was instituted and field hospitals set up close to the troops. He told everyone—from corps and division commanders to company and platoon leaders—that from now on, the Eighth Army would move as a unit, with all parts supporting each other.

He told his officers that they had become too road-bound. He was particularly insistent that no units be out of communication. If radios don't work and telephone wires have been cut, he said, use runners. Stay in touch with the rest of the army even if it means using smoke signals.

He reviewed the performance of his subordinates and replaced a number of them. One minor problem was Ned Almond. When Walker commanded the Eighth Army, Almond's conduct bordered on insubordinate, and he ran the X Corps as if it were a private army. Walker was a lieutenant general and army commander. Almond was a major general and corps commander, but Almond was also MacArthur's chief of staff. Ridgway had a meeting with Almond and made it clear that X Corps was part of the Eighth Army and that no corps commander would henceforth enjoy a favored position. "Almond came out of that meeting a very sober guy," said Col. William McCaffrey, the X Corps commander's deputy chief of staff.[20]

The ROK divisions were a particular problem. Most of the higher officers were political appointees. They had been promoted without regard for their military merit, and they often fled at the first sign of trouble. Their men followed their example. As ROKs made up about half of the U.N. army, their performance was a serious problem for Ridgway.

Ridgway knew that the Eighth Army was not ready to take the offensive, and he was sure the Chinese would launch another attack as soon as they resupplied themselves. He ordered a new defense line constructed south of the current battle line. If pressed, the Eighth Army could retire to that. There would be no more routs.

As expected, the Chinese attacked on New Year's Eve. As feared, some ROK units bolted. But Ridgway had set up a line of American MPs to halt the retreating troops. He reorganized the defeated ROKs, fed them, rearmed them and sent them back to the front, where they fought well. The U.N. troops retreated, but they retreated in good order. Seoul had to be evacuated, but the Chinese didn't get very far before they again ran out of supplies.

On January 22, Ridgway struck back. A task force of 1st Cavalry Division troops advanced on Inch'on. Three days later, Ridgway launched Operation Thunderbolt, a major reconnaissance in force. The tactics were traditional, but new to Korea. There were no more columns moving up roads. The troops advanced overland, each unit in contact with its flankers, under cover of the Eighth Army's built-up firepower. Masses of artillery, tanks, mortars and automatic weapons blasted Communist-held hills. Air strikes hit any enemy troops who were located.

The Chinese launched another offensive. The ROK divisions flanking the U.S. 2nd Division fled, but "the 2nd Division performed in the finest tradition of its service in both World Wars," Ridgway reported.[21] The performance of the 23rd Regimental Combat Team (an infantry regiment with its own artillery and armor) he found especially commendable.

This Chinese offensive sputtered out even sooner than the last one, although the Chinese had announced their intention of driving all the U.N. forces into the sea. Meanwhile, Ridgway had asked FECOM staff for a study on "the desirable location of major elements of the Eighth Army for the period February 20 to August 31, 1951."[22]

The staff recommended that the Eighth Army hold its present position until winter was over, then withdraw to the Pusan Perimeter. MacArthur's people still believed the war had been lost. Ridgway was thinking of moving in the other direction. "I disapproved it [the study] at once," he reported.[23]

Ridgway's plan was quite different. The Communists greatly outnumbered the U.N. forces: as many as nine Chinese field armies eventually entered Korea. But the Eighth Army had enormously increased its firepower.[24] Ridgway's objective was clear from the offensive's code name: Operation Killer. He planned to use the UN's firepower, including air power, to inflict the maximum damage to the enemy while keeping U.N. losses to a minimum. Gaining territory was no object. MacArthur approved the plan, but added one modification: recapture Seoul. Possession of Kimpo Airport, which served Seoul, would be a great advantage. Also, the recapture of Seoul would make headlines.

After weeks of meticulous planning, Ridgway was ready to go. He ordered the attack. Just before the troops moved out, MacArthur arrived in Korea. As usual, he was surrounded by a horde of correspondents.

"I have just ordered a resumption of the offensive," said the man who, the month before, had told his superiors the U.N. force would be crowded into a tiny beachhead and annihilated. The offensive had already been planned and ordered by Ridgway, but MacArthur, as usual, got the credit.

At first, Operation Killer seemed to be living up to its name. In one week the IX Corps, operating in the Yang-pyang and Hujin sector, killed 5,000 Chinese while sustaining only small losses. Ridgway hoped to push the Chinese and North Koreans so close they would not have a chance to regroup and resupply. Even if the Chinese were short of equipment, they were not short of brains. They held forward positions with a light screen of troops who nevertheless fought ferociously to delay the U.N. advance. Ridgway continued pressing. Operation Killer was followed by Operation Ripper. Ripper was another killer. All units performed well, even the ROKs. The 1st Battalion of the 2nd ROK Regiment annihilated an enemy battalion without losing a single man. Among other things, the ROKs captured four artillery pieces and seven mortars. But the main enemy forces did not stick around to be ground up by Eighth Army firepower.

"Old Iron Tits" repeatedly tried to envelop Communist units only to find they had melted away before he could close the trap. An airborne drop, intended to cut off retreating Chinese, had to be cancelled when Ridgway learned the Chinese had already left the area. Although capturing ground was no object, the U.N. troops, slogging through Korea's "mud season," soon found themselves just below the 38th parallel.

MacArthur's last blast

Truman decided to issue a public declaration that the U.N. Command was willing to consider a cease-fire. On March 19, the Joint Chiefs of Staff discussed a draft that had been prepared by the State Department. The draft was then circulated to U.N. members participating in the war. On March 20, the Joint Chiefs sent a message to MacArthur:

> *"State planning presidential announcement shortly that, with clearing of bulk of South Korea of aggressors, United Nations now prepared to discuss conditions of settlement in Korea. Strong U.N. feeling persists that further diplomatic effort towards settlement should be made before any advance with major forces north of the 38th parallel. Time will be required to determine diplomatic reactions and permit new negotiations that may develop. Recognizing that parallel has no military significance, State has asked JCS what authority you should have to permit sufficient freedom of action for next few weeks to provide security for U.N. forces and maintain contact with enemy. Your recommendations desired."[25]*

MacArthur replied:

> *Recommend that no further military restrictions be imposed upon the United Nations Command in Korea. The inhibitions which already exist should not be increased. The military disadvantage arising from the restrictions upon the scope*

of our air and naval operations coupled with the disparity between the size of our command and the enemy ground potential renders it completely impracticable to attempt to clear North Korea or make any appreciable effort to that end. My present directives, establishing the security of the command as the paramount consideration, are adequate to cover the two points raised by the State Department.[26]

If the U.S. Government was willing to discuss a cease-fire at the 38th parallel, it was obviously not aiming to "clear North Korea," so MacArthur's complaints were completely irrelevant. Nobody was asking him to conquer North Korea. That had been his own idea from the first. His answer to the Joint Chiefs's query was that his current orders were fine.

There was a great shock in Washington, then among the Joint Chiefs, State Department, and Truman himself when they learned that MacArthur had sabotaged the planned presidential declaration. On March 24, MacArthur had issued a declaration of his own.

It opened with bombast: "Even under inhibitions which now restrict the activity of the United Nations forces and the corresponding military advantages which accrue to Red China, it has shown its complete inability to accomplish by force of arms the conquest of Korea." Then MacArthur inserted his own foreign policy: "The enemy therefore must now be painfully aware that a decision of the United Nations to depart from its tolerant effort to contain the war to the area of Korea through expansion of our military operations to his coastal areas and interior bases would doom Red China to the risk of imminent military collapse." Finally, he set himself—not the United Nations or the President of the United States—as the master of peace and war: "Within my area of authority as military commander, however, it should be needless to say I stand ready at any time to confer in the field with the commander-in-chief of the enemy forces in an earnest effort to find any military means whereby the realization of the political objectives of the United Nations in Korea, to which no nation may justly take exception, might be accomplished without further bloodshed."[27]

MacArthur was far from a fool. He knew that the insulting and arrogant tone he had adopted would prevent the Chinese authorities from even considering Truman's planned cease-fire offer.

At best, MacArthur's declaration was the most blatant example of a military leader defying the civilian government in American history. At worst, it may have caused the deaths of some 20,000 American soldiers and hundreds of thousands of others, both soldiers and civilians.[28]

To say that "Give'em Hell" Harry Truman was furious would be a grave understatement. MacArthur was replaced. Ridgway moved to Tokyo to replace MacArthur, and Lt. Gen. James Van Fleet replaced Ridgway as Eighth Army commander.

Truman's opponents in Congress tried to use MacArthur's replacement to get Truman politically. That presented the strange spectacle of Senator Robert Taft (R. Ohio), the country's arch isolationist, embracing MacArthur, who believed the United States should get *more* involved with Asia. MacArthur tried to make it sound as if the Joint Chiefs of Staff agreed with him but were handcuffed by the civilians, Truman, and Secretary of State Dean Acheson. Unfortunately for MacArthur, the Joint Chiefs also testified. They agreed with Truman. The "Old Soldier" faded away.

And the war ground on. In spite of the efforts of Ridgway and the Eighth Army, the Chinese and North Koreans were able to resupply and reorganize themselves. Once again, Chinese bugles blared through the night air; once again North Koreans filtered through mountain forests in the darkness. U.N. troops were again pushed back. But they weren't pushed back so far this time.

"I been up and down this peninsula like a yo-yo," old-timers used to tell new U.S. replacements. But each time the yo-yo went down, it didn't go as far as the last time. And each time it came up, it went higher.

The Communist offensive petered out; there was some seesaw fighting, and by May the Eighth Army, now under Van Fleet, was again on the offensive. At the end of May, with the U.N. still advancing well north of the 38th parallel, there were new peace explorations. This time, they were between American diplomat George Kennan and Russian diplomat Yakov Malik. The Russian could not do anything directly, but he went through channels to the Chinese government and came back with the word that it would probably consider an armistice.

Talking peace, making war

Alan G. Kirk, the U.S. ambassador to Moscow, met Soviet Foreign Minister Andrei Gromyko. Gromyko said the Soviet Union favored an armistice, although he thought the initial talks should concern only the military solution, with political matters to be discussed at a later conference. He said he couldn't speak for the Chinese government. Kirk knew, however, that the ultra-cautious Russians would never have said that much unless they were pretty sure the Chinese would agree to cease-fire.

On June 28, Washington told Ridgway to offer to discuss a cease-fire with the Chinese and North Koreans. He did. After some preliminary bickering, the talks got underway early in July—first at Kaesong, later at Panmunjom.

What followed was perhaps the most surreal episode of this surreal war. The talks continued for more than two years. And all that time, the fighting went on. In fact, the bloodiest fighting of the whole war began right after the peace talks opened. Van Fleet wanted to straighten his line by taking a mass of mountains in eastern Korea. They later became known as Bloody Ridge, Heartbreak Ridge, and the Punchbowl. The Punchbowl, an ancient extinct volcano crater, got its name for its shape. The other two, from what taking them involved.

This time, the Eighth Army did not encounter screening forces designed to delay them. This time, they hit the North Korean Army main force, which was solidly dug in. The area was heavily mined, and the North Koreans fought from almost-invisible bunkers—deep pits, roofed with heavy logs and dirt showing nothing but small loopholes, behind which there were usually machine guns. Nothing but a direct hit from a 155-mm gun could knock out such a bunker. Every inch of the ridges was zeroed in by the North Korean mortars, including their great 120-mm mortar—a weapon much larger than any mortar on the U.N. side. The struggle for the ridges began in July. It ended in October. Other heavy fighting took place in the Pyonggang-Chorwon-Kumwha "Iron Triangle" and at the "Bloody Angle," just west of Chorwon. During this period, the U.N. forces sustained 60,000 casualties, 22,000 of them being American. Estimated Chinese and North Korean losses for the period were 234,000. For comparison, for the whole beginning of the war, from the first North Korean offensive until Chinese offensive November 25, 1950, American casualties totaled fewer than 28,000.[29]

The forgotten war

The winter of 1951/1952 was followed by a long period of apparent stalemate. Most of the news concerned wrangling over exchange of POWs and a couple of riots at POW camps. Ridgway, with a fourth star, was sent to Europe to replace Dwight D. Eisenhower as commander of NATO forces. But the war hadn't ended. Both the U.N. and Communist armies had dug in. Miles of barbed wire and trenches stretched unbroken across Korea from sea to sea. Dotting the trenches a few yards apart were fighting bunkers, dug into the ground, framed with logs, and covered with sandbags on the U.N. side and soil on the Communist side. On the reverse side of the ridges were other bunkers where the troops lived. On the Communist side, there were large underground command posts and there were tunnels through the mountains. In the tunnels were field artillery pieces and anti-tank guns which the Chinese and North Koreans used to snipe at tanks or Eighth Army soldiers. On the U.N. side were tanks, which had been hauled up to the ridgelines and used as pillboxes. In front of both main lines of resistance (MLRs) were hundreds of square miles of minefields and devilish napalm flares. Between the lines were outposts, listening posts, and artillery forward observer posts. It was, in short, World War I all over again. In 1918, the tank had broken the stalemate of trench warfare, but 1918 did not have the masses of land mines that infested the Korean front, nor the anti-tank guns and the bazookas. Most important, Flanders fields were flat; there were no 6,000-foot mountains.

The last two years of the Korean War did not resemble the 1940 "phony war" in France. There was nothing phony about war in 1952 and 1953. Every night there were at least half a dozen platoon-, company-, or battalion-size actions along the front—usually fights over outposts. These fights were, for the numbers engaged, very bloody. There were "contact patrols" that had no purpose but to draw the enemy's fire. For a period in the summer of 1953, troops of the 5th RCT were pulling two contact patrols a day.

Van Fleet felt that such action was necessary to keep up the combat efficiency of the army. He later said, "A sitdown army is subject to collapse at the first sign of an enemy effort. I couldn't allow my forces to become soft and dormant."[30] Instead, he got a lot of them dead for no good reason. The Chinese launched a few fair-size attacks against ROK divisions in 1952, but the ROKs held firm. In 1953, the Chinese again delivered some major attacks, again mostly against ROK units. They gained a few yards of ground and thousands of casualties.[31] It became obvious that the Communists were not going to go anywhere. Then the Chinese and North Koreans agreed to sign an armistice.

On July 27, 1953, the cease fire began. It is still in effect. The Korean War cost 54,246 American lives. When the peace talks began, the United States had suffered 75,000 casualties. In August 1952, a year after the talks began, there were 41,000 more casualties. When the war ended, there were, in total, 157,530 American casualties.[32]

"Listening Post Alice," the main bunker of sandbag castle, only 10 yards from the enemy line, before September 6, 1952, when it was destroyed by a North Korean battalion—all of whom were killed. (Photo by the author.)

Reported American casualties have always been a sore point with veterans of the Korean War. The Joint Chiefs of Staff, in their Korean Highlights of July 27, 1953, estimated that 24,965 Americans were killed. Even added to the 12,939 missing and presumed dead, that falls far short of the actual total, as does their count of 101,368 wounded but not fatally.[33] That figure of 24,965 was used quite a bit before the records keepers revised it upwards. After that, the favorite figure was the 33,629 "battle deaths." That made it sound as if the other 20,000 or so service people died of whooping cough or the DTs. They died of collapsing bunkers and peritonitis caused by shell fragments and bullets; they were frozen to death in 1950's winter retreat. They died of innumerable causes, but all of the deaths had one thing in common: they wouldn't have happened if the troops had not been in combat in Korea. Nobody worried about "battle deaths" and "other deaths" when reporting on the Vietnam War. They reported that 58,151 Americans died in the Vietnam War, and that's the way they should have reported it.

Most of the casualties in Korea were army casualties. Most of the fighting was infantry fighting and the army furnished 86 percent of the infantry. The marines

Living bunkers on the reverse slope of Heartbreak Ridge in Korea, 1952. The apparent quiet is an illusion. (National Archives)

made up the other 14 percent. The army took 86 percent of the infantry casualties; the marines took 14 percent. Air Force casualties amounted to a bit less than a quarter of the marine casualties, but air force "battle deaths" were slightly higher than a quarter. When you're hit while in the air, you're less likely to live through it. Navy casualties were quite small. Infantry "battle deaths," whether they were army or marine, Korea or World War II, were approximately three times the amount of "other deaths." In Korea, army troops suffered 27,704 "battle deaths" and 9,429 "other deaths." There was a smaller proportion of "other deaths" in Vietnam. That reflects the improved state of combat medicine. The Vietnam totals were 30,904 to 7,274. The total of army deaths in Korea and Vietnam, 37,173 and 38,178 respectively, is quite close. Vietnam lasted more than five times as long as Korea, and the number of men serving in Korea was a small fraction of those serving in Vietnam.

Korea was a very bloody war. The U.S. government for a long time tried to keep that fact buried. In 1952, the FECOM newspaper, *Pacific Stars and Stripes* would print almost anything but combat news. The U.S. government wanted everyone to think that MacArthur's 1950 offensive had knocked the North Koreans out of the war. That line went over pretty well, because Pentagon communiques hardly ever mentioned North Koreans after 1950.[34]

There are a number of reasons why the Korean War is the "forgotten war." For one thing, few people had television. And after the "yo-yo" stopped bouncing up and down, there wasn't much to interest the newspapers. Further, the public had just lived through World War II. It was emotionally jaded. Korea did not involve defense of the country, either. But a very big reason Korea is forgotten is that Uncle Sam wanted us to forget it. Dwelling on a war fought half-way around the world in which thousands of people were killed uselessly is not good for public morale.

Who won?

Bevin Alexander subtitled his book *The First War We Lost*. He maintains that there were two wars. The first, the United States vs. North Korea, we won. We drove North Korea out of South Korea. The second war, the United States vs. China, we lost. China's only aim, he says, was to maintain a buffer state in North Korea.

But our original aim was to save South Korea. We did. Then we let MacArthur pursue his reckless advance to the Yalu. Red China entered the war and drove us back below the 38th parallel. So far, Alexander's thesis is reasonable. But Red China caught the "MacArthur disease" and announced it was going to wipe out the U.N. army. North Korea had been a Soviet satellite. China saw the opportunity to turn all of Korea into a Chinese satellite. But instead of conquering South Korea, it got pushed back well north of the 38th parallel. It finally signed the cease-fire after it piled up thousands upon thousands of Chinese and North Korean bodies fruitlessly trying to break the U.N. line. That may not be an American victory, but it certainly wasn't a defeat.

There is only one reason we *didn't* lose the Korean War.

His name is Matthew Ridgway.

10

A Visitor From the Black World: Edward Lansdale

Allies confer

Vietnam was falling apart. The French had built a poorly-sited fortress at a place called Dien Bien Phu, hoping the Communist Viet Minh would attack it in force so they could be slaughtered. The Viet Minh attacked it in force. They overwhelmed the fortress.[1] The French agreed to leave Vietnam.

The war against the Viet Minh was unpopular in France. French troops in the Southeast Asian colony had to operate on a shoestring. One of the ways they maintained their hold in Vietnam was by enlisting the armies of local warlords. The warlords were affiliated with either of two religious factions (the Hoa Hao or the Cao Dai) or a criminal syndicate (the Binh Xuyen).

On the eve of the French departure, the factions were attempting to take over the government. At the same time, Bao Dai, the former puppet emperor who was now chief of state, was trying to remove his prime minister, Ngo Dinh Diem. Diem didn't want to leave, and the army of the new state had been, for months, on the verge of a coup d'etat.

As the French were withdrawing their support, their allies, the Americans, were starting to aid the newly independent nation. On this day in February, 1955, the French commander in South Vietnam, a General Gambiez, was meeting with a U.S. Air Force colonel named

Lansdale. Edward Lansdale, the French knew, was a much more important person than his rank indicated. The two were meeting to discuss the problem posed by the rebellious factions. The way it began was typical of French-American relations. Lansdale later recalled:

> *A large Alsatian dog...eyed me warily. General Gambiez told me cheerily that he was a guard dog who could attack and kill me at one word from him. I commented just as cheerily that the reason my hands were in my pockets as I sat down was that I had a tiny .25-caliber automatic in my pocket and I hoped the dog didn't make my trigger finger itchy since the gun was aimed at my host's stomach or perhaps a little lower down. Gambiez laughed and took the dog over to the other side of the room. I politely put my hands on top of the table.*[2]

Nobody was mauled by a dog or shot at the meeting, but other than that, it had few positive results. The French hated to leave Vietnam, and they bitterly resented the fact that the Americans were taking their place. At this stage of his career, Lansdale was to find his French "allies" a more difficult and dangerous foe than all of Ho Chi Minh's battalions. And he was not unaccustomed to dangerous foes.

The Philippines

Lansdale had held an Army Reserve commission before World War II, but during the Depression he found that his efforts to make ends meet didn't allow him time for his military duties. He resigned his commission. Later, when the United States entered the war, he tried to have it reinstated. While he was waiting for reinstatement, he joined the new Office of Strategic Services (OSS, the ancestor of the CIA). When he received his commission, it was as an Army intelligence officer, and he continued to work for the OSS. He seems to have been primarily involved with analyzing information in the United States, but the record on his wartime activities is very, very murky.[3]

When the war ended and the OSS was disbanded, Lansdale continued as an Army intelligence officer. In 1945, immediately after Japan's surrender, he was sent to the Philippines, where the United States was trying to help its former colony begin life as an independent country.[4]

Lansdale's brother Ben had served in the Philippines during the war. During a conversation with Ben before he left the States, Ed Lansdale pulled out a pocket harmonica asked his brother if he could remember any songs the Filipino soldiers had sung. Ben said he was too busy with other things to think about songs. He asked Ed why he cared. Ed said he wanted to communicate with Filipinos and it would help "to know their songs, something they hold dear to their hearts."[5] Lansdale, like Orde Wingate, knew that the best source of intelligence about a country is the people who live there.

Lansdale's technique of mixing with the local people produced good results. In his first few weeks in the Philippines, Lansdale completed 23 staff studies for his headquarters or the Pentagon about economic, social, political and military conditions in the Philippines, published a weekly Philippine press analysis and wrote several studies on conditions on the Ryukyu Islands between Okinanwa and Japan.

One assignment took him to the Ryukyus with an Army Counter Intelligence Corps agent, a photographer, and a Nisei soldier acting as an interpreter. He discovered that the local official in charge with distributing food to the islanders was selling it on the black market—while his countrymen were trying to survive on grass soup. He called a public meeting and denounced the official before the crowd of islanders. As he was speaking, his interpreter, Matsue Yagawa, whispered to him that the official had a pistol in the drawer of a desk at which he was sitting. Yagawa had noticed his hand inching toward the drawer.

Edward Lansdale, the CIA's troubleshooter extraordinaire. Working behind the scenes, Lansdale saved democracy in the Philippines and established Diem in Vietnam. (Library of Congress)

"Tell him I know he's got a gun in there and I'm waiting for him to get it," Lansdale said, glancing at the .45 caliber automatic he wore in shoulder holster. "Tell him I want him to take a shot at me so I can kill him right in front of the people."

The official understood English. Before Lansdale's words could be translated into Japanese, he jumped up and shouted, "I don't have a gun! I don't have a gun!"

Lansdale arrested him on the spot. The Americans hustled the Japanese official away from the cheering crowd to a waiting boat. As they proceeded to the nearest jail, the interpreter asked Major Lansdale, "How fast are you on the draw?"

"I don't know," Lansdale replied. "I've never tried one of these holsters." He reached for the gun and tried to whip it out. The gun didn't move. Try as he might, Lansdale wasn't able to tug it free.

"Oh jeez," said Yagawa, his hopes of seeing a modern Wild Bill Hickock crushed, "I thought you were lightning fast. You would have been creamed."[6]

Most of Lansdale's work was in the Philippines. A Communist guerrilla movement, the Hukbo ng Bayan Laban Sa Hapan (Hukbalahap for short and Huk for shorter) had begun during the war. By war's end, the Huks controlled a large part of central Luzon. For a while, they tried to take over the new government by peaceful means. But in 1946, they began an armed rebellion. One time, Lansdale was passing through a village where a Huk agitator was denouncing "American imperialism" as the cause of all ills in the islands. Lansdale stopped his jeep and got out.

"What's the matter," he asked the Huk, "didn't you ever have an American friend?"

Instead of attacking Lansdale, the mob (including the speaker) crowded around him and talked about Americans they knew and liked.

"I teased them with the reminder that these folks they had known were the 'American imperialists' they had been denouncing. They assured me that not a single one of them was. It was a long time before I could get away from the gossipy friendliness," Lansdale later wrote.[7]

Another time, he tried to meet the Huk's "El Supremo," Luis Taruc. He heard that Taruc was visiting his sister, so he drove to her house. He took off his shoes, as a polite Filipino would, and looked inside. He was instantly surrounded by armed men.

"You're a spy," one of them said.

"Don't shoot," Lansdale said. "Look at the floor. You'll get it bloody and she'll have to clean it up! If you're going to shoot me do it outside." The men hesitated. "I didn't say that to be a smart aleck," Lansdale continued. "I was well brought up, too."

He admitted he was an American intelligence officer. His job, he said, was to learn facts and write reports which were read by the president of the United States. It was similar to what they did when they gave news releases to newspapers in Manila. If their news stories were very good, they were picked up by wire services and were published in the United States. The most important ones were read by the president of the United States. But his reports got to the president much faster than their news stories. So, he asked them, "What do you want me to tell the president of the United States?"[8]

But by the time the guerrillas had finished talking, Taruc had departed.

Not all his encounters with the Huks were so friendly. One time, he returned home from a business trip with his car riddled with bullet holes. His wife, Helen, never happy about the Army or the Philippines, became extremely upset.

Back to the Black World

In spite of his wife, Lansdale decided he liked the military life. He applied for, and got, a commission in the regular Army. Then, he asked for a transfer to the newly created U.S. Air Force. He expected the Air Force to be less hidebound than the Army. The Air Force, however, took him out of the Philippines and the work he loved and made him an instructor at its Strategic Intelligence School at Lowry Air Force Base, near Denver.

Meanwhile, the government created a new organization, the Central Intelligence Agency, to coordinate intelligence gathering. Unlike its predecessor, the OSS, the CIA did not at first get involved in paramilitary activities. It might suggest such activities to a committee composed of representatives of the Defense and State departments. Carrying out suggested "dirty tricks" was another and even more secret agency known by the deliberately confusing name: Office of Policy Coordination.

While he was instructing at the intelligence school, Lansdale was bending every ear he could about the Philippines' need for help against Communist rebels. He pointed out that aid had been given to Greece when it was involved in the same sort of struggle. Finally, the Air Force loaned him to the OPC, which a short time later sent him back to the Philippines.

Lansdale returned to Manila wearing the uniform of an Air Force lieutenant colonel, but he was really back in what the regular military call the "black world," the secret milieu of spies, spymasters and covert propagandists.

"Magsaysay is my guy"

While Lansdale was still working at OPC headquarters in Washington, a Filipino friend, Maj. Mamerto Montemayor, brought a young Filipino congressman to visit him. Montemayor said the congressman, Ramon Magsaysay (mag SIGH sigh), who was in Washington to lobby for Filipino war veterans, had some good ideas about fighting the Huks. Magsaysay made an impressive appearance. He was a big man, six feet tall and powerfully built—a giant in the Philippines. Lansdale found his mind even more impressive.

They had a conversation that lasted well into the night. The next day, Lansdale told his superiors about Magsaysay, an auto mechanic who became a guerrilla leader against the Japanese and went into politics after the war.

"I decided he should be the guy to handle [the Huk war] out in the Philippines," Lansdale recalled later, "because of his feeling toward the people and the enemy. He understood the problem, which very few Filipinos or Americans ever did."[9]

Officials from the State Department, the Defense Department, the Air Force and OPC met Lansdale and Magsaysay. As a result, they pressured Philippine President Elpidio Quirino to appoint the congressman secretary of national defense. And Lansdale went back to the Philippines as an intelligence officer with the Joint U.S. Military Advisory Group (JUSMAG). That was his cover—he actually reported directly to the Defense and State departments through the OPC. His mission was to help the new secretary against the Huks and build a power base for Magsaysay.

When Lansdale got to Manila, Magsaysay was out in the field. The American found the Philippine cabinet officers somewhat less than enlightening. The Huks were obviously much stronger than when he had left the islands, but nobody could tell him anything about them or how they had become so powerful. He looked up journalists and politicians he had known during his previous tour. They told him the government was totally corrupt, that Quirino's election was characterized by mind-boggling fraud, that Quirino's brother, Tony, headed a gang of thugs who beat up or murdered any of the President's critics. The government, they said, had lost the support of the people.

After the Huks killed all the personnel at an army hospital and then hacked up the patients with bolo knives, Lansdale drove to the town where the massacre occurred to see what the people thought of the Huks. He was shocked to learn that they still favored the guerrillas. They said the Huks had asked them politely to get off the street, because they were going to attack the soldiers and didn't want any villagers to get hurt. As for the soldiers, they stole the villagers' chickens and pigs, beat up anyone who didn't show what they considered proper respect, or in some cases, shot such people.

Magsaysay had also been out in the field. When he returned to Manila, Lansdale went to his office. As he walked up the steps to the defense secretary's office, he heard running feet and shouts of "sonnamabeech!" He saw Magsaysay chasing a terrified Filipino around his office. When he saw Lansdale, the secretary paused, and the other man leaped out of a window, landed on a first story roof, and jumped to the ground.

"Hey, I was only joking," he yelled. "Can't you take a joke?" Then he dashed for his car.

"He tried to bribe me," Magsaysay explained.[10]

The last thing the Huks wanted was an honest, dynamic official like Magsaysay in the government. Honesty did not commend him to Tony Quirino's thugs, either. Lansdale was able to persuade Magsaysay to send his family to the country for safety and move in with Lansdale at Camp Murphy. There the two had long conversations, and Lansdale was able to suggest ways of making war on the enemy's mind.

Psywar

Lansdale continued getting intelligence personally. He was not a member of the Philippine government so technically he was not an enemy of the Hukbalahaps. Actually, he was the leading representative of "American imperialism"—the Huks' prime bete noire and so a prime target for assassination. They even put a price on his head.

When he heard that Luis Taruc was planning to extend his operations from Luzon to the Visayan Islands in the center of the archipelago, Lansdale took a "holiday" at the farm of a friend on Panay, in the Visayans. Right after he left, the Huks arrived. They heard that an American had been in the vicinity. "Was he a U.S. Air Force colonel?" they asked the local people. The locals didn't think so. This American just played

Visayan songs on the harmonica for them. If he were a colonel, it must be in the Salvation Army.[11] A few days after that, Guillermo Capadocia, the Huk commander on Panay, was killed in an ambush based on data Lansdale had collected. Capadocia's second in command took over. Confused by his new responsibilities, he asked two trusted officers what he should do. They advised him to surrender. He did. The two trusted officers were agents Lansdale had planted among the Huks.

Charlie Company of the Philippine Army's 7th Battalion Combat Team used the phony Huk scam on a grand scale. They wore old, nondescript clothing, did not shave or cut their hair and went barefoot. They lived in the swamps, sang Huk songs and mingled with the real Huks. They provided valuable information and, when conditions were right, engaged their surprised "comrades" in hand-to-hand combat.

At this stage of the war, most of the rifles, cartridges and grenades the Huks used came from the Philippine Army. Lansdale and Magsaysay eventually located the guerrillas' clandestine source of supply. They arranged to have doctored munitions sent to the Huks. A few days later, Huk ambush parties found their grenades exploding prematurely and their rifles blowing up.

The usual response to Communist demonstrations was for police and soldiers to show up with rifles, bayonets, and tear gas. Lansdale tried something new. A supporter of the demonstrations would show up with cauldrons of hot coffee and hot chocolate for the demonstrators. The drinks contained a powerful laxative.

Lansdale's spies were often able to obtain the names of members of particular Huk units. That made possible the "eye of God" gambit. A government officer in a light plane flew over a Hukbalahap unit fleeing from a Philippine Army battalion. He called out the names of Huk officers and told them they were doomed because the government knew all about them. Then he added, "Thank you, our friend in your squadron, for all the information."[12] The Huks held an immediate court of inquiry and executed three of their members who were actually innocent of any treason.

Some of Lansdale's dirty tricks were distinctly grisly. To get a Huk squadron to move out of a particular area, his agents spread the rumor that the forest was haunted by an *asuang*, a Philippine vampire. Then an Army ambush grabbed the last man in a Huk patrol, punched two holes in his neck, drained out his blood and left the body where the next Huk patrol would see it.

Psychological warfare, "psywar" in OPC terminology, involved far more than dirty tricks, however. Lansdale and Magsaysay aimed to eliminate the Huks' support among the villagers.

Reform

The most important thing to do was reform the Philippine Army. No outsider could have done that by giving orders. But Lansdale never gave orders. Instead, he gave coffee klatches. Military and civil leaders often gathered at his house to talk to Magsaysay. While they were waiting to see the secretary, Lansdale served coffee and stimulated conversation. Naturally the talk centered on the war. Many ideas were thrown around.

"He would sit quietly and listen to you talk," said a friend. Then he would sum up what had been said, putting emphasis on points he wanted to make. "Suddenly, you are getting a revelation. You think, 'Oh my God, why didn't I think of this?' Then I made my own judgment. Where did that come from? From myself! But he helped! That's why I would trust a man like him."[13]

Among the ideas that came out of these sessions was using Philippine Army doctors to treat villagers wounded in the fighting and Army lawyers to help poor villagers with legal problems. Until then, the poor were at the mercy of the rich who alone could afford lawyers.

Another idea was the 10 centavo telegram. Any peasant with a problem could send a telegram, at a rate anyone could afford, to the secretary of national defense.

Once Magsaysay complained that whenever he made an inspection of a military post, the soldiers were expecting him. Lansdale suggested surprise inspections. The next thing he knew, Magsaysay was waking him up in the middle of the night to go tearing off to some jungle outpost. Magsaysay discovered a lot of irregularities that way. He responded by transferring and sacking commanding officers. The army began to shape up. Soldiers no longer treated villagers like serfs.

Magsaysay himself came up with the psychological bombshell of the Huk war. Any guerrilla who surrendered and was not wanted on some other criminal charge would be given a chance to farm undeveloped land. If he worked at farming and stayed out of trouble, he would get title to the land. Lansdale was worried because the secretary of national defense had no authority to make such an offer. Making Magsaysay's offer a reality became the main subject of Lansdale's coffee klatches. Enough powerful Filipinos became interested in the idea to have the government create the Economic Development Corporation (EDCOR) and give it public land in the big southern island of Mindanao. The government had preempted the Hukbalahap slogan, "land for the landless."

Honest elections

Lansdale and his friends then took on another Communist slogan. The previous elections had been so corrupt the Huks had been saying that the only way to change the government was with "bullets, not ballots."

In the off-year election, November 1951, Filipinos would elect a third of their senate and many local officials. Lansdale and Magsaysay determined that this would be an honest election. Lansdale flew back to Washington and sought help at OPC headquarters. He came back with Gabriel Kaplan, a New York politician with lots of experience in working with civic groups. Kaplan went to Filipino chambers of commerce, veterans' groups, jaycees, and other organizations, and taught them how vote cheating could be held to a minimum. He urged them to organize and instruct voters. His listeners formed the National Movement for Free Elections (NAMFREL). They taught voters how to make thumb prints on their ballots so election officials could not throw them out because of smudged prints. They also taught them how to spot attempts to smudge prints. Volunteers with cameras would watch polling places to photograph any hanky-panky.

Then Lansdale made up forged Hukbalahap leaflets, using a captured Huk typewriter and a Huk mimeograph machine, urging voters in Manila to boycott the election. Finally, Magsaysay sent soldiers to the polling places to prevent any strong-arm tactics.

Out of five and a half million voters, four and a half million cast ballots. Quirino's party lost heavily. And the Huks lost credibility. Magsaysay was now a national hero.

In the next election, in 1953, Magsaysay ran for president. Elderly citizens sported buttons reading "Magsaysay is my guy" and young women wore buttons proclaiming "I sigh for Magsaysay." Magsaysay traveled to the United States, a trip Lansdale made sure was highly publicized, and had a meeting with U.S. President Harry Truman.

Meanwhile, in 1952, the CIA had absorbed the OPC. Relations between the two agencies had never been warm, and someone in the CIA, reportedly Allen Dulles himself, had told Quirino that Lansdale was not merely an Air Force colonel, but a high-level U.S. spook. Quirino threatened to declare Lansdale persona non grata. John Foster Dulles tried to block that move, but in Manila Gen. Albert Pierson, the current head of JUSMAG, opposed Lansdale's continued use of his agency as a cover. When Lansdale arrived in Manila, Pierson unexpectedly told the press that Lansdale was no longer a member of JUSMAG. That was not a smart move on Pierson's part. Lansdale got a new cover job as assistant Air Force historian in Manila. Pierson lost his command.

The new chief of JUSMAG was no Pierson. Gen. Robert Cannon sent U.S. troops out to watch the polling places in case Quirino's henchmen tried to subvert the Philippine military. An attempt was made to assassinate Magsaysay, and Tony Quirino's men almost got Lansdale, but the election was held.

Magsaysay won in a landslide—2,912,992 to 1,313,991.

Lansdale returned to the United States after Magsaysay's inauguration, ending his long separation from his wife and two sons. A few weeks later, Luis Taruc surrendered. The Huk war was over.

If Ramon Magsaysay was one of the fathers of the Republic of the Philippines, Lansdale was one of the godfathers. In the upper reaches of the CIA, the State Department and the Defense Department, the colonel was considered almost a miracle man.

Lansdale's hope of spending time with his family was shattered when Magsaysay asked that he be sent back to the Philippines temporarily to help implement some of his reforms. Lansdale was in the Philippines when he got an urgent call to go to Vietnam.

Vietnam

The United States had been aiding France in its struggle with the Communist Viet Minh. By the later stages of the war, U.S. taxpayers were financing almost 80 percent of the war's cost. Understanding the situation requires a quick glance at Vietnamese history.

France had conquered Vietnam, along with Laos and Cambodia, in the 19th century. It ruled Vietnam—which it had divided into three parts called Tonkin, Annam, and Cochin China—through a puppet emperor. During World War II, the Vichy government of France allowed its "ally," Japan, to occupy its Southeast Asian colonies, collectively known as French Indochina. French officials governed the country under Japanese supervision. The puppet emperor, Bao Dai, remained a puppet emperor under Japan. The Japanese organized a Vietnamese militia, which they may have planned to use in World War II, but the war ended before that could happen.[14]

Just before the war ended, the Japanese suspected their French collaborators were planning to betray them. They threw all the French in jail and attempted to continue ruling through Bao Dai. But then the Vietnamese militia, led by Ho Chi Minh, proclaimed Vietnam a republic. The Japanese, knowing the war was almost over, did not try to suppress the revolt. Bao Dai abdicated.

When the war was over, French troops, aided by the British, returned to Vietnam.[15] Bao Dai returned, not as emperor but as "head of state."[16] Ho Chi Minh's troops, the Viet Minh, resisted the renewal of French rule. At this point, the Viet Minh was dominated by Communists, but it was not entirely Communist. When the Communists took over all of China, Viet Minh strength increased enormously.

France asked for more American aid but was eventually forced to discuss peace in Geneva. The day after the Geneva talks began, Dien Bien Phu fell. The conferees agreed that Vietnam should be temporarily divided along the 17th parallel, with the Viet Minh controlling the north and the French the south. A plebiscite would be held to determine the fate of the nation.

Nobody had any doubts about the result of a plebiscite between Ho Chi Minh's disciplined Viet Minh and the handful of sycophants around the playboy Bao Dai, who spent most of his time on the Riviera and spoke Vietnamese with a French accent. The Eisenhower Administration was horrified at the prospect. Something had to be done. Ike sent Lansdale to Vietnam.

No friendly place

It didn't take Lansdale long to realize he wasn't in the Philippines. First, there were the Americans. Lansdale's cover was assistant air attache. But the air attache was hostile. He said Lansdale was a CIA man impersonating an officer. When he learned otherwise, he said he outranked Lansdale and had to be shown that Lansdale became a full colonel before he did.

Lansdale really had little to do with the air attache. The CIA station chief was more of a problem. The station chief, Emmett McCarthy, said Lansdale, like the rest of the OPC alumni, was an amateur who didn't understand his craft. He didn't recognize that Lansdale was chief of his own team. In a short time, McCarthy, like General Pierson, took an unexpected trip back to the United States. He was replaced by a more amenable CIA man.

Then there were the Vietnamese. They were heirs to an ancient culture, but technologically, they were far behind the Filipinos. Their school system was atrocious, and most of them were illiterate. Politically, they were light years behind the Filipinos. Under the French, any political activity meant exile, prison, or the guillotine. There were no political parties—only conspiratorial cells. There were sects, though. The Hoa Hao (pronounced "wah how") was a reformed Buddhist group. The Cao Dai ("cow yie") was a syncretic religion with a pantheon of saints—from Confucius to Victor Hugo. Both had been part of the Japanese-sponsored Vietnam militia; both had private armies; and both had factories that manufactured pistols, rifles, submachine guns, machine guns, and mortars.

The sects had been wooed away from the Viet Minh by Captain Antoine Savani of the French secret service. The Binh Xuyen ("bean zwin") is often called a sect, but it was about as religious as the Luchese Crime Family. It was a gang of criminals. All of these groups had connections to the French. However, in the case of the Binh Xuyen, they had very interesting connections.

Like the sects, the Binh Xuyen had been incorporated into the Japanese-sponsored militia. Like the sects, they stayed affiliated with the Viet Minh when the Japanese went home. Unlike the sects, they refused to collaborate with the French. But before long, they had a falling out with the Communists in the Viet Minh. To save themselves, they reached an accommodation with the French. They would, with French help, fight the Viet Minh but only on their own territory. To venture on to French-controlled territory would make them collaborators, and that they would not be. The French ceded them territory on the edge of Saigon. As the war went on, the French gave them more and more territory until they owned almost all of Saigon.[17] And, of course, they controlled all opium, prostitution, and gambling in Saigon, including the biggest casino in the Orient. Finally, the leader of the Bihn Xuyen, Le Van "Bay" Vien, purchased from Bao Dai the position of Saigon police chief for one of his lackeys (with French approval, of course). That accomplished, Bay Vien purged the force of honest detectives. He intended to kill them, but most escaped and found haven with the Vietnam Army. The "good cops" then organized the Military Security Service (MSS) and waited for a change in fortune.[18]

Finally, there were the French. National honor wasn't the only reason they hated to leave Vietnam. They had a financial stake—a big, ugly, financial stake. At least, the secret service, which was part of the French Army, did. The French people were happy to get out of Vietnam. The French government, if not happy, was at least willing. The French Army was unhappy. But the French secret service tried desperately to hang on. To finance the war effort, the French secret service had gotten into the drug trade. Major Roger Trinquier, charged with organizing the hill tribes to fight the Viet Minh, had encouraged them to grow opium and arranged for transportation of the drug to local and world markets. Profits from the opium trade would buy guns for the tribes and provide subsidies to the sects. Captain Savani, known to brother officers as "the Corsican bandit," kept the Binh Xuyen supplied with dope for their opium dens. Opium and its derivative, heroin, went to the Corsican criminal syndicates in Saigon, which sent the drugs to their colleagues in Marseille.

Lansdale had learned of the opium trade on a short inspection trip in Vietnam before his present assignment. He suggested an investigation. In reply, his superiors said, "Don't you have anything else to do? We don't want to open up this keg of worms since it will be a major embarrassment to a friendly government. So drop your investigation."[19]

For years, the United States had been the world leader in the movement to ban narcotics and other drugs.[20] Because of this, the French secret service was against letting Americans have any say in Vietnam. And the Corsican and Vietnamese gangsters would fight to the death against American control in Vietnam.

Lansdale's ostensible job as a member of the American Military Assistance Advisory Group (MAAG) was helping the Vietnam Army organize its psychological warfare section. Under the arrangement worked out with the French, American advisers were paired with French advisers. As time went on, American involvement in the Vietnam Army was scheduled to get heavier and French involvement lighter. But at this point, there was some question about what the French were *really* involved with. Lansdale quickly learned that all of his French colleagues were really secret service agents whose only job was to keep track of him. As in the Philippines, he traveled all over the country to get information. But it was harder here. English was the second language of most Filipinos. In Vietnam the second language was French, which Lansdale did not understand. He always traveled with an interpreter.

A few weeks after Lansdale arrived, the Americans, working through the French, pressured Bao Dai into appointing Ngo Dinh Diem premier. Before the war, Diem had been Bao Dai's interior minister. He resigned in disgust after the puppet emperor forgot about all the reforms he had promised at the time of his coronation. The Japanese asked Diem to be puppet premier in 1944. He refused. Ho Chi Minh offered him a cabinet post when the Japanese left. Diem, an ardent Catholic whose brother had been killed by the Communists, again refused. He tried to form an anti-Communist political party and failed, going into exile in 1950. Since then, he had lived mostly in foreign monasteries. A host of Americans, including Sen. John F. Kennedy and his father, Joseph, Sen. Mike Mansfield and Justice William O. Douglas, considered Diem a hero. Lansdale quickly became the premier's friend, although he recognized that he lacked the political talent and imagination of Magsaysay.

On one occasion, Lansdale, concerned that Diem controlled little more than his official residence and its grounds while Bay Vien controlled almost all of Saigon and its twin city, Cholon, called on the ganglord with a proposition:

> *I suggested that the Binh Xuyen figuratively beat their swords into plow-shares. Their private army could lay down its weapons and, with equipment and material bought with the sale of their underworld enterprises, it might build a much-needed superhighway from Saigon to the sea at Cap St. Jacques (where the Binh Xuyen owned much property). The highway, as their donation to the country, could bear the name of the Binh Xuyen leader.*[21]

Amazingly, Bay Vien liked the idea. He asked Lansdale to arrange a meeting with Diem. Lansdale was congratulating himself on a major psychological coup when Bay Vien stormed out of the premier's palace. He was indescribably furious. One of his advisors said the wrong thing, and Bay Vien shot him on the spot.

Lansdale rushed to Diem's office and asked what had happened. Diem said the gangster had made some sort of "silly" proposal about going straight and using his resources to build a highway. Lansdale pointed out that he had told Diem that was what Bay Vien was going to offer.

"I said that I didn't believe him. I turned it down. After all, the man's a scoundrel."[22]

The factions remained a problem, but Lansdale considered the plebiscite, scheduled to take place in two years, his most pressing problem. He had to build a political base for Diem. He knew that Vietnam's large Catholic minority was strongly anti-Communist, but most of them were in the north, where their votes might easily be "lost" by the Viet Minh. He spread horror stories about what would happen when Ho Chi Minh took over. Hordes of northerners abandoned their homes and moved south of the 17th parallel. (It was all in vain. After Lansdale left, Diem refused to participate in an all Vietnam plebiscite.)

Working with Diem, Lansdale instituted a civic action program that had city-raised civil servants going out to the villages and getting their hands dirty helping the villagers with construction projects. He got Filipino doctors, nurses, and technicians to come to Vietnam to train the local people.[23]

The French had feared that Diem would be an American tool, but they didn't expect the monk-like premier to last long. They still controlled the Vietnam Army, and Diem appeared to exist on the sufferance of the Binh Xuyen and the sects. But Lansdale was making Diem stronger every day. He was outbidding the French for the support of the sect generals. The French were not about to challenge the Americans by ousting the premier. They'd let the Vietnam Army do it.

Lansdale heard rumors of a coup. He called on Trinh Minh The, a guerrilla hunted by both the French and the Viet Minh. Earlier, he had defeated the Viet Minh in battle, but was later betrayed by the French. Now he fought both. He had assassinated a French general in 1951, and in 1953 tried to kill French officials by blowing up the Saigon opera house. Lansdale visited The several times. The guerrilla general said he would call on Lansdale.

That day, Lansdale noticed French security people loitering all over his street. They told him they knew The was on his way, and when he arrived, they'd kill him. With any luck, they added, they'd also kill Lansdale in the melee. The arrived, but he came disguised as the chauffeur for one of his men the French didn't recognize. He agreed to support Diem, and left without the French knowing he'd ever been there. If there were a coup, Diem could escape to The's territory.

Lansdale defused the coup. Just before it was to take place, he invited the commanding general, Nguyen Van Hinh, to come to Manila for a brief visit. Hinh regretted that he wouldn't be able to visit Manila, particularly its night clubs, but said Lansdale could take some of his staff. Lansdale chose the officers who would be key players in the coup. He introduced the officers to President Magsaysay who arranged to keep them busy for a week. The coup never materialized. Under strong American pressure, the French government transferred Hinh, who was also an officer in the French Air Force, to France. Lansdale then had Diem weed out unreliable officers and replace them with others. The American colonel was gradually taking over the training and administration of the Vietnam Army.

The French secret service agents didn't give up. They got Bay Vien to call a meeting of all the factions. Most of them responded to the Binh Xuen leader. The sect-and-gangster convention demanded that Diem include them in the government, take a figurehead position and give the Binh Xuyen vice lords the leading position in the government.

Bay Vien's timing was not very good. His nonnegotiable demands were issued right after the French government gave up all its leadership positions in the Vietnam Army and turned the Army's pay and maintenance over to the Americans. Lansdale had been increasing his hold on the Vietnam Army. Now it was complete.

The Battle of Saigon

About this time, a new American ambassador arrived to complicate the situation. "Lightning Joe" Collins, former U.S. Army chief of staff, arrived on special assignment from Eisenhower. He apparently did not give much weight to the ideas of a mere colonel—certainly not as much as those of his old friend, General Paul Ely, the top French commander. And Collins's ideas about international relations were full of inside-the-Beltway cliches. He talked about the Vietnamese civil service as if there were a real civil service instead of a handful of clerks who never left Saigon. Worst of all, he wanted to give up on Diem because he wouldn't form a "coalition government." A coalition government in Saigon at that time would be like having cabinet officers, senators and congressmen representing the Mafia, the Crips, the Bloods and the Montana and Michigan Militias in present-day Washington.

Collins had been assured by the French officers he knew that the Vietnam Army hated Diem and would not fight for him if it came to a confrontation with Bay Vien and his sect allies. He advised Washington and told Lansdale not to discuss any "substantive" issues with Diem.

From his home on the Riviera, Bao Dai, at the urging of the French secret service, announced that he was replacing Diem. Diem ignored him. Bao Dai sent an officer of his personal bodyguard to take command of the Army. The Army ignored him. Bao Dai, it turned out, had told Bay Vien that he was deposing Diem before Diem got the message.

At midnight on March 29, 1955, Binh Xuyen mortars opened fire on Diem's quarters. The gangsters also attacked army installations at several points. Lansdale rushed to the premier's headquarters and noticed that French tanks were blocking Vietnam Army units from reinforcing the government troops. He told Collins what was happening, and the ambassador said Ely was imposing a cease-fire on the two sides. As Lansdale wrote:

> *I told him that this humanitarian impulse of the French military was coming at a strangely late time. French military men were in close liaison with the Binh Xuen, under the orders of General Ely, and could easily have stopped the Binh Xuyen from initiating the attack on Diem and the Vietnamese Army. It was patently implausible that the Binh Xuyen would have started this fight without tacit French approval. I must conclude that these French military men believed their own fiction that the Vietnamese Army was a pushover for the Binh Xuyen. When that army, caught in ambush and attacked by large forces, showed it was no pushover and started fighting back vigorously, I imagined the heart started to go out of the Binh Xuyen soldiery and that this had shocked the French. A few more Vietnamese troops in town would have chased the Binh Xuyen right out of the city, but the French had prevented this reinforcement.*[24]

Lansdale predicted that a cease-fire would only postpone the day of reckoning, which would be bloodier than anything that would have happened that night. The French put 30,000 men and 400 tanks into Saigon to keep the government and gangster forces apart. The government army had a disadvantage: It had no formal intelligence agency as it had relied on the French secret service. It also had an advantage: The city's population hated the gangsters almost as much as they hated the French.

Lansdale was getting information about the Binh Xuyen and its allies from his own agents, including informers in the enemy organization. He learned that there was dissention. Several of the sect's warlords came over to Diem. Lansdale's information was better than the ambassador's.

On April 26, Collins left for Washington to tell Eisenhower that Diem was finished.

April 28, fighting broke out again. Diem telephoned General Ely and told him his palace was under fire. He said he wanted Ely to know that he had not broken the truce. Then he hung up.

The Vietnam Army counterattacked. Lansdale was right. The fighting was bloody. Much of downtown Saigon was pulverized by mortars and demolition charges in the house-to-house fighting. Most of Bay Vien's sect allies got out of the fighting early, leaving the gangsters to their own devices. Before long the Binh Xuyen were throwing away their identifying green berets and running. In nine hours of fighting, they were driven out of Saigon and were seeking safety in the largely Chinese city of Cholon. The government soldiers pursued them through Cholon and into their original hide-out, a swamp known as Rung Sat, "the Forest of the Assassins."

While the battle was raging, John Foster Dulles, taken in by Collins's report, sent a telegram ordering the embassy to stop cooperating with Diem. Eventually, it dawned on the embassy personnel that Diem was winning. They told Washington. Dulles rescinded his order. The embassy staff burned his first telegram.

Antoine Savani of the French secret service had not forgotten his proteges, the Binh Xuyen. He was with them all through the fighting in Saigon. When the Vietnam Army stormed the Grand Monde casino, they captured 37 members of a French *colon* militia organization Savani had organized. Desperately trying to prevent the complete rout of the Binh Xuyen, Savani took command of their defense in Cholon. It didn't help. The fighting would continue for several more days, but the Binh Xuyen, a criminal organization that had existed for 15 years, was being annihilated.

While the struggle was going on in Saigon, Bay Vien offered a reward for Lansdale. Dead or alive—but preferably alive. The gang lord promised to disembowel the American, fill his body with mud and throw it in the canal. Early the next morning, Col. Jean Leroy, a French-Vietnamese guerrilla leader who had been friendly with Lansdale, appeared at the colonel's house and said he was taking him to the Bien Xuyen. Outside the house was a heavily armed squad of Leroy's soldiers.

"No thanks. I'm not coming," Lansdale said.[25] He then advised the guerrilla that he should disappear, because the Army was pushing the Binh Xuyen back everywhere. While they talked, Lansdale moved closer to a box of hand grenades he had hidden. Then several members of Lansdale's team entered. One of them said he didn't need all those armed men in front of the house, because the Binh Xuyen were in full flight.

"I put my arm around Leroy's shoulders and walked him to the door, where we said farewell," Lansdale recalled.[26]

Diem's revolution

The Binh Xuyen were finished. So were the sect factions that stayed with Bay Vien. Wiser warlords had come over to Diem. Lansdale organized the warlords and other nationalists for another move. They declared that Bao Dai, the non-emperor, was deposed. On May 2, while Ambassador Collins was returning to Saigon, the warlords called on Diem and demanded that he bow to the will of the people and order a plebiscite on the monarchy. At the same time, Nguyen Van Vy, the officer who had tried to take over the Army for Bao Dai, was demanding that Diem leave the country. Vy was saved by old friends in the Army, who took him to dinner, but the process of turning Vietnam into a republic had begun.

The fat lady hadn't sung yet. Two French secret service officers approached Cao Dai warlords trying to get them to turn against Diem. Shots were fired at Americans, and a Frenchman who looked like Lansdale was murdered in front of his house. The shooting was being done by Corsican gangsters and French secret service agents. It stopped after Lansdale arranged to have a number of bombs go off in front of the secret service agents' homes.

In the summer of 1955, the French Army started to go home. In November Diem held the plebiscite on the monarchy, "bowing to the will of the people." To nobody's surprise, Bao Dai was deposed. The vote was 5,721,735 for Diem, 63,017 for Bao Dai. Neil Sheehan says Lansdale "helped Diem rig a plebiscite to depose Bao Dai."[27] Maybe, but it scarcely seems worthwhile to rig an election against anyone as obviously worthless as Bao Dai.[28] And Lansdale was far too sophisticated to rig an election so that his candidate got more than 98 percent of the vote.

The curse of Cassandra

When Lansdale returned from the Philippines, official Washington considered him something of a rainmaker. When he returned from Vietnam, he was the rain god himself. He *was* a prophet, a prophet like Cassandra, the Trojan priestess cursed by Apollo. Apollo would let her see into the future, and she would always speak the truth. But no one would believe her.

Lansdale knew that all was not sweetness and light in Vietnam. He had gotten Diem's approval for a number projects. Army personnel were starting to engage in civic action programs, such as those in the Philippines. Other soldiers went to the Philippines to learn how to fight a "people's war." He established communication lines with allies in the villages and tried to anticipate enemy guerrilla moves by the Viet Minh.[29] He got Diem to agree to the formation of village self-defense forces which would allow the country's traditionally autonomous villages to protect themselves. (After Lansdale left, Diem, on the advice of this brother, Ngo Dinh Nhu, destroyed village autonomy by appointing village officials.)

But Lansdale also knew that Diem's brother, Ngo Dinh Nhu, had too much influence on the new president. Nhu wanted to set up a one-party state. He controlled a secret police force which arrested, imprisoned, tortured, or killed opposition politicians. He founded a party, Can Lao, to which all politicians had to belong. Its initiation included kissing a picture of Diem and swearing undying loyalty to him. Nhu suspected the loyalty of the country's Buddhist majority and began a low-level persecution. Nhu also controlled the secret intelligence service. And like the French secret service agents before him, Nhu revived the drug trade to finance his operations.

Diem, unfortunately was devoted to his brother. Lansdale believed that the president—idealistic, scrupulously honest personally, and strong-willed—would be an excellent leader if he could be removed from Nhu's influence. He proposed a way to do that to two Kennedy Administration officials, W. Averill Harriman and John Kenneth Galbraith: establish an academic position for Nhu at Harvard. Nhu, who fancied himself an intellectual, would be unable to resist. He'd go to Cambridge and Diem would be able to run the country properly. Harriman loved the idea, but Galbraith became angry.

"We don't do that at Harvard!" he said.[30]

The regular U.S. Army had taken over training the Vietnam Army. They were turning it into a mirror image of the U.S. Army. Lansdale said that was all wrong. The U.S. Army was created to serve the United States. The United States did not have a population that for generations had ardently hated its government, and saw its military as oppressors. Vietnam did. Vietnam, he said, needed a native army that actively helped the people as the Philippine Army under Magsaysay did. The U.S. Army gave lip service to the principle of winning "the hearts and minds of the people," but as the grunts in the field put it, "If you get 'em by the balls, the hearts and minds will follow."

Lansdale had been fighting a new kind of war. It wasn't the kind of war the U.S. Army was prepared to fight. The U.S. Army was prepared to fight another Korea. The CIA and the State Department were unprepared for Lansdale's free-wheeling person-to-person style. So the Pentagon gave him a job as an Air Force staff officer in the Pentagon. He was promoted to brigadier general. He tried to get an assignment in the Far East, but the heads of the military and diplomatic establishments overseas wanted nothing to do with him—he upset the established order.

It got worse after the publication of three books. The first, *The Ugly American*, by William J. Lederer and Eugene Burdick, featured a harmonica-playing Air Force colonel who could only have been modeled on Lansdale. His name was Edwin B. Hillandale. Hillandale was a hero, a model of how America's representatives should conduct themselves in a poor Southeast Asian country. But the book was nothing but trouble for Lansdale. Before this, he had been known only in some rather shadowy military and intelligence circles. Now he was famous. This proved, according to his enemies, that he was not only a disruptive force but a publicity-hound.

Next was Graham Greene's *The Quiet American*. That was worse. Greene's character, Alden Pyle, was a naive CIA agent who innocently created death and destruction.

Finally, there was Jean Larteguy's *Le mal jaune*, published in the United States as *Yellow Fever*. Larteguy's Lansdale alias, Col. Lionel Teryman, was a villain: a brutal, uncouth, and fanatically anti-French CIA agent.

On October 31, 1963, after six years of frustration, Lansdale retired from the Air Force with the rank of major general. Soon after, he returned to the States, Lansdale's friend, Ramon Magsaysay, was killed in an airplane crash. Shortly after he retired, on November 2, 1963, another friend, Ngo Dinh Diem, was killed in a coup d'etat. To Lansdale, the coup was a disaster. It would have been a disaster even if Diem were not murdered. The coup destroyed what was left of the Vietnam Constitution that he had helped write.

He returned to Vietnam one last time as an assistant to U.S. ambassadors Henry Cabot Lodge and Ellsworth Bunker. But by that time, U.S. policy had gone so far down the wrong path that nobody could have saved the situation. The British had just put down a guerrilla movement in Malaya by herding villagers into "strategic hamlets," which were surrounded by barbed wire and guard posts. The hamlets weren't like Valeriano Weyler's concentration camps—the villagers could work in the fields during the day, but the guerrillas couldn't come to them at night.

Only Lansdale seems to have noticed the differences between the situation in Malaya and that in Vietnam. The guerrilla forces in Malaya were manned and supported only by Chinese immigrants (who were a despised minority) and not by native Malayans. The Chinese villagers had no attachment to a particular location. To the rural Vietnamese, his village and his fields were integral parts of his being. His ancestors were buried there. His village was part of his family. It was sacred.

The Americans had found the Vietnamese Army didn't come up to their standards of efficiency, so they took over the war. To the rural Vietnamese, these tall white-skinned or black-skinned men looked precisely like the French soldiers, the hated strangers who had oppressed their people for generations. They would help anyone to get rid of them.

Mao Zedong once said the guerrilla depends on the people the way the fish depends on the sea. Lansdale had tried to dry up the sea. The U.S. Army had raised the sea to a comfortable temperature for the "fish" and filled it with nutrients.

Lansdale came home for the last time in 1968. The Tet Offensive, which made obvious years of official lying, had guaranteed that the Vietnam War was lost.[31]

Since then, an effort has been made to remember the sacrifices made by the Americans who fought in that war. But there has been no effort to remember the man who tried so hard to prevent the government's mistakes. So Ed Lansdale, America's greatest fighter of "people's wars," is almost forgotten today.

But as one who always sought the shadows and spurned the limelight, that's probably how he would like it to be.

Afterword

Afterword

The phrase "New World Order" was popularized by George Bush (the first), but it was given a sinister slant by spokesmen for Christian fundamentalism and the militia movement. These scare merchants told tales of conspiracy featuring wild radicals—such as Bush. Traitors in Washington were supposed to be bringing in foreign troops, who were already patrolling in black helicopters. They would disarm the U.S. population and turn the government over to the United Nations. Of course, there has never been the slightest evidence for any of that. There are no black helicopters nor plans for a takeover of the U.S. by the U.N.

There is a new world order, though. Look at the illustrations in Richard Meinertzhagen's books, *Army Diary* and *Kenya Diary*. Those photographs of Kikuyu warriors, carrying spears, shields, swords, and clubs—but wearing absolutely nothing—seem as far from today's world as statues of Athenian warriors in helmet and breastplate. When World War II began, there was but one country in Africa, Liberia, that was not bound to a European nation by some sort of colonial tie. Today there are no colonies in Africa.

Today, India and Pakistan, homelands of Jan Christiaan Smuts's despised "coolies," are independent countries. They have fought each other repeatedly with jet planes and tanks and are now threatening each other with nuclear missiles. Central Asia, long under the heel of Russia, and Southeast Asia, and long dominated by Britain, France, and the Netherlands, are free and independent. The grim

233

and purposeful Chinese Army that faced Matthew Ridgway was light years from the bluster-and-boast Imperial armies of the Taiping Rebellion.

True enough, but most of those changes occurred well after the people mentioned in this volume. How are they involved?

Change comes slowly, but it has to start somewhere. A sense of nationality has to grow in places like Central Africa where there was only a tribal outlook or in Central America where there wasn't even that. Even so, the nationalism Walker stimulated in Central America forced the British to give Ruatan back to Honduras while Walker was still alive. That, in fact, set up the chain of events that led to his death. Nationalism still hasn't totally replaced tribalism in Africa, as that continent's gory record of civil strife attests. But African countries managed to gain their independence anyhow.

Before the Africans could fight for independence, they had to believe they could do it successfully. Defeat after defeat had led them to believe they could not beat the white men. Von Lettow-Vorbeck taught them they could, and Wingate reinforced the lesson.

The Chinese did not lack a sense of nationality. Pride led them to fight against the European encroachers. However, their armies were hopeless. Ward taught them that Chinese could fight in the Western manner and do it successfully. Mishandling of the Ever Victorious Army by his British successors and suspicion by their Chinese superiors destroyed Ward's creation. But the idea lingered on. When China fought Japan in 1894, it had modern warships. It lost that war, but the war that began in 1937 was a different story. In spite of being beset by civil war, China became an insoluble problem for Japan, leading to its desperate attack on Pearl Harbor.[1] Today, China is universally recognized as one of the world's greatest powers.

Of course, a nation needs more than confidence to win its independence. Weapons are a big help. Former colonial countries were always outgunned when they began their struggles for independence.[2] That's where Childers came in. He proved that a weak power could win its independence by appealing to world opinion.

Not all the leaders celebrated here wanted to end colonialism. Funston certainly didn't. But by "winning the hearts and minds" of Filipinos, he started their islands on the road to democracy, which made independence inevitable. That's something the French never did in their Indochinese colonies. A couple of generations later, Lansdale came along and completed Funston's work in the Philippines. He failed in Indochina, which became independent—but undemocratic and hostile.

Mosby fought for the Confederacy, which was based on slavery—an evil that made people even less free than colonialism. But as a diplomat, he fought against the excesses of Westerners in colonial Hong Kong. And as a federal official in the West, he fought a kind of American feudalism that is today largely forgotten.[3]

These shadowy soldiers accomplished far more than giving colonialism a shove on the road to oblivion. They were, after all, soldiers, and most of their accomplishments are military. Wingate, besides being one of the founders of Israel, broke new ground in strategy. His air-supplied "strongholds" were precursors of the U.S. Army's "air cavalry" tactics, even though he had no helicopters. Childers waged what is probably the most effective psychological warfare campaign in modern times. Lansdale and Funston both excelled in the seldom-successful skill of counterinsurgency, and they did it without resorting to the brutality of General Weyler or Lord Kitchner. Captain Jack is the only Native American leader who, though vastly outnumbered, made fools of the U.S. Army. Fred Ward invented new tactics based on river boats that were even more successful than those used shortly afterward in the American Civil War. Under von Lettow-Vorbeck, German East Africa introduced an astonishing array of innovations, from truck tires made of rope and raw latex to salt distilled from wild plants and a whiskey distillery in the jungle.

All have done their part to create the modern world.

Endnotes

Endnotes

CHAPTER 1: THE "GRAY-EYED MAN OF DESTINY"

1. Richard Harding Davis in *Real Soldiers of Fortune* (p. 187) attributes a last statement to Walker. Noel B. Gerson in *Sad Swashbuckler: The Life of William Walker* (p. 148) says Walker declined to make a statement. So does Albert Z. Carr in *The World and William Walker*, p. 271. Walker's alleged statement: "I die a Roman Catholic. In making war upon you at the invitation of the people of Ruatan I was wrong. Of your people I ask pardon. I accept my punishment with resignation. I would like to think my death will be for the good of society." That sounds like something cooked up by what passed for the propaganda ministry of the Honduras government.

2. Gerson, p. 148, says there were three volleys.

3. See William Weir, *Written With Lead*, pp. 14-35.

4. "Filibuster" comes from the Dutch *Vrijbuiter*, which stems from *vrij* (free) and *buit* (booty). The meaning is the same as its English derivative, "freebooter" ("pirate," not, as some believe, "wanderer"). The Spanish took the Dutch word and modified it to make it easier for Spanish speakers to pronounce—*filibusteros*. It still meant pirate. The Americans took the Spanish word, only slightly modified, to describe those adventurers, primarily American, who pursued the soldier of fortune's trade in foreign countries, primarily in Latin America. The behavior of all filibusters was obstreperous, so "filibuster" came to be applied to the obstreperous behavior of legislators who tried to block or delay legislation. (See Anne H. Soukhanov, *Word Mysteries & Histories*, pp. 85-86.)

5. William Walker, *The War in Nicaragua*, Foreword by Robert Houston, p. 3.

6. Frederic Rosengarten, Jr., *Freebooters Must Die!* p. 1. Some say that universities at that time were little better than high schools. If so, Walker would still be precocious, but not as precocious as it might seem. But consider two points:

   1. Few people graduated from high school in those days, and far fewer from universities;

   2. To be admitted to the University of Nashville, the student had to be proficient in Latin and Greek as well as English grammar and mathematics.

   Once in, the student studied calculus, navigation, astronomy, chemistry, geology, philosophy, logic, constitutional and international law, rhetoric, oratory, natural history, and, of course, more Greek and Roman classics. William O. Scroggs, *Filibusters and Financiers*, p. 11.

7. Walker, *The War in Nicaragua*, Foreward by Robert Houston, p. 2.

8. Gerson, p. 41.

9. Gerson, p. 42.

10. The author, a pretty good, but far from sensational pistol shot, can cut a playing card edgewise at well over eight paces while using the typical duelist's standing, one-hand stance. For anyone to unintentionally miss a man-size target at that distance is almost unthinkable.

11. Gerson, p. 44; James Jeffrey Roche in *By-Ways of War*, p. 58-59, says Walker was hit in the foot, but tried to hide the blood from the wound. Roche apparently confuses this duel with a later one that occurred right before Walker embarked for Mexico. In that duel he was hit in the foot, and the wound hindered his preparations for the expedition.

12. Gerson, p. 45.

13. The silver ore in northern Sonora was supposed to be so rich you could find nuggets of pure silver in it.

14. A few years before this, Americans had annexed almost half of Mexico.

15. Melendrez was later to write a self-serving memoir about how he drove Walker out of Mexico. He was the first of a string of Latin "heroes" who accomplished deeds on paper they never would have dared to do when Walker was alive.

16. Ward's biographer, Caleb Carr, in *The Devil Soldier* (p. 59) quotes one of the deserters who said the men left because Walker was "vain," "weak-minded" and "cruel." Carr says Walker was "a confirmed advocate of slavery," which is the opposite of the truth. Walker not only endangered his job and his life by campaigning against slavery in New Orleans, he also campaigned against a proposal to annex Cuba and make it a slave state. In California, Walker aligned himself with the anti-slavery wing of the Democratic Party. When he addressed the Democratic state convention in 1854, pro-slavery elements started a riot. Carr says

Ward's "shame at having served under the 'King of the Filibusters' was very real." His shame at having deserted his comrades before the going got rough may have been real. After the exodus of half of Walker's first recruits, the loyalty of his remaining followers under the most trying circumstances in Mexico and later in Nicaragua is remarkable.

17. Davis, p. 158.

18. E. Alexander Powell, *Gentleman Rovers*, p. 190; Davis, p.159; Roche, p. 71.

19. Gerson, p. 61.

20. Lucius Beebe and Charles Clegg, *The American West*, p. 68. After 1855, a trans-Panama railroad was available to travelers.

21. In the 1850s, Britain controlled most of the world's maritime bottlenecks: the Straits of Gibraltar, the Cape of Good Hope, Aden, Singapore, and—through its base on the Falkland Islands—Cape Horn. There was also heavy settlement of British nationals in Patagonia and strong British influence in the sheikdoms of the Persian Gulf. Control of these choke points enabled Britain to dominate international commerce.

22. After Napoleon had been disposed of, the British government called on the Duke of Wellington for advice on how to handle the Americans. Wellington studied the appropriate maps and advised the ministers to make peace as quickly as possible.

23. Among other tests, he hired an extremely pretty young woman as a receptionist. Any potential filibusters who ogled her were automatically rejected. See Gerson, pp. 64-65.

24. Gerson, p. 69; Carr, pp. 124-127.

25. The type of rifle is not known, but some or all of them were probably the Sharps, a breech-loader that was the favorite weapon of buffalo hunters, target shooters, and Free Soil guerrillas in "Bleeding Kansas." The Sharps was by far the best breech-loader of the pre-metallic cartridge era, and was noted for its accuracy, power, and—although not a repeater—rapidity of fire.

26. Walker, p. 53.

27. Davis, p. 163; Gerson, p.70; Albert Z. Carr, p. 126; Wallace, p. 167.

28. Davis, p. 164; Gerson, p. 70.

29. Walker, p. 94.

30. C.W. Doubleday, *Reminiscences of the "Filibuster" War in Nicaragua*, p. 163.

31. Albert Z. Carr, p. 131; Gerson, p. 73; Wallace, p. 170; Davis, p. 169; C.W. Doubleday, p. 163. James Carson Jamison, *With Walker in Nicaragua*, p. 39, says 80 enemy dead were buried.

32. Albert Z. Carr, p. 147.

33. "Conscription" resembled the old English press gang. In *The War in Nicaragua*, p. 72, Walker says, "There is scarcely any labor a Nicaraguan will not do to keep

out of the clutches of the press-gang; and their immunity from this dreaded evil by the presence of the Americans in the country, gave the latter much of the moral power they possessed over the native population. The laborers and small proprietors run more risks to escape military duty than they are generally required to meet, if they are so unlucky as to be caught by the recruiting sergeant."

34. The Costa Rican army included a number of English, French, and German mercenaries. Roche, p. 134

35. Gerson, p. 93; Albert Z. Carr, p.176; Scroggs, p. 183; Walker, pp. 181-185.

36. Walker, p. 197.

37. Albert Z. Carr, pp. 178-179; Walker, p. 204.

38. Scroggs, p. 193, cites documents proving that the new weapons were rifles, rather than smooth-bore muskets.

39. Walker, p. 207, says that the Costa Ricans got cholera because they dumped dead bodies down wells. Maybe. He was there, after all. But the story defies common sense. Cholera had been raging in Nicaragua before the invasion. Large numbers of wounded men with lowered resistance in hospitals with poor sanitation would have produced a virulent outbreak in Rivas. Walker was later to have the same trouble in Granada.

40. As if the Costa Ricans had ever been merciful.

41. Walker, p. 211; Wallace, p. 195, says only 400.

42 Albert Z. Carr, pp. 185-190; Scroggs, pp. 196-197.

43. The ship is often described as a Costa Rican vessel. It was not. Salazar was a Nicaraguan citizen, and he was pretending the ship was a United States vessel. A state of war still existed between Nicaragua and Costa Rica, and Salazar was guilty of trading with the enemy.

44. In their correspondence, the Leon faction accused Walker of wanting to destroy Central America's language, culture and religion. Walker spoke their language, had adopted their culture, and soon would convert to their religion.

45. They, too, had powerful friends. When local authorities in Greytown gave the Transit Company trouble. In May 1854, they arranged for the U.S. Navy to send a warship to bombard Greytown.

46. Vanderbilt had juggled the books so that all the profits from taking people across Nicaragua went to the ocean-going steamship line, with none to the Transit Company. As for the $10,000 annual payment—Vanderbilt's answer to that and to any other inconveniences was summed up in his most famous statement: "The public be damned."

47. Walker, p. 255.

48. Walker, p. 266, is brutally frank about his desire to curry favor with the Southern states while keeping Nicaragua an independent country. "While the slavery

decree was calculated to bind the Southern States to Nicaragua, as if she were one of themselves, it was also a disavowal of any desire for annexation to the Federal Union."

49. Vanderbilt eventually discontinued the Panama route after the company that had pioneered the route agreed to pay him a $40,000 a month "subsidy" (a polite word for a kickback).

50. Albert Z. Carr, p. 204.

51. Walker, pp. 288-289.

52. Jamison, p. 133.

53. Wallace, p. 219.

54. The Minie rifle was one that used the bullet invented by Captain Charles Claude Etienne Minie of the French army. Most muzzle-loading rifles were slow to load, because the bullet had to fit the bore tightly so the rifling could spin it. Minie's bullet had a hollow base. It was easy to load, because it was smaller than the bore, but when the powder ignited, the explosion expanded the hollow base to fit the bore. The Minie rifle wasn't as good as the rather rare and expensive breech-loaders, but it was far better than any other muzzle-loader.

55. Walker, p. 349.

56. Albert Z. Carr, p. 216.

57. Albert Z. Carr, p. 217.

58. Albert Z. Carr, p. 218.

59. He probably would have been, but he didn't realize it at the time. If he had, he wouldn't have surrendered.

60. Actually, he had become president the way most Nicaraguan presidents had, and he had lost his office the same way.

61. It did, of course, but such niceties have never bothered major powers when dealing with small countries.

62. Walker, Foreword by Robert Houston, p. 11.

63. Albert Z. Carr, p. 270.

64. Davis, p. 186.

65. Powell, p. 215; Walker, Foreword by Houston, p. 11.

CHAPTER 2: THE YANKEE GOD OF WAR

1. Chinese authorities had boarded a Chinese schooner, the *Arrow,* with a Chinese crew and arrested several crew members. Because the schooner had once been registered in Hong Kong, the British decided that their flag had been violated although the registration was no longer valid. It made no difference that the sailors were released soon after their arrest. See Byron Farwell, *Queen Victoria's*

Little Wars, p. 138. In the First Opium War, the British sacked China's major coastal cities and forced it to open five ports for trade. China had to pay $21 million for opium it had destroyed, as well as give Hong Kong to Britain. China still refused to legalize opium although it was afraid to enforce laws against it. After the Second Opium War, it legalized the drug, gave the British Kowloon on the mainland opposite Hong Kong, and paid massive indemnities to Britain and France. See Alfred W. McCoy, *The Politics of Heroin*, pp. 86-87.

2. The very fact that Chinese officials in central China could ask for assistance from the same nations that were invading their country in the north shows the near-anarchy that existed in China at the time.

3. When the British took Hong Kong, they began a campaign against the pirates who infested the South China Sea. The pirates moved inland and conducted their business on China's great rivers. See Jonathan Spence, *God's Chinese Son*, pp. 81-84.

4. As it was when the Imperialists captured a city.

5. Caleb Carr, *The Devil Soldier*, p. 69.

6. A.A. Hayes, a Shanghai merchant, quoted in Carr, p. 65.

7. All governmental and social rank in China depended on proficiency in government examinations on the Confucian classics.

8. Spence, pp. 42-43.

9. Spence, p. 127.

10. Carr, pp. 85-86.

11. Charles Schmidt, an officer who served with the Ward Corps from beginning to end, said of Vicente Macanaya: "If real bravery consists of an undauntedness of spirit, a cool presence of mind, and active physical exertion, then all these qualities are combined in Vincente [sic] to a degree that leaves no doubt on the minds of the many friends who know him, and have seen him so fearless in the midst of danger." Carr, p. 91.

12. E. Alexander Powell, *Gentlemen Rovers*, p. 230; Carr, p. 108.

13. Charles Schmidt, quoted in Carr, p. 119.

14. Carr, p. 119.

15. Carr, p. 148.

16. Carr, p. 156.

17. Chinese military units at the time carried banners identifying themselves. Ward's troops chose a banner with a single Chinese ideogram, "Hwa."

18. Saxton T. Pope, *Bows and Arrows*, pp. 23-27. Pope says of a bow he tested, "Apparently the Chinese conception of warfare entailed the use of dreadful appearances and intimidation, and that these principles applied to bows do not make them more efficient engines of destruction." Pope says the bow appeared to "have

been constructed for some giant in strength." He stated that "When braced, no white man could pull it." By strapping the bow to his feet and pulling with both hands, Pope, a world-famous archer, was able to shoot the bow. But the arrow flew only 100 yards while arrows from an ordinary English longbow flew 250 yards.

19. Carr, p. 190.

20. Carr, p. 208. The mandarin did not explain how Ward was able to "gun down" the two officers with a rattan stick.

21. Carr, p. 248.

22. Augustus Lindley, the English Taiping, wrote of Nan-ch'iao: "Mercy seems never to have entered the minds of these Christian warriors, who loudly inveighed against the Taipings as "blood thirsty monsters," &c., &c....while those who had thrown down their arms were vainly trying to hide or flee from the deadly rifle, or stood blocked in the gateway of the tower, the valorous conquerors calmly and easily continued to shoot them so long as they remained within range." Carr, p. 263. A British officer said of the French at Che-lin: "since the death of Admiral Protet, the French have been behaving like fiends, killing indiscriminately men, women, and children. Truth demands the confession that British sailors likewise have been guilty of the commission of similar revolting barbarities—not only on the Taipings but on the inoffensive helpless country people." Carr, p. 264.

23. Carr, pp. 264-265.

24. Carr, p. 269.

25. Carr, p. 271.

26. Carr, p. 272.

27. Forester claimed he had climbed a tower to see where the enemy troops were. If so, it wasn't a very smart move. The enemy troops were all around him. Lindley claims he went back to retrieve some treasure, but Lindley is hardly a reliable source concerning his enemies' motives.

28. Carr, p. 288.

29. Carr, p. 293.

30. Carr, p. 310.

31. Carr, p. 309.

32. Lytton Strachey, *Eminent Victorians*, p. 251.

33. John Keegan and Andrew Wheatcroft, *Who's Who in Military History*, p.139.

CHAPTER 3: THE DIFFERENT DRUMMER

1. Kevin H. Siepel, *Rebel*, p. 11.

2. John S. Mosby, *The Memoirs of Colonel John S. Mosby*, p. 118.

3. Siepel, p. 57.

4. Stuart never liked the idea of Mosby's men being partisans. He urged the guerrilla leader to call his force "Mosby's Regulars." Siepel, pp. 77-78; Virgil Carrington Jones, *Ranger Mosby*, pp. 108-109.

5. James M. McPherson, *Battle Cry of Freedom*, p. 738.

6. The Spencer was a repeater holding seven rounds in the stock. With most models, all seven rounds could be loaded into the rifles at once, instead of one at a time, as with Henry's and other repeaters.

7. After the Civil War, the U.S. Army made a distinction between European-style war and frontier war. In the former, troops were to be armed with two single-shot pistols and a saber. In the latter, a carbine and a revolver. See Edward C. Ezell, *Handguns of the World*, p. 50. This was *after* the revolver had proved its superiority in the "European-style" fighting of the Civil War.

8. For more on Custer, see William Weir, *Written With Lead*, pp. 64-81.

9. The men to be executed were chosen by lot. One so chosen was a drummer boy. Mosby, when told of this, excused the lad, and lots were drawn again for the last victim. Mosby did not witness the executions. After hanging three men, the executioners decided to shoot the rest. When the last man was to be shot, the gun of his executioner misfired. The intended victim, Sergeant Charles Marvin, of the Second New York Cavalry, hit his would-be executioner as hard as he could and escaped. Mosby did not try to recapture him and ordered no more executions. He had made his point.

10. Peterson, *Arms and Armor in Colonial America*, p. 262.

11. The rifle, because it required a tight-fitting ball was slow to load. Even when the rifleman used a slightly undersized ball wrapped in a greased patch, his weapon had a much lower rate of fire than a smoothbore musket. Consequently, the rifle was used only by light infantry. Not until the invention of the Minie bullet could rifles be loaded fast enough to serve as the principal infantry weapon.

12. See Weir, *Fatal Victories*, pp. 142-143, 145-146, for more on Wilder and his brigade.

13. Peterson, *Arms and Armor in Colonial America*, p. 262.

14. Ezell, *Handguns of the World*, p. 49.

15. Mosby did not kill the other student, who himself had been arrested for a number of assaults, some with weapons. There was some evidence that Mosby acted in self-defense, but he was convicted of "unlawful shooting" and sentenced to a year in jail, along with a $500 fine. The governor pardoned him after appeals by Mosby's family and friends, a majority of the jury that convicted him, and the lieutenant governor, who said that under the circumstances Mosby faced, he would have done the same thing himself.

16. Siepel, p. 81.
17. Siepel, p. 82; see also Mosby, pp. 193-195.
18. Siepel, p. 102.
19. Ezell, *Small Arms of the World*, 12th Edition, p. 46.
20. Siepel, p. 100.
21. Siepel, p. 92.
21. Siepel, p. 122.
22. Mosby, p. 253.
23. Siepel, pp. 134-135.
24. Siepel, pp. 137-38; Jones, pp. 245-250.
25. Siepel, p. 146.
26. An unknown person shot at him as he got off a train at Warrenton. Jones, p. 299.
27. Siepel, p. 242.

CHAPTER 4: TREACHERY IN THE BADLANDS

1. Cyrus Townsend Brady, *Northwestern Fights and Fighters*, p. 233; Major F.A. Boutelle, *The Duel With Scar-Faced Charley*, in Brady, *Northwestern Fights and Fighters*, p. 265.
2. Brady, p. 233.
3. Brady, p. 233.
4. Boutelle in Brady, p. 266.
5. In *Bury My Heart at Wounded Knee*, Dee Brown says Captain Jack did appear and was told by Jackson he had to return to the reservation. Brown quotes the chief as agreeing to go, although protesting the soldiers' surprise appearance. But Brown's account is based on W.S. Nye's in *Carbine and Lance*, which is ultimately based on the account by A.B. Meacham. Meacham played an important part in the Modoc War, but he was not present at the first encounter. All who were present say the chief did not appear until after the gunfire.
6. Boutelle in Brady, p. 266.
7. Boutelle in Brady, p. 270.
8. "Modoc" is said to mean "stranger." The name was apparently how other Indians referred to them. That was how many tribes acquired the names by which they are usually known. "Navajo," "Apache," and "Sioux" all mean "enemy." "Mohawk" means "cannibal." See Brady, footnote, p. 225.
9. *New York Times*, March 22, 1998, "Less to Celebrate at this Gold Rush Anniversary," by James Brooke.
10. Brown, p. 220.

11. Brown, p. 221.
12. Brown, p. 225.
13. Brady, p. 236.
14. Brady, p. 236.
15. David Perry, "Battles in the Lava Beds," in Brady, p. 296.
16. Brown, p. 228, quoting A.B. Meacham, *Wigwam and Warpath*, Boston, 1875, p. 441.
17. Brown, p. 229, quoting Albert Britt, *Great Indian Chiefs*, New York, 1938, pp. 235-36.
18. Brown, p. 230, quoting Sherman to Canby, March 12, 1873.
19. Brown, pp. 231-233, quoting Meacham, *Wigwam and Warpath*, p. 441.
20. Brown, p. 234.
21. Brady, pp. 249-250.
22. Brown, p. 238.
23. Brown, p. 239, quoting Jeff C. Riddle, *The Indian History of the Modoc War*, 1914, pp. 143-144.
24. Brown, p. 239.
25. Brown, p. 239.
26. Brady, p. 254.
27. Brady, p. 254.

CHAPTER 5: "DAMN, DAMN, DAMN THE FILIPINO"

1. Brian McAllister Linn, *The U.S. Army and Counterinsurgency in the Philippine War, 1899-1902*, p.63.
2. G.J.A. O'Toole, *The Spanish War*, p. 36.
3. David F. Trask, *The War With Spain in 1898*, p. 437.
4. O'Toole, p. 96; Bain, *Sitting in Darkness*, p. 57.
5. O'Toole, p. 91.
6. To appreciate the irony of this prejudice, compare the percentage of the U.S. population of Indian descent with that of the Mexican population of Indian descent. The breakdown of the Mexican population of Indian descent: Mestizos (Caucasian and Indian), 60 percent; Indian, 30 per cent. The United States, in the last census listed American Indian and Alaskan Native population at 1 percent. Incidentally, Mexico is a large country, with a population of approximately 98,552,776 people. Thirty percent of that number is a hell of a lot of people.
7. O'Toole, p. 56.
8. McKinley was able to deceive most of his contemporaries as well as many future historians, but he did not deceive a contemporary historian, Henry Adams, who

called him the "first genius of manipulation." See David Haward Bain, *Sitting in Darkness*, p. 56.

9. Bain, p. 57.

10. Bain, p. 59.

11. Parts of *Maine's* hull were bent inward, indicating an external explosion, but parts were bent outward. The first American commission investigating the explosion stressed the parts bent inward. The Spanish commission stressed those bent outward. The Spanish also noted that no geyser of water was seen, nor were there any dead fish where the explosion took place—both of which would have been inevitable features of an external explosion. Almost a century later, a commission headed by Admiral Hyman Rickover concluded the explosion was internal. The latest evidence, discussed in *Smithsonian*, Feb. 1998, "Remember the *Maine*," by Tom Miller, and *The National Geographic*, Feb. 1998, "Remember the *Maine*?" by Thomas B. Allen, is ambiguous, but favors the internal explosion theory.

12. Spain still had a handful of ships in Spanish waters. After the Battle of Manila Bay, they were sent east, through the Suez Canal, to reinforce the Philippines, but they turned back after reaching the Red Sea, because the Spanish government was afraid of an American attack on the coasts of Spain.

13. Bain, p. 72. McKinley was in the habit of writing notes to himself. George Cortelyou, one of his aides during negotiations with Spain on the peace treaty, remarked to McKinley how, after many discussions by U.S. diplomats the terms sent to Spain had finally evolved. McKinley then "took from his pocket...a memorandum in his own handwriting, made on the day of the receipt of the Spanish note, or about that time, in which he stated what he would require as terms of peace. These...were exactly those which were finally transmitted." In other words, the president knew what he wanted and manipulated his advisers into thinking they had hammered out peace terms in their discussions. See Trask, p. 431.

14. American settlers in Hawaii had overthrown the queen and established a republic. The Hawaiian settlers then concluded a treaty of annexation with the United States. However, President Grover Cleveland, learning that the "revolution" was really a coup d'etat engineered by the American minister to the islands, withdrew the treaty. McKinley revived it. The islands were annexed after a joint resolution of Congress.

15. Bain, p. 72.

16. See reproductions in *Gun Digest Annual, 1992*, "Guns of the Philippine Wars" by William Weir.

17. And although they were primitive in many respects, the Igorots built what is perhaps the world's most sophisticated system for rice cultivation in unlikely terrain.

18. As a result of peace talks, the Spanish government agreed to institute reforms and make payments to the rebels, and Aguinaldo agreed to go into exile. But the government never got around to all the reforms and the fighting picked back up

again. Oscar F. Williams, American consul in Manila, reported that after Aguinaldo was banished, "War exists, battles are of almost daily occurrence, ambulances bring in many wounded and hospitals are full....Insurgents are being armed and drilled and are rapidly increasing in numbers and efficiency. See Trask, p. 397.

19. Dewey had been promoted to admiral after his victory.

20. Trask, p. 409.

21. The first American troops in the Philippines were volunteers, not regulars. The regulars had Krag-Jorgensen repeating rifles which used smokeless powder. Most of the volunteer had the old black powder Springfields.

22. Bain, p. 77.

23. O'Toole, p. 386.

24. Trask, p. 409.

25. Samuel Eliot Morison, *The Oxford History of the American People,* p. 806.

26. *Civilization,* April-May 1998, "God was Present at the Founding," by Nicholas von Hoffman.

27. Bain, pp. 184-85; O'Toole, p. 388.

28. Bain, p. 185.

29. Bain, pp. 185-86.

30. Many of the Filipino rebels had removed the sights on their rifles to make carrying them more convenient.

31. Trask, on p. 394, repeats this canard. Trask, at the time of writing, was Director of the Office of the Historian of the U.S. State Department.

32. Bain, p. 21.

33. The Hotchkiss 12-pounder weighed not 12, but 218 pounds. The shell fired from its three-inch bore weighed 12 pounds. The carriage body weighed 205 pounds and each wheel weighed 62 pounds. It was light enough to be dragged by the men in its crew if necessary, and it could be disassembled and packed on mule back. Although it was a breech-loader, there was no shield to shelter a crew. Taking shelter behind the gun would have been dangerous, because the whole weapon recoiled when fired. It did not have an efficient recoil-absorbing mechanism. (*Bannerman Catalogue of Military Goods—1927,* p. 135.)

34. Dynamite, especially gelatin dynamite, is an extremely powerful but sensitive explosive. It is too powerful to be used as a filling in an ordinary shell, because the explosion of the propelling powder would detonate the shell while in the gun barrel. The Sims-Dudley gun used a powder charge in a lower barrel to compress air which was bled into the upper barrel holding the dynamite shell. The compressed air propelled the shell. Bannerman, p. 145.

35. Bain, p. 47; Thomas W. Crouch, *A Yankee Guerrillero,* p. 50.

36. O'Toole, pp. 57-58.

37. The volunteer system was a traditional way of raising troops in time of need. All males between 16 and 60 were in the unorganized militia and could be called for military service to defend the United States from invasion. They could not be used in foreign wars. For fighting overseas, the government relied on citizens who organized themselves into military units, which were then taken into the army as units. The volunteer army was separate from the regular army, and volunteer officers—such as volunteer enlisted men—would have no standing in the regular army when the emergency had ended.

38. Those qualifications were, unfortunately, extremely rare in the army we sent to Cuba.

39. Crouch, *A Leader of Volunteers*, pp. 12-13.

40. Crouch, p. 121.

41. Bain, p. 87.

42. Bain, p. 89.

43. Bain, p. 90.

44. Linn, pp. 57-58.

45. Linn, p. 76.

46. Linn, p. 76.

47. Bain p. 98.

48. According to one story, the Macabebes were descended from Mexican Indians brought to the Philippines by the Spanish in the 16th century.

49. Bain, p. 210.

50. O'Toole, p. 394.

51. O'Toole, p. 395.

52. Roosevelt and Funston had exchanged many admiring letters. In one, Roosevelt expressed the desire to serve under Funston in the next war.

53. Linn, pp. 85-86.

CHAPTER 6: THE AFRICAN GHOST

1. Olga Anastasia Pelensky, *Isak Dinesen*, p. 7.

2. Isak Dinesen, *Letters from Africa, 1914-1931*, p. 10.

3. The Mauser 71/84 was another black powder gun—essentially the 71 with a tubular magazine under the barrel. The Model 88 was an 8-mm smokeless powder repeater loaded with a clip. Before enough to arm all of Germany's regular and reserve troops in Europe could be produced, Germany adopted the greatly superior Mauser 98. In 1914, the only rifles Germany could spare were the Mauser 71s. Some of these went to Africa, others were sold to Irish rebels.

4. Edwin P. Hoyt, *Guerrilla*, p. 9.
5. Richard Meinertzhagen, *Army Diary*, p. 110.
6. Peter Hathaway Capstick, *Warrior*, p. 61.
7. Judith Thurman, *Isak Dinesen*, p. 147.
8. Thurman, p. 132.
9. Dinesen, p. 23.
10. Kitchener made his reputation by mowing down a horde of poorly armed Arabs with machine guns in the Sudan. He then stamped out the last embers of Boer resistance in South Africa by adopting Spanish General Valeriano (the Butcher) Weyler's invention of concentration camps in Cuba. Under Kitchener in South Africa, thousands of Afrikaner women and children died of starvation and disease in those camps. Kitchener's military exploits demonstrate plenty of cruelty, but precious little genius.
11. Meinertzhagen, p. 82.
12. Meinertzhagen, p. 84; Hoyt, p. 31.
13. Hoyt, p. 39; Meinertzhagen, p. 89.
14. Hoyt, p. 39.
15. Meinertzhagen, p. 93; Capstick, p. 188.
16. Hoyt, p. 118.
17. Meinertzhagen, p. 112; Hoyt, p. 53.
18. Hoyt, p. 88.
19. Hoyt, p. 84.
20. The South Africans did, in fact, get a mandate over German Southwest Africa (now called Namibia).
21. Meinertzhagen, p. 165.
22. Not to be confused with sleeping sickness. See Peter Capstick, *Death in the Long Grass*, p. 173.
23. Meinertzhagen, p. 184.
24. Hoyt, p. 116.
25. Hoyt, p. 133.
26. Meinertzhagen, pp. 109-110.
27. John Toland, *Ships in the Sky*, p. 56.
28. Gaza, on the Mediterranean coast, was the logical place to attack. The British planned to attack the other end of the line at Beersheba. Meinertzhagen plotted an elaborate series of deceptions to make the Turks think otherwise. To cap the deception, he allowed himself to be pursued by a Turkish patrol, during which he "lost" forged orders.

29. Mark Cocker, *Richard Meinertzhagen*, p. 94.

30. Errol Trzebinksi, *Silence Will Speak*, pp. 117-119.

31. Hoyt, p. 164.

32. Hoyt, p. 5.

33. T.E. Lawrence, *Seven Pillars of Wisdom*, pp. 385-386.

34. Meinertzhagen, p. 296.

35. In 1948, at the birth of the State of Israel, Meinertzhagen was in the Holy Land as an observer. Fighting broke out between Jewish defense forces and Arab armies. On hearing firing, the 70-year-old Meinertzhagen dashed up to the Israeli firing line, seized a rifle and shot three Arab soldiers before others in his party hustled him back to their ship.

36. William Stevenson, *The Ghosts of Africa*, p. 393.

CHAPTER 7: THE PEN AND THE SWORD

1. Burke Wilkinson, *The Zeal of the Convert*, p. 109.

2. Still another private force in Ireland was the Citizen Army, commanded by a Socialist labor leader, James Connolly. The Citizen Army was originally organized to provide protection for striking workers, but it quickly became Republican.

3. The IRB at this time was a small and almost moribund secret society. Regardless, it had infiltrated the leadership of the Volunteers. Members of the IRB gave their first loyalty to the society, which recognized its own chief as the president of an Irish Republic. This, of course, was a rather arrogant position, as the people had no voice in the selection of such a president. It was, however, to have a strong influence on Irish politics as Republican sentiment increased and the society grew in membership. During the Civil War, Michael Collins was head of the IRB.

4. Frank O'Connor, *An Only Child*, p. 212.

5. O'Connor, p. 211.

6. Quite a few of the "upper crust" actors in this drama had American wives. Among them, Randolph Churchill, Michael O'Rahilly, and Sir John Lavery.

7. It was theoretically a joint effort by Childers and his friend, Basil Williams, but Childers did most of the writing.

8. In 1898, another amateur soldier, Winston Churchill, reached the same conclusion. Charging with the 21st Lancers at Omdurman, Churchill substituted a Mauser C 96 automatic pistol for a lance or a sword. He was happy with the choice of weapons. After one charge, his regiment dismounted and used their carbines. Later, Churchill reflected on "the futility of the much vaunted *arme blanche*." Winston S. Churchill, *My Early Life*, p. 194.

9. Peter de Rosa, *Rebels*, p. 34.

10. The rifles the Volunteers took were empty. Hobson had withheld the ammunition because he thought the Volunteers had not yet had enough training on how to use the weapons. On the way home, the Volunteers were met by police and soldiers, who demanded that they surrender the rifles. The Volunteers refused. There was a scuffle, but no one was seriously hurt. The police managed to seize 16 rifles, but they gave them back the next day. There was a rumor (which is untrue) that the soldiers bayonetted many Volunteers. After that incident, a crowd gathered and began throwing rocks and banana skins at the troops as they were marching away. The official report held that the soldiers should have marched with the police, because the police would have had no trouble dispersing the crowd. Instead, the troops fired on the crowd. This happened in downtown Dublin, a long way from Howth. Three persons were killed and 38 were injured, 15 seriously. See Aodogan O'Rahilly, *Winding the Clock*, pp. 125-29. Incidentally, O'Rahilly, whose father, The O'Rahilly, was in charge of arming the Volunteers and was one of the masterminds of the gun-running, says: "Pride of place in the operation goes to Erskine Childers. He was one of the few men in Ireland who had the technical skill, the dedication, the courage, the integrity, and the commitment to carry out this self-imposed duty." O'Rahilly, p. 119.

11. See Weir, *Fatal Victories*, pp. 178-99.

12. There were a few skirmishes outside of Dublin, but they amounted to nothing.

13. Some sources call the weapon a revolver, but that was a common Irish term for any handgun; some say it was a .22 automatic, but there were no such pistols at that time. O'Connor calls it a Spanish pistol, but the Free State military tribunal charged Childers with "being in unlawful possession of a Colt automatic pistol." (Dorothy Macardle, *The Irish Republic*, p. 812.) The .25 caliber pistol was the only Colt small enough to wear pinned to a suspender—Childers's usual method of carrying it.

14. Wilkinson, p. 217.

15. Calton Younger, *Ireland's Civil War*, p. 108.

16. Collins was director of military intelligence for the IRA, adjutant general of the army and minister for finance for the Republic, as well as chairman of the supreme council of the IRB. He was a workaholic with a mind like a computer and was the real leader of the republic, especially while de Valera was fundraising in the United States.

17. Andrew Boyle, *The Riddle of Erskine Childers*, p. 265, quoting Tom Jones, *Whitehall Diary*, vol. 3, p. 17.

18. Boyle, p. 265.

19. The term "Irish Republican Army" dates from just before the 1916 Rising, when the troops of Pearse and Connolly proclaimed a republic and declared that they were the Irish Republican Army. The IRA of the Black and Tan War and the Civil War traced its origins directly to the men of 1916.

20. O'Connor, *The Big Fellow*, p. 96.

21. Wilkinson, p. 165.

22. Wilkinson, p. 165.

23. Wilkinson, p. 173.

24. Boyle, p. 267.

25. Wilkinson, p. 179; Jim Ring, *Erskine Childers*, p. 239.

26. The day the letter was sent, de Valera had been arrested (for the third time). Just as was the case with Childers, he was immediately released.

27. Ring, p. 239.

28. There are nine counties in the historical province of Ulster. Six were split off because that was the largest area in which the Carsonites could maintain a majority. If all nine counties were detached, there would be no Protestant majority in Northern Ireland.

29. Cathal Brugha, like Childers, was the son of an English father and an Irish mother. He was originally named Charles Burgess. He gave Childers the idea of changing his name to a Gaelic equivalent, but after consulting scholars Childers learned that there was no way to translate Erskine Childers into the Irish language.

30. Younger, p. 167. The theory that de Valera chose Collins for the negotiating team so he could take the blame for what was bound to yield less than a republic seems as baseless as the counter theory that the negotiations, the split in the cabinet and the split in the Dáil followed a master plan by the IRB to put Collins at the head of the state. See Boyle, pp. 300-303.

31. Boyle, p. 288, quoting Childers's diary. Childers recorded: "A.G. insolent to me about altering drafts. Attacks me about *Riddle of the Sands*. Says I caused the European War and now want to cause another....Griffith broke out about allegiance, saying he was willing to save the country from our (the Republicans) war—personally willing. He implied he was willing to tell LL.G. this, but Robert Barton put it to him then he said No."

32. Wilkinson, p. 203; Younger, p. 235; Boyle, p. 303.

33. Tim Pat Coogan, *Michael Collins*, p. 309.

34. O'Connor, *The Big Fellow*, pp. 145-146; Wilkinson, p. 201.

35. Wilkinson, pp. 212-213.

36. O'Connor, *An Only Child*, p. 232.

37. Wilkinson, pp. 213-214; Ring, p. 278.

38. Wilkinson, p. 206.

39. Terence De Vere White, O'Higgins' biographer, attempted to prove the affair existed only in Lady Lavery's mind, but there's too much evidence to the contrary. See Tim Pat Coogan, *Michael Collins*, pp. 288-291. Collins, too, had an affair with Hazel Lavery, but he wasn't married—and he never pretended to be a saint.

40. Coogan, pp. 288-289.

41. Wilkinson, pp. 214-215; Boyle, p. 316; Macardle, pp. 802-803.

42. O'Higgins had joined the volunteers after the 1916 rising, but he had never been involved in fighting. He was arrested once for making a seditious speech, but was soon released.

43. Wilkinson, p. 219.

44. O'Connor, *An Only Child*, p. 232.

45. Wilkinson, p. 222; Macardle, p. 812.

46. Wilkinson, p. 197.

47. Wilkinson, p. 222; Macardle, p. 811.

48. De Valera's new attitude toward the oath illustrates the workings of his complex mind. He had to sign an oath to be admitted to the Dáil, but he maintained, "I signed it the same way I would sign an autograph in a newspaper." He said it was not an oath in the eyes of God, but merely a humiliating formality the Free State government required. At the signing, he had been given a Bible on which to swear the oath. He had pushed the Bible away and said, "I am not going to take an oath. I am prepared to put my name down in this book in order to get permission to go into the Dáil, but it has no other significance." See J. Bowyer Bell, *The Secret Army*, p. 62.

CHAPTER 8: CRAZY ORDE

1. Trevor Royle, *Orde Wingate: Irregular Soldier*, p. 56.

2. Wingate thought that Britain was planning to annex Ethiopia to the Empire as it had annexed Palestine after the First World War. That would have put him in the same position as his distant cousin, T.E. Lawrence, who also thought he was fighting for the liberation of an oppressed people. Whether or not Wingate's suspicion was justified is debatable. What is certain, however, is that there was a conscious effort to play down the Ethiopian campaign.

3. Royle, p. 79.

4. Not anti-Semitic. The Arabs are more truly Semitic than most Jews.

5. Christopher Sykes, *Orde Wingate*, p. 136.

6. Leonard Mosley, *Gideon Goes to War*, p. 48.

7. Mosley, p. 49.

8. Mosley, p. 57.

9. Mosley, p. 58.

10. Hugh Foot, *A Start in Freedom*, p. 52.

11. Christopher Sykes, *Orde Wingate*, p. 147.

12. Mosley, pp. 74-76, details one instance; Sykes, pp. 547-551, refutes it.

13. Mosley, pp. 63-64.

14. Mosley, p. 78.

15. Mosley, p. 95.

16. Mosley, pp. 95-96.

17. Wingate's contact with VIPs in England was a result of the work he and Lorna did with the Zionist leaders.

18. Mosley, pp. 107-108; Sykes, pp. 248-249; Royle, pp. 182-183.

19. Mosley, pp.127-129; see also Sykes, p. 291.

20. Mosley, p. 109.

21. Mosley, p. 112.

22. Royle, p. 187.

23. Mosley, p. 133; Royle, p. 201.

24. Mosley, p. 132.

25. Mosley, p. 137.

26. As soon as he got on the throne, Haile Selassie made short work of that plan. He was a tiny man physically, but he understood political power. He made his own appointments and ignored the British recommendations. They did not dare to appear to be in open conflict with the Emperor-martyr.

27. Mosley, p. 136.

28. Royle, p. 215.

29. Mosley, p. 141.

30. Mosley, p. 141.

31. Wingate, as usual, was highly critical of the men he got. The 13th King's Regiment, he said, was too old, physically unfit and lacked esprit d'corps. The Gurkhas, he added, were "slow of wit, raw, untrained." Mosley, pp. 187-188; see also Royle, p. 260.

32. The author, a former combat soldier, finds this hard to believe.

33. The Chindits returned safely, but few—including Wingate—were in good shape. That they eventually recovered was largely due to the efficiency of an army head nurse, whom Wingate's biographer Trevor Royle calls "the legendary Matron Agnes McGeary." Later, when Wingate came down with typhoid fever, Matron McGeary, at the request of Lorna Wingate, flew from Britain to India to supervise the general's treatment.

34. Derek Tulloch, *Wingate in Peace and War*, p. 91.

35. Cochran was the original "Flip Corkin" of the comic strip *Terry and the Pirates*.

36. Tulloch, p. 128.

37. In spite of apparent unity, each of the four Allies—the United States, Britain, China, and the Soviet Union—had a separate agenda. The British had always relegated the Far East to secondary importance. They felt little should be done until things were settled in Europe. Churchill, for some reason known only to himself, would rather have had an amphibious landing on Sumatra than an offensive in Burma.

The Russians, incessantly clamoring for a second front in Europe, were appeasing Japan to avoid a second front in Siberia.

Chiang Kai-Shek wanted to avoid committing any resources outside of China—even to open the Burma Road.

Officially, the United States agreed that Europe should get priority, although Japan had attacked the center of U.S. military power, the Pacific Fleet. The United States reacted strongly: the most powerful U.S. naval units went to the Pacific and stayed there. The Pacific war was pretty much an American-Japanese show.

The American people reacted emotionally. In his otherwise excellent book, Derek Tulloch suggests that if China were knocked out of the war, the Allies might negotiate a peace with Japan. To Americans, a negotiated peace with Japan would have been unthinkable. In short, no matter what it proclaimed in international conferences, the United States never put the war against Japan on the back burner.

The American counteroffensive began in 1942 and continued steadily while U.S. troops were also fighting in Africa and Europe. A month after the war in Europe was over, Japan had been pushed out of all its post-Pearl Harbor conquests, and American troops were occupying Okinawa, a Japanese island.

Japan's merchant fleet had been annihilated; its navy almost annihilated. Its aircraft factories had all been destroyed and its oil supplies had disappeared. All its largest cities had been bombed flat. All that was required was a pair of nuclear bombs to give the country a face-saving reason to surrender.

Except for the fighting in Burma, Britain's contribution to the defeat of Japan was negligible. The Soviet Union's cynical last-minute declaration of war was utterly useless—as far as defeating Japan, that is. As shown in Chapter 9, it created a world of new troubles.

Some American politicians, notably Henry Stimson, professed to believe that Hitler had told the Japanese to attack Pearl Harbor. The Japanese leaders took no orders from Hitler or anyone else. Japanese membership in the Rome-Berlin-Tokyo Axis was a marriage of convenience. It was caused by the American embargo on Japan, cutting off, among other things, the Island Empire's main supply of oil. Japanese leaders thought that the Axis pact would give them an excuse to grab the oil in the Dutch East Indies, as the Netherlands was an enemy of their new ally, Germany. The Netherlands and France had been knocked out and Britain was hanging on the ropes in 1940. But the United

States threatened war if Japan moved into Southeast Asia. As the Japanese saw it, their only alternative was to attack the U.S. fleet. For more on this, see William Weir, *Fatal Victories*, pp. 200-219.

38. Tulloch, p. 175.

39. Royle, p. 289.

40. Tulloch, p. 205.

41. Tulloch, p. 277.

42. Royle, p. 319.

43. Tulloch, p. 265.

CHAPTER 9: FROM THE JAWS OF DEFEAT (AND DUGOUT DOUG)

1. Literally. See Matthew B. Ridgway, *The Korean War*, pp. 89, 119.

2. For an early example of that ability, consider this note to Gen. Leonard Wood, who had just retired as army chief of staff, from MacArthur, then a captain serving in the Vera Cruz occupation force:

   > General Funston is handling things very well...but I miss the inspiration, my dear General, of your own clean-cut decisive methods. I sincerely hope that affairs will shape themselves so that you will shortly take the field for the campaign which, if death does not call you, can have but one ending—the White House.

   (Walter Millis, *Arms and Men*, p. 192.)

3. The location of the International Date Line makes the dates somewhat confusing, but the Philippine attack was an actual eight hours after the Hawaii attack.

4. William Weir, *Fatal Victories*, p. 217.

5. Bevin Alexander, in *Korea*, blames the politically correct and strategically stupid slogan "Unconditional Surrender" for much of the subsequent trouble. He believes the Japanese would have surrendered in 1944 or, at latest, early 1945 if they did not believe that unconditional surrender would have meant the execution of the Emperor, who was regarded as a deity by most Japanese. President Harry Truman eventually did exempt the Emperor, but only after the second atomic bomb. Before that, President Franklin Roosevelt, because he felt that the Japanese would resist unconditional surrender to the last, demanded that the Soviet Union enter the war against Japan. The Russians fulfilled their pledge after the second atomic bomb, guaranteeing them a maximum of spoils for a minimum of effort. The great men at Yalta never bothered to explain why Korea, which had been conquered by Japan in 1910, should be governed by great power trustees instead of liberated. Alexander, pp. 8-9.

6. During the evacuation, three North Korean propeller-driven fighters attacked four U.S. jet fighters covering the airlift of civilians. The Americans promptly

shot all three down. Later in the day they shot down four more North Korean fighters. So even before the United States officially intervened, American fighters destroyed one-sixth of North Korea's fighter fleet.

7. Instead of three infantry regiments, the divisions (except the 24th) had two. Instead of a tank battalion, each division had two companies. Instead of three 4.2 inch mortar platoons, they had two. Instead of a light artillery battalion, they had two batteries. Infantry regiments had two battalions instead of three. Artillery batteries had four 105-mm howitzers. See Alexander, p. 47; Ridgway, p. 29.

8. The 105-mm howitzer was a relatively low-velocity artillery piece, unable to penetrate the armor of a modern tank. But the HEAT (high explosive anti-tank) shell had a shaped charge. The front part of the shell's explosive charge was shaped to direct a jet of hot gas straight ahead. This would burn through the armor like an acetylene torch, but it does so instantaneously. The low-velocity bazooka rocket killed tanks the same way. Some newspaper accounts at the time told of bazooka shells that penetrated a tank but did not explode. That is absolutely impossible. Even Alexander, who was in the Korean War, writes of bazooka rockets and high explosive shells "bouncing off" North Korean tanks. Such missiles seldom bounce; they may explode harmlessly against tank armor. In the first days of the Korean War, many, many did.

9. Alexander, p. 148.

10. Ridgway, p. 40.

11. As a General of the Army, MacArthur outranked all the Chiefs. At 70 years old, he was also considerably older than any of them.

12. A fact that was a subject of bitter humor for the "cops" in the foxholes and bunkers of Korea.

13. Alexander, p. 368.

14. Alexander, p. 372.

15. Alexander, p. 377.

16. Alexander, p. 378.

17, Alexander, p. 383.

18. Alexander, p. 384.

19. Ridgway, p. 87.

20. Clay Blair, *The Forgotten War*, p. 573.

21. Ridgway, p. 106.

22. Ridgway, p. 104.

23. Ridgway, p. 105.

24. Weaponry in the Eighth Army came to exceed army TO&E (table of organization and equipment) requirements. In the last two years of the war, the typical infantry regiment had an automatic weapon—a .50 caliber machine

gun, a .30-caliber water-cooled machine gun, a .30-caliber air-cooled machine gun, a Browning automatic rifle, or at least an M-2 carbine—in every hole or fighting bunker. In contrast, some Chinese infantrymen had no guns and were armed only with hand grenades.

25. Alexander, pp. 405-406.

26. Alexander, p. 406.

27. Alexander, pp. 406-407.

28. The Korean War, which lasted three years, one month, and two days, killed 54,246 U.S. servicepeople. The Pentagon, in its effort to deemphasize the war, has stressed what it called "battlefield deaths," which it puts at 33,629. The other 20,617 it says, died of "other causes." Other causes include such things as bunkers collapsing in the spring thaws or the summer rains and deaths in hospitals from wounds incurred on the firing line. Very few of those deaths would have occurred if the troops were not in combat in Korea. For comparison, in the Vietnam War which, for the purpose of compiling casualties, the Pentagon considers everything from Jan. 1, 1961 through Sept. 30, 1977 (which includes the Mayaguez incident), there were 58,151 American deaths. Vietnam, of course, saw a vastly larger number of U.S. servicepeople.

   After the peace talks began in July, there were 12,300 American "battlefield deaths." If the proportion of those to "other deaths" is the same as before, there were about 20,000 deaths after the peace talks began. And the peace talks began three months after MacArthur had been sacked.

   Of course, MacArthur's sabotage of the cease-fire proposal would not have caused all those deaths if cease-fire negotiations were conducted as they later were—talking peace while making war.

29. Alexander, p. 447.

30. Alexander, p. 440. Van Fleet's words are those of a man who had never been an infantry rifleman and who had for decades had no contact with infantry riflemen. He had no idea of the terrible effect continual, useless contact patrols could have on morale.

31. Estimated Communist casualties in June and July 1953 were 108,000. Alexander, p. 481.

32. For more on U.S. casualties and the "forgotten war" period, see *War, Literature and the Arts*, Spring/Summer 1998, "Memoir: Public Information," by William R. Weir. For a typical incident in that period, see *Military History*, August 1986, "Defending Sandbag Castle," by William Weir.

33. Alexander, p. 483.

34. Communiques from the Pentagon discussing actions involving the 25th Infantry Division during most of 1952 invariably described their North Korean opponents as Chinese. *War, Literature and the Arts*, Spring/Summer 1998.

CHAPTER 10: A VISITOR FROM THE BLACK WORLD

1. The fortress was built in a valley overlooked by hills on all sides. The French knew that the hills would be perfect observation posts if the Viet Minh had artillery, but they were sure the Communist guerrillas had no artillery. They were wrong.

2. Edward Geary Lansdale, *In the Midst of Wars*, p. 249. See also Alfred McCoy, *The Politics of Heroin*, p. 159.

3. Cecil B. Currey, *Edward Lansdale*, pp. 23-26.

4. Under heavy American tutelage. The United States retained a number of military bases and had trade concessions.

5. Currey, p. 27.

6. Currey, p. 29.

7. Lansdale, p. 10.

8. Currey, pp. 43-44.

9. Currey, p. 71.

10. Lansdale, p. 33.

11. Lansdale, p. 83.

12. Lansdale, p. 74.

13. Currey, p. 87.

14. The Japanese also tried to create a puppet Philippine army, but even the most ardent collaborators in their puppet government refused to collaborate.

15. It was more than mere aid. The British actually returned the French to Vietnam. The British force was much stronger than the original French Expeditionary Force.

16. Bao Dai still wanted to be called "Your Majesty," but since he had abdicated, he maintained he was no longer an emperor. The Empire of Vietnam was now the State of Vietnam. It didn't matter much to Bao Dai, because he was seldom in the country.

17. For a detailed description of this strange process see McCoy, pp. 150-155.

18. They later became the nucleus of Diem's reformed Saigon police force.

19. McCoy, p. 140.

20. See William Weir, *In the Shadow of the Dope Fiend*, pp. 26-66.

21. Lansdale, p. 177.

22. Lansdale, p. 177.

23. At first Diem objected. "How can nightclub entertainers help us?" he asked. Most of the rock bands in Southeast Asia are composed of Filipinos. Even the well traveled and relatively sophisticated Diem thought in stereotypes.

24. Lansdale, pp. 264-265.

25. Lansdale, p. 295.

26. Lansdale, p. 296. Ten years later, Lansdale met Leroy in Washington. The guerrilla leader had taken his men to France, where they became building contractors. Lansdale and Leroy had a drink together for old times' sake.

27. Neil Sheehan, *A Bright Shining Lie*, p. 141.

28. One day, Bao Dai was informed that his current favorite, a buxom blonde, was seen drunk in public while entertaining several Frenchmen. "Yes, I know," the non-emperor said. "She's only plying her trade. Of the two, I am the real whore." Sheehan, p. 171.

29. The Communist guerrillas who later operated in South Vietnam after Lansdale left were called Viet Cong, which is merely Vietnamese for "Vietnamese Communists." By that time, the Viet Minh were the North Vietnamese government.

30. Currey, p. 254.

31. See William Weir, *Fatal Victories*, pp. 220-237 for details on the Tet Offensive and its aftermath.

AFTERWORD

1. See Weir, *Fatal Victories*, pp. 200-219.

2. The biggest exception to that rule is the United States, and that was two centuries ago. The British were hampered by primitive transportation, 3,000 miles of ocean, and the inability to put nearly as many soldiers in the field as the Americans because the British economy couldn't spare the men.

3. See Helen Huntington Smith, *The War on Powder River*, for a description of the feudal society that developed in Wyoming in the 1880s and 1890s.

Bibliography

Bibliography

Books

Alexander, Bevin. *Korea: The First War We Lost*. New York: Hippocrene Books, 1996.

Bain, David Haward. *Sitting in Darkness: Americans in the Philippines*. Boston: Houghton Mifflin, 1984.

Bannerman, Francis Sons, Inc. *Bannerman Catalog of Military Goods, 1927* (reproduction). Northfield, Ill.: DBI Books, 1980.

Beebe, Lucius and Clegg, Charles. *The American West*. New York: Dutton, 1955.

Bell, J. Bowyer. *The Secret Army*. New York: John Day, 1971.

Blair, Clay. *The Forgotten War: America in Korea, 1950-1953*. New York: Times Books, 1987.

Boyle, Andrew. *The Riddle of Erskine Childers*. London: Hutchinson, 1977.

Bruce-Briggs, B. *The Shield of Faith: Strategic Defense from Zeppelins to Star Wars*. New York: Simon & Schuster, 1988.

Brady, Cyrus Townsend. *Northwestern Fights and Fighters*. Williamstown, Mass.: Corner House, 1974.

Brice, Martin. *Forts and Fortresses*. New York: Facts on File, 1990.

Brown, Dee. *Bury My Heart at Wounded Knee: An Indian History of the American West*. New York: Holt, Rinehart & Winston, 1970.

Brownstone, David and Franck, Irene. *Timelines of War: A Chronology of War from 100,000 BC to the Present*. Boston: Little, Brown, 1994.

Capstick, Peter Hathaway. *Death in the Long Grass*. New York: St. Martin's, 1977.

———. *Warrior: The Legend of Colonel Richard Meinertzhagen*. New York: St. Martin's, 1998.

Carr, Albert Z. *The World and William Walker*. New York: Harper & Row, 1963.

Carr, Caleb. *The Devil Soldier: The American Soldier of Fortune Who Became a God in China*. New York: Random House, 1992.

Caulfield, Max. *The Easter Rebellion: Dublin 1916*. Boulder, Colo.: Roberts Rinehart, 1995.

Chandler, David. *The Art of Warfare on Land*. New York: Hamlyn, 1974.

Chandler, David, ed. *Dictionary of Battles*. New York: Henry Holt, 1988.

Childers, Erskine. *The Riddle of the Sands*. New York: Dover, 1976.

Churchill, Winston S. *My Early Life: A Roving Commission*. New York: Scribner's, 1958.

Cocker, Mark. *Richard Meinertzhagen: Soldier, Scientist and Spy*. London: Secker & Warburg, 1989.

Colby, William, with Forbath, Peter. *Honorable Men: My Life in the CIA*. New York: Simon & Schuster, 1978.

Coogan, Tim Pat. *Michael Collins: The Man Who Made Ireland*. Boulder, Colo.: Roberts Rinehart, 1996.

Cox, Tom. *Damned Englishman: A Study of Erskine Childers (1870-1922)*. Hicksville, N.Y.: Exposition Press, 1975.

Crouch, Thomas W. *A Leader of Volunteers: Frederick Funston and the 20th Kansas in the Philippines, 1898-1899*. Lawrence, Kans.: Coronado Press, 1984.

———. *A Yankee Guerrillero: Frederick Funston and the Cuban Insurrection. 1896-1897*, Memphis, Tenn.: Memphis State University Press, 1975.

Currey, Cecil B. *Edward Lansdale: The Unquiet American*. Boston: Houghton Mifflin, 1988.

Davis, Richard Harding. *The Notes of a War Correspondent*. New York: Scribner's, 1911.

———. *Real Soldiers of Fortune*. New York: Scribner's, 1906.

Delbruck, Hans. *History of the Art of War*. Lincoln, Nebr.: University of Nebraska Press, 1982.

DeRosa, Peter. *Rebels: The Irish Rising of 1916*. London: Corgi, 1991.

Derry, T.K. and Williams, Trevor I. *A Short History of Technology*. New York: Oxford University Press, 1960.

DeVoto, Bernard. *The Year of Decision 1846*. Boston: Little, Brown, 1943.

Diagram Group, The. *Weapons: An International Encyclopedia from 5000 BC to 2000 AD*. New York: St. Martins, 1990.

Dinesen, Isak. *Letters from Africa, 1914-1931*. Chicago: University of Chicago Press, 1981.

Donelson, Linda. *Out of Isak Dinesen in Africa: The Untold Story*. Iowa City, Iowa: Coulsong List, 1995.

Doubleday, C.W. *Reminiscences of the "Filibuster" War in Nicaragua*. New York: Putnam's, 1886.

Dugan, James and Lafore, Laurence. *Days of Emperor and Clown: The Italo-Ethiopian War 1935-1936*. Garden City, N.Y.: Doubleday, 1973.

Duncan, David Douglas. *This is War: A Photo-Narrative of the Korean War*. Boston: Little, Brown, 1990.

Eden, Steven. *Military Blunders: Wartime Fiascoes from the Roman Age through World War I*. New York: Metro Books, 1995.

Eggenberger, David. *An Encyclopedia of Battles*. New York: Dover, 1985.

Ellis, John. *The Social History of the Machine Gun*. New York: Pantheon, 1975.

Esposito, Vincent J. *The West Point Atlas of American Wars*. New York: Praeger, 1960.

Ezell, Edward C. *Handguns of the World*. New York: Barnes & Noble, 1993.

——. *Small Arms of the World: A Basic Manual of Small Arms*, 12th Revised Edition. Harrisburg, Pa.: Stackpole, 1983.

Farwell, Byron. *Queen Victoria's Little Wars*. London: W.W. Norton, 1985.

Foner, Philip S. *The Spanish-Cuban-American War and the Birth of American Imperialism*. New York: Monthly Review Press, 1972.

Foot, Hugh. *A Start in Freedom*. New York: Harper & Row, 1964.

Forty, George. *At War in Korea*. New York: Bonanza, 1985.

Fuller, J.F.C. *A Military History of the Western World*. New York: DaCapo, 1987.

——. *The Conduct of War 1789-1961*. New Brunswick, N.J.: Rutgers University Press, 1961.

Funston, Frederick. *Memories of Two Wars*. New York: Scribners, 1911.

Gerson, Noel B. *Sad Swashbuckler: The Life of William Walker*. Nashville, Tenn.: Thomas Nelson, 1976.

Glubb, John Bagot. *A Soldier With the Arabs*. New York: Harper, 1957.

Goodrich, L. Carrington. *A Short History of the Chinese People*. New York: Harper & Row, 1963.

Greene, Graham. *The Quiet American*. New York: Viking, 1956.

Grousset, Rene. *The Rise and Splendor of the Chinese Empire*. Berkeley: University of California Press, 1959.

Hoyt, Edwin P. *Guerrilla: Colonel von Lettow-Vorbeck and Germany's East African Empire*. New York: Macmillan, 1981.

Jamison, James Carson. *With Walker in Nicaragua or Reminiscences of an Officer of the American Phalanx*. Columbia, Mo.: E.W. Stephens, 1909.

Jennings, Patrick. *Pictorial History of World War II*. Norwalk, Conn.: Longmeadow, 1975.

Jobe, Joseph, ed. *Guns: An Illustrated History of Artillery*. Greenwich, Conn.: New York Graphic Society, 1971.

Jones, Virgil Carrington. *Ranger Mosby*. Chapel Hill, N.C.: University of North Carolina Press, 1944.

Keegan, John. *A History of Warfare*. New York: Vintage Books, 1993.

———. *The Second World War*. New York: Penguin, 1989.

Keegan, John and Wheatcroft, Andrew. *Who's Who in Military History*. New York: Morrow, 1976.

Kennedy, Paul. *The Rise and Fall of the Great Powers: Economic Change and Military Conflict from 1500 to 2000*. New York: Random House, 1987.

Lansdale, Edward Geary. *In the Midst of Wars: An American's Mission to Southeast Asia*. New York: Harper & Row, 1972.

Lawrence, T.E. *Seven Pillars of Wisdom: A Triumph*. New York: Dell, 1962.

Lederer, William J. and Burdick, Eugene. *The Ugly American*. New York: W.W. Norton, 1958.

Liddell-Hart, Basil. *Great Captains Unveiled: from Genghis Khan to General Wolfe*. London: Greenhill Books, 1989.

———. *The Real War: 1914 to 1918*. Boston: Little, Brown, 1930.

———. *Strategy*. New York: Praeger, 1960.

Linn, Brian McAllister. *The U.S. Army and Counterinsurgency in the Philippine War, 1899-1902*. Chapel Hill, N.C.: University of North Carolina Press, 1989.

Macardle, Dorothy. *The Irish Republic*. New York: Farrar, Straus and Giroux. 1965.

Marshall, S.L.A. *The American Heritage History of World War I*. New York: American Heritage, 1964.

McCoy, Alfred W. *The Politics of Heroin: CIA Complicity in the Global Drug Trade*. Brooklyn, N.Y.: Lawrence Hill, 1991.

McNeil, William H. *The Pursuit of Power*. Chicago: University of Chicago Press, 1982.

McPherson, James M. *Battlecry of Freedom: The Civil War Era*. New York: Ballentine, 1988.

Meinertzhagen, Richard. *Army Diary (1899-1926)*. Edinburgh: Oliver and Boyd, 1960.

——. *Kenya Diary (1902-1906)*. New York: Hippocrene Books, 1984.

Millis, Walter. *Arms and Men: A Study of American Military History*. New York: Mentor, 1958.

Mitchell, Joseph B. and Creasy, Edward. *Twenty Decisive Battles of the World*. New York: Macmillan, 1964.

Montross, Lynn. *War Through the Ages*. New York: Harper & Row, 1960.

Moody, T.W. and Martin, F.X. *The Course of Irish History*. Cork: Mercier, 1978.

Morison, Samuel Eliot. *The Oxford History of the American People*. New York: Oxford University Press, 1965.

Morris, Edmund. *The Rise of Theodore Roosevelt*. New York: Coward, McCann & Geoghegan, 1979.

Mosby, John S. *The Memoirs of Colonel John S. Mosby*. Bloomington, Ind.: Indiana University Press, 1959.

Mosley, Leonard. *Gideon Goes to War: The Story of Major-General Orde C. Wingate*. New York: Scribner's, 1955.

Neumann, Alfred. *Strange Conquest*. New York: Ballentine, 1954.

Ni Dhonnchadha, Mairin and Dorgan, Theo, eds. *Revising the Rising*. Derry, Ireland: Field Day, 1991.

Nowlan, Kevin B., ed. *The Making of 1916: Studies in the History of the Rising*. Dublin: Stationery Office, 1969.

O'Brien, Conor Cruise. *States of Ireland*. New York: Random House, 1972.

O'Broin, Leon. *Dublin Castle and the 1916 Rising*. New York: New York University Press, 1971.

O'Connor, Frank. *An Only Child*. Boston: G.K. Hall, 1985.

——. *The Big Fellow: Michael Collins and the Irish Revolution*. Dublin: Clonmore & Reynolds, 1965.

Ogburn, Charlton, Jr. *The Marauders*. New York: Harper Brothers, 1959.

O'Rahilly, Aodogan. *Winding the Clock: O'Rahilly and the 1916 Rising*. Dublin, Ireland: Lilliput Press, 1991.

O'Toole, G.J.A. *The Spanish War: An American Epic, 1898*. New York: W.W. Norton, 1984.

Pakenham, Thomas. *The Boer War*. New York: Random House, 1979.

——. *The Scramble for Africa: The White Man's Conquest of the Dark Continent from 1876 to 1912*. New York: Random House, 1991.

Pelensky, Olga Anastasia. *Isak Dinesen: The Life and Imagination of a Seducer*. Athens, Ohio: Ohio University Press, 1991.

Pitt, Barrie and Frances. *The Month-by-Month Atlas of World War II*. New York: Summit, 1989.

Pope, Dudley. *Guns*. London: Hamlyn, 1969.

Pope, Saxton T. *Bows and Arrows*. Berkeley: University of California Press, 1962.

Powell, E. Alexander. *Gentlemen Rovers*. New York: Scribner's, 1913.

Pratt, Fletcher. *The Battles that Changed History*. Garden City, N.Y.: Doubleday, 1956.

Preston, Richard A., Wise, Sydney F., and Werner, Herman O. *Men in Arms: A History of Warfare and its Interrelationships with Western Society, rev. ed.* New York: Praeger, 1962.

Regan, Geoffrey. *Snafu: Great American Military Disasters*. New York: Avon, 1993.

———. *The Guinness Book of More Military Blunders*. Enfield, England: Guinness, 1994.

———. *The Guinness Book of Naval Blunders*. Enfield, England: Guinness, 1994.

Reid, William. *Weapons Through the Ages*. New York: Crescent, 1976.

Ridgway, Matthew B. *The Korean War: How We Met the Challenge; How All-Out Asian War Was Averted; Why MacArthur Was Dismissed; Why Today's War Objectives Must Be Limited.* Garden City, N.Y.: Doubleday, 1967.

Ring, Jim. *Erskine Childers*. London: John Murray, 1996.

Roche, James Jeffrey. *By-Ways of War: The Story of the Filibusters*. Boston: Sherman, French & Co., 1907.

Rosengarten, Frederic, Jr. *Freebooters Must Die! The Life and Death of William Walker, the Most Notorious Soldier of Fortune of the Nineteenth Century.* Wayne, Pa.: Haverford House, 1976.

Royle, Trevor. *Orde Wingate, Irregular Soldier*. London: Weidenfeld & Nicolson, 1995.

Scroggs, William O. *Filibusters and Financiers: The Story of William Walker and His Associates*. New York: Macmillan, 1916.

Sheehan, Neil. *A Bright Shining Lie: John Paul Vann and America in Vietnam*. New York: Random House, 1988.

Siepel, Kevin H. *Rebel: The Life and Times of John Singleton Mosby*. New York: St. Martin's, 1983.

Smith, Helen Huntington. *The War on Powder River*. Lincoln, Nebr.: University of Nebraska Press, 1966.

Smith, W.H.B. *Small Arms of the World: A Basic Manual of Military Small Arms*. Harrisburg, Pa.: Stackpole, 1960.

Soukhanov, Anne H., ed. *Word Mysteries & Histories*. Boston: Houghton Mifflin, 1986.

Spence, Jonathan D. *God's Chinese Son: The Taiping Heavenly Kingdom of Hong Xiuquan*. New York: W.W. Norton, 1996.

Stevenson, William. *The Ghosts of Africa*. New York: Harcourt Brace Jovanovich, 1980.

Stone, I.F. *The Hidden History of the Korean War 1950-51*. Boston: Little, Brown, 1988.

Strachey, Lytton. *Eminent Victorians*. New York: Harcourt, Brace, 1969.

Sulzberger, C.L. *The American Heritage Picture Book of World War II*. New York: American Heritage, 1966.

Sykes, Christopher. *Orde Wingate*. London: Collins, 1959.

Tarassuk, Leonid and Blair, Claude, ed. *The Complete Encyclopedia of Arms & Weapons*. New York: Bonanza, 1979.

Taylor, A.J.P. *English History 1914-1945*. New York: Oxford University Press, 1965.

Taylor, Telford. *Sword and Swastika: Generals and Nazis in the Third Reich*. New York: Barnes & Noble, 1980.

Taylor, Thomas. *Born of War*. New York: McGraw-Hill, 1988.

Thayer, Charles W. *Guerrilla*. New York: Harper & Row, 1963.

Thompson, William Irwin. *The Imagination of an Insurrection: Dublin, Easter 1916*. New York: Harper & Row, 1972.

Thurman, Judith. *Isak Dinesen: The Life of a Storyteller*. New York: St. Martin's, 1982.

Toland, John. *Ships in the Sky: The Story of the Great Dirigibles*. New York: Holt, 1957.

Trask, David F. *The War with Spain in 1898*. New York: Macmillan, 1981.

Trevelyan, G.M. *The English Revolution, 1688-1689*. New York: Oxford University Press, 1968.

Trzebinski, Errol. *Silence Will Speak: A Study of the Life of Denys Finch Hatton and His Relationship With Karen Blixen*. Chicago: University of Chicago Press, 1977.

Tulloch, Derek. *Wingate in Peace and War*. London: Macdonald, 1972.

van Creveld, Martin. *Technology and War: From 2000 B.C. to the Present*. New York: Free Press, 1989.

Vetter, Hal. *Mutiny on Koje Island*. Rutland, Vt.: Tuttle, 1965.

Voorhees, Melvin B. *Korean Tales*. New York: Simon & Schuster, 1952.

Walker, William. *The War in Nicaragua*. Tucson, Ariz.: University of Arizona Press, 1985.

Wallace, Edward S. *Destiny and Glory*. New York: Coward-McCann, 1957.

Walsh, John E. *The Philippine Insurrection: America's Only Try for an Overseas Empire*. New York: Watts, 1973.

Weintraub, Stanley. *MacArthur's War: Korea and the Undoing of an American Hero*. New York: Simon & Schuster, 2000.

Weir, William. *Fatal Victories*. Hamden, Conn.: Archon, 1993.

——. *In the Shadow of the Dope Fiend: America's War on Drugs*. North Haven, Conn.: Archon, 1995.

——. *Written With Lead: Legendary American Gunfights and Gunfighters*. Hamden, Conn.: Archon, 1992.

White, Terence de Vere. *Kevin O'Higgins*. London: Methuen, 1948.

Wilkinson, Burke. *The Zeal of the Convert: The Life of Erskine Childers*. Sag Harbor, N.Y.: Second Chance Press, 1985.

Young, Peter. *Atlas of the Second World War*. New York: Berkley Windhover, 1977.

——. *The Machinery of War*. New York: Crescent, 1973.

Young, Peter and Lawford, J.P. (eds.). *History of the British Army*. New York: Putnam's, 1970.

Younger, Calton. *Ireland's Civil War*. London: Fontana Press, 1979.

Periodicals

American Heritage, June, 1957, "The Defeat, the Lesson, the Victory," by Walter Waller Edwards.

——. Dec., 1957, "The Gray-Eyed Man of Destiny," by Edward S. Wallace.

Gun Digest Annual, 1992, "The Guns of the Philippine Wars," by William Weir.

Military History, Aug. 1986, "Defending Sandbag Castle," by William Weir.

National Geographic, Feb., 1998, "Remember the *Maine*?" by Thomas B. Allen.

New York Times, Jan. 3, 1859, schooner *Susan*, carrying filibusters, leaves from Mobile.

——. Jan. 4, 1859, more on *Susan*.

——. Jan. 8, 1859, more on filibuster escape; French and U.S. plans for canal in Nicaragua.

——. Jan. 11, 1859, *Susan* reported wrecked.

New York Times, Jan. 17, 1859, British assert right to search U.S. ship for filibusters.

——. Jan. 20, 1859, more on British right to search.

——. Jan. 27, 31, Feb. 2, 12, 22, Mar. 14, 21, Apr. 14, May 6, 16, Aug. 29, 1859, U.S. and French maneuvering on trans Nicaragua canal.

——. June 25, Oct. 5, 1859, Walker plans for filibustering expedition.

——. June 27, 30, July 28, Aug. 1, 1859, U.S. demands rejected.

——. Aug. 29, 1859, U.S.-British treaty negotiations.

——. Oct. 6, 7, British to protect Nicaragua.

——. Oct. 8, 10, filibusters arrested.

——. Oct. 11, filibusters escape.

——. Oct. 14, 24-26, more on filibusters.

——. Oct. 29, 1859, Guzman elected president of Nicaragua.

——. Jan. 5, 1860, Review of William Walker's *The War in Nicaragua*.

——. Aug. 21, 1860, Walker invades Honduras.

——. Aug. 22, 1860, editorial on Walker.

——. Aug. 27, 1860, Walker captures Truxillo.

——. Aug. 29, 1860, Walker proclamation: intends to overthrow Guariola.

——. Sept. 1, 1860, Walker in Honduras.

——. Sept. 6, 1860, Walker attacked by Hondurans and British.

——. Sept. 11, 1860, Walker surrenders; editorial on Walker.

——. Sept. 12, 1860, editorial on Walker.

——. Sept. 17, 1860, Walker executed.

——. Sept. 18, 1860, more details on Walker execution.

——. Sept. 21, 1860, still more details on execution of William Walker; editorial on execution of William Walker.

——. Sept. 22, 1860, obituary on William Walker.

——. Sept. 29, 1860, report on documents found concerning William Walker; editorial on William Walker.

——. Oct. 2, 1860, more details on execution of Walker.

——. Nov. 1, 1860, quotes *Times of London* on Walker.

——. Nov. 2, 1860, editorial on foreign reaction to Walker's death.

——. Dec. 19, 1860, editorial on Walker.

——. March 22, 1998, "Less to Celebrate at this Gold Rush Anniversary," by James Brooke.

Smithsonian, Oct., 1997, "Bang! Bang! You're Dead," by Barbara Holland.

———. Feb., 1998, "Remember the *Maine*," by Tom Miller.

The New Yorker, Jan. 27, 1975, "Profiles—Son and Father," by Anthony Bailey.

War, Literature and the Arts, Spring/Summer, 1998, "Memoir: Public Information," by William R. Weir.

Index

C

G

Gadsden Purchase, 24
Gadsden, James, 24
Garcia, Calixton, 107
Garrison, Cornelius, 33
Gatling gun, 109
General Act of Berlin, 121
George, Lloyd, 153, 156
German East Africa, 120-122, 125-126, 134, 235
German Influence on British Cavalry, 147
Gettysburg, 75
Gideon Force, 174-178
"God Worshiping Society," 53
Gomez, Maximo, 105-107
Good Words for Exhorting the Age, 45
Gordon, Charles George, 61-62
Grant, Ulysses S., 75
Graziani, Rudolfo, 170
"Green Banner," 57
Griffith, Arthur, 149-151, 156-157, 159-160
Guam, 100
Guardiola, Santos, 28, 30, 41
guerillas, 131
  guerilla warfare, 68-71, 73
  orders concerning in Civil War, 69-70
Guild, Lafayette, 77
Guofan, Zeng, 50, 53, 56, 59

H

HAC in South Africa, The, 147
Hacohen, David, 167
"Haganah," 167
Halleck, Henry W., 76
Hanna, Mark, 97
Hathaway, James, 70
Havana, 99

Hayes, Rutherford B., 79
Heartbreak Ridge, 205, 208
Heavenly Kingdom, the, 45-46
Hendreck, Sean, 158
Henningson, Charles Frederick, 36-38
Hicks, Graham, 22
Hire, Henry, 50
Hitler, Adolf, 13
Hoa Hao, 221
Hodge, John, 194
Home Rule, 144, 147, 150
Hongzhang, Li, 79
Honorable Artillery Company, 147
Honzhang, Li, 57-59
Hooker Jim, 82, 84, 86-91
Hooker, "Fighting Joe," 73
Hope, Sir James, 50-51, 55-56, 58
Hoskins, Reginald, 136
Hotchkiss revolving cannons, 109
Hsiao-t'ang, 55
Huan Hsueh, 43, 47, 49
Hukbo ng Bayan Laban Sa Hapan, 214-217
Huoxiu, Hong, 45

I

Igorots, 101,
In the Ranks of the CIV, 146
Inch'on, 196-198
Influence of Sea Power on History, The, 97
Insurrectos, 101-104, 110
Irish Bulletin, 151, 154
"Irish Question," the, 149-150
Irish Republican Army (IRA), 151-153, 156-159
Irish Republican Brotherhood, 157
Irish Volunteers, 144-145, 148-149, 153
Iron Triangle, 206
Ironside, Sir Edmund, 169-170

N

O

T

X

Y

About the Author

*S*oldiers in the Shadows is William Weir's second book for Career Press/New Page Books, the first being *50 Battles that Changed the World.* A former newspaper reporter and Army combat correspondence in the Korean War, he has also written many magazine articles, mostly about military subjects, weapons, or crime. Although a retired public relations executive, he jokingly refers to himself as a "crime and violence specialist." His earlier books include *Written With Lead: Legendary American Gunfights and Gunfighters; Fatal Victories; In the Shadow of the Dope Friend;* and *A Well Regulated Militia: The Battle Over Gun Control.* He and his wife, Anne, live in Connecticut, where they take pride in their three children, Alison, an Air Force officer; Joan, a special education teacher; and Bill, a newspaper reporter.